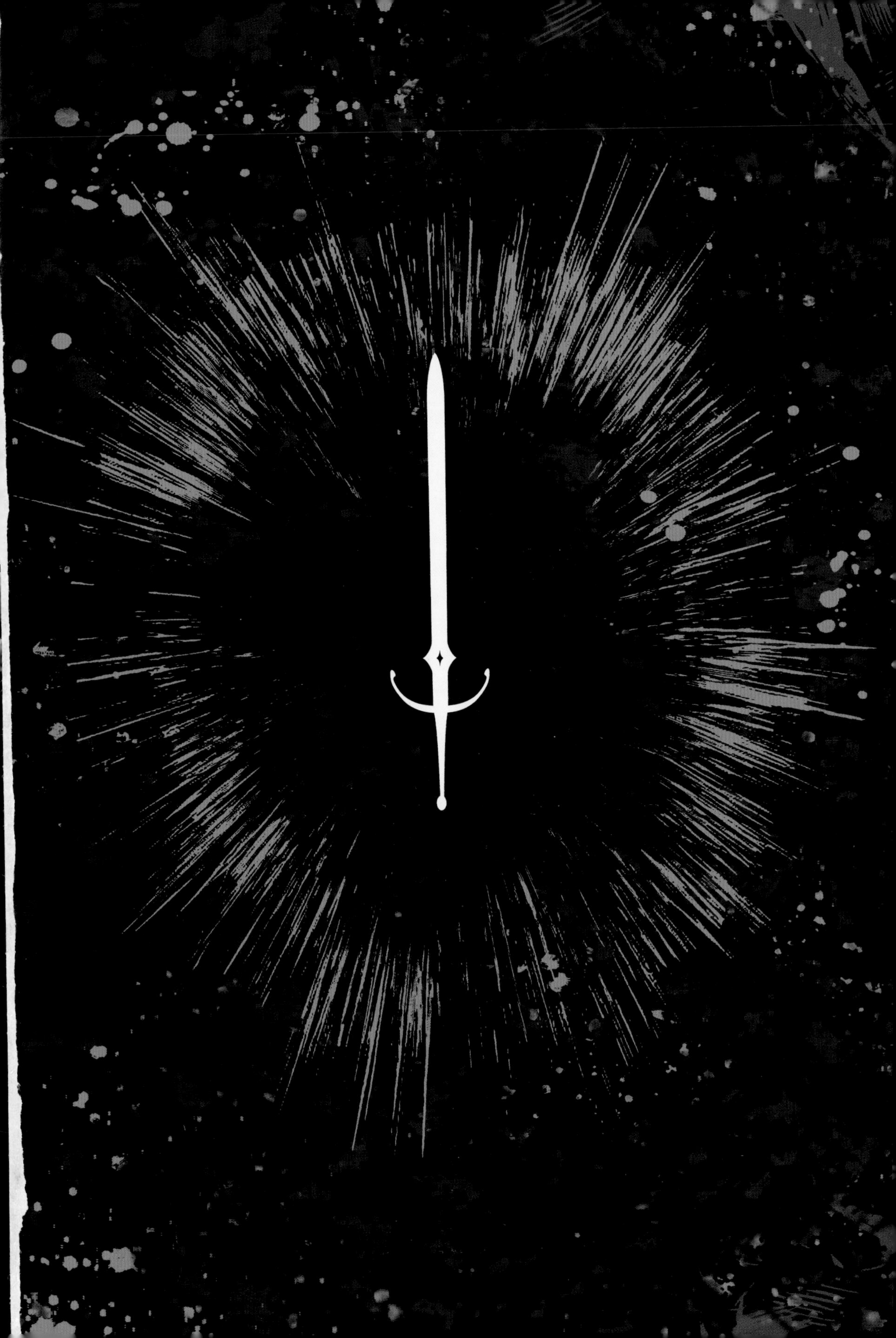

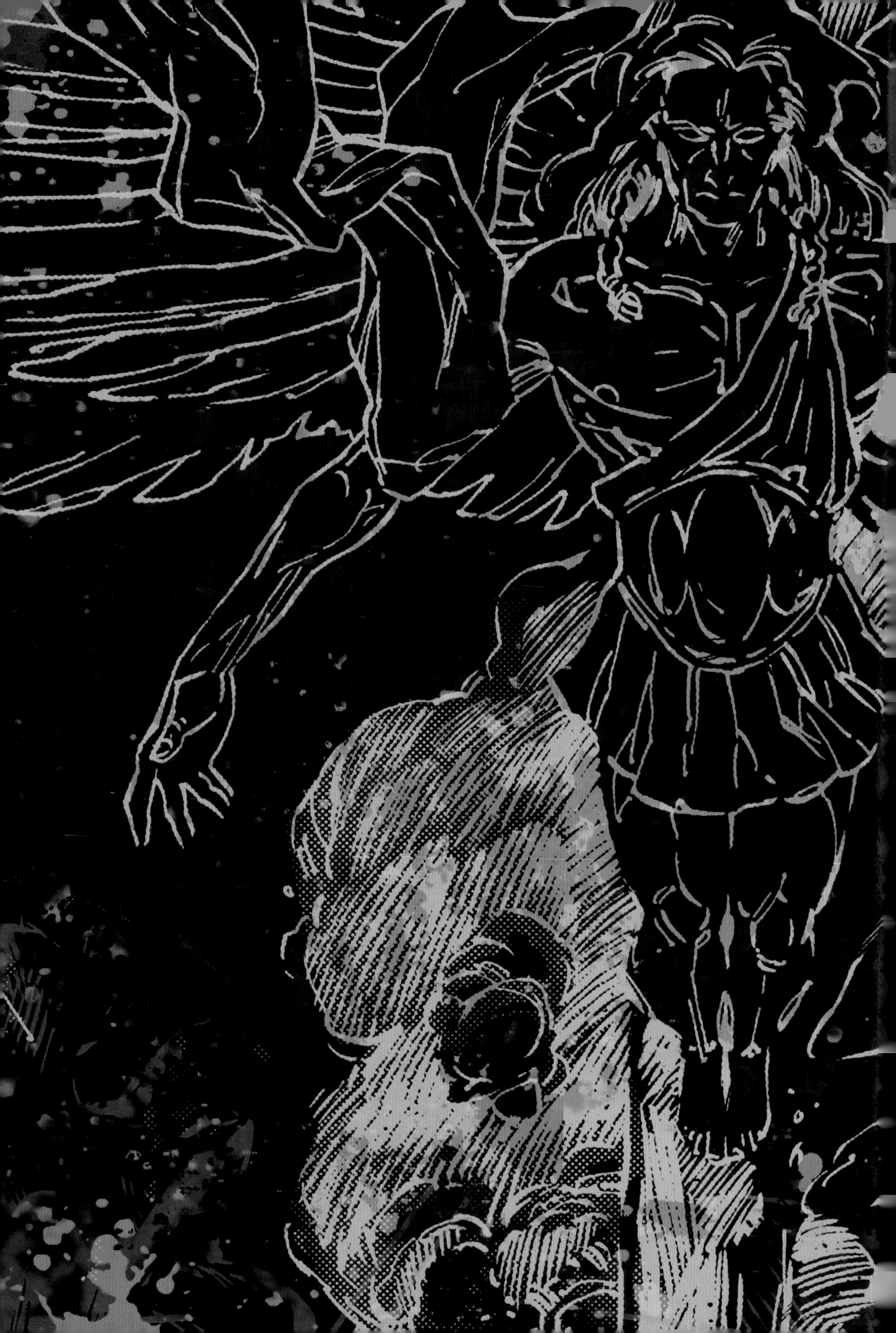

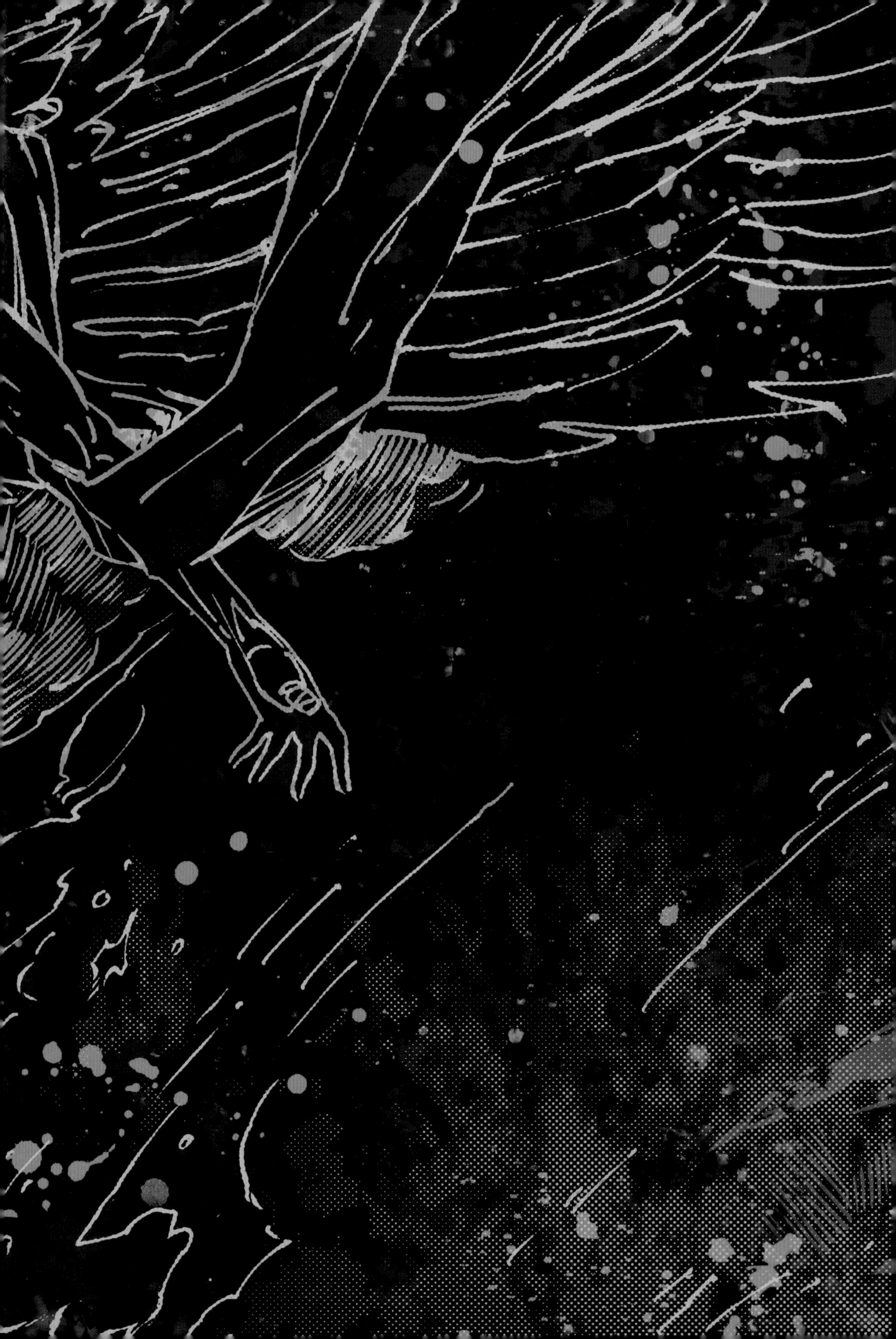

MESSENGER

THE LEGEND OF JOAN OF ARC

MESSENGER

THE LEGEND OF JOAN OF ARC

A GRAPHIC NOVEL

WRITTEN BY
TONY LEE

ILLUSTRATED BY
SAM HART

COLORED BY
SAM HART WITH **FLAVIO COSTA**

LETTERED BY
CADU SIMÕES

CANDLEWICK PRESS

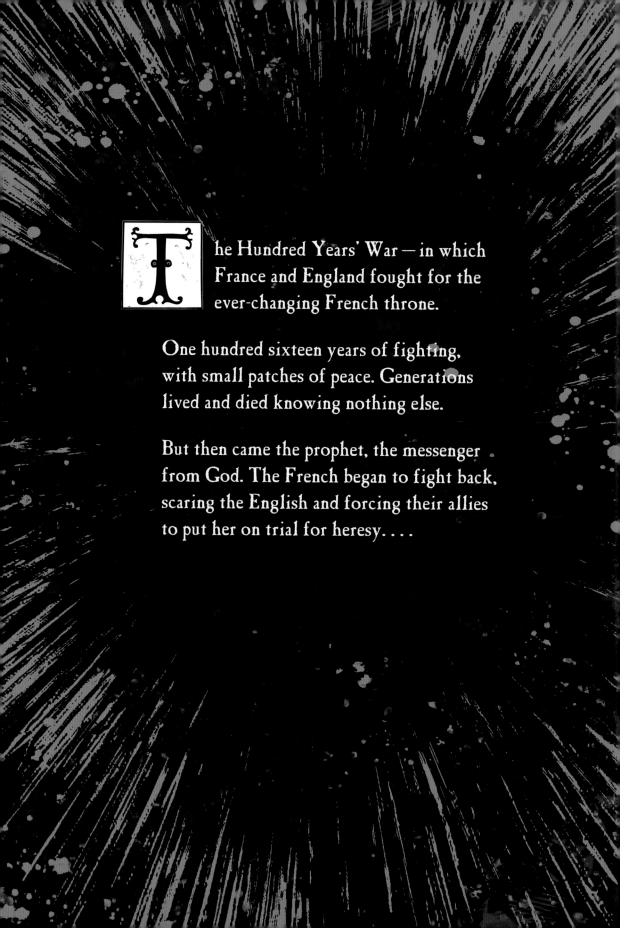

The Hundred Years' War — in which France and England fought for the ever-changing French throne.

One hundred sixteen years of fighting, with small patches of peace. Generations lived and died knowing nothing else.

But then came the prophet, the messenger from God. The French began to fight back, scaring the English and forcing their allies to put her on trial for heresy....

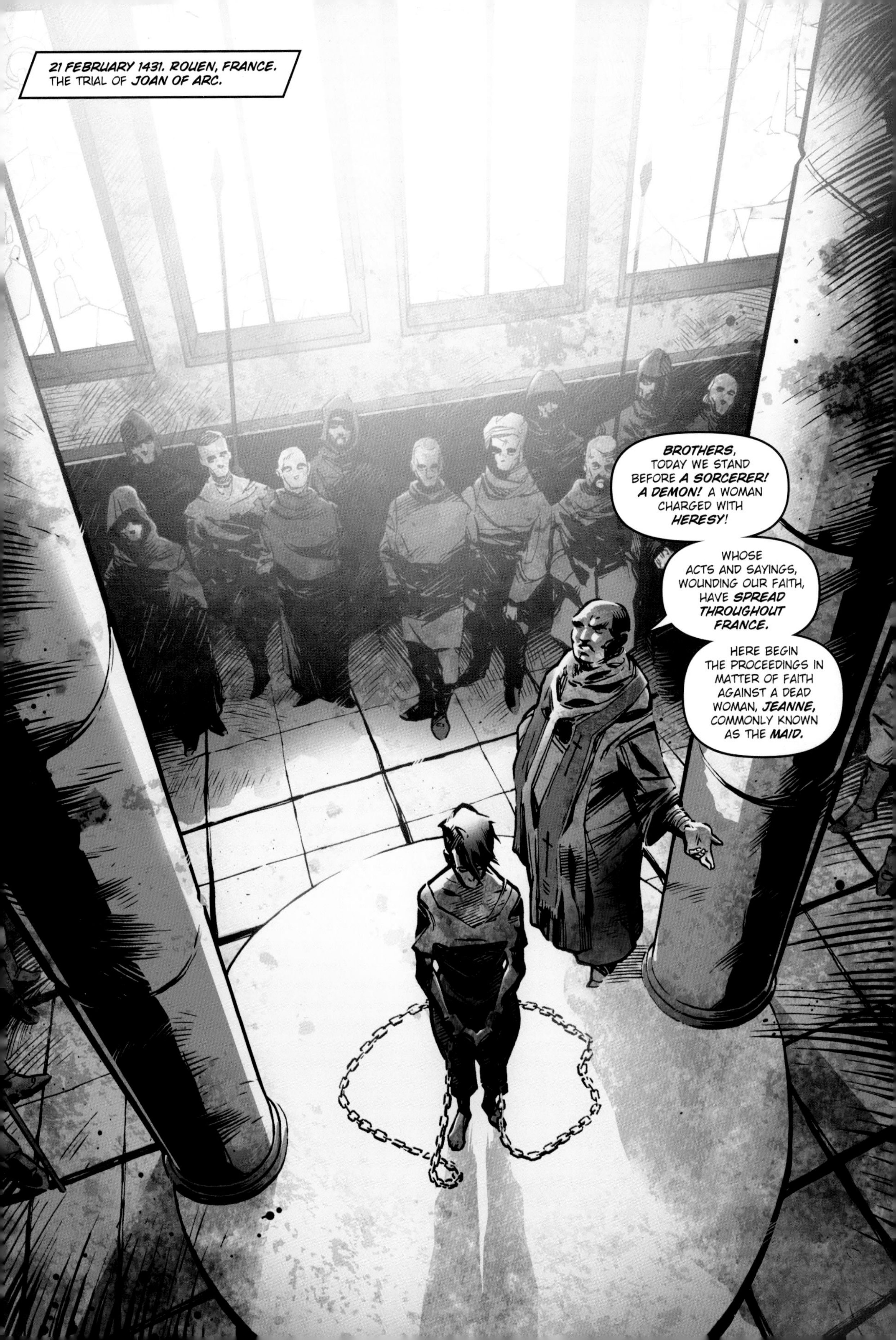
21 FEBRUARY 1431. ROUEN, FRANCE. THE TRIAL OF JOAN OF ARC.
BROTHERS, TODAY WE STAND BEFORE A SORCERER! A DEMON! A WOMAN CHARGED WITH HERESY!
WHOSE ACTS AND SAYINGS, WOUNDING OUR FAITH, HAVE SPREAD THROUGHOUT FRANCE.
HERE BEGIN THE PROCEEDINGS IN MATTER OF FAITH AGAINST A DEAD WOMAN, JEANNE, COMMONLY KNOWN AS THE MAID.

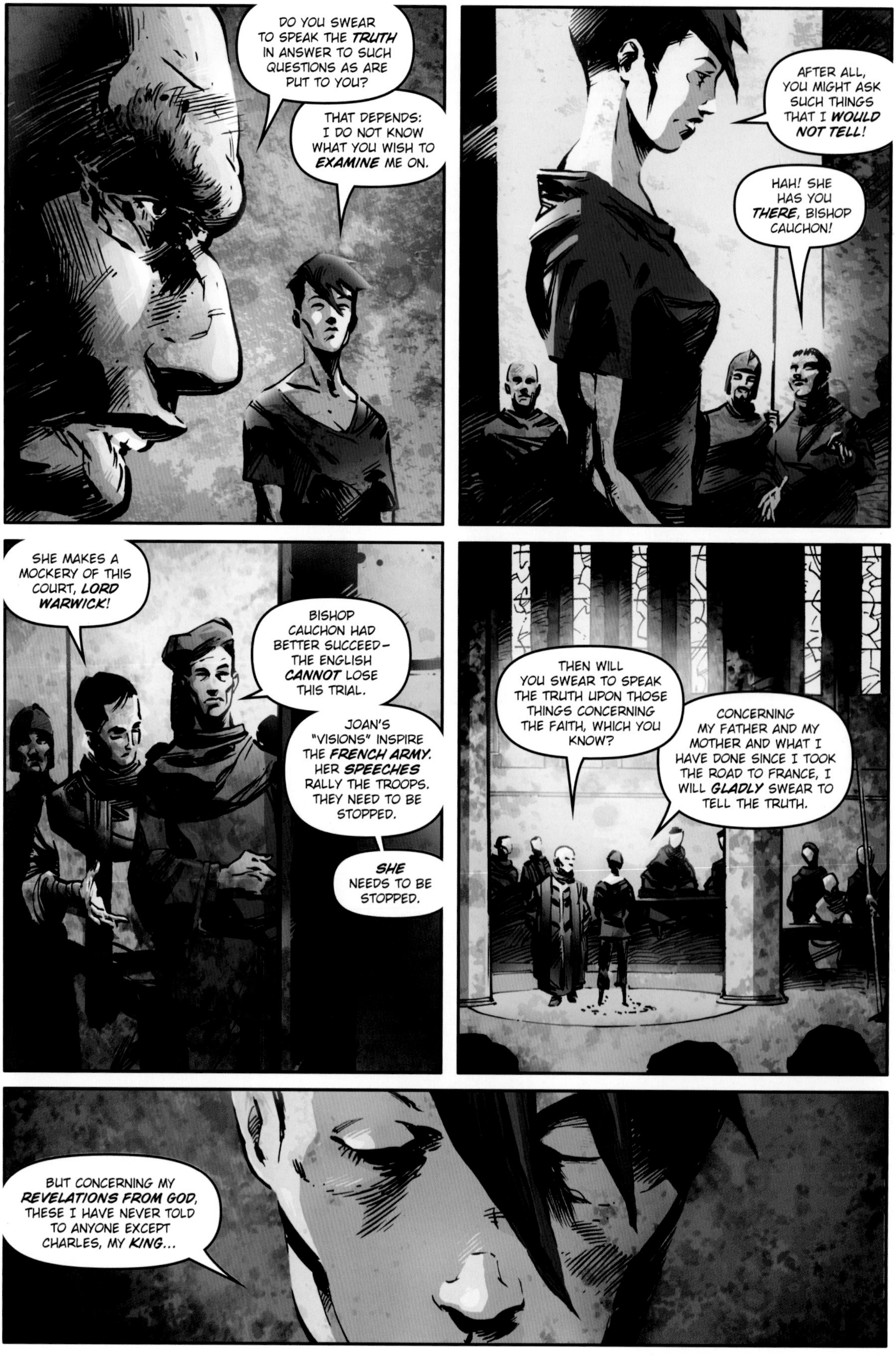
DO YOU SWEAR TO SPEAK THE TRUTH IN ANSWER TO SUCH QUESTIONS AS ARE PUT TO YOU?
THAT DEPENDS: I DO NOT KNOW WHAT YOU WISH TO EXAMINE ME ON.
AFTER ALL, YOU MIGHT ASK SUCH THINGS THAT I WOULD NOT TELL!
HAH! SHE HAS YOU THERE, BISHOP CAUCHON!
SHE MAKES A MOCKERY OF THIS COURT, LORD WARWICK!
BISHOP CAUCHON HAD BETTER SUCCEED— THE ENGLISH CANNOT LOSE THIS TRIAL.
JOAN'S "VISIONS" INSPIRE THE FRENCH ARMY. HER SPEECHES RALLY THE TROOPS. THEY NEED TO BE STOPPED.
SHE NEEDS TO BE STOPPED.
THEN WILL YOU SWEAR TO SPEAK THE TRUTH UPON THOSE THINGS CONCERNING THE FAITH, WHICH YOU KNOW?
CONCERNING MY FATHER AND MY MOTHER AND WHAT I HAVE DONE SINCE I TOOK THE ROAD TO FRANCE, I WILL GLADLY SWEAR TO TELL THE TRUTH.
BUT CONCERNING MY REVELATIONS FROM GOD, THESE I HAVE NEVER TOLD TO ANYONE EXCEPT CHARLES, MY KING...

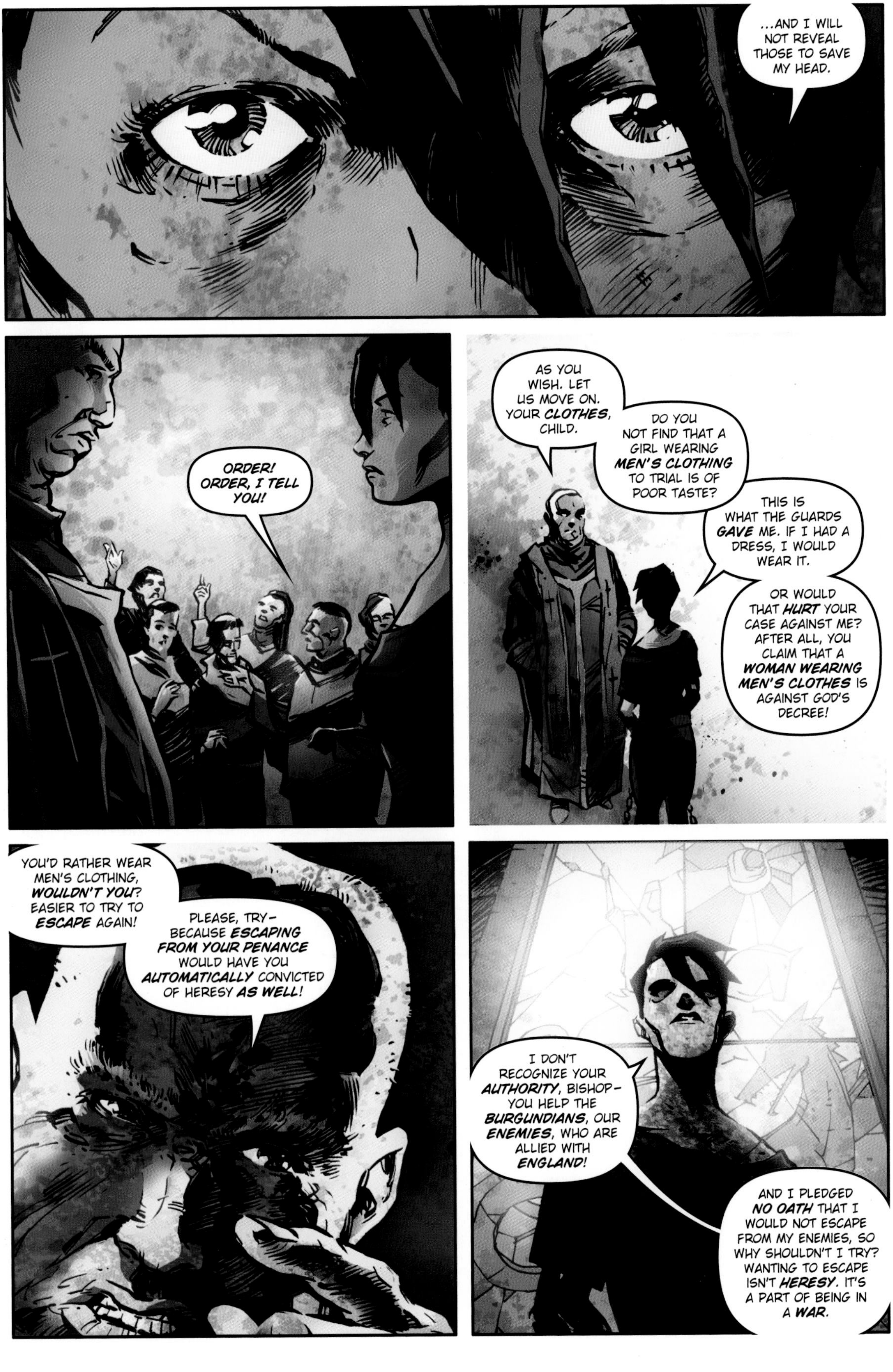
...AND I WILL NOT REVEAL THOSE TO SAVE MY HEAD.
ORDER! ORDER, I TELL YOU!
AS YOU WISH. LET US MOVE ON. YOUR CLOTHES, CHILD.
DO YOU NOT FIND THAT A GIRL WEARING MEN'S CLOTHING TO TRIAL IS OF POOR TASTE?
THIS IS WHAT THE GUARDS GAVE ME. IF I HAD A DRESS, I WOULD WEAR IT.
OR WOULD THAT HURT YOUR CASE AGAINST ME? AFTER ALL, YOU CLAIM THAT A WOMAN WEARING MEN'S CLOTHES IS AGAINST GOD'S DECREE!
YOU'D RATHER WEAR MEN'S CLOTHING, WOULDN'T YOU? EASIER TO TRY TO ESCAPE AGAIN!
PLEASE, TRY-BECAUSE ESCAPING FROM YOUR PENANCE WOULD HAVE YOU AUTOMATICALLY CONVICTED OF HERESY AS WELL!
I DON'T RECOGNIZE YOUR AUTHORITY, BISHOP-YOU HELP THE BURGUNDIANS, OUR ENEMIES, WHO ARE ALLIED WITH ENGLAND!
AND I PLEDGED NO OATH THAT I WOULD NOT ESCAPE FROM MY ENEMIES, SO WHY SHOULDN'T I TRY? WANTING TO ESCAPE ISN'T HERESY. IT'S A PART OF BEING IN A WAR.

LET US TALK OF YOUR *CHILDHOOD*. BORN IN *DOMRÉMY*, YOU LIVED A NORMAL LIFE, DID YOU NOT?

YOUR FATHER, *JACQUES D'ARC*, WAS A VILLAGE OFFICIAL.

HE WAS A *FARMER*, YES—WE OWNED NEARLY FIFTY ACRES OF LAND.

HE WAS IN CHARGE OF THE LOCAL *MILITIA* AND COLLECTED THE TAXES, AMONG OTHER THINGS.

DOMRÉMY WAS—*IS*—LOYAL TO THE FRENCH, BUT AT THE TIME WAS SURROUNDED BY *BURGUNDIAN* TERRITORY.

WE WERE OFTEN RAIDED, ATTACKED BY BANDITS. ON ONE OCCASION THEY TRIED TO *BURN DOWN OUR VILLAGE*.

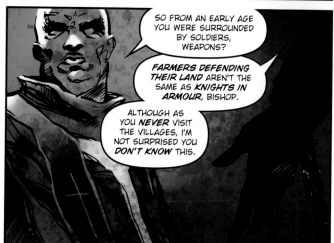

SO FROM AN EARLY AGE YOU WERE SURROUNDED BY SOLDIERS, WEAPONS?

FARMERS DEFENDING THEIR LAND AREN'T THE SAME AS *KNIGHTS IN ARMOUR*, BISHOP.

ALTHOUGH AS YOU *NEVER* VISIT THE VILLAGES, I'M NOT SURPRISED YOU *DON'T KNOW* THIS.

HA HA HA HA HA HA

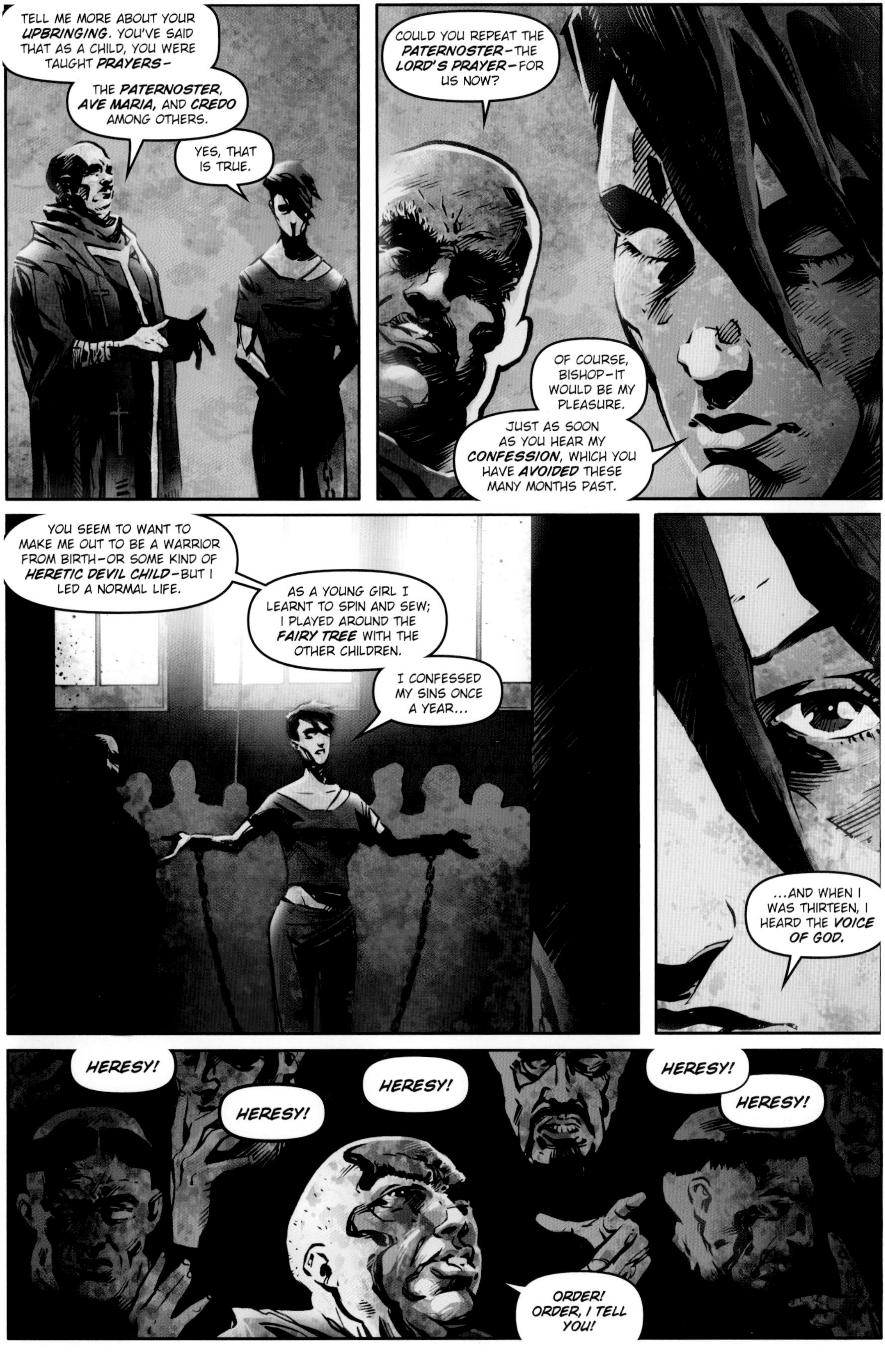
TELL ME MORE ABOUT YOUR UPBRINGING. YOU'VE SAID THAT AS A CHILD, YOU WERE TAUGHT PRAYERS-
THE PATERNOSTER, AVE MARIA, AND CREDO AMONG OTHERS.
YES, THAT IS TRUE.
COULD YOU REPEAT THE PATERNOSTER—THE LORD'S PRAYER—FOR US NOW?
OF COURSE, BISHOP—IT WOULD BE MY PLEASURE.
JUST AS SOON AS YOU HEAR MY CONFESSION, WHICH YOU HAVE AVOIDED THESE MANY MONTHS PAST.
YOU SEEM TO WANT TO MAKE ME OUT TO BE A WARRIOR FROM BIRTH—OR SOME KIND OF HERETIC DEVIL CHILD—BUT I LED A NORMAL LIFE.
AS A YOUNG GIRL I LEARNT TO SPIN AND SEW; I PLAYED AROUND THE FAIRY TREE WITH THE OTHER CHILDREN.
I CONFESSED MY SINS ONCE A YEAR...
...AND WHEN I WAS THIRTEEN, I HEARD THE VOICE OF GOD.
HERESY!
HERESY!
HERESY!
HERESY!
HERESY!
ORDER! ORDER, I TELL YOU!

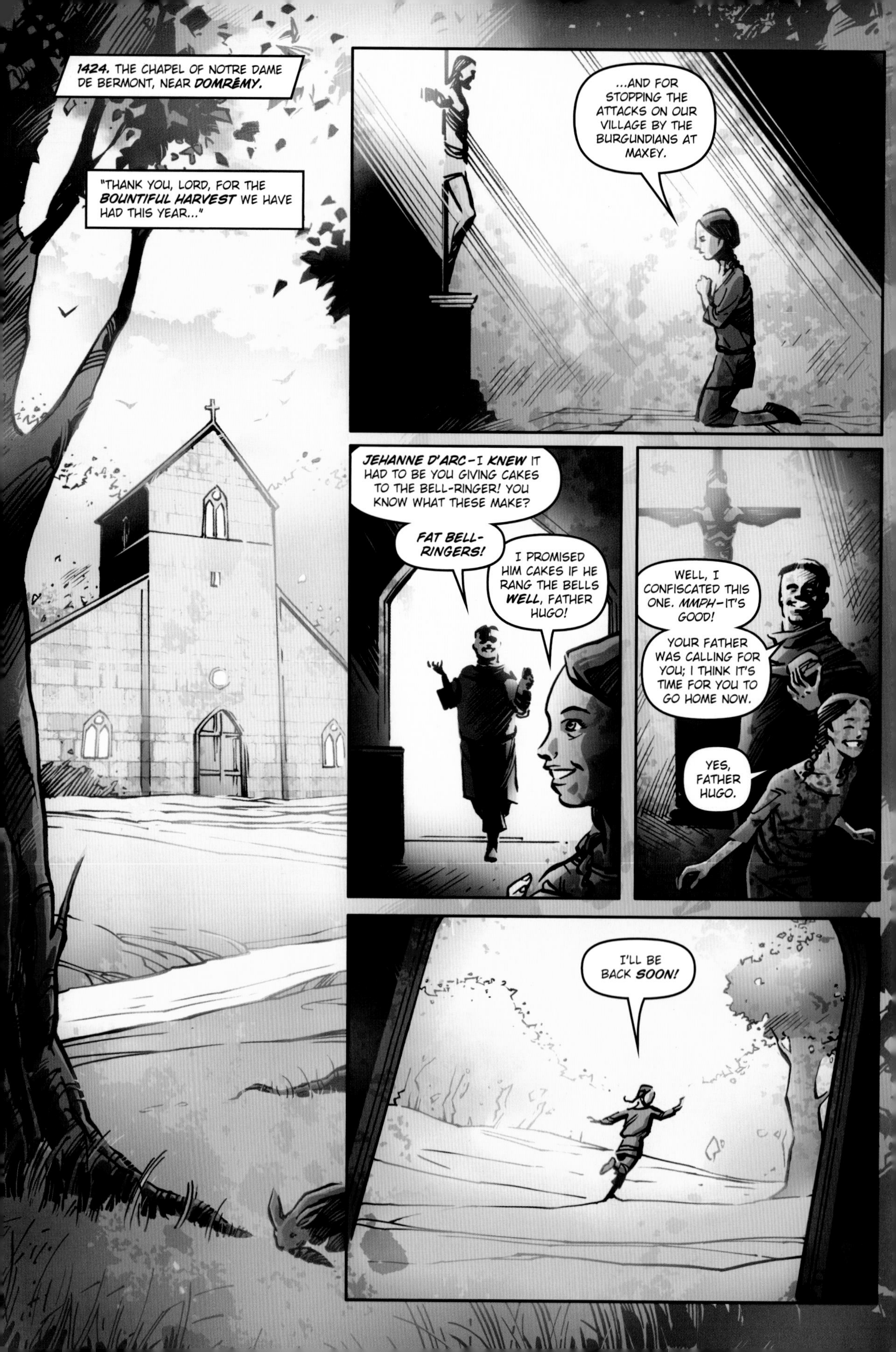
1424. THE CHAPEL OF NOTRE DAME DE BERMONT, NEAR DOMRÉMY.
"THANK YOU, LORD, FOR THE BOUNTIFUL HARVEST WE HAVE HAD THIS YEAR..."
...AND FOR STOPPING THE ATTACKS ON OUR VILLAGE BY THE BURGUNDIANS AT MAXEY.
JEHANNE D'ARC—I KNEW IT HAD TO BE YOU GIVING CAKES TO THE BELL-RINGER! YOU KNOW WHAT THESE MAKE?
FAT BELL-RINGERS!
I PROMISED HIM CAKES IF HE RANG THE BELLS WELL, FATHER HUGO!
WELL, I CONFISCATED THIS ONE. MMPH—IT'S GOOD!
YOUR FATHER WAS CALLING FOR YOU; I THINK IT'S TIME FOR YOU TO GO HOME NOW.
YES, FATHER HUGO.
I'LL BE BACK SOON!

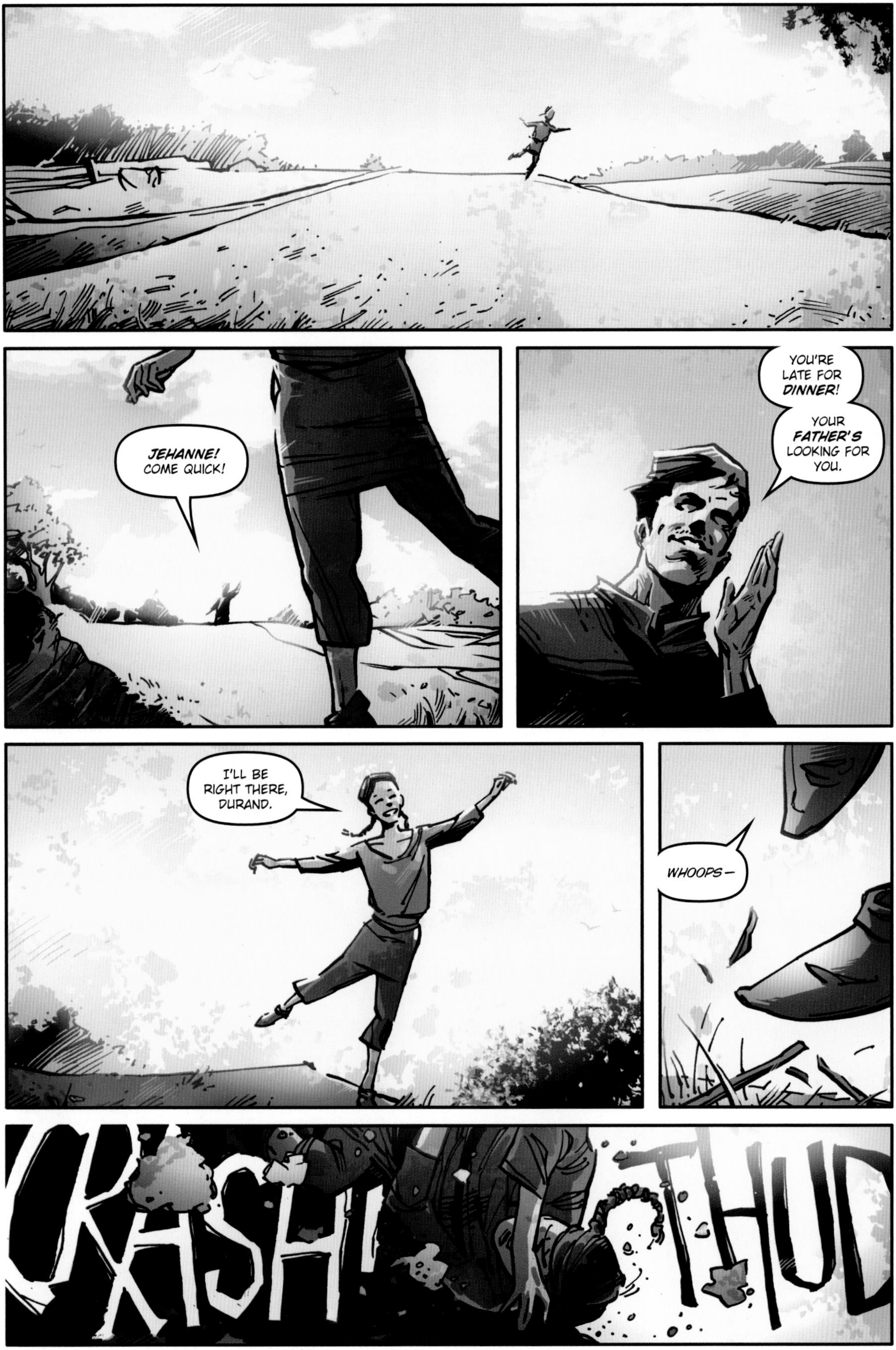
JEHANNE! COME QUICK!
YOU'RE LATE FOR DINNER!
YOUR FATHER'S LOOKING FOR YOU.
I'LL BE RIGHT THERE, DURAND.
WHOOPS—
CRASH!
THUD

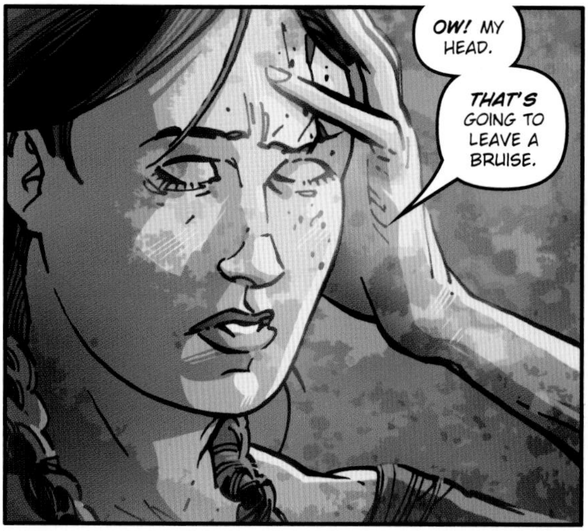
OW! MY HEAD.
THAT'S GOING TO LEAVE A BRUISE.

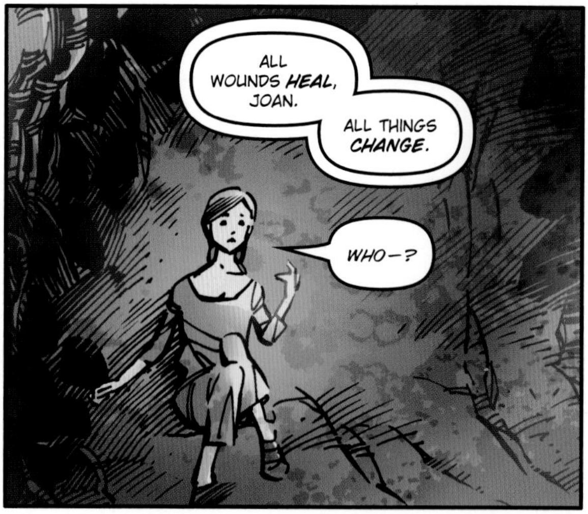
ALL WOUNDS HEAL, JOAN.
ALL THINGS CHANGE.
WHO—?

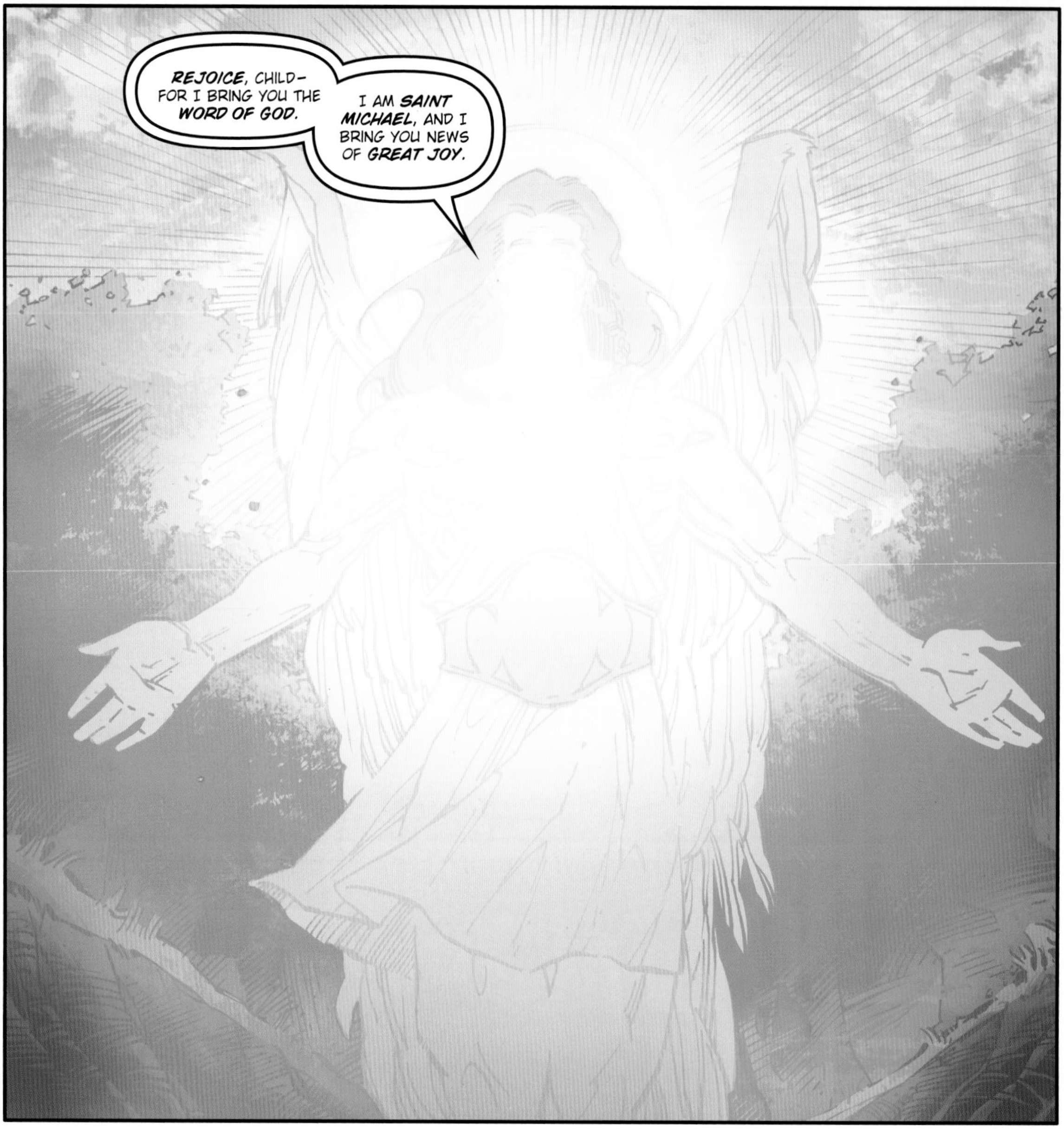
REJOICE, CHILD—FOR I BRING YOU THE WORD OF GOD.
I AM SAINT MICHAEL, AND I BRING YOU NEWS OF GREAT JOY.

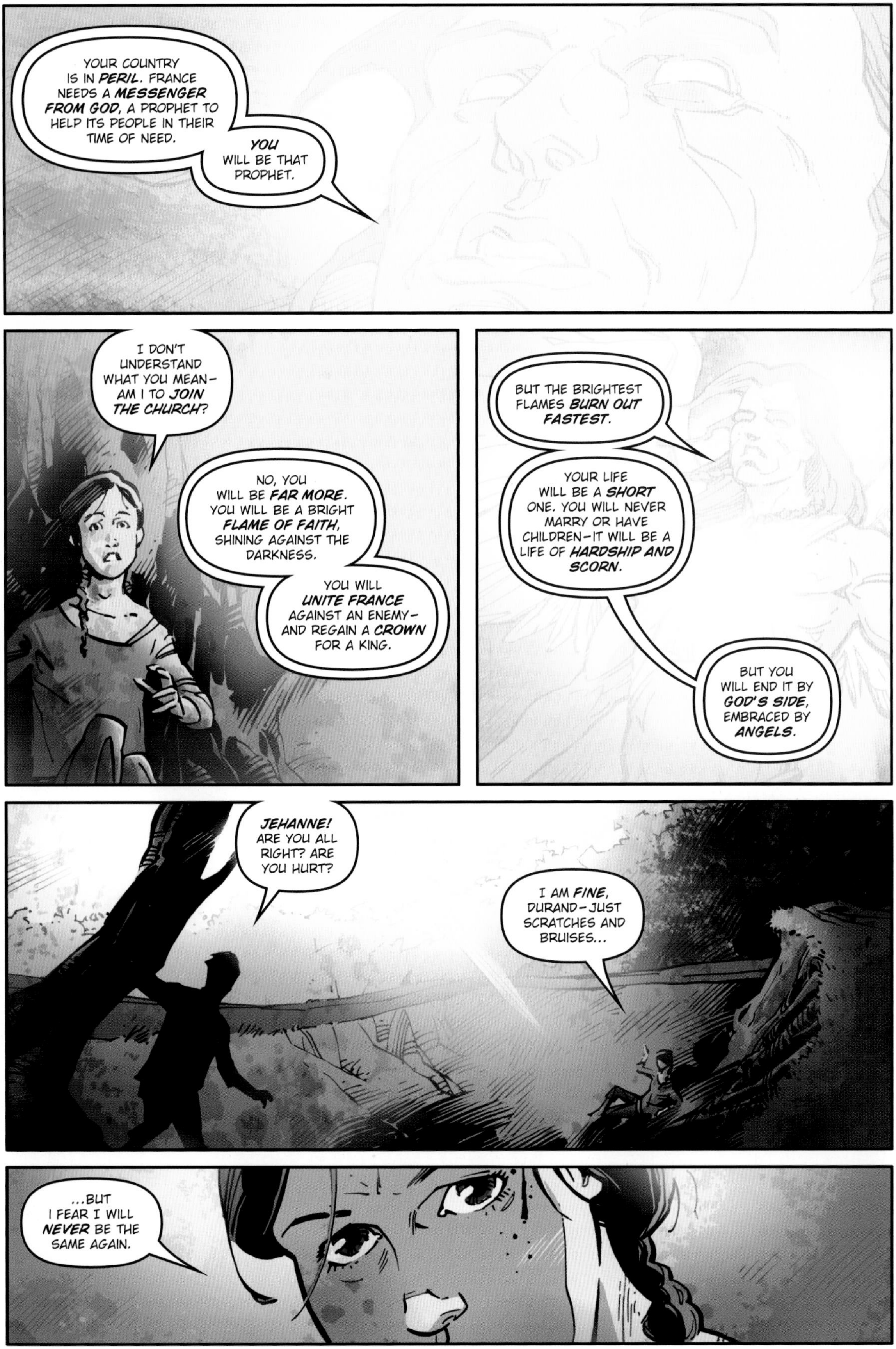
YOUR COUNTRY IS IN PERIL. FRANCE NEEDS A MESSENGER FROM GOD, A PROPHET TO HELP ITS PEOPLE IN THEIR TIME OF NEED.
YOU WILL BE THAT PROPHET.
I DON'T UNDERSTAND WHAT YOU MEAN—AM I TO JOIN THE CHURCH?
NO, YOU WILL BE FAR MORE. YOU WILL BE A BRIGHT FLAME OF FAITH, SHINING AGAINST THE DARKNESS.
YOU WILL UNITE FRANCE AGAINST AN ENEMY—AND REGAIN A CROWN FOR A KING.
BUT THE BRIGHTEST FLAMES BURN OUT FASTEST.
YOUR LIFE WILL BE A SHORT ONE. YOU WILL NEVER MARRY OR HAVE CHILDREN—IT WILL BE A LIFE OF HARDSHIP AND SCORN.
BUT YOU WILL END IT BY GOD'S SIDE, EMBRACED BY ANGELS.
JEHANNE! ARE YOU ALL RIGHT? ARE YOU HURT?
I AM FINE, DURAND—JUST SCRATCHES AND BRUISES...
...BUT I FEAR I WILL NEVER BE THE SAME AGAIN.

YOUR COUSIN *WORRIES* US WITH NEWS OF YOUR ACCIDENT. ARE YOU SURE YOU'RE NOT HURT, JEHANNE?

I'M FINE, FATHER. THE *ANGEL* MADE ME BETTER, ANYWAY!

ANGEL?

WELL, MORE OF A *SAINT*, REALLY. MICHAEL. HE CAME WITH WORDS FROM *GOD.*

I'M GOING TO BE A *MESSENGER.* HE TOLD ME THINGS ABOUT MY FUTURE.

YOU DON'T FEEL *FEVERISH*, YET YOU'RE *DELIRIOUS!*

NOT AT ALL, MOTHER! GOD WILL *GUIDE* ME— EVERYTHING WILL BE OK!

I UNDERSTAND MY *ROLE* NOW.

ENOUGH!

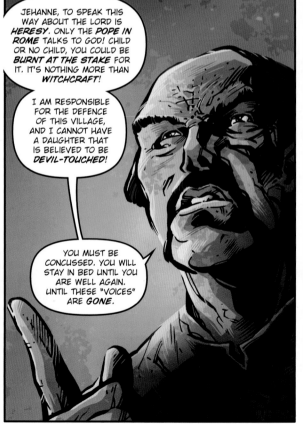

JEHANNE, TO SPEAK THIS WAY ABOUT THE LORD IS *HERESY.* ONLY THE *POPE IN ROME* TALKS TO GOD! CHILD OR NO CHILD, YOU COULD BE *BURNT AT THE STAKE* FOR IT. IT'S NOTHING MORE THAN *WITCHCRAFT!*

I AM RESPONSIBLE FOR THE DEFENCE OF THIS VILLAGE, AND I CANNOT HAVE A DAUGHTER THAT IS BELIEVED TO BE *DEVIL-TOUCHED!*

YOU MUST BE CONCUSSED. YOU WILL STAY IN BED UNTIL YOU ARE WELL AGAIN. UNTIL THESE "VOICES" ARE *GONE.*

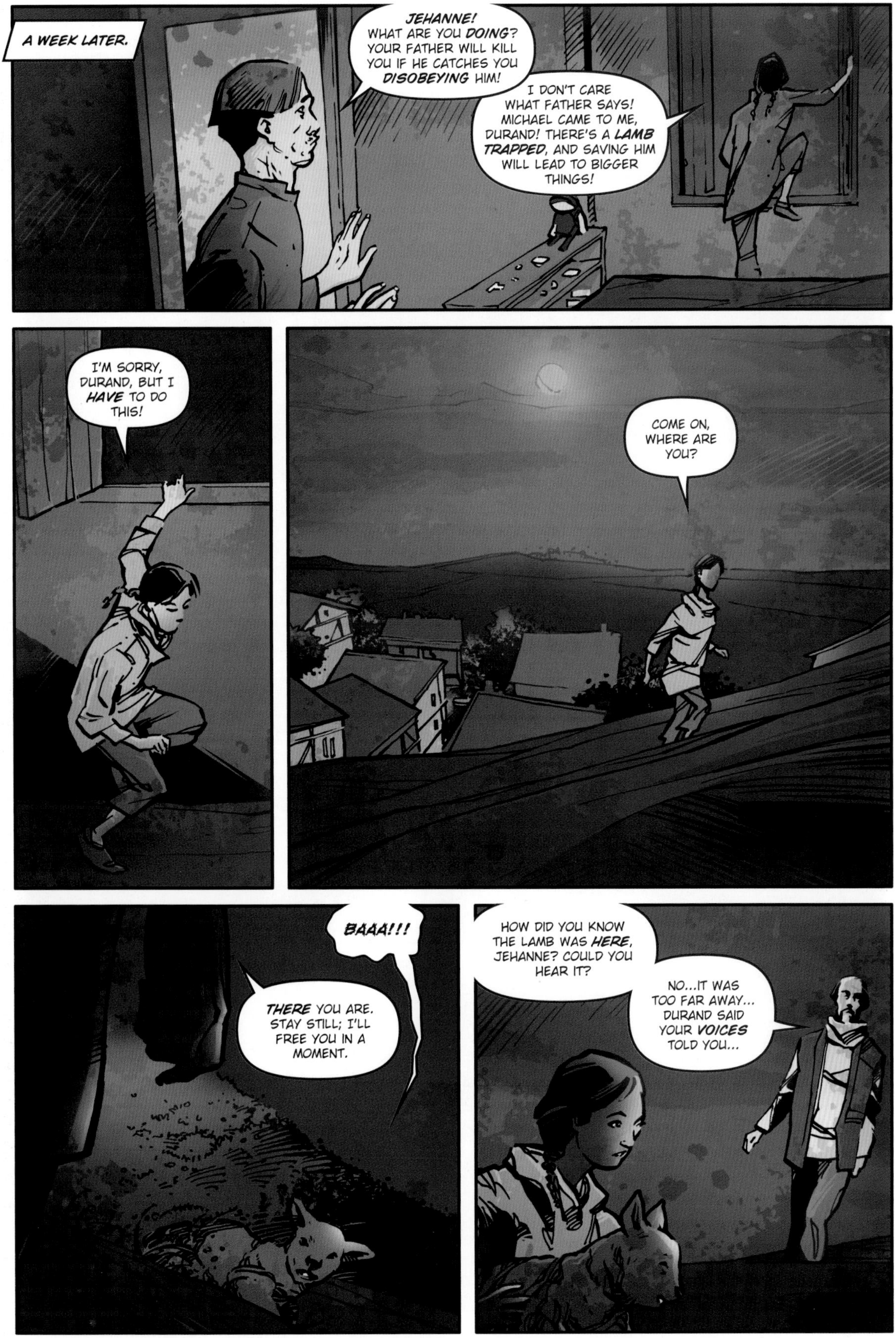
A WEEK LATER.
JEHANNE! WHAT ARE YOU DOING? YOUR FATHER WILL KILL YOU IF HE CATCHES YOU DISOBEYING HIM!
I DON'T CARE WHAT FATHER SAYS! MICHAEL CAME TO ME, DURAND! THERE'S A LAMB TRAPPED, AND SAVING HIM WILL LEAD TO BIGGER THINGS!
I'M SORRY, DURAND, BUT I HAVE TO DO THIS!
COME ON, WHERE ARE YOU?
BAAA!!!
THERE YOU ARE. STAY STILL; I'LL FREE YOU IN A MOMENT.
HOW DID YOU KNOW THE LAMB WAS HERE, JEHANNE? COULD YOU HEAR IT?
NO...IT WAS TOO FAR AWAY... DURAND SAID YOUR VOICES TOLD YOU...

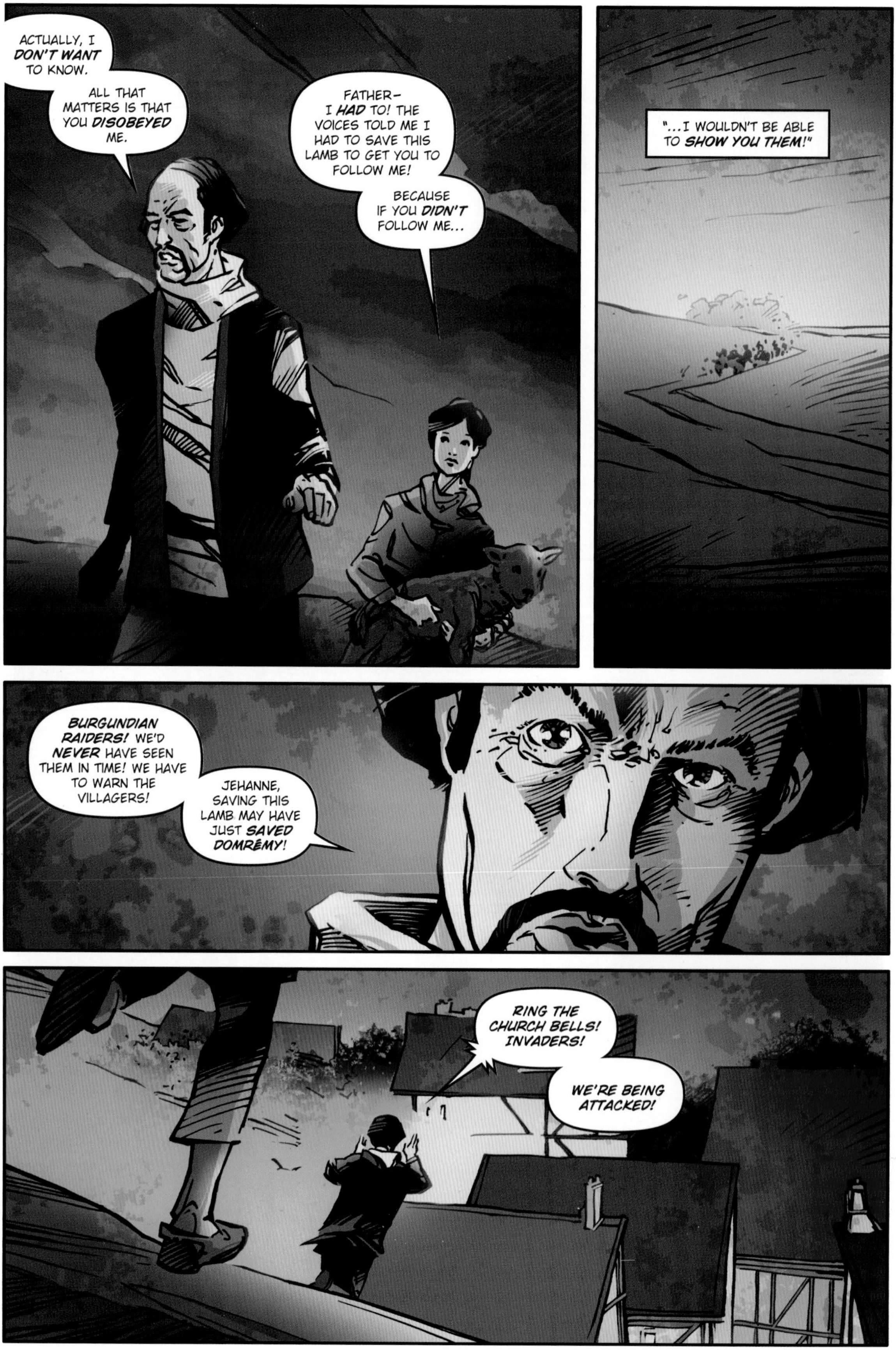

ACTUALLY, I DON'T WANT TO KNOW.
ALL THAT MATTERS IS THAT YOU DISOBEYED ME.
FATHER— I HAD TO! THE VOICES TOLD ME I HAD TO SAVE THIS LAMB TO GET YOU TO FOLLOW ME!
BECAUSE IF YOU DIDN'T FOLLOW ME...
"...I WOULDN'T BE ABLE TO SHOW YOU THEM!"
BURGUNDIAN RAIDERS! WE'D NEVER HAVE SEEN THEM IN TIME! WE HAVE TO WARN THE VILLAGERS!
JEHANNE, SAVING THIS LAMB MAY HAVE JUST SAVED DOMRÉMY!
RING THE CHURCH BELLS! INVADERS!
WE'RE BEING ATTACKED!

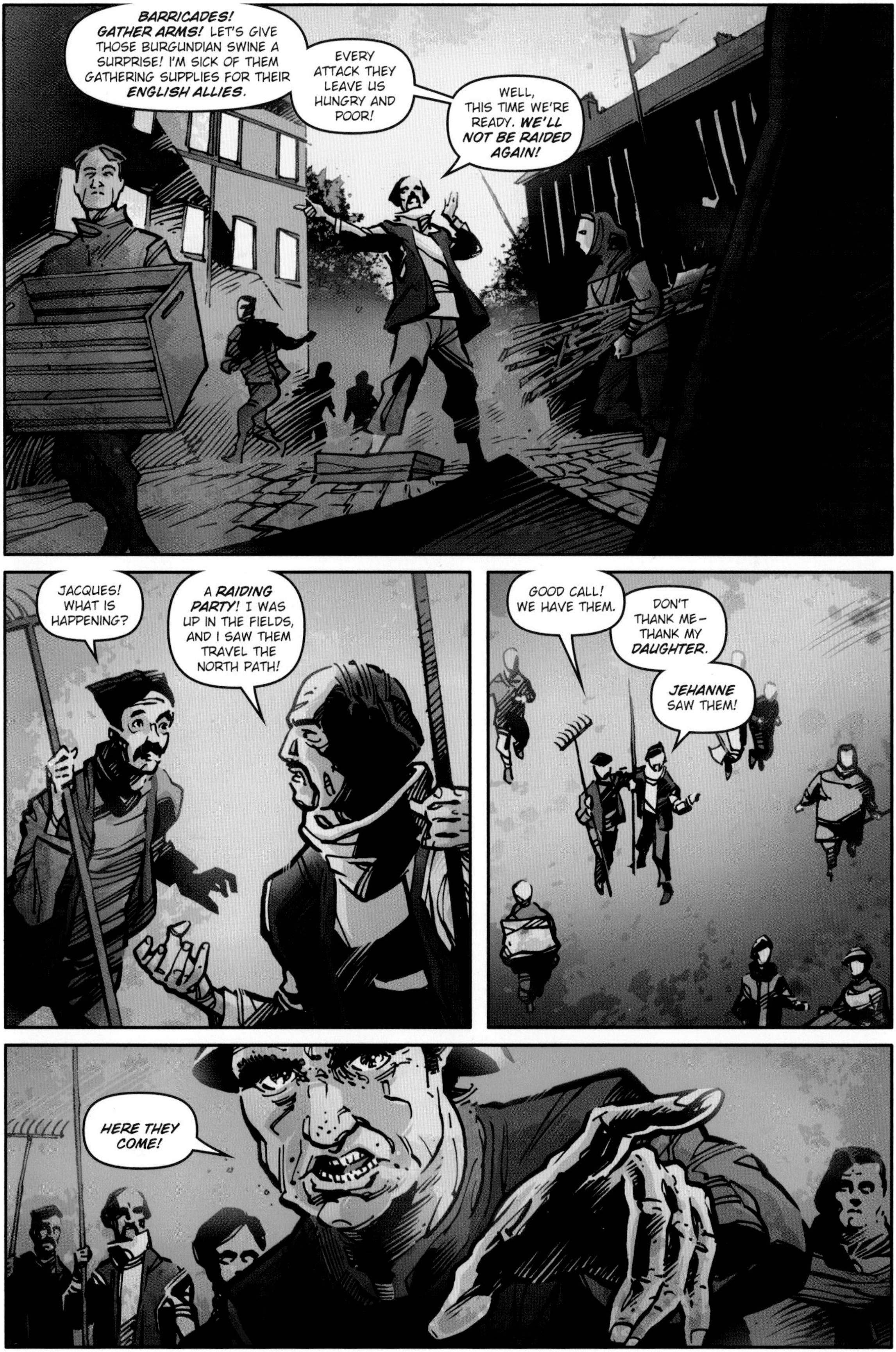
BARRICADES! GATHER ARMS! LET'S GIVE THOSE BURGUNDIAN SWINE A SURPRISE! I'M SICK OF THEM GATHERING SUPPLIES FOR THEIR ENGLISH ALLIES.
EVERY ATTACK THEY LEAVE US HUNGRY AND POOR!
WELL, THIS TIME WE'RE READY. WE'LL NOT BE RAIDED AGAIN!
JACQUES! WHAT IS HAPPENING?
A RAIDING PARTY! I WAS UP IN THE FIELDS, AND I SAW THEM TRAVEL THE NORTH PATH!
GOOD CALL! WE HAVE THEM.
DON'T THANK ME— THANK MY DAUGHTER.
JEHANNE SAW THEM!
HERE THEY COME!

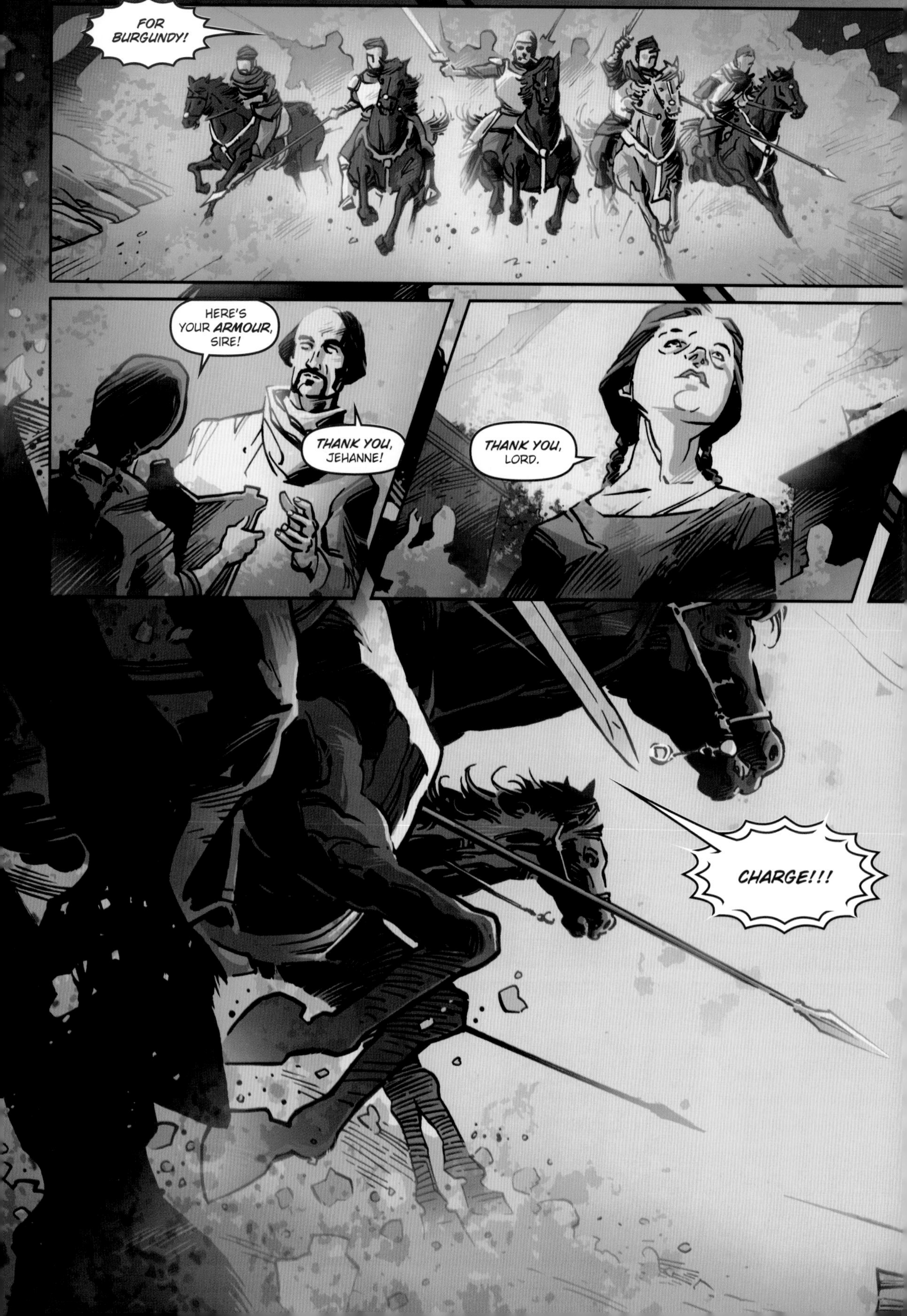
FOR BURGUNDY!
HERE'S YOUR ARMOUR, SIRE!
THANK YOU, JEHANNE!
THANK YOU, LORD.
CHARGE!!!

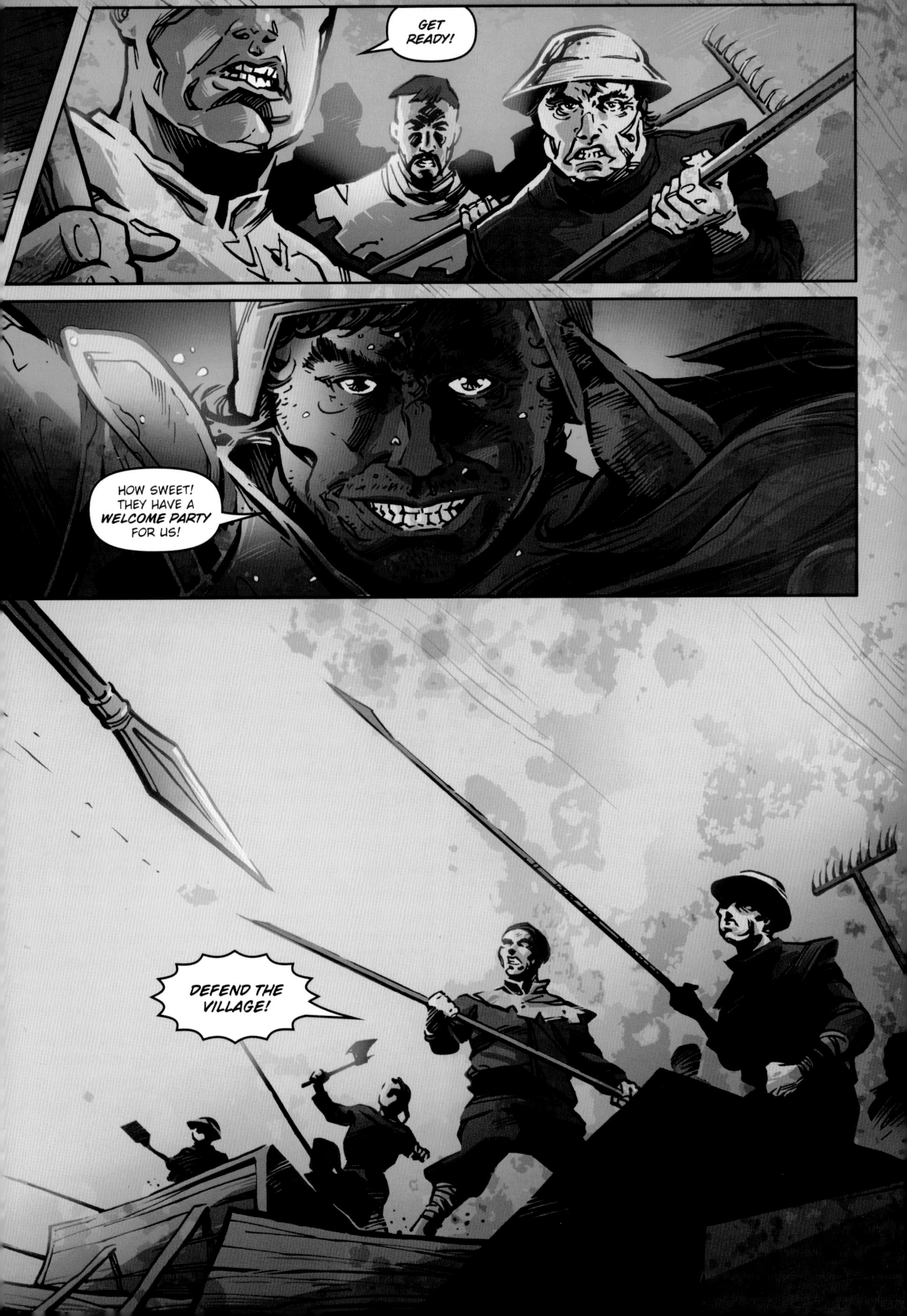
GET READY!
HOW SWEET! THEY HAVE A WELCOME PARTY FOR US!
DEFEND THE VILLAGE!

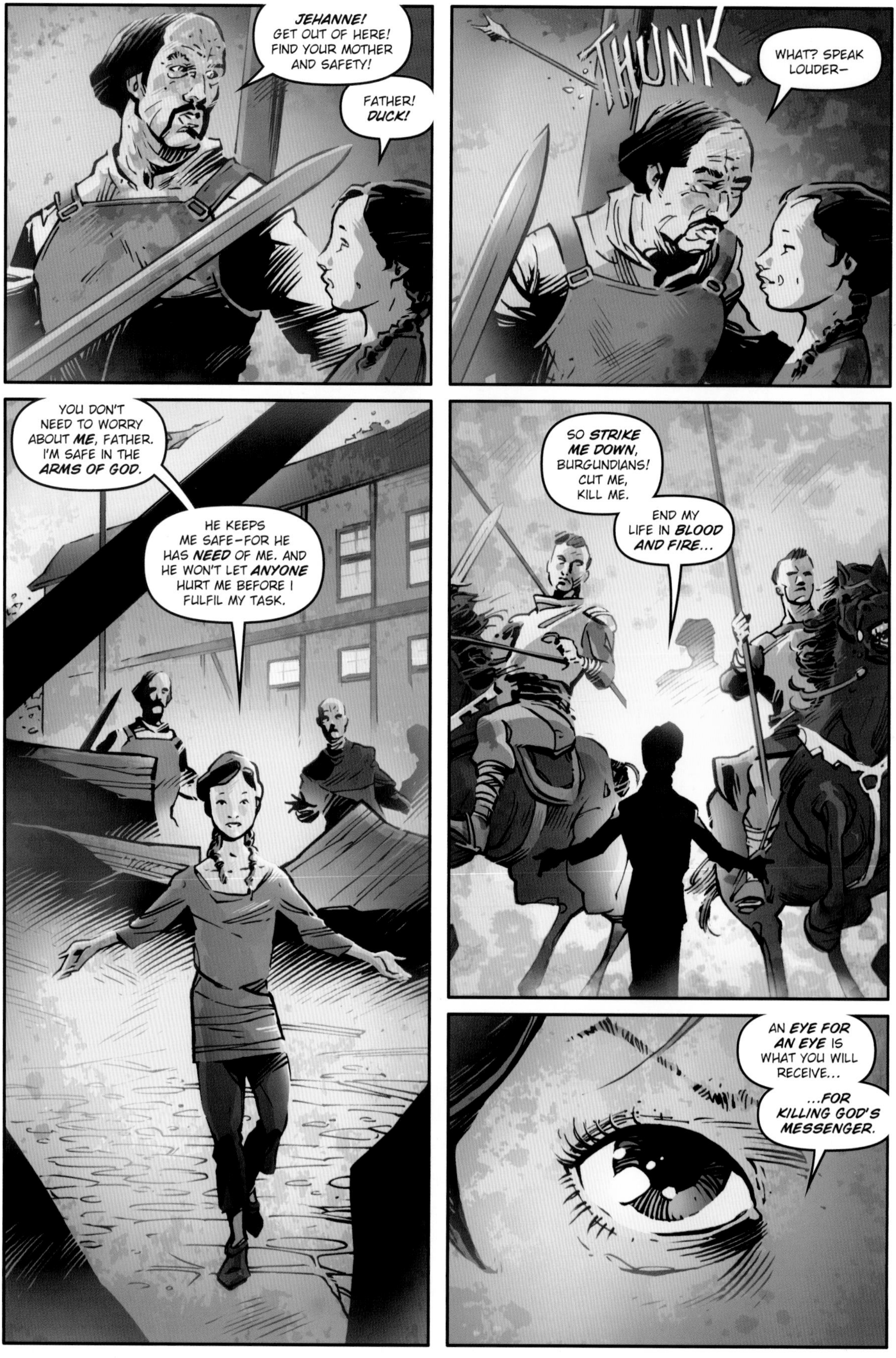
JEHANNE! GET OUT OF HERE! FIND YOUR MOTHER AND SAFETY!
FATHER! DUCK!
THUNK
WHAT? SPEAK LOUDER–
YOU DON'T NEED TO WORRY ABOUT ME, FATHER. I'M SAFE IN THE ARMS OF GOD.
HE KEEPS ME SAFE–FOR HE HAS NEED OF ME. AND HE WON'T LET ANYONE HURT ME BEFORE I FULFIL MY TASK.
SO STRIKE ME DOWN, BURGUNDIANS! CUT ME, KILL ME.
END MY LIFE IN BLOOD AND FIRE...
AN EYE FOR AN EYE IS WHAT YOU WILL RECEIVE...
...FOR KILLING GOD'S MESSENGER.

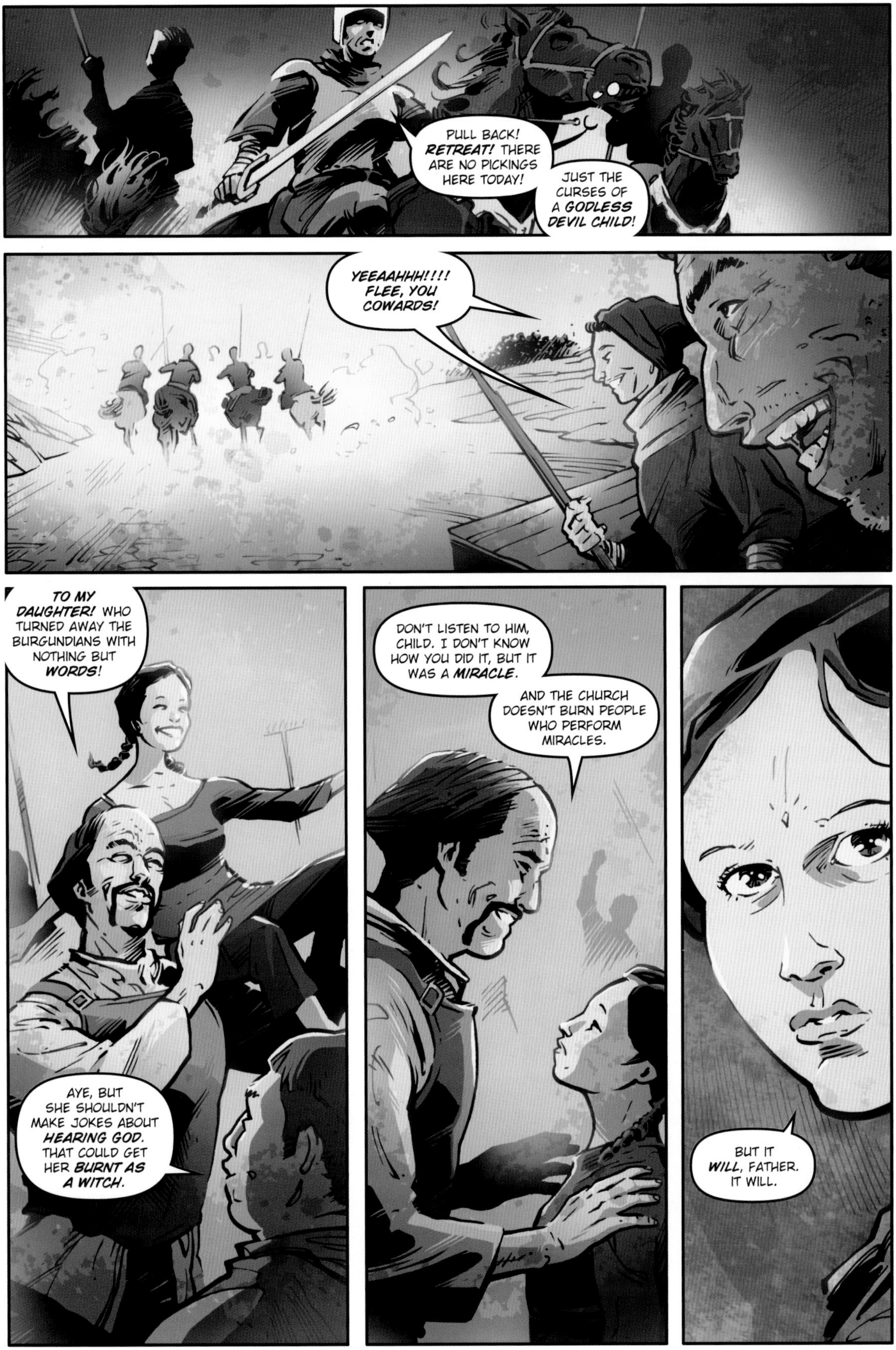
PULL BACK! RETREAT! THERE ARE NO PICKINGS HERE TODAY!
JUST THE CURSES OF A GODLESS DEVIL CHILD!
YEEAAHHH!!!! FLEE, YOU COWARDS!
TO MY DAUGHTER! WHO TURNED AWAY THE BURGUNDIANS WITH NOTHING BUT WORDS!
AYE, BUT SHE SHOULDN'T MAKE JOKES ABOUT HEARING GOD. THAT COULD GET HER BURNT AS A WITCH.
DON'T LISTEN TO HIM, CHILD. I DON'T KNOW HOW YOU DID IT, BUT IT WAS A MIRACLE.
AND THE CHURCH DOESN'T BURN PEOPLE WHO PERFORM MIRACLES.
BUT IT WILL, FATHER. IT WILL.

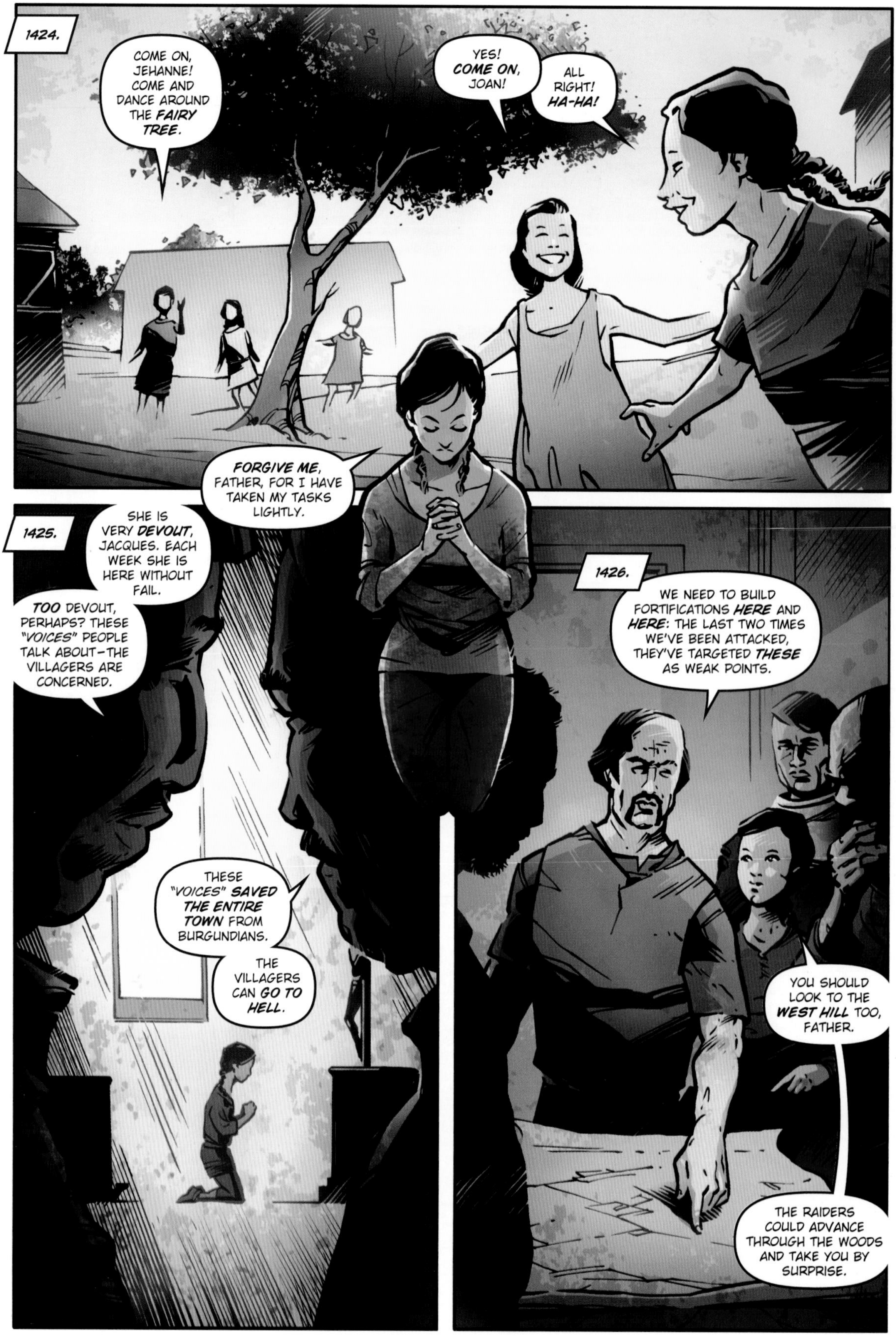
1424.
COME ON, JEHANNE! COME AND DANCE AROUND THE FAIRY TREE.
YES! COME ON, JOAN!
ALL RIGHT! HA-HA!
FORGIVE ME, FATHER, FOR I HAVE TAKEN MY TASKS LIGHTLY.
1425.
SHE IS VERY DEVOUT, JACQUES. EACH WEEK SHE IS HERE WITHOUT FAIL.
TOO DEVOUT, PERHAPS? THESE "VOICES" PEOPLE TALK ABOUT—THE VILLAGERS ARE CONCERNED.
THESE "VOICES" SAVED THE ENTIRE TOWN FROM BURGUNDIANS.
THE VILLAGERS CAN GO TO HELL.
1426.
WE NEED TO BUILD FORTIFICATIONS HERE AND HERE: THE LAST TWO TIMES WE'VE BEEN ATTACKED, THEY'VE TARGETED THESE AS WEAK POINTS.
YOU SHOULD LOOK TO THE WEST HILL TOO, FATHER.
THE RAIDERS COULD ADVANCE THROUGH THE WOODS AND TAKE YOU BY SURPRISE.

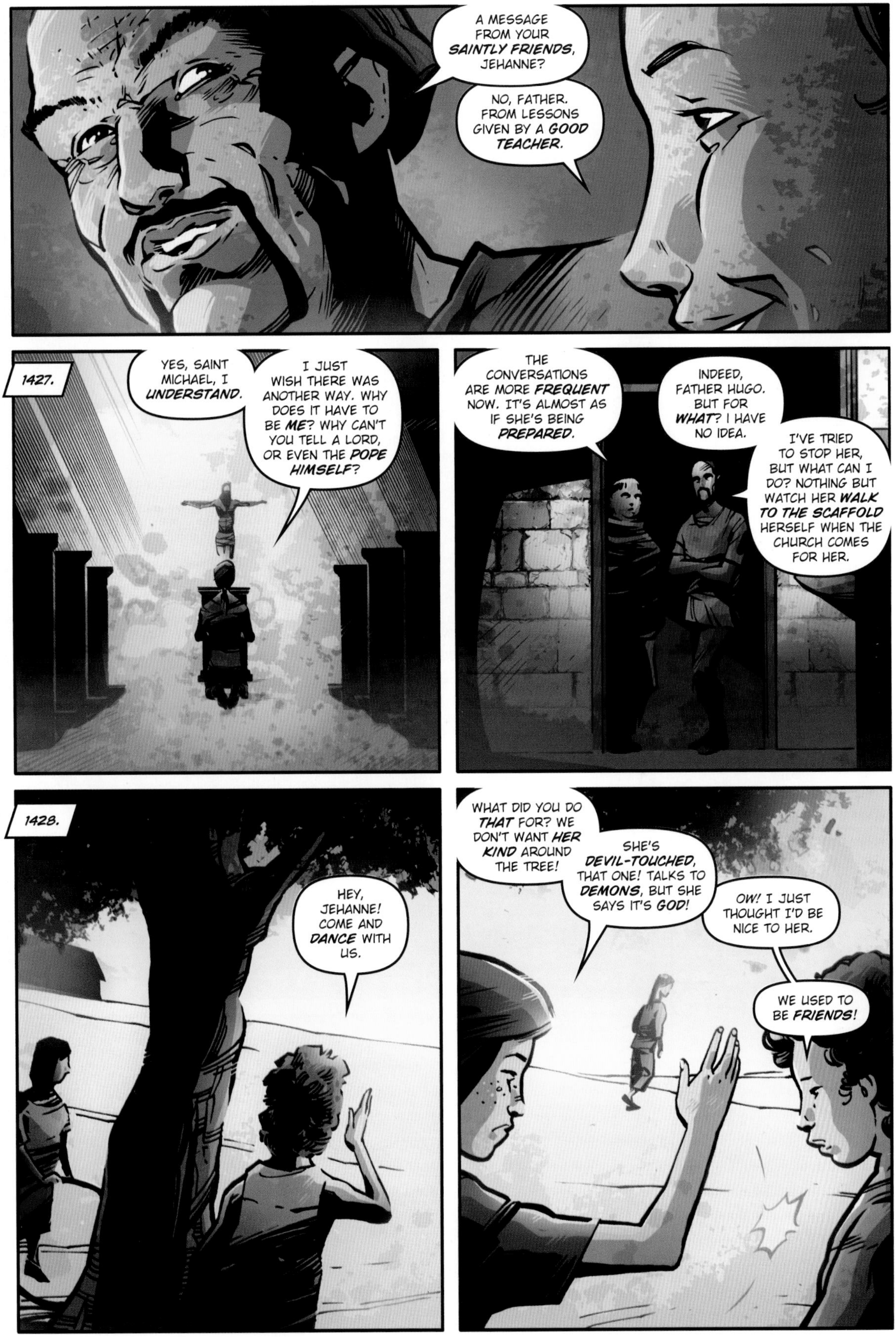
A MESSAGE FROM YOUR SAINTLY FRIENDS, JEHANNE?
NO, FATHER. FROM LESSONS GIVEN BY A GOOD TEACHER.
1427.
YES, SAINT MICHAEL, I UNDERSTAND.
I JUST WISH THERE WAS ANOTHER WAY. WHY DOES IT HAVE TO BE ME? WHY CAN'T YOU TELL A LORD, OR EVEN THE POPE HIMSELF?
THE CONVERSATIONS ARE MORE FREQUENT NOW. IT'S ALMOST AS IF SHE'S BEING PREPARED.
INDEED, FATHER HUGO. BUT FOR WHAT? I HAVE NO IDEA.
I'VE TRIED TO STOP HER, BUT WHAT CAN I DO? NOTHING BUT WATCH HER WALK TO THE SCAFFOLD HERSELF WHEN THE CHURCH COMES FOR HER.
1428.
HEY, JEHANNE! COME AND DANCE WITH US.
WHAT DID YOU DO THAT FOR? WE DON'T WANT HER KIND AROUND THE TREE!
SHE'S DEVIL-TOUCHED, THAT ONE! TALKS TO DEMONS, BUT SHE SAYS IT'S GOD!
OW! I JUST THOUGHT I'D BE NICE TO HER.
WE USED TO BE FRIENDS!

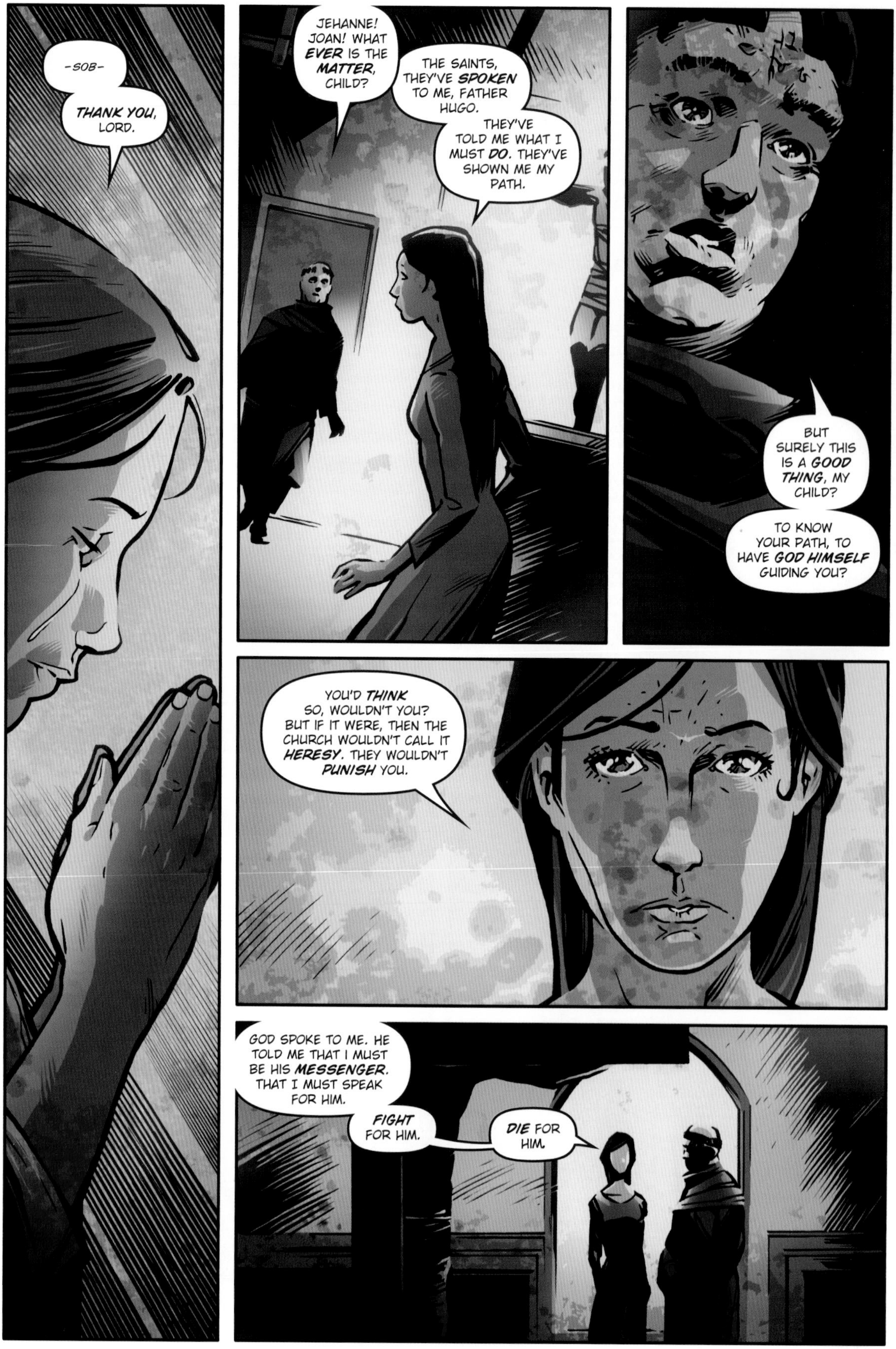
-SOB-
THANK YOU, LORD.
JEHANNE! JOAN! WHAT EVER IS THE MATTER, CHILD?
THE SAINTS, THEY'VE SPOKEN TO ME, FATHER HUGO.
THEY'VE TOLD ME WHAT I MUST DO. THEY'VE SHOWN ME MY PATH.
BUT SURELY THIS IS A GOOD THING, MY CHILD?
TO KNOW YOUR PATH, TO HAVE GOD HIMSELF GUIDING YOU?
YOU'D THINK SO, WOULDN'T YOU? BUT IF IT WERE, THEN THE CHURCH WOULDN'T CALL IT HERESY. THEY WOULDN'T PUNISH YOU.
GOD SPOKE TO ME. HE TOLD ME THAT I MUST BE HIS MESSENGER. THAT I MUST SPEAK FOR HIM.
FIGHT FOR HIM.
DIE FOR HIM.

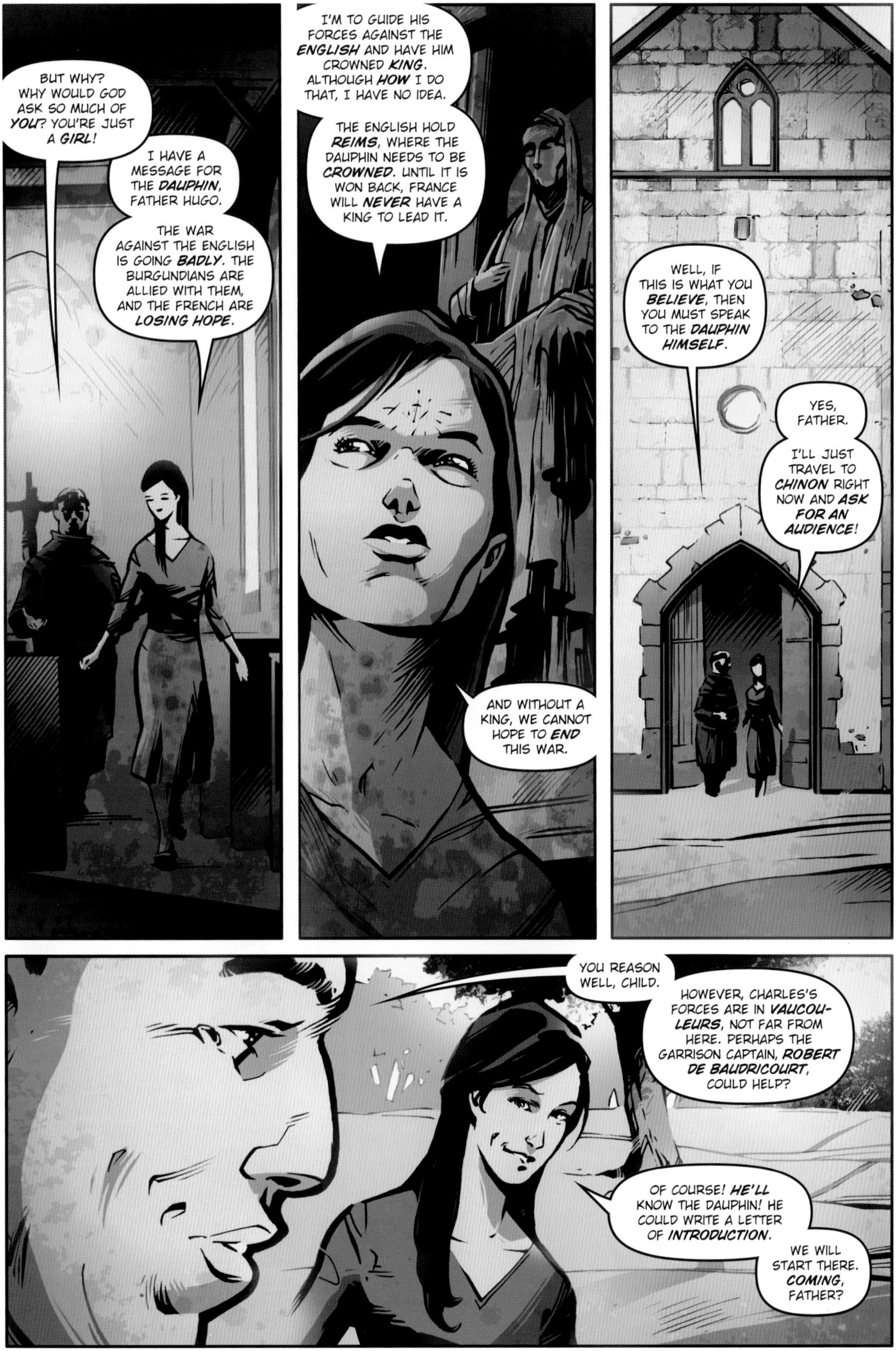
BUT WHY? WHY WOULD GOD ASK SO MUCH OF YOU? YOU'RE JUST A GIRL!
I HAVE A MESSAGE FOR THE DAUPHIN, FATHER HUGO.
THE WAR AGAINST THE ENGLISH IS GOING BADLY. THE BURGUNDIANS ARE ALLIED WITH THEM, AND THE FRENCH ARE LOSING HOPE.
I'M TO GUIDE HIS FORCES AGAINST THE ENGLISH AND HAVE HIM CROWNED KING. ALTHOUGH HOW I DO THAT, I HAVE NO IDEA.
THE ENGLISH HOLD REIMS, WHERE THE DAUPHIN NEEDS TO BE CROWNED. UNTIL IT IS WON BACK, FRANCE WILL NEVER HAVE A KING TO LEAD IT.
AND WITHOUT A KING, WE CANNOT HOPE TO END THIS WAR.
WELL, IF THIS IS WHAT YOU BELIEVE, THEN YOU MUST SPEAK TO THE DAUPHIN HIMSELF.
YES, FATHER.
I'LL JUST TRAVEL TO CHINON RIGHT NOW AND ASK FOR AN AUDIENCE!
YOU REASON WELL, CHILD.
HOWEVER, CHARLES'S FORCES ARE IN VAUCOULEURS, NOT FAR FROM HERE. PERHAPS THE GARRISON CAPTAIN, ROBERT DE BAUDRICOURT, COULD HELP?
OF COURSE! HE'LL KNOW THE DAUPHIN! HE COULD WRITE A LETTER OF INTRODUCTION.
WE WILL START THERE. COMING, FATHER?

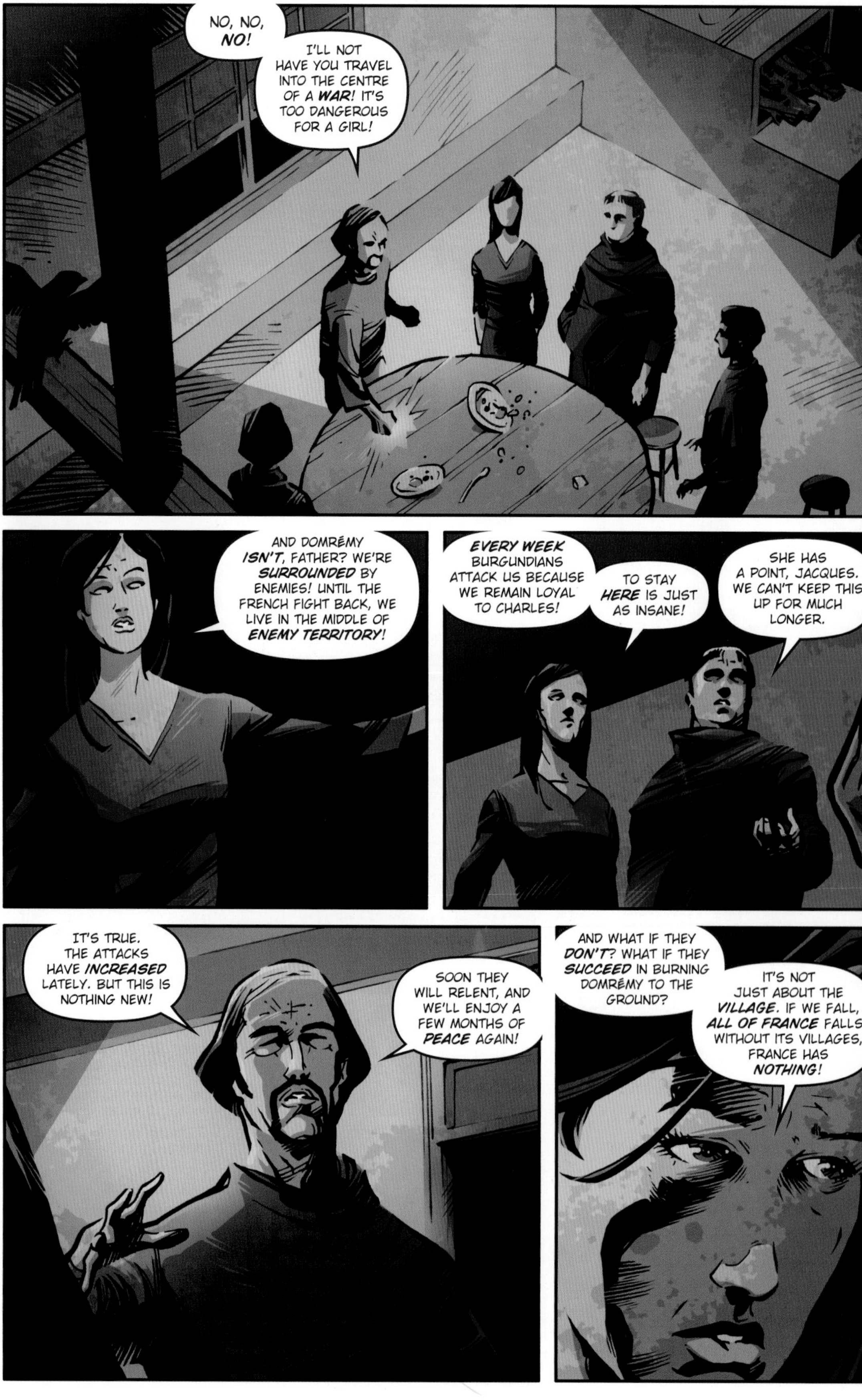
NO, NO, NO!
I'LL NOT HAVE YOU TRAVEL INTO THE CENTRE OF A WAR! IT'S TOO DANGEROUS FOR A GIRL!
AND DOMRÉMY ISN'T, FATHER? WE'RE SURROUNDED BY ENEMIES! UNTIL THE FRENCH FIGHT BACK, WE LIVE IN THE MIDDLE OF ENEMY TERRITORY!
EVERY WEEK BURGUNDIANS ATTACK US BECAUSE WE REMAIN LOYAL TO CHARLES!
TO STAY HERE IS JUST AS INSANE!
SHE HAS A POINT, JACQUES. WE CAN'T KEEP THIS UP FOR MUCH LONGER.
IT'S TRUE. THE ATTACKS HAVE INCREASED LATELY. BUT THIS IS NOTHING NEW!
SOON THEY WILL RELENT, AND WE'LL ENJOY A FEW MONTHS OF PEACE AGAIN!
AND WHAT IF THEY DON'T? WHAT IF THEY SUCCEED IN BURNING DOMRÉMY TO THE GROUND?
IT'S NOT JUST ABOUT THE VILLAGE. IF WE FALL, ALL OF FRANCE FALLS! WITHOUT ITS VILLAGES, FRANCE HAS NOTHING!

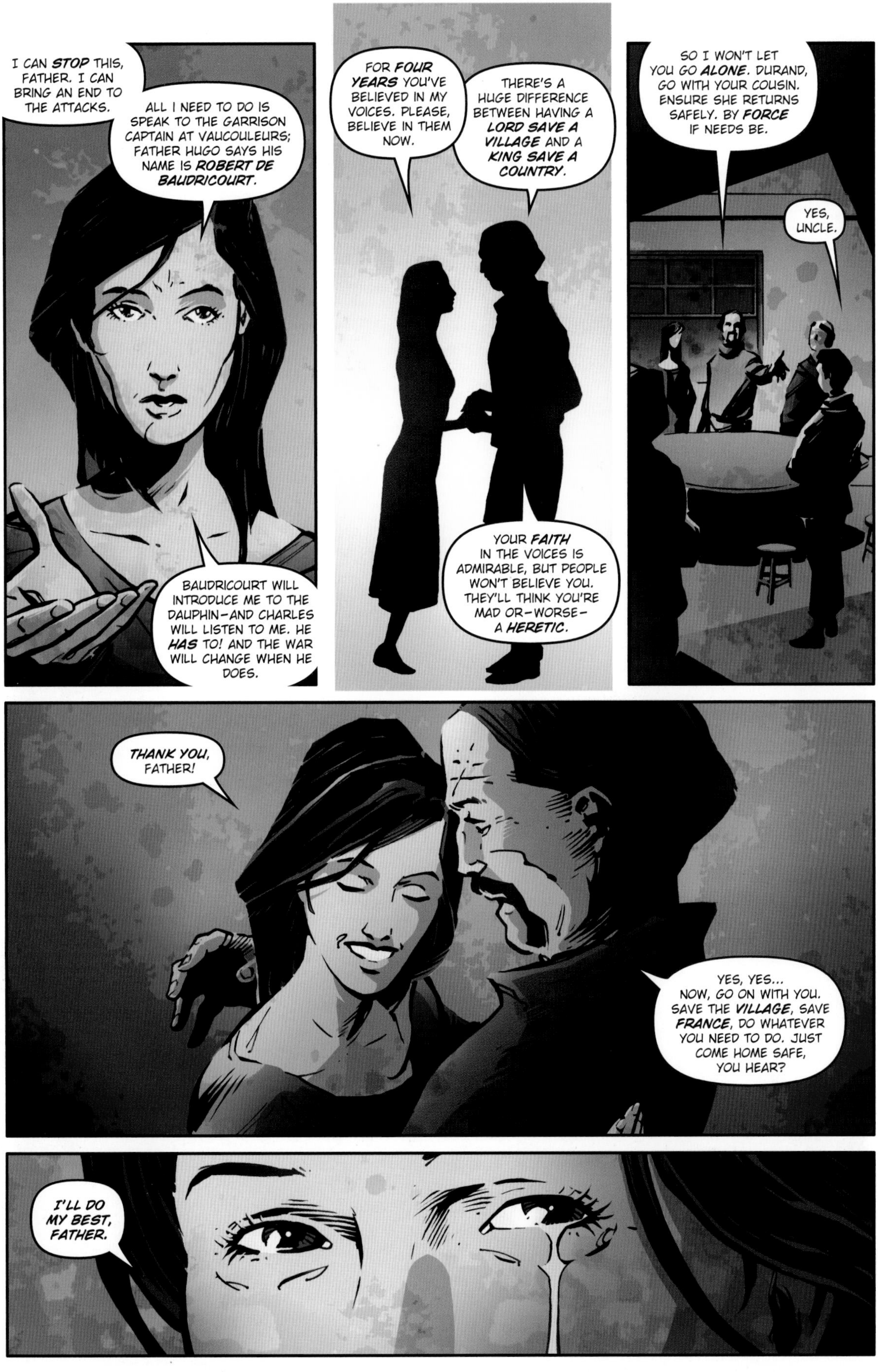
I CAN STOP THIS, FATHER. I CAN BRING AN END TO THE ATTACKS.
ALL I NEED TO DO IS SPEAK TO THE GARRISON CAPTAIN AT VAUCOULEURS; FATHER HUGO SAYS HIS NAME IS ROBERT DE BAUDRICOURT.
BAUDRICOURT WILL INTRODUCE ME TO THE DAUPHIN—AND CHARLES WILL LISTEN TO ME. HE HAS TO! AND THE WAR WILL CHANGE WHEN HE DOES.
FOR FOUR YEARS YOU'VE BELIEVED IN MY VOICES. PLEASE, BELIEVE IN THEM NOW.
THERE'S A HUGE DIFFERENCE BETWEEN HAVING A LORD SAVE A VILLAGE AND A KING SAVE A COUNTRY.
YOUR FAITH IN THE VOICES IS ADMIRABLE, BUT PEOPLE WON'T BELIEVE YOU. THEY'LL THINK YOU'RE MAD OR—WORSE—A HERETIC.
SO I WON'T LET YOU GO ALONE. DURAND, GO WITH YOUR COUSIN. ENSURE SHE RETURNS SAFELY. BY FORCE IF NEEDS BE.
YES, UNCLE.
THANK YOU, FATHER!
YES, YES... NOW, GO ON WITH YOU. SAVE THE VILLAGE, SAVE FRANCE, DO WHATEVER YOU NEED TO DO. JUST COME HOME SAFE, YOU HEAR?
I'LL DO MY BEST, FATHER.

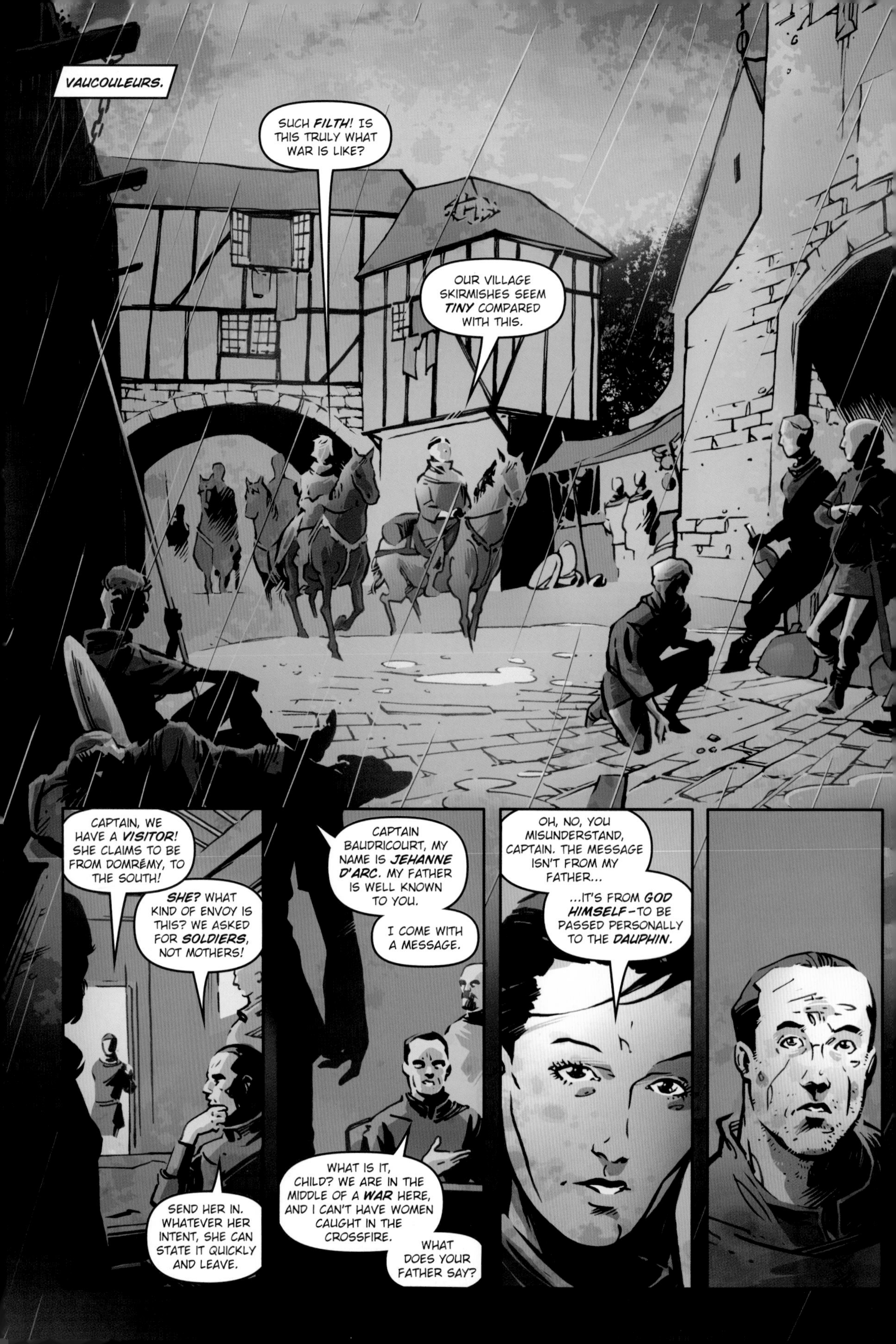
VAUCOULEURS.
SUCH FILTH! IS THIS TRULY WHAT WAR IS LIKE?
OUR VILLAGE SKIRMISHES SEEM TINY COMPARED WITH THIS.
CAPTAIN, WE HAVE A VISITOR! SHE CLAIMS TO BE FROM DOMRÉMY, TO THE SOUTH!
SHE? WHAT KIND OF ENVOY IS THIS? WE ASKED FOR SOLDIERS, NOT MOTHERS!
SEND HER IN. WHATEVER HER INTENT, SHE CAN STATE IT QUICKLY AND LEAVE.
CAPTAIN BAUDRICOURT, MY NAME IS JEHANNE D'ARC. MY FATHER IS WELL KNOWN TO YOU.
I COME WITH A MESSAGE.
WHAT IS IT, CHILD? WE ARE IN THE MIDDLE OF A WAR HERE, AND I CAN'T HAVE WOMEN CAUGHT IN THE CROSSFIRE.
WHAT DOES YOUR FATHER SAY?
OH, NO, YOU MISUNDERSTAND, CAPTAIN. THE MESSAGE ISN'T FROM MY FATHER...
...IT'S FROM GOD HIMSELF–TO BE PASSED PERSONALLY TO THE DAUPHIN.

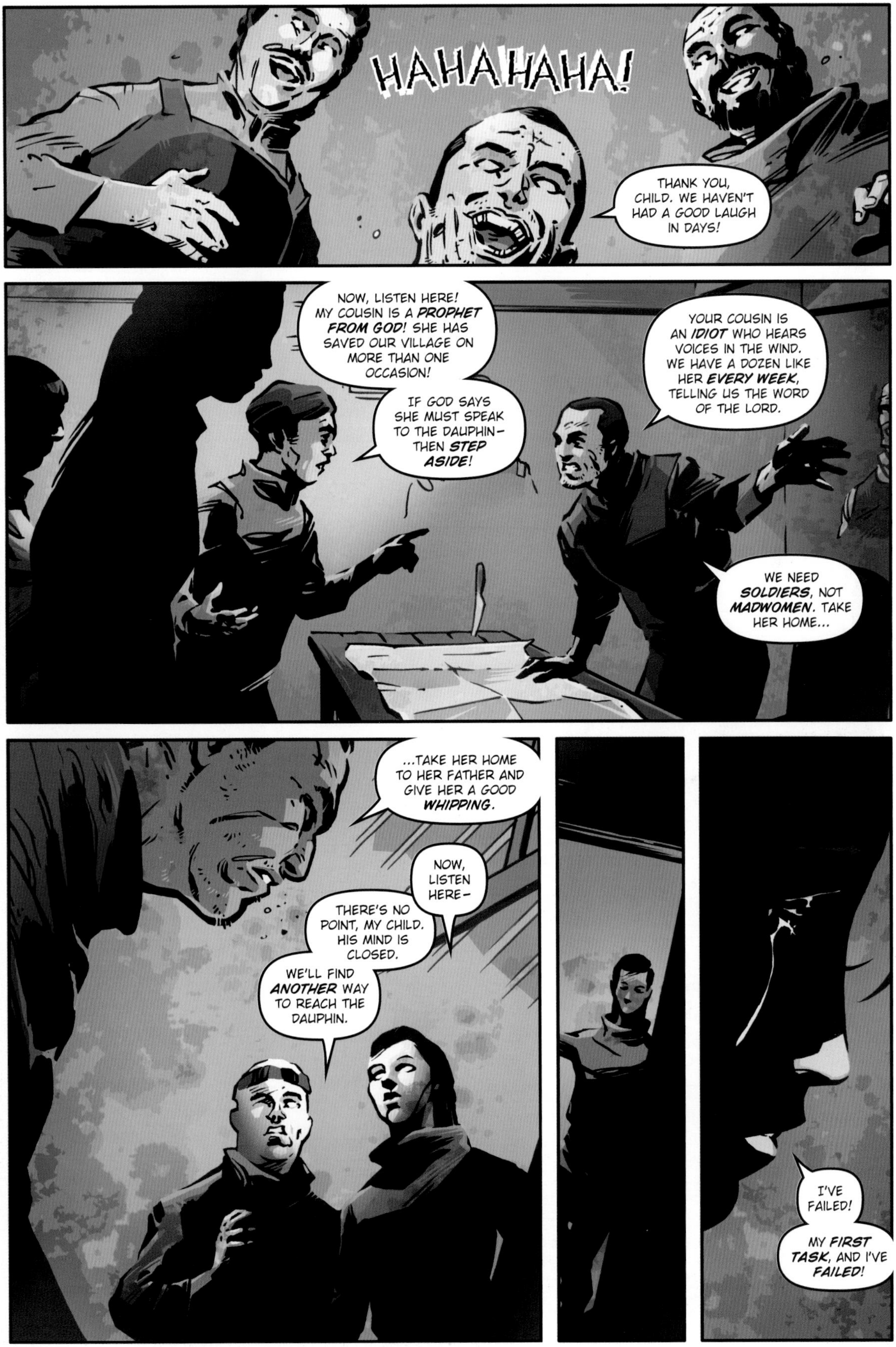
HAHAHAHA!
THANK YOU, CHILD. WE HAVEN'T HAD A GOOD LAUGH IN DAYS!
NOW, LISTEN HERE! MY COUSIN IS A PROPHET FROM GOD! SHE HAS SAVED OUR VILLAGE ON MORE THAN ONE OCCASION!
IF GOD SAYS SHE MUST SPEAK TO THE DAUPHIN— THEN STEP ASIDE!
YOUR COUSIN IS AN IDIOT WHO HEARS VOICES IN THE WIND. WE HAVE A DOZEN LIKE HER EVERY WEEK, TELLING US THE WORD OF THE LORD.
WE NEED SOLDIERS, NOT MADWOMEN. TAKE HER HOME...
...TAKE HER HOME TO HER FATHER AND GIVE HER A GOOD WHIPPING.
NOW, LISTEN HERE—
THERE'S NO POINT, MY CHILD. HIS MIND IS CLOSED.
WE'LL FIND ANOTHER WAY TO REACH THE DAUPHIN.
I'VE FAILED!
MY FIRST TASK, AND I'VE FAILED!

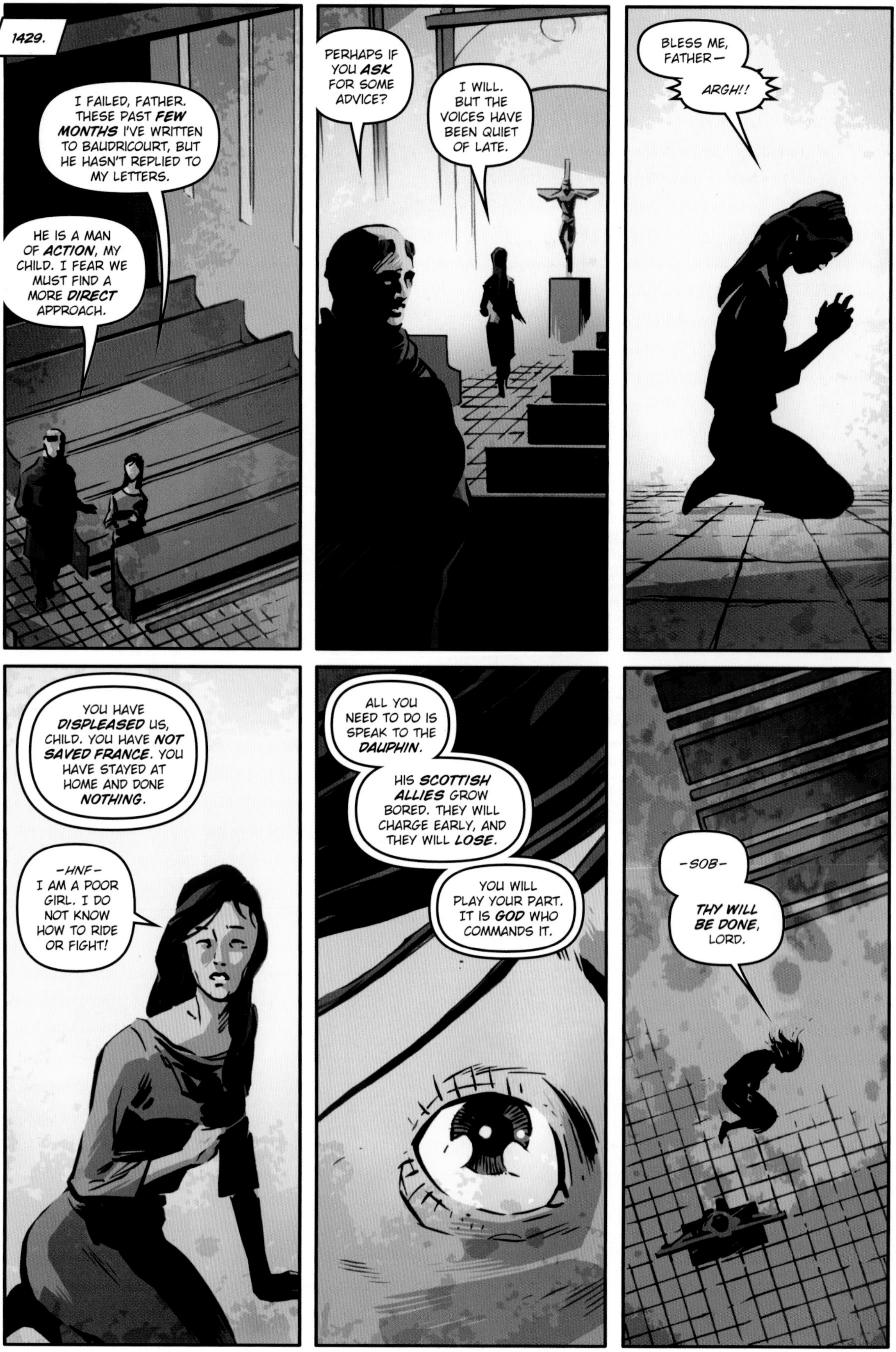
1429.
I FAILED, FATHER. THESE PAST FEW MONTHS I'VE WRITTEN TO BAUDRICOURT, BUT HE HASN'T REPLIED TO MY LETTERS.
HE IS A MAN OF ACTION, MY CHILD. I FEAR WE MUST FIND A MORE DIRECT APPROACH.
PERHAPS IF YOU ASK FOR SOME ADVICE?
I WILL. BUT THE VOICES HAVE BEEN QUIET OF LATE.
BLESS ME, FATHER—
ARGH!!
YOU HAVE DISPLEASED US, CHILD. YOU HAVE NOT SAVED FRANCE. YOU HAVE STAYED AT HOME AND DONE NOTHING.
-HNF- I AM A POOR GIRL. I DO NOT KNOW HOW TO RIDE OR FIGHT!
ALL YOU NEED TO DO IS SPEAK TO THE DAUPHIN.
HIS SCOTTISH ALLIES GROW BORED. THEY WILL CHARGE EARLY, AND THEY WILL LOSE.
YOU WILL PLAY YOUR PART. IT IS GOD WHO COMMANDS IT.
-SOB-
THY WILL BE DONE, LORD.

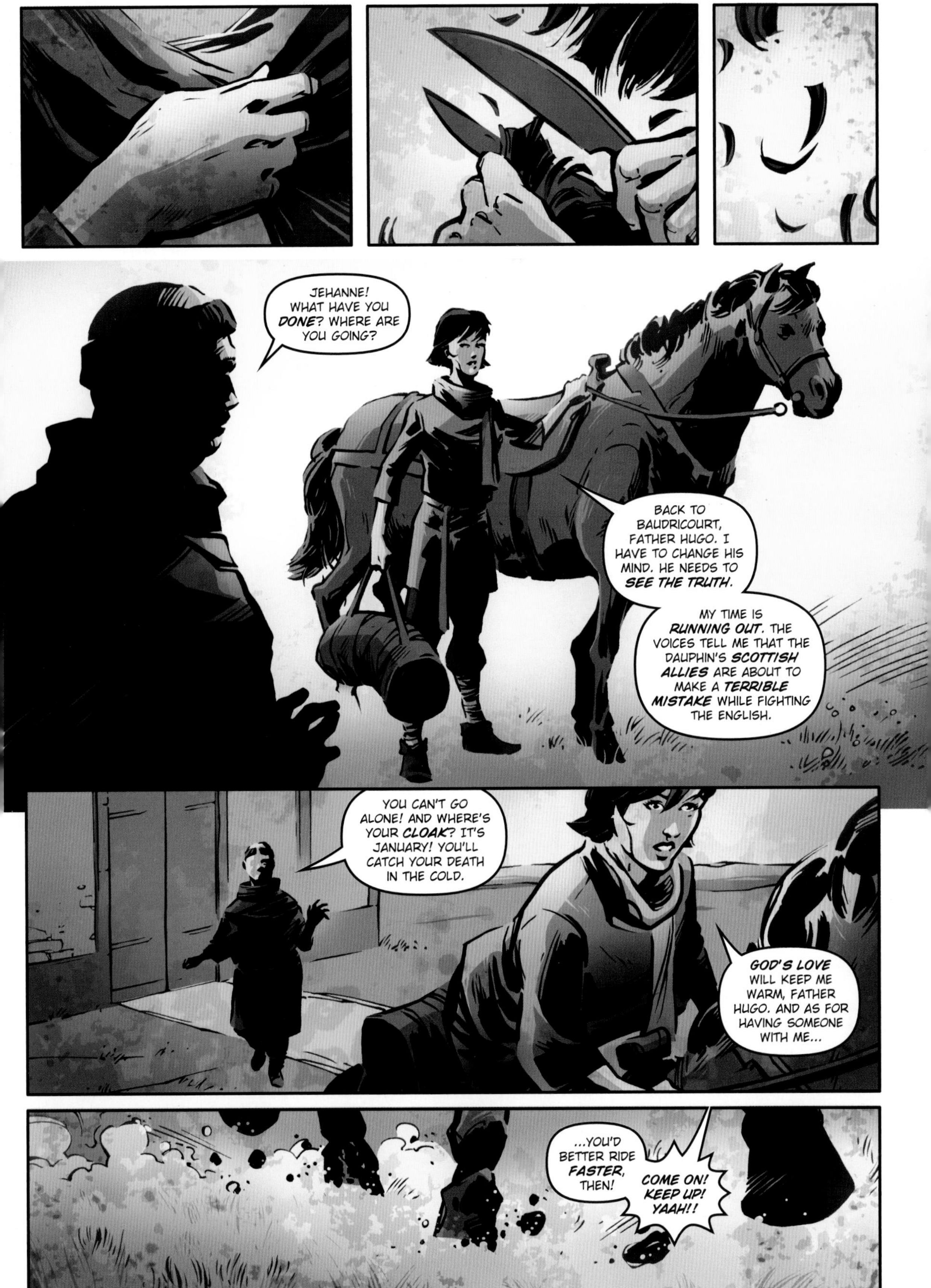

JEHANNE! WHAT HAVE YOU DONE? WHERE ARE YOU GOING?
BACK TO BAUDRICOURT, FATHER HUGO. I HAVE TO CHANGE HIS MIND. HE NEEDS TO SEE THE TRUTH.
MY TIME IS RUNNING OUT. THE VOICES TELL ME THAT THE DAUPHIN'S SCOTTISH ALLIES ARE ABOUT TO MAKE A TERRIBLE MISTAKE WHILE FIGHTING THE ENGLISH.
YOU CAN'T GO ALONE! AND WHERE'S YOUR CLOAK? IT'S JANUARY! YOU'LL CATCH YOUR DEATH IN THE COLD.
GOD'S LOVE WILL KEEP ME WARM, FATHER HUGO. AND AS FOR HAVING SOMEONE WITH ME...
...YOU'D BETTER RIDE FASTER, THEN!
COME ON! KEEP UP! YAAH!!

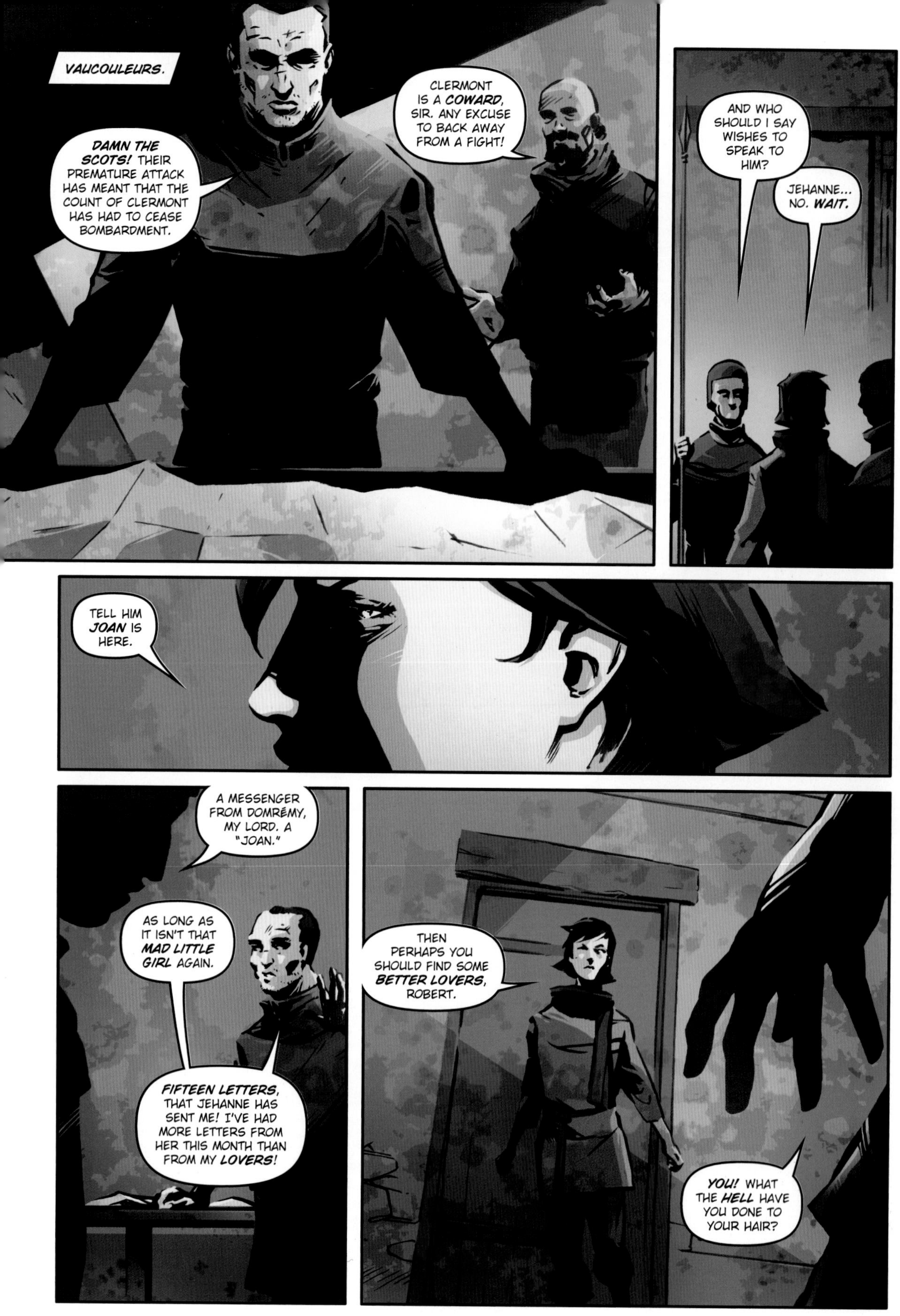
VAUCOULEURS.
DAMN THE SCOTS! THEIR PREMATURE ATTACK HAS MEANT THAT THE COUNT OF CLERMONT HAS HAD TO CEASE BOMBARDMENT.
CLERMONT IS A COWARD, SIR. ANY EXCUSE TO BACK AWAY FROM A FIGHT!
AND WHO SHOULD I SAY WISHES TO SPEAK TO HIM?
JEHANNE... NO. WAIT.
TELL HIM JOAN IS HERE.
A MESSENGER FROM DOMRÉMY, MY LORD. A "JOAN."
AS LONG AS IT ISN'T THAT MAD LITTLE GIRL AGAIN.
FIFTEEN LETTERS, THAT JEHANNE HAS SENT ME! I'VE HAD MORE LETTERS FROM HER THIS MONTH THAN FROM MY LOVERS!
THEN PERHAPS YOU SHOULD FIND SOME BETTER LOVERS, ROBERT.
YOU! WHAT THE HELL HAVE YOU DONE TO YOUR HAIR?

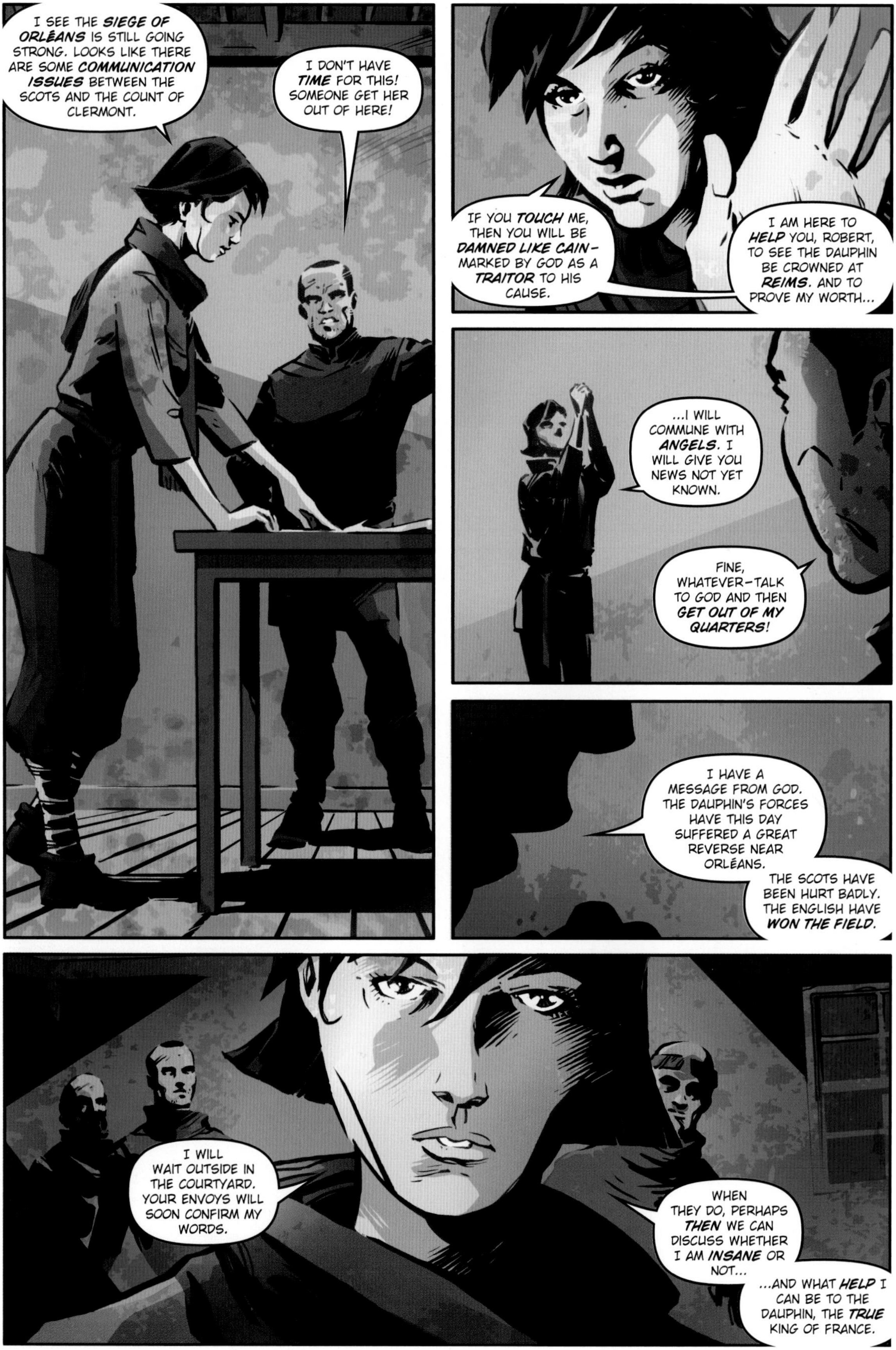
I SEE THE SIEGE OF ORLÉANS IS STILL GOING STRONG. LOOKS LIKE THERE ARE SOME COMMUNICATION ISSUES BETWEEN THE SCOTS AND THE COUNT OF CLERMONT.
I DON'T HAVE TIME FOR THIS! SOMEONE GET HER OUT OF HERE!
IF YOU TOUCH ME, THEN YOU WILL BE DAMNED LIKE CAIN–MARKED BY GOD AS A TRAITOR TO HIS CAUSE.
I AM HERE TO HELP YOU, ROBERT, TO SEE THE DAUPHIN BE CROWNED AT REIMS. AND TO PROVE MY WORTH...
...I WILL COMMUNE WITH ANGELS. I WILL GIVE YOU NEWS NOT YET KNOWN.
FINE, WHATEVER–TALK TO GOD AND THEN GET OUT OF MY QUARTERS!
I HAVE A MESSAGE FROM GOD. THE DAUPHIN'S FORCES HAVE THIS DAY SUFFERED A GREAT REVERSE NEAR ORLÉANS.
THE SCOTS HAVE BEEN HURT BADLY. THE ENGLISH HAVE WON THE FIELD.
I WILL WAIT OUTSIDE IN THE COURTYARD. YOUR ENVOYS WILL SOON CONFIRM MY WORDS.
WHEN THEY DO, PERHAPS THEN WE CAN DISCUSS WHETHER I AM INSANE OR NOT...
...AND WHAT HELP I CAN BE TO THE DAUPHIN, THE TRUE KING OF FRANCE.

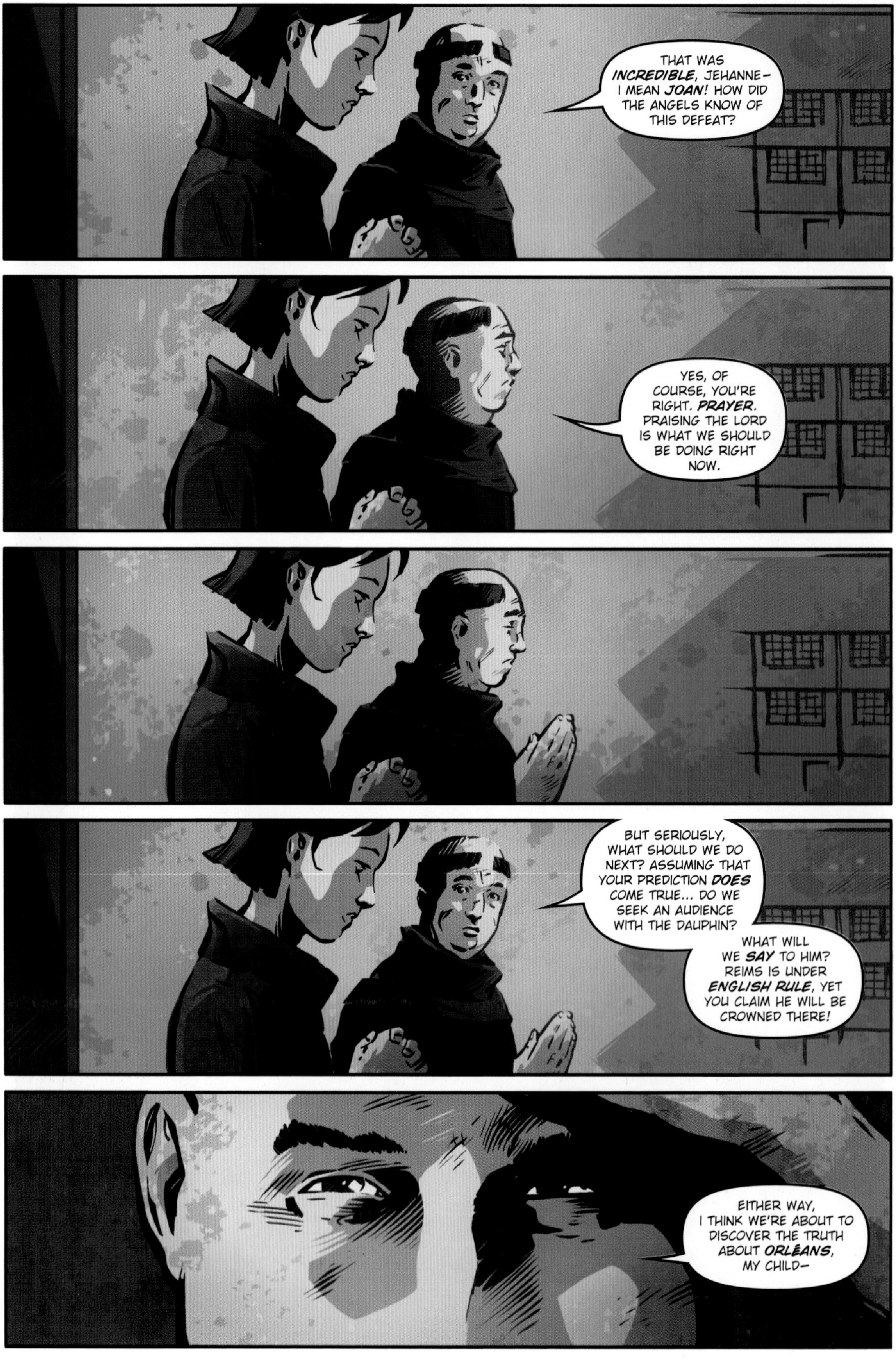
THAT WAS INCREDIBLE, JEHANNE— I MEAN JOAN! HOW DID THE ANGELS KNOW OF THIS DEFEAT?
YES, OF COURSE, YOU'RE RIGHT. PRAYER. PRAISING THE LORD IS WHAT WE SHOULD BE DOING RIGHT NOW.
BUT SERIOUSLY, WHAT SHOULD WE DO NEXT? ASSUMING THAT YOUR PREDICTION DOES COME TRUE... DO WE SEEK AN AUDIENCE WITH THE DAUPHIN?
WHAT WILL WE SAY TO HIM? REIMS IS UNDER ENGLISH RULE, YET YOU CLAIM HE WILL BE CROWNED THERE!
EITHER WAY, I THINK WE'RE ABOUT TO DISCOVER THE TRUTH ABOUT ORLÉANS, MY CHILD—

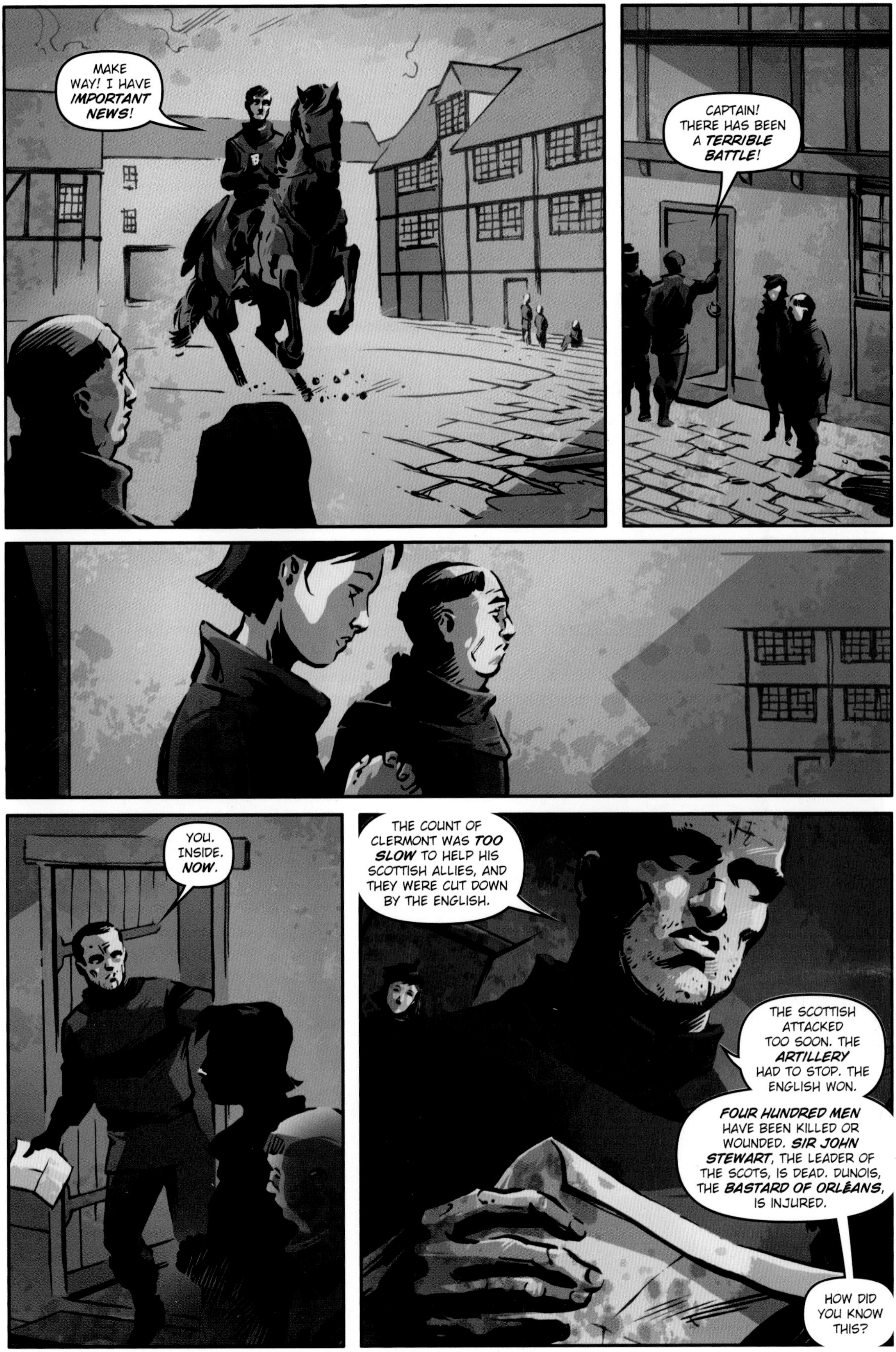
MAKE WAY! I HAVE IMPORTANT NEWS!
CAPTAIN! THERE HAS BEEN A TERRIBLE BATTLE!
YOU. INSIDE. NOW.
THE COUNT OF CLERMONT WAS TOO SLOW TO HELP HIS SCOTTISH ALLIES, AND THEY WERE CUT DOWN BY THE ENGLISH.
THE SCOTTISH ATTACKED TOO SOON. THE ARTILLERY HAD TO STOP. THE ENGLISH WON.
FOUR HUNDRED MEN HAVE BEEN KILLED OR WOUNDED. SIR JOHN STEWART, THE LEADER OF THE SCOTS, IS DEAD. DUNOIS, THE BASTARD OF ORLÉANS, IS INJURED.
HOW DID YOU KNOW THIS?

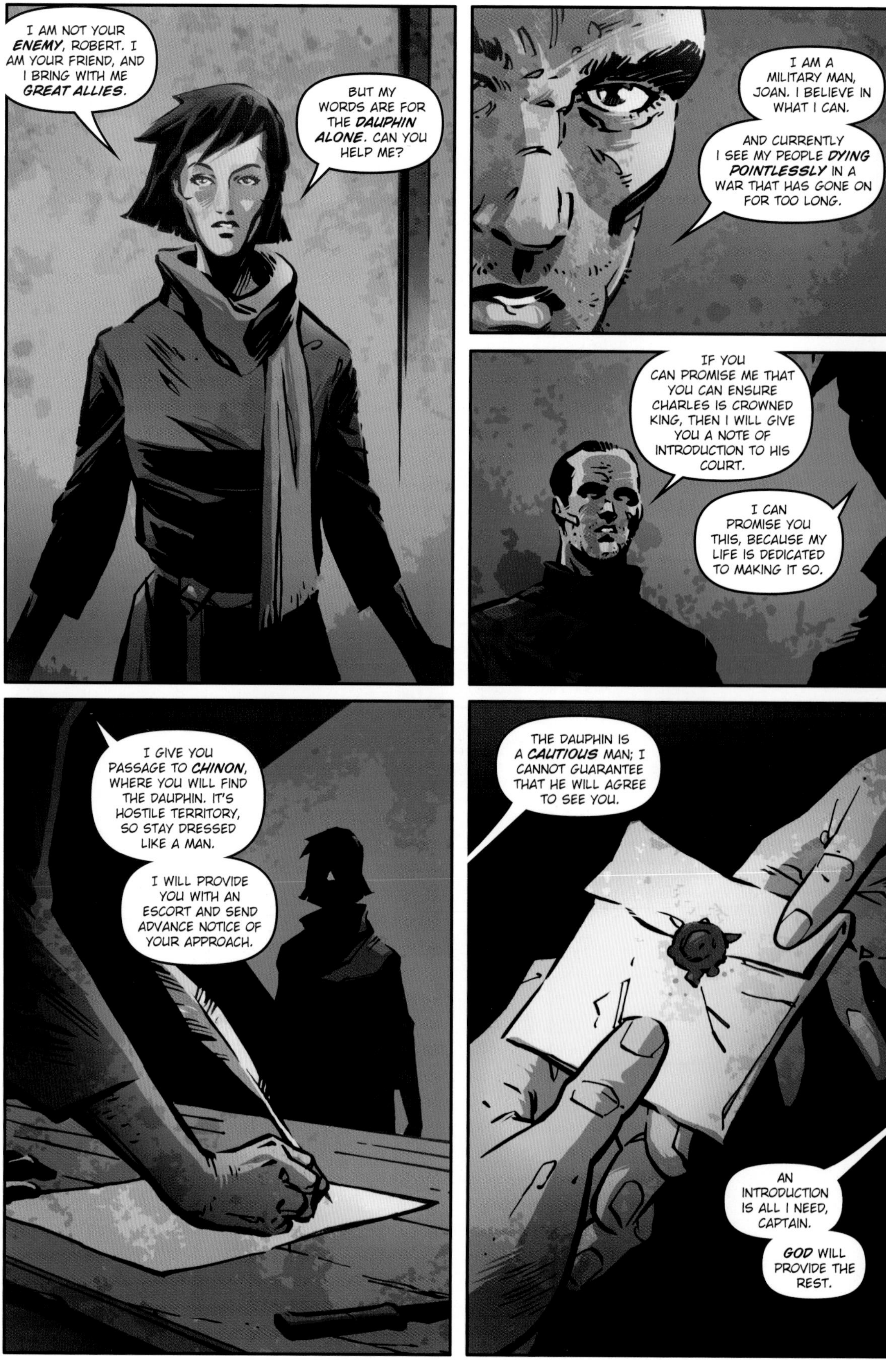

I AM NOT YOUR ENEMY, ROBERT. I AM YOUR FRIEND, AND I BRING WITH ME GREAT ALLIES.
BUT MY WORDS ARE FOR THE DAUPHIN ALONE. CAN YOU HELP ME?
I AM A MILITARY MAN, JOAN. I BELIEVE IN WHAT I CAN.
AND CURRENTLY I SEE MY PEOPLE DYING POINTLESSLY IN A WAR THAT HAS GONE ON FOR TOO LONG.
IF YOU CAN PROMISE ME THAT YOU CAN ENSURE CHARLES IS CROWNED KING, THEN I WILL GIVE YOU A NOTE OF INTRODUCTION TO HIS COURT.
I CAN PROMISE YOU THIS, BECAUSE MY LIFE IS DEDICATED TO MAKING IT SO.
I GIVE YOU PASSAGE TO CHINON, WHERE YOU WILL FIND THE DAUPHIN. IT'S HOSTILE TERRITORY, SO STAY DRESSED LIKE A MAN.
I WILL PROVIDE YOU WITH AN ESCORT AND SEND ADVANCE NOTICE OF YOUR APPROACH.
THE DAUPHIN IS A CAUTIOUS MAN; I CANNOT GUARANTEE THAT HE WILL AGREE TO SEE YOU.
AN INTRODUCTION IS ALL I NEED, CAPTAIN.
GOD WILL PROVIDE THE REST.

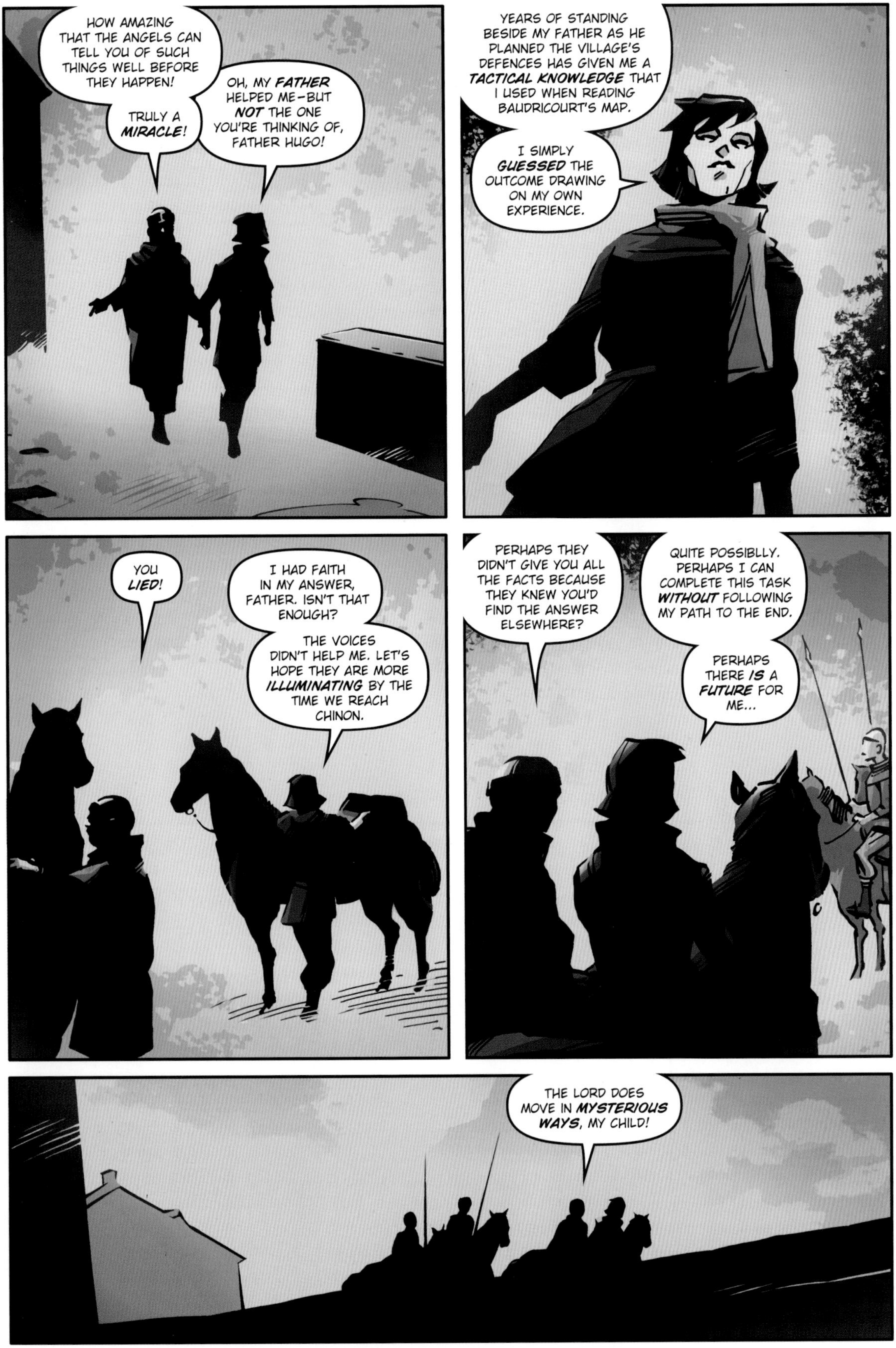
HOW AMAZING THAT THE ANGELS CAN TELL YOU OF SUCH THINGS WELL BEFORE THEY HAPPEN!
TRULY A ***MIRACLE***!
OH, MY ***FATHER*** HELPED ME—BUT ***NOT*** THE ONE YOU'RE THINKING OF, FATHER HUGO!
YEARS OF STANDING BESIDE MY FATHER AS HE PLANNED THE VILLAGE'S DEFENCES HAS GIVEN ME A ***TACTICAL KNOWLEDGE*** THAT I USED WHEN READING BAUDRICOURT'S MAP.
I SIMPLY ***GUESSED*** THE OUTCOME DRAWING ON MY OWN EXPERIENCE.
YOU ***LIED***!
I HAD FAITH IN MY ANSWER, FATHER. ISN'T THAT ENOUGH?
THE VOICES DIDN'T HELP ME. LET'S HOPE THEY ARE MORE ***ILLUMINATING*** BY THE TIME WE REACH CHINON.
PERHAPS THEY DIDN'T GIVE YOU ALL THE FACTS BECAUSE THEY KNEW YOU'D FIND THE ANSWER ELSEWHERE?
QUITE POSSIBLLY. PERHAPS I CAN COMPLETE THIS TASK ***WITHOUT*** FOLLOWING MY PATH TO THE END.
PERHAPS THERE ***IS*** A ***FUTURE*** FOR ME...
THE LORD DOES MOVE IN ***MYSTERIOUS WAYS***, MY CHILD!

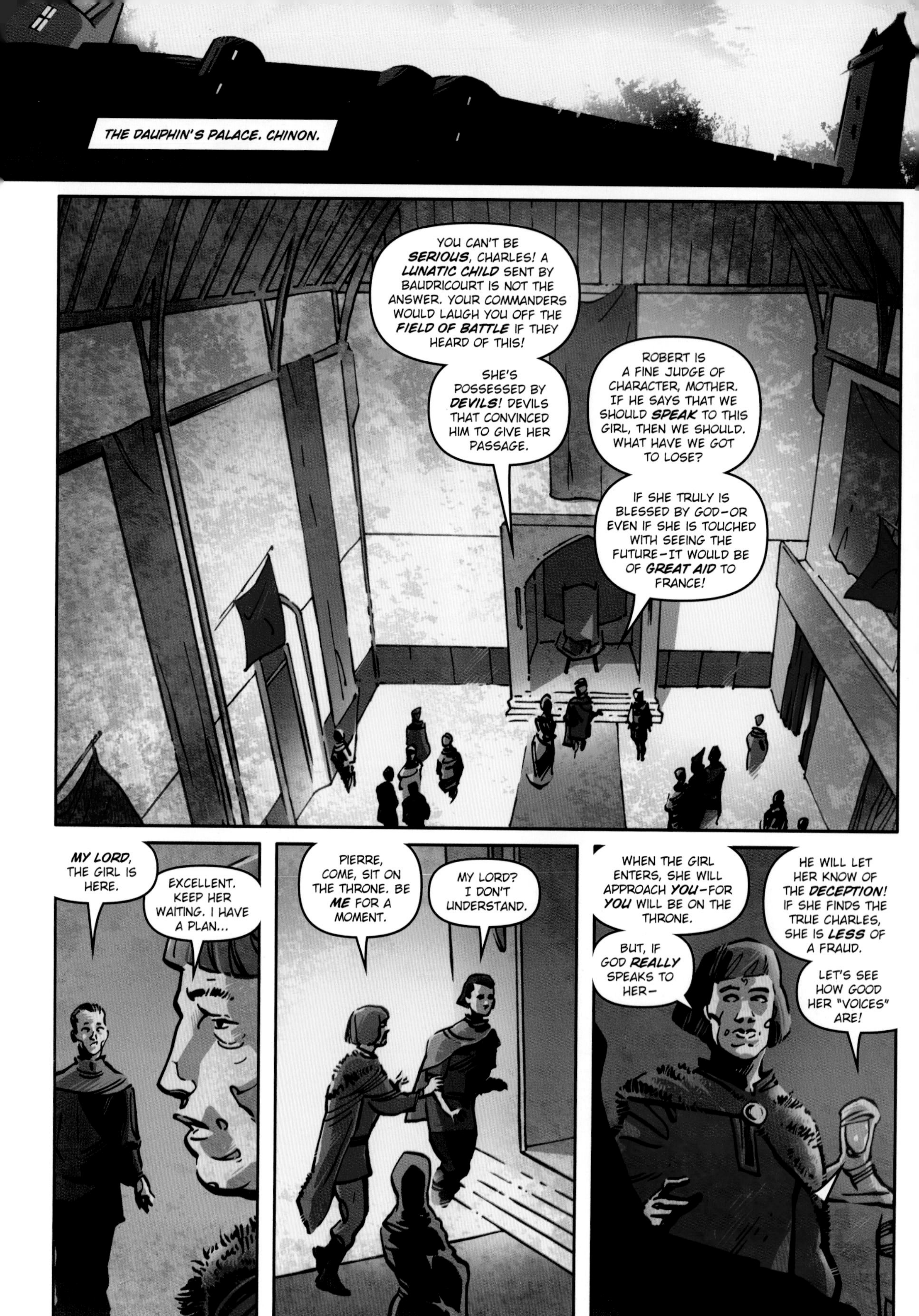
THE DAUPHIN'S PALACE. CHINON.
YOU CAN'T BE SERIOUS, CHARLES! A LUNATIC CHILD SENT BY BAUDRICOURT IS NOT THE ANSWER. YOUR COMMANDERS WOULD LAUGH YOU OFF THE FIELD OF BATTLE IF THEY HEARD OF THIS!
SHE'S POSSESSED BY DEVILS! DEVILS THAT CONVINCED HIM TO GIVE HER PASSAGE.
ROBERT IS A FINE JUDGE OF CHARACTER, MOTHER. IF HE SAYS THAT WE SHOULD SPEAK TO THIS GIRL, THEN WE SHOULD. WHAT HAVE WE GOT TO LOSE?
IF SHE TRULY IS BLESSED BY GOD—OR EVEN IF SHE IS TOUCHED WITH SEEING THE FUTURE—IT WOULD BE OF GREAT AID TO FRANCE!
MY LORD, THE GIRL IS HERE.
EXCELLENT. KEEP HER WAITING. I HAVE A PLAN...
PIERRE, COME, SIT ON THE THRONE. BE ME FOR A MOMENT.
MY LORD? I DON'T UNDERSTAND.
WHEN THE GIRL ENTERS, SHE WILL APPROACH YOU—FOR YOU WILL BE ON THE THRONE.
BUT, IF GOD REALLY SPEAKS TO HER—
HE WILL LET HER KNOW OF THE DECEPTION! IF SHE FINDS THE TRUE CHARLES, SHE IS LESS OF A FRAUD.
LET'S SEE HOW GOOD HER "VOICES" ARE!

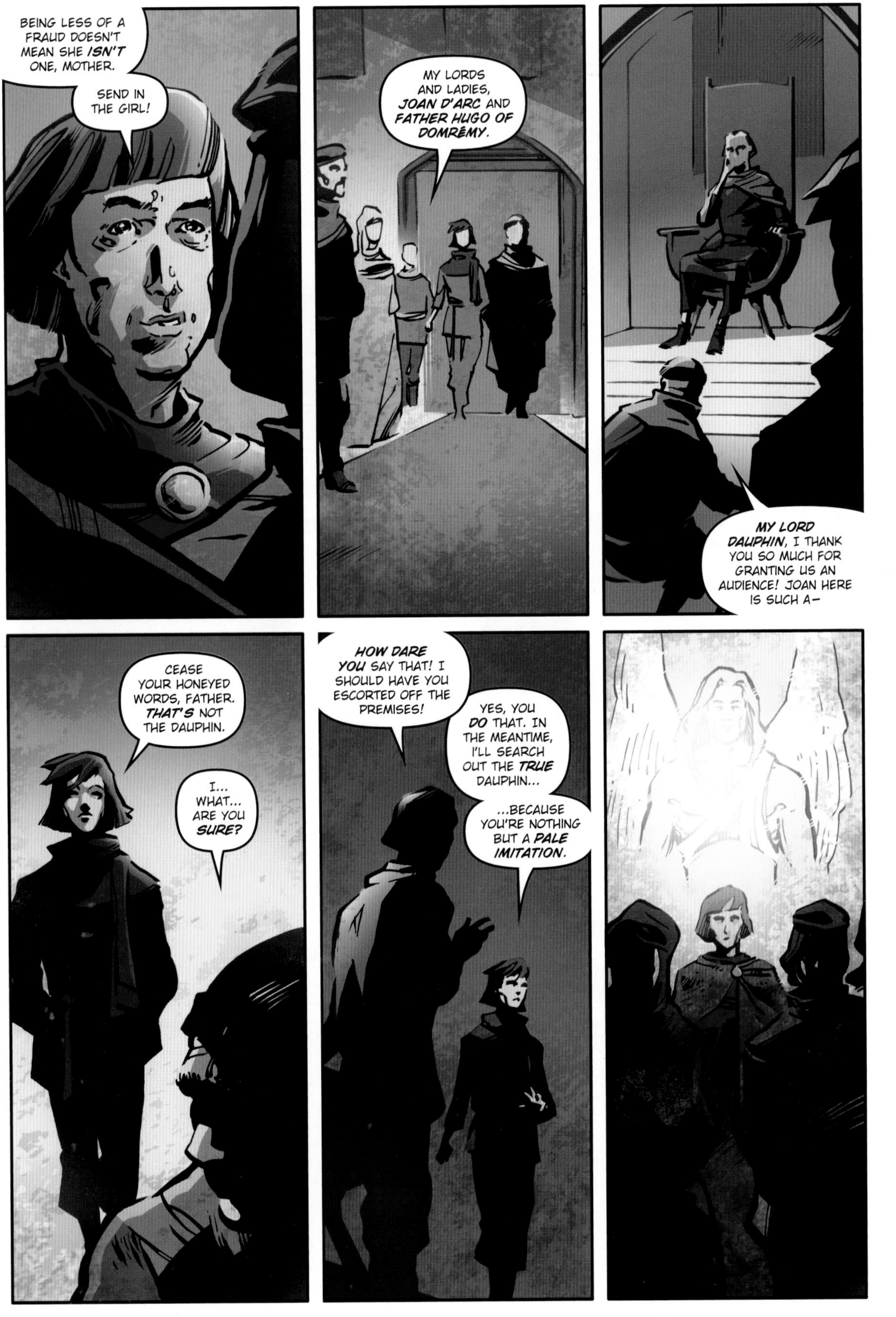
BEING LESS OF A FRAUD DOESN'T MEAN SHE *ISN'T* ONE, MOTHER.
SEND IN THE GIRL!
MY LORDS AND LADIES, ***JOAN D'ARC*** AND ***FATHER HUGO OF DOMRÉMY***.
MY LORD DAUPHIN, I THANK YOU SO MUCH FOR GRANTING US AN AUDIENCE! JOAN HERE IS SUCH A–
CEASE YOUR HONEYED WORDS, FATHER. ***THAT'S*** NOT THE DAUPHIN.
I... WHAT... ARE YOU ***SURE?***
HOW DARE YOU SAY THAT! I SHOULD HAVE YOU ESCORTED OFF THE PREMISES!
YES, YOU ***DO*** THAT. IN THE MEANTIME, I'LL SEARCH OUT THE ***TRUE*** DAUPHIN...
...BECAUSE YOU'RE NOTHING BUT A ***PALE IMITATION***.

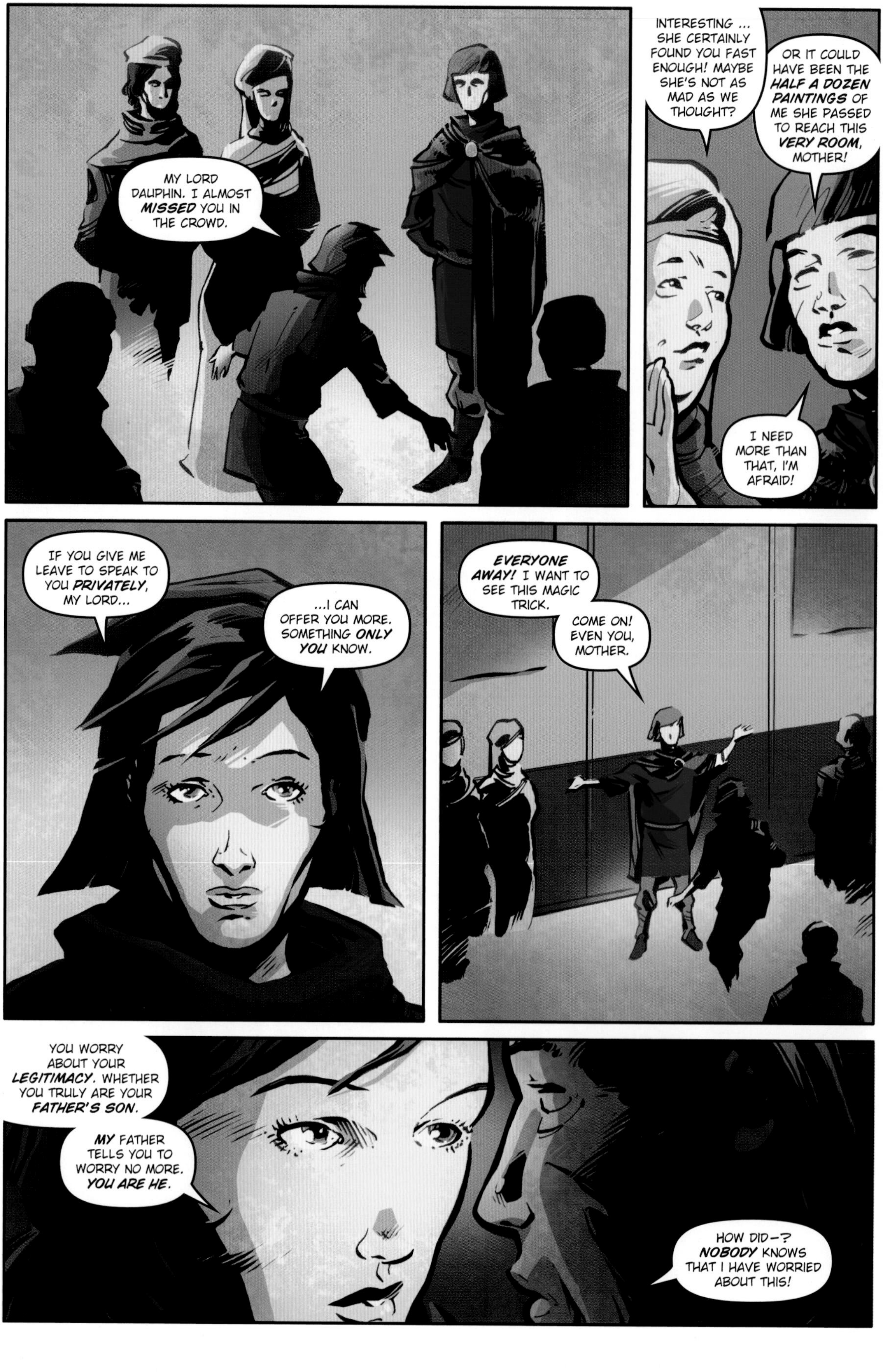
MY LORD DAUPHIN. I ALMOST MISSED YOU IN THE CROWD.
INTERESTING ... SHE CERTAINLY FOUND YOU FAST ENOUGH! MAYBE SHE'S NOT AS MAD AS WE THOUGHT?
OR IT COULD HAVE BEEN THE HALF A DOZEN PAINTINGS OF ME SHE PASSED TO REACH THIS VERY ROOM, MOTHER!
I NEED MORE THAN THAT, I'M AFRAID!
IF YOU GIVE ME LEAVE TO SPEAK TO YOU PRIVATELY, MY LORD...
...I CAN OFFER YOU MORE. SOMETHING ONLY YOU KNOW.
EVERYONE AWAY! I WANT TO SEE THIS MAGIC TRICK.
COME ON! EVEN YOU, MOTHER.
YOU WORRY ABOUT YOUR LEGITIMACY. WHETHER YOU TRULY ARE YOUR FATHER'S SON.
MY FATHER TELLS YOU TO WORRY NO MORE. YOU ARE HE.
HOW DID—? NOBODY KNOWS THAT I HAVE WORRIED ABOUT THIS!

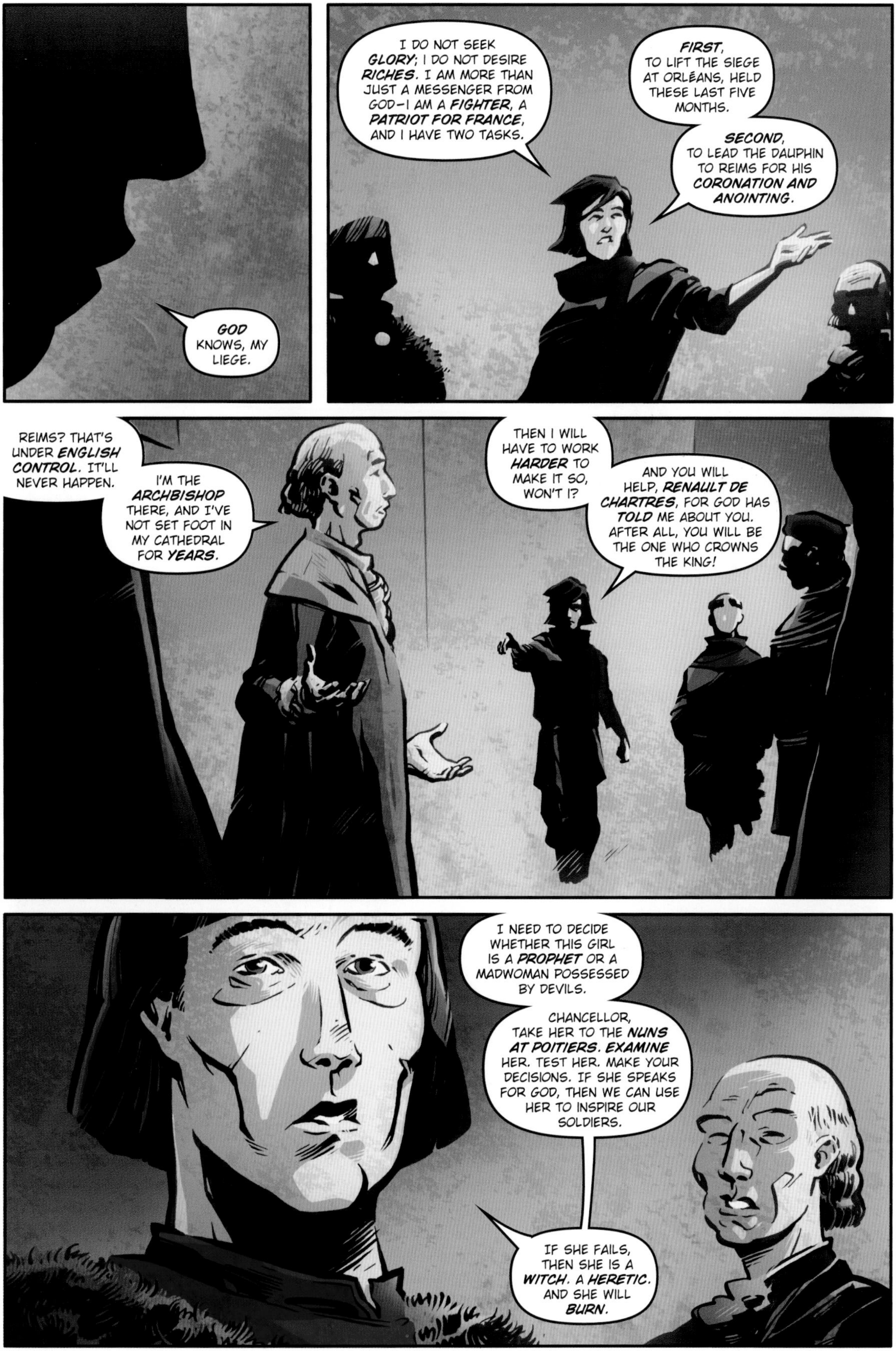
GOD KNOWS, MY LIEGE.
I DO NOT SEEK GLORY; I DO NOT DESIRE RICHES. I AM MORE THAN JUST A MESSENGER FROM GOD—I AM A FIGHTER, A PATRIOT FOR FRANCE, AND I HAVE TWO TASKS.
FIRST, TO LIFT THE SIEGE AT ORLÉANS, HELD THESE LAST FIVE MONTHS.
SECOND, TO LEAD THE DAUPHIN TO REIMS FOR HIS CORONATION AND ANOINTING.
REIMS? THAT'S UNDER ENGLISH CONTROL. IT'LL NEVER HAPPEN.
I'M THE ARCHBISHOP THERE, AND I'VE NOT SET FOOT IN MY CATHEDRAL FOR YEARS.
THEN I WILL HAVE TO WORK HARDER TO MAKE IT SO, WON'T I?
AND YOU WILL HELP, RENAULT DE CHARTRES, FOR GOD HAS TOLD ME ABOUT YOU. AFTER ALL, YOU WILL BE THE ONE WHO CROWNS THE KING!
I NEED TO DECIDE WHETHER THIS GIRL IS A PROPHET OR A MADWOMAN POSSESSED BY DEVILS.
CHANCELLOR, TAKE HER TO THE NUNS AT POITIERS. EXAMINE HER. TEST HER. MAKE YOUR DECISIONS. IF SHE SPEAKS FOR GOD, THEN WE CAN USE HER TO INSPIRE OUR SOLDIERS.
IF SHE FAILS, THEN SHE IS A WITCH. A HERETIC. AND SHE WILL BURN.

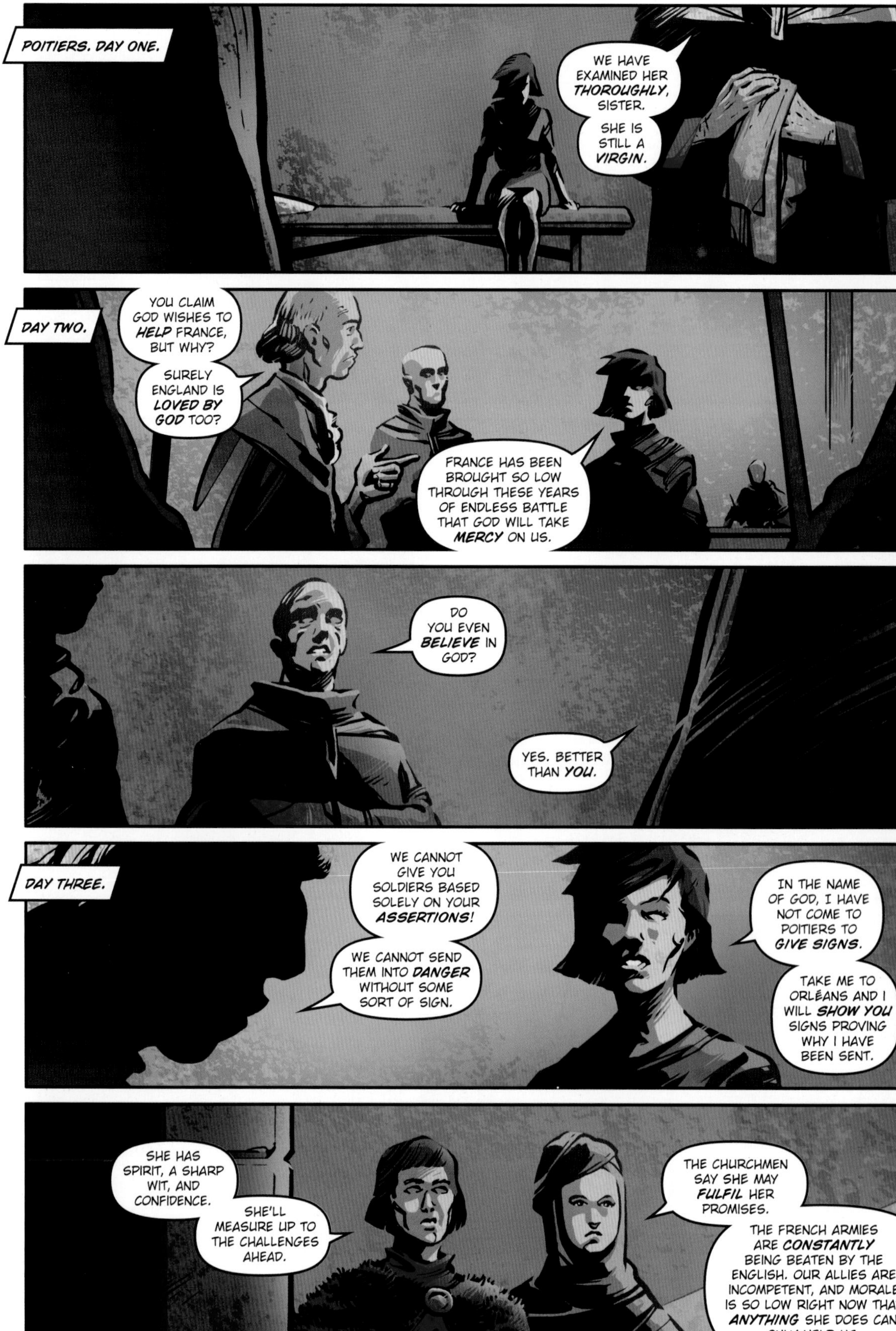
POITIERS. DAY ONE.
WE HAVE EXAMINED HER THOROUGHLY, SISTER.
SHE IS STILL A VIRGIN.
DAY TWO.
YOU CLAIM GOD WISHES TO HELP FRANCE, BUT WHY?
SURELY ENGLAND IS LOVED BY GOD TOO?
FRANCE HAS BEEN BROUGHT SO LOW THROUGH THESE YEARS OF ENDLESS BATTLE THAT GOD WILL TAKE MERCY ON US.
DO YOU EVEN BELIEVE IN GOD?
YES. BETTER THAN YOU.
DAY THREE.
WE CANNOT GIVE YOU SOLDIERS BASED SOLELY ON YOUR ASSERTIONS!
WE CANNOT SEND THEM INTO DANGER WITHOUT SOME SORT OF SIGN.
IN THE NAME OF GOD, I HAVE NOT COME TO POITIERS TO GIVE SIGNS.
TAKE ME TO ORLÉANS AND I WILL SHOW YOU SIGNS PROVING WHY I HAVE BEEN SENT.
SHE HAS SPIRIT, A SHARP WIT, AND CONFIDENCE.
SHE'LL MEASURE UP TO THE CHALLENGES AHEAD.
THE CHURCHMEN SAY SHE MAY FULFIL HER PROMISES.
THE FRENCH ARMIES ARE CONSTANTLY BEING BEATEN BY THE ENGLISH. OUR ALLIES ARE INCOMPETENT, AND MORALE IS SO LOW RIGHT NOW THAT ANYTHING SHE DOES CAN ONLY HELP US.

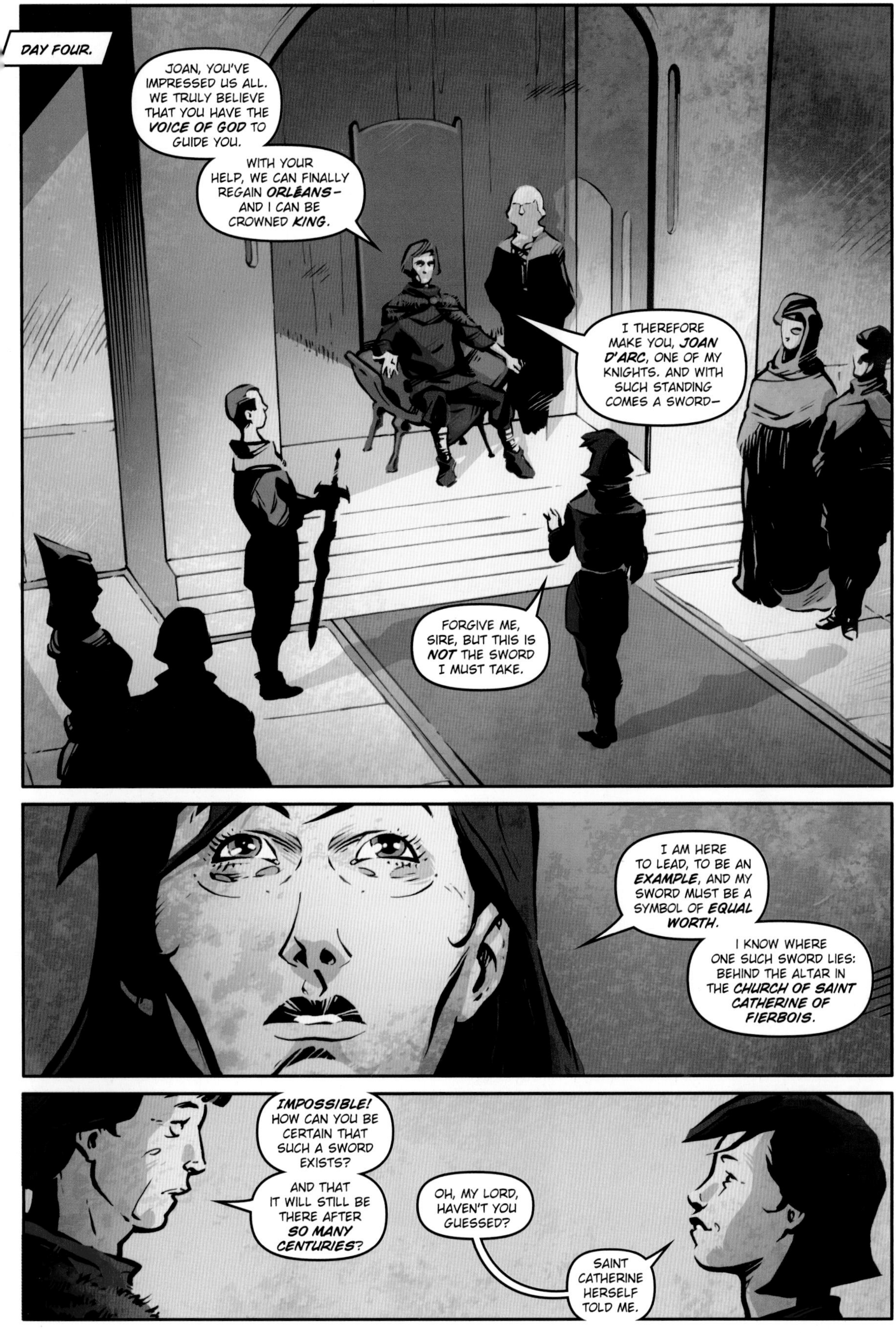
DAY FOUR.
JOAN, YOU'VE IMPRESSED US ALL. WE TRULY BELIEVE THAT YOU HAVE THE VOICE OF GOD TO GUIDE YOU.
WITH YOUR HELP, WE CAN FINALLY REGAIN ORLÉANS— AND I CAN BE CROWNED KING.
I THEREFORE MAKE YOU, JOAN D'ARC, ONE OF MY KNIGHTS. AND WITH SUCH STANDING COMES A SWORD—
FORGIVE ME, SIRE, BUT THIS IS NOT THE SWORD I MUST TAKE.
I AM HERE TO LEAD, TO BE AN EXAMPLE, AND MY SWORD MUST BE A SYMBOL OF EQUAL WORTH.
I KNOW WHERE ONE SUCH SWORD LIES: BEHIND THE ALTAR IN THE CHURCH OF SAINT CATHERINE OF FIERBOIS.
IMPOSSIBLE! HOW CAN YOU BE CERTAIN THAT SUCH A SWORD EXISTS?
AND THAT IT WILL STILL BE THERE AFTER SO MANY CENTURIES?
OH, MY LORD, HAVEN'T YOU GUESSED?
SAINT CATHERINE HERSELF TOLD ME.

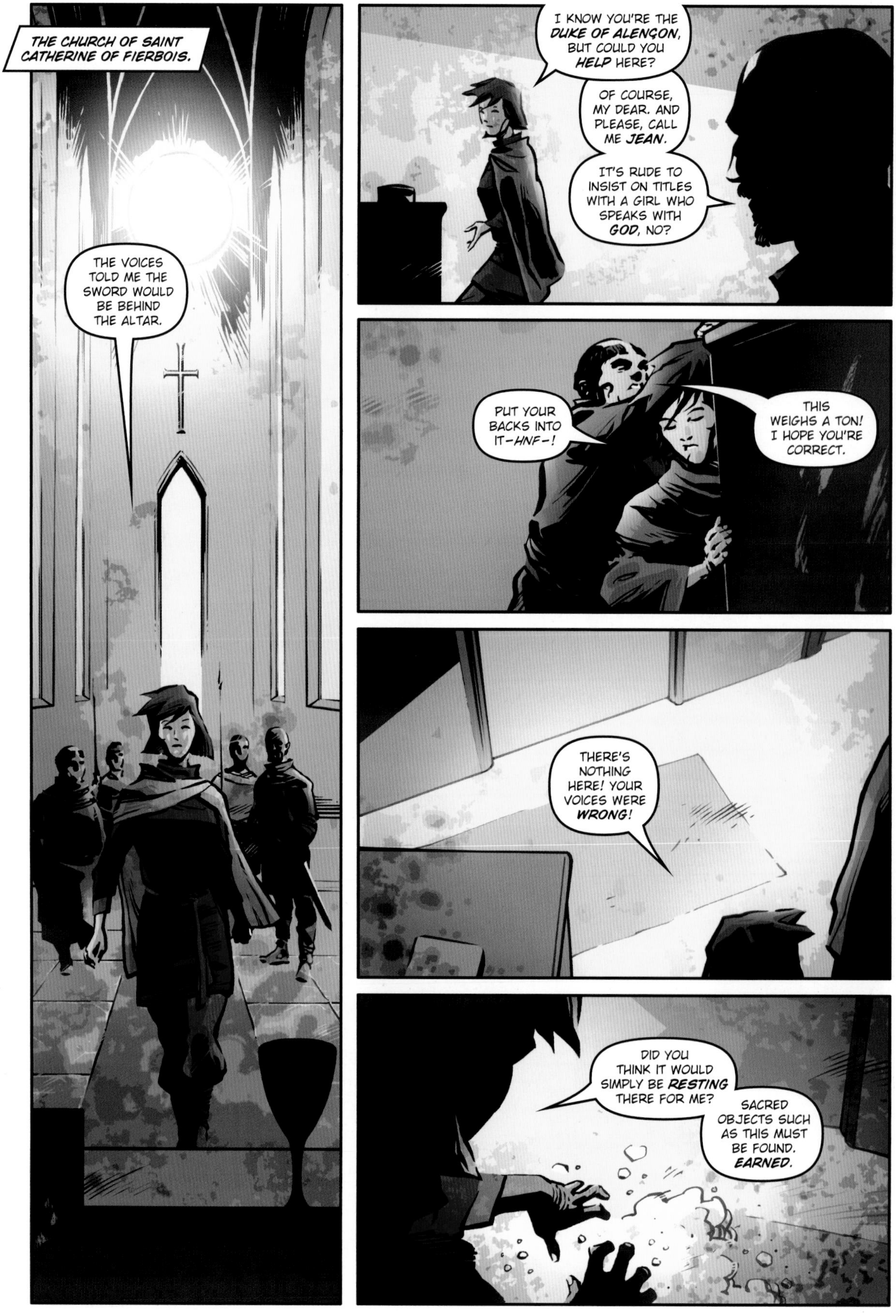
THE CHURCH OF SAINT CATHERINE OF FIERBOIS.
THE VOICES TOLD ME THE SWORD WOULD BE BEHIND THE ALTAR.
I KNOW YOU'RE THE DUKE OF ALENÇON, BUT COULD YOU HELP HERE?
OF COURSE, MY DEAR. AND PLEASE, CALL ME JEAN.
IT'S RUDE TO INSIST ON TITLES WITH A GIRL WHO SPEAKS WITH GOD, NO?
PUT YOUR BACKS INTO IT–HNF–!
THIS WEIGHS A TON! I HOPE YOU'RE CORRECT.
THERE'S NOTHING HERE! YOUR VOICES WERE WRONG!
DID YOU THINK IT WOULD SIMPLY BE RESTING THERE FOR ME?
SACRED OBJECTS SUCH AS THIS MUST BE FOUND. EARNED.

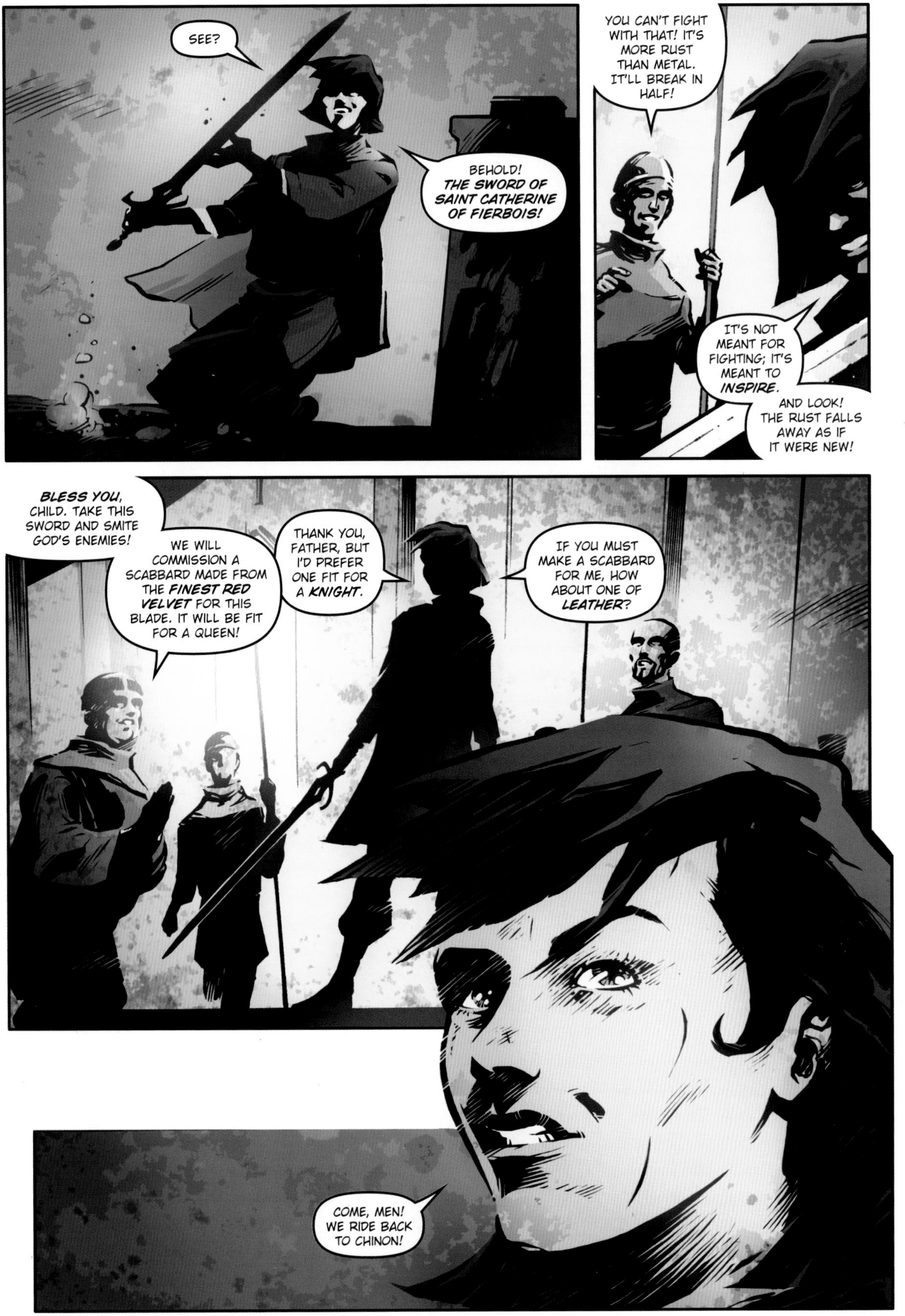
SEE?
BEHOLD! THE SWORD OF SAINT CATHERINE OF FIERBOIS!
YOU CAN'T FIGHT WITH THAT! IT'S MORE RUST THAN METAL. IT'LL BREAK IN HALF!
IT'S NOT MEANT FOR FIGHTING; IT'S MEANT TO INSPIRE.
AND LOOK! THE RUST FALLS AWAY AS IF IT WERE NEW!
BLESS YOU, CHILD. TAKE THIS SWORD AND SMITE GOD'S ENEMIES!
WE WILL COMMISSION A SCABBARD MADE FROM THE FINEST RED VELVET FOR THIS BLADE. IT WILL BE FIT FOR A QUEEN!
THANK YOU, FATHER, BUT I'D PREFER ONE FIT FOR A KNIGHT.
IF YOU MUST MAKE A SCABBARD FOR ME, HOW ABOUT ONE OF LEATHER?
COME, MEN! WE RIDE BACK TO CHINON!

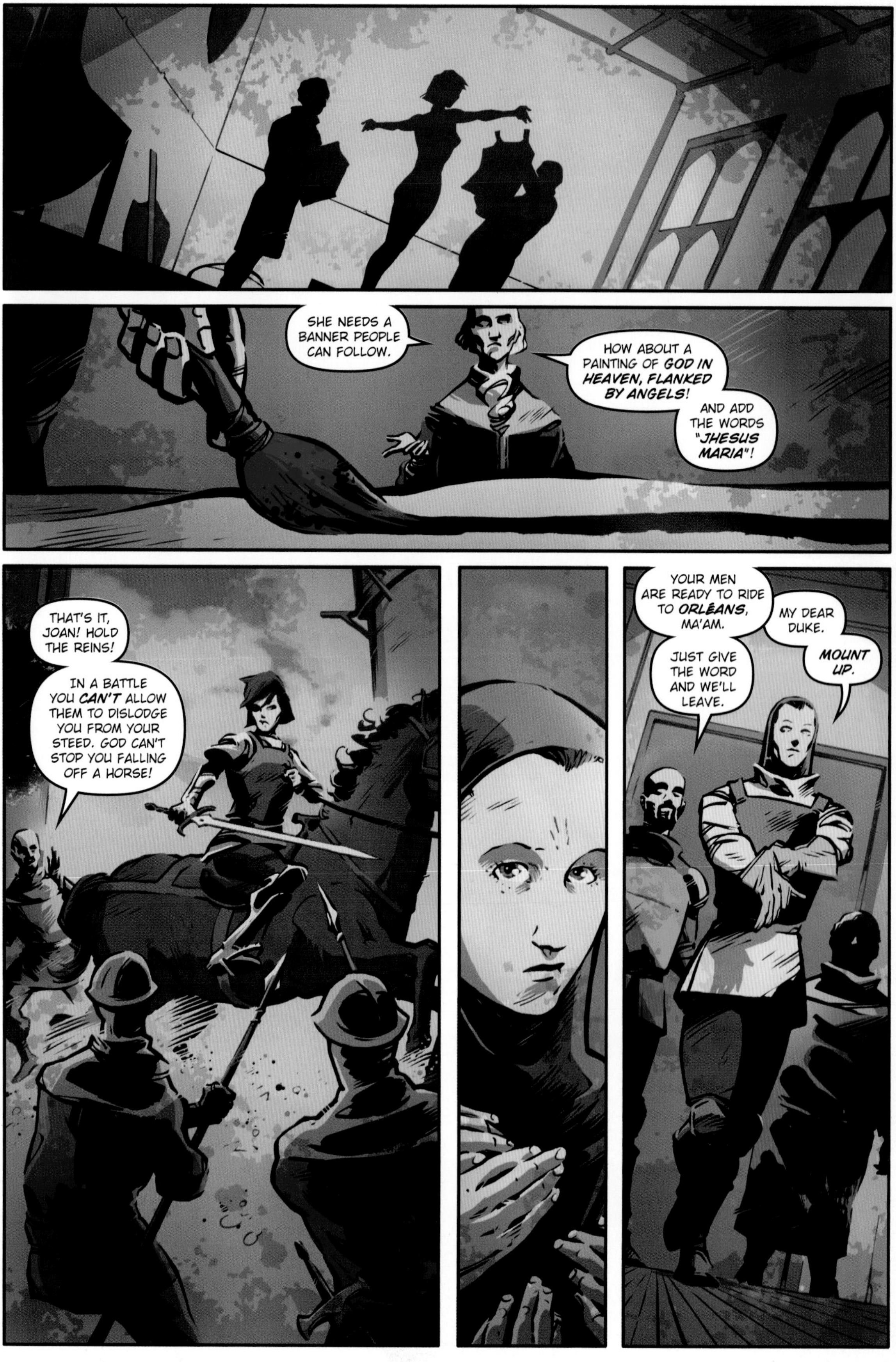
SHE NEEDS A BANNER PEOPLE CAN FOLLOW.
HOW ABOUT A PAINTING OF **GOD IN HEAVEN, FLANKED BY ANGELS**!
AND ADD THE WORDS "**JHESUS MARIA**"!
THAT'S IT, JOAN! HOLD THE REINS!
IN A BATTLE YOU **CAN'T** ALLOW THEM TO DISLODGE YOU FROM YOUR STEED. GOD CAN'T STOP YOU FALLING OFF A HORSE!
YOUR MEN ARE READY TO RIDE TO **ORLÉANS**, MA'AM.
JUST GIVE THE WORD AND WE'LL LEAVE.
MY DEAR DUKE.
MOUNT UP.

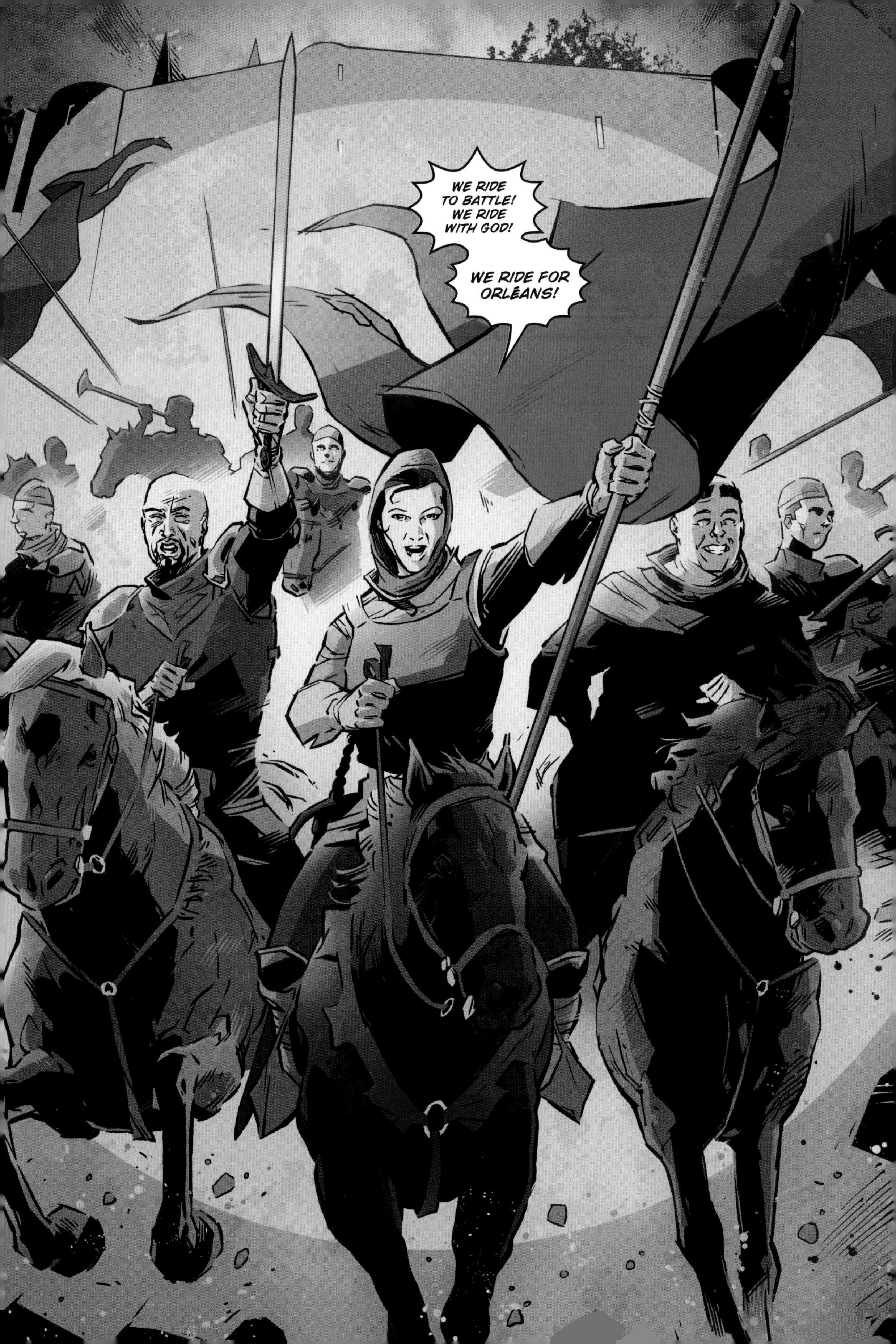
WE RIDE TO BATTLE! WE RIDE WITH GOD!
WE RIDE FOR ORLÉANS!

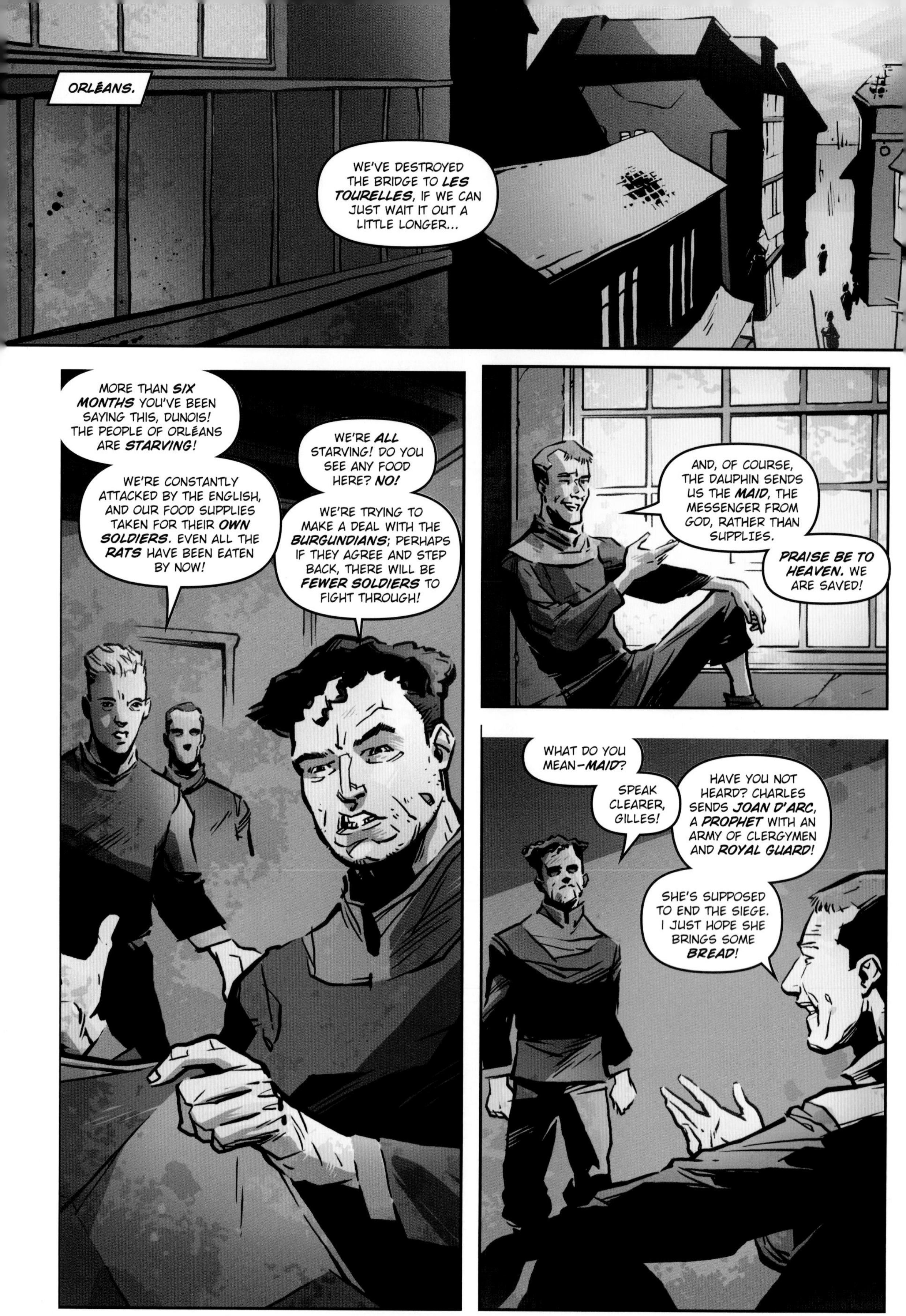
ORLÉANS.
WE'VE DESTROYED THE BRIDGE TO LES TOURELLES, IF WE CAN JUST WAIT IT OUT A LITTLE LONGER...
MORE THAN SIX MONTHS YOU'VE BEEN SAYING THIS, DUNOIS! THE PEOPLE OF ORLÉANS ARE STARVING!
WE'RE CONSTANTLY ATTACKED BY THE ENGLISH, AND OUR FOOD SUPPLIES TAKEN FOR THEIR OWN SOLDIERS. EVEN ALL THE RATS HAVE BEEN EATEN BY NOW!
WE'RE ALL STARVING! DO YOU SEE ANY FOOD HERE? NO!
WE'RE TRYING TO MAKE A DEAL WITH THE BURGUNDIANS; PERHAPS IF THEY AGREE AND STEP BACK, THERE WILL BE FEWER SOLDIERS TO FIGHT THROUGH!
AND, OF COURSE, THE DAUPHIN SENDS US THE MAID, THE MESSENGER FROM GOD, RATHER THAN SUPPLIES.
PRAISE BE TO HEAVEN. WE ARE SAVED!
WHAT DO YOU MEAN—MAID?
SPEAK CLEARER, GILLES!
HAVE YOU NOT HEARD? CHARLES SENDS JOAN D'ARC, A PROPHET WITH AN ARMY OF CLERGYMEN AND ROYAL GUARD!
SHE'S SUPPOSED TO END THE SIEGE. I JUST HOPE SHE BRINGS SOME BREAD!

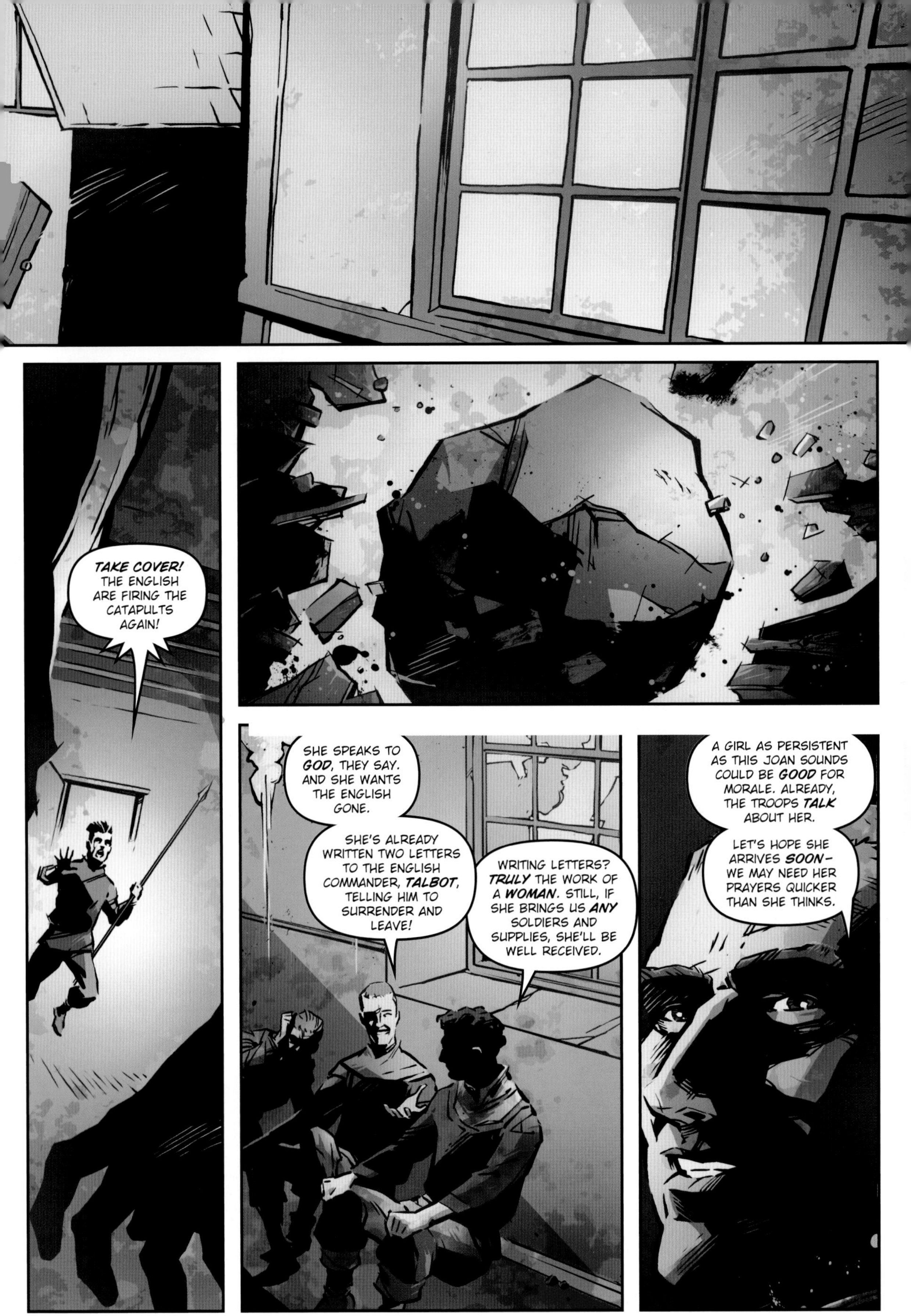

TAKE COVER! THE ENGLISH ARE FIRING THE CATAPULTS AGAIN!
SHE SPEAKS TO GOD, THEY SAY. AND SHE WANTS THE ENGLISH GONE.
SHE'S ALREADY WRITTEN TWO LETTERS TO THE ENGLISH COMMANDER, TALBOT, TELLING HIM TO SURRENDER AND LEAVE!
WRITING LETTERS? TRULY THE WORK OF A WOMAN. STILL, IF SHE BRINGS US ANY SOLDIERS AND SUPPLIES, SHE'LL BE WELL RECEIVED.
A GIRL AS PERSISTENT AS THIS JOAN SOUNDS COULD BE GOOD FOR MORALE. ALREADY, THE TROOPS TALK ABOUT HER.
LET'S HOPE SHE ARRIVES SOON— WE MAY NEED HER PRAYERS QUICKER THAN SHE THINKS.

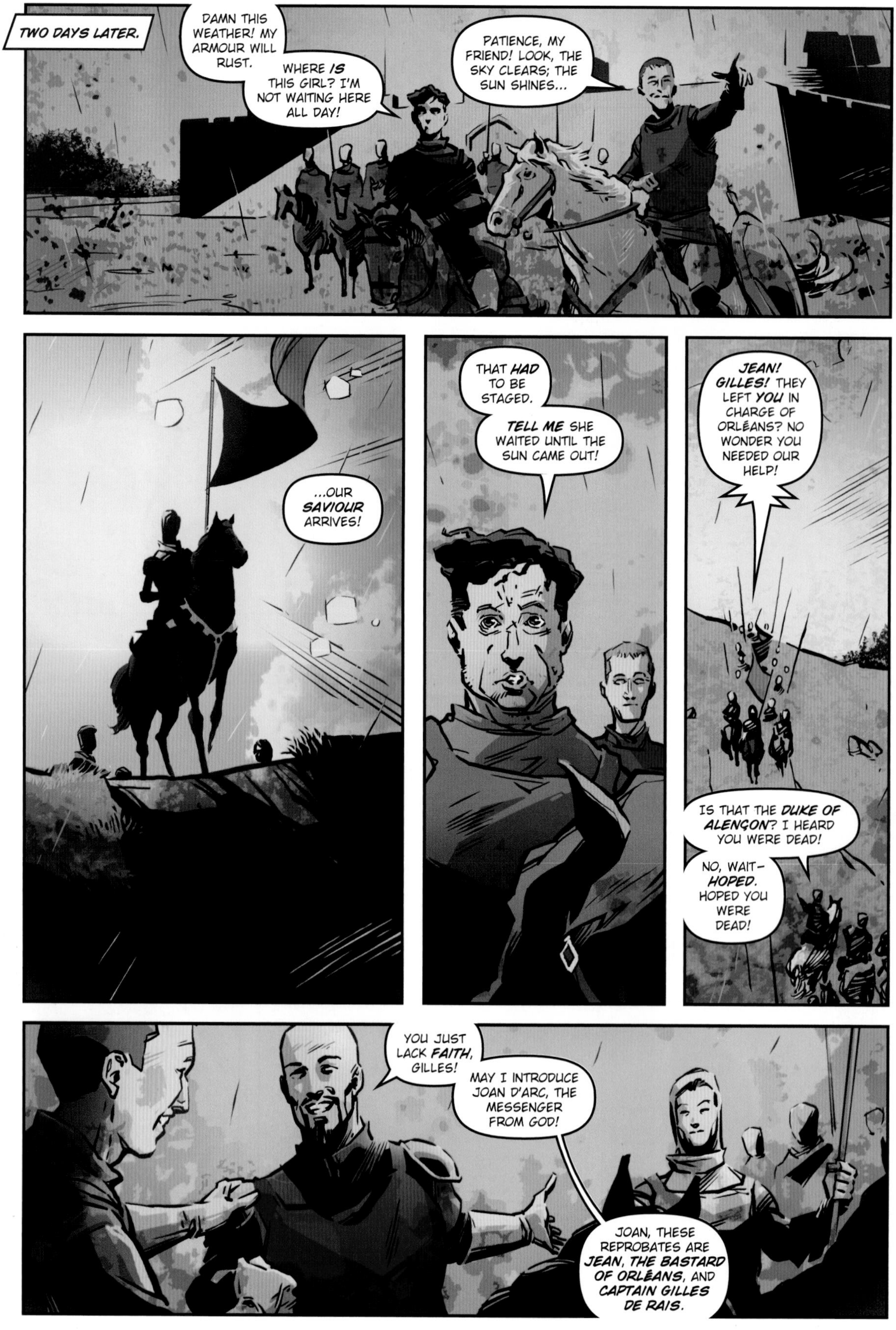

TWO DAYS LATER.
DAMN THIS WEATHER! MY ARMOUR WILL RUST.
WHERE IS THIS GIRL? I'M NOT WAITING HERE ALL DAY!
PATIENCE, MY FRIEND! LOOK, THE SKY CLEARS; THE SUN SHINES...
...OUR SAVIOUR ARRIVES!
THAT HAD TO BE STAGED.
TELL ME SHE WAITED UNTIL THE SUN CAME OUT!
JEAN! GILLES! THEY LEFT YOU IN CHARGE OF ORLÉANS? NO WONDER YOU NEEDED OUR HELP!
IS THAT THE DUKE OF ALENÇON? I HEARD YOU WERE DEAD!
NO, WAIT– HOPED. HOPED YOU WERE DEAD!
YOU JUST LACK FAITH, GILLES!
MAY I INTRODUCE JOAN D'ARC, THE MESSENGER FROM GOD!
JOAN, THESE REPROBATES ARE JEAN, THE BASTARD OF ORLÉANS, AND CAPTAIN GILLES DE RAIS.

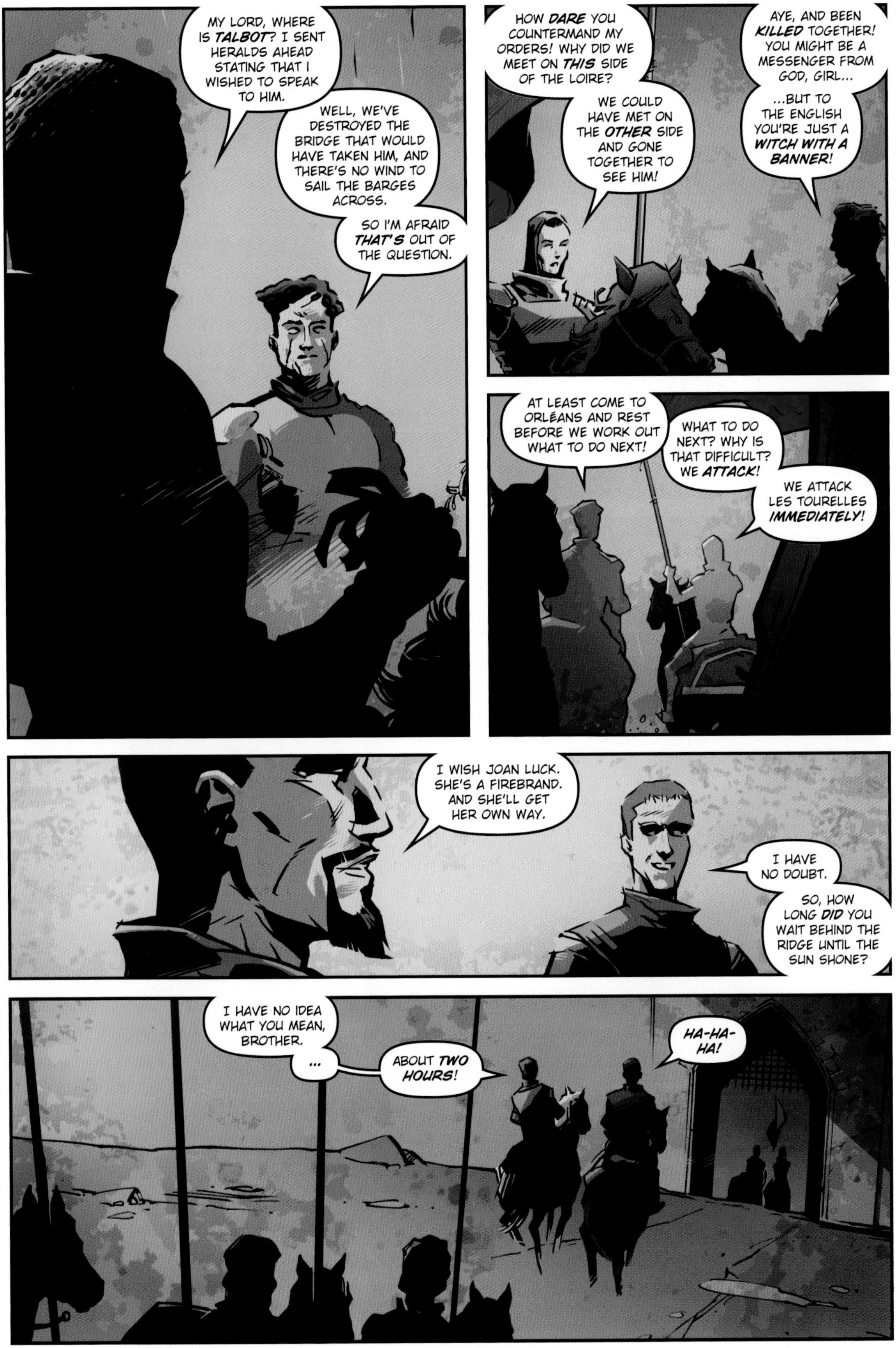

MY LORD, WHERE IS ***TALBOT***? I SENT HERALDS AHEAD STATING THAT I WISHED TO SPEAK TO HIM.
WELL, WE'VE DESTROYED THE BRIDGE THAT WOULD HAVE TAKEN HIM, AND THERE'S NO WIND TO SAIL THE BARGES ACROSS.
SO I'M AFRAID ***THAT'S*** OUT OF THE QUESTION.
HOW ***DARE*** YOU COUNTERMAND MY ORDERS! WHY DID WE MEET ON ***THIS*** SIDE OF THE LOIRE?
WE COULD HAVE MET ON THE ***OTHER*** SIDE AND GONE TOGETHER TO SEE HIM!
AYE, AND BEEN ***KILLED*** TOGETHER! YOU MIGHT BE A MESSENGER FROM GOD, GIRL...
...BUT TO THE ENGLISH YOU'RE JUST A ***WITCH WITH A BANNER***!
AT LEAST COME TO ORLÉANS AND REST BEFORE WE WORK OUT WHAT TO DO NEXT!
WHAT TO DO NEXT? WHY IS THAT DIFFICULT? WE ***ATTACK***!
WE ATTACK LES TOURELLES ***IMMEDIATELY***!
I WISH JOAN LUCK. SHE'S A FIREBRAND. AND SHE'LL GET HER OWN WAY.
I HAVE NO DOUBT.
SO, HOW LONG ***DID*** YOU WAIT BEHIND THE RIDGE UNTIL THE SUN SHONE?
I HAVE NO IDEA WHAT YOU MEAN, BROTHER.
...
ABOUT ***TWO HOURS***!
HA-HA-HA!

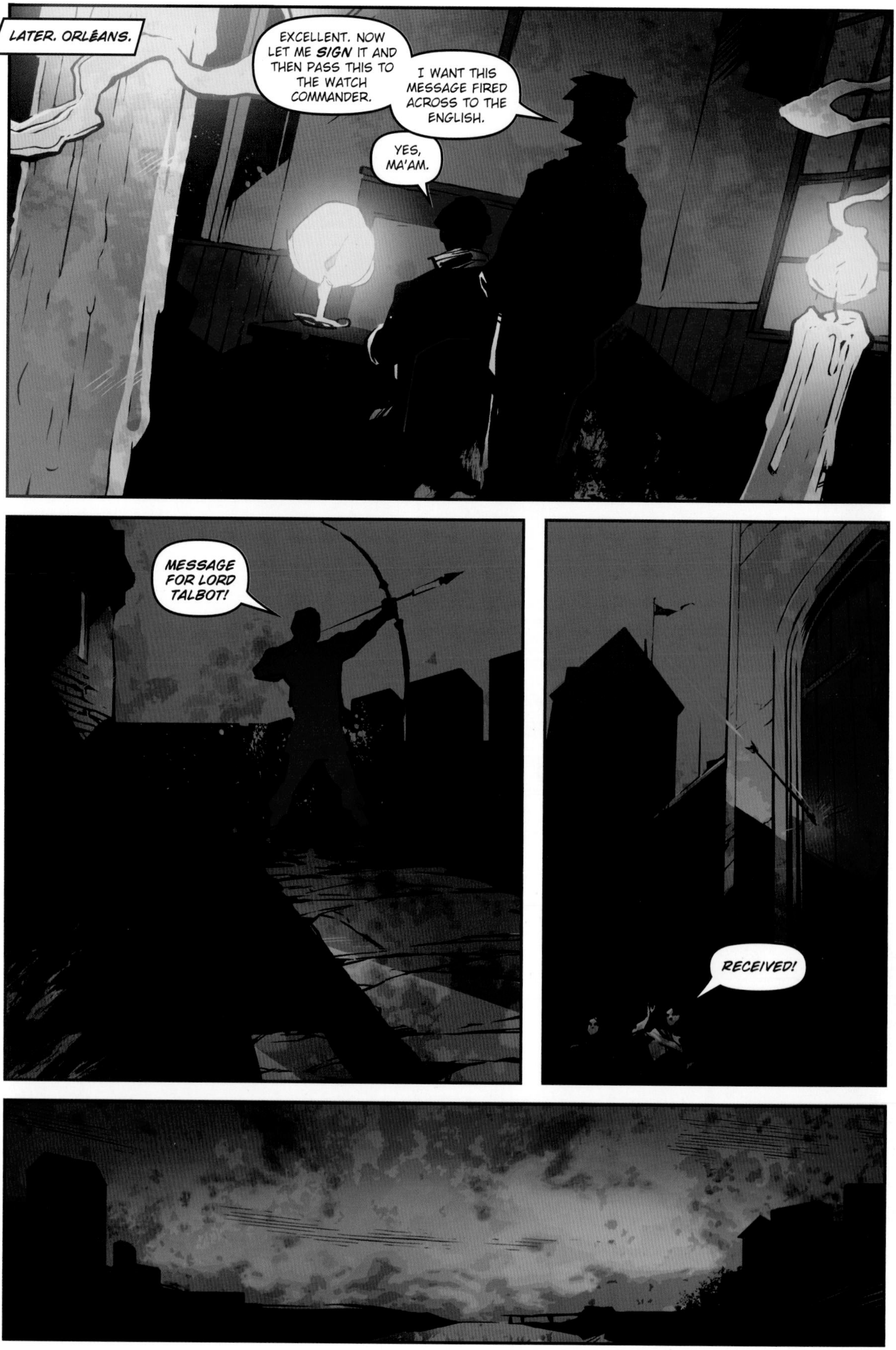
LATER. ORLÉANS.
EXCELLENT. NOW LET ME SIGN IT AND THEN PASS THIS TO THE WATCH COMMANDER.
I WANT THIS MESSAGE FIRED ACROSS TO THE ENGLISH.
YES, MA'AM.
MESSAGE FOR LORD TALBOT!
RECEIVED!

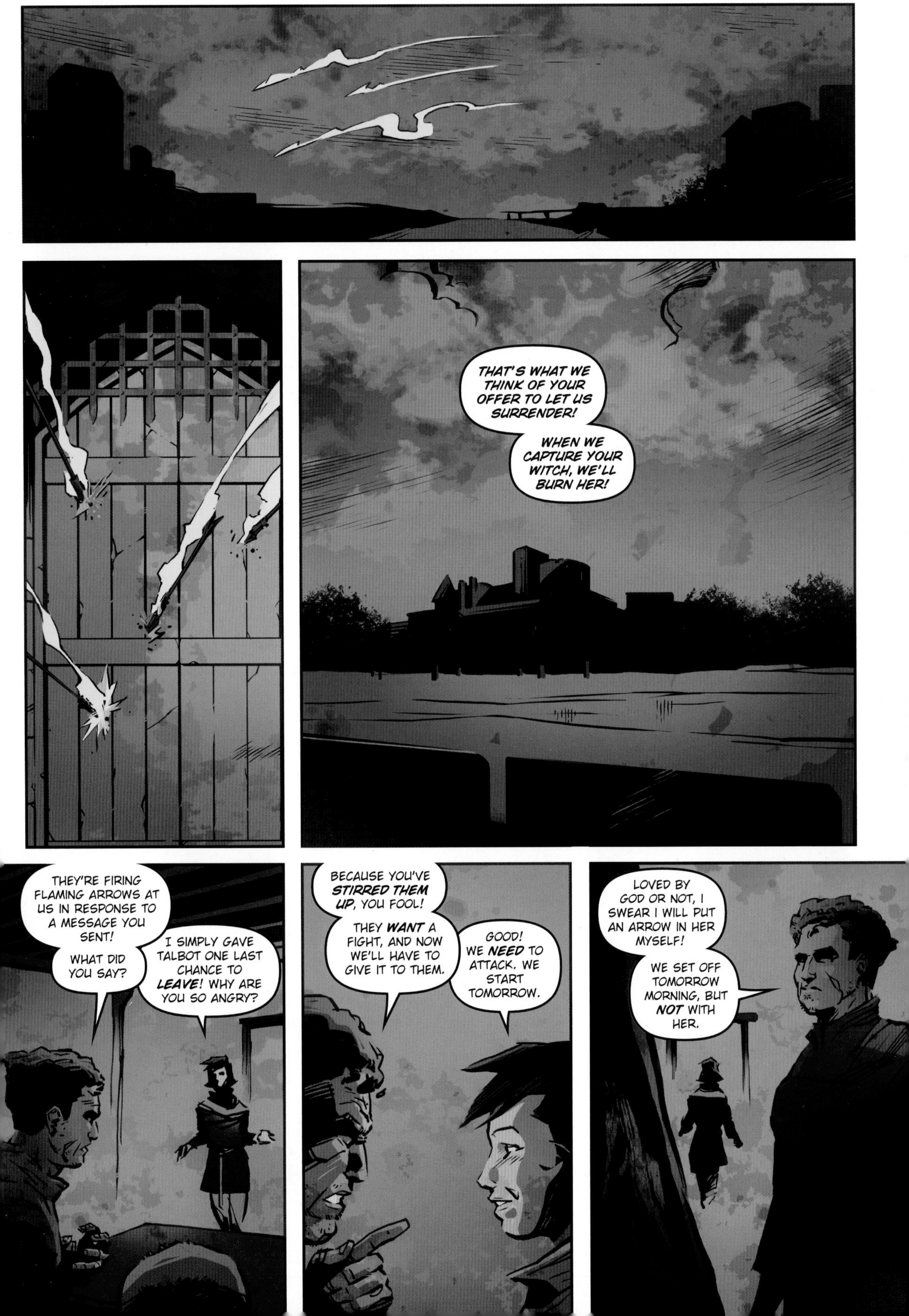
THAT'S WHAT WE THINK OF YOUR OFFER TO LET US SURRENDER!
WHEN WE CAPTURE YOUR WITCH, WE'LL BURN HER!
THEY'RE FIRING FLAMING ARROWS AT US IN RESPONSE TO A MESSAGE YOU SENT!
WHAT DID YOU SAY?
I SIMPLY GAVE TALBOT ONE LAST CHANCE TO LEAVE! WHY ARE YOU SO ANGRY?
BECAUSE YOU'VE STIRRED THEM UP, YOU FOOL!
THEY WANT A FIGHT, AND NOW WE'LL HAVE TO GIVE IT TO THEM.
GOOD! WE NEED TO ATTACK. WE START TOMORROW.
LOVED BY GOD OR NOT, I SWEAR I WILL PUT AN ARROW IN HER MYSELF!
WE SET OFF TOMORROW MORNING, BUT NOT WITH HER.

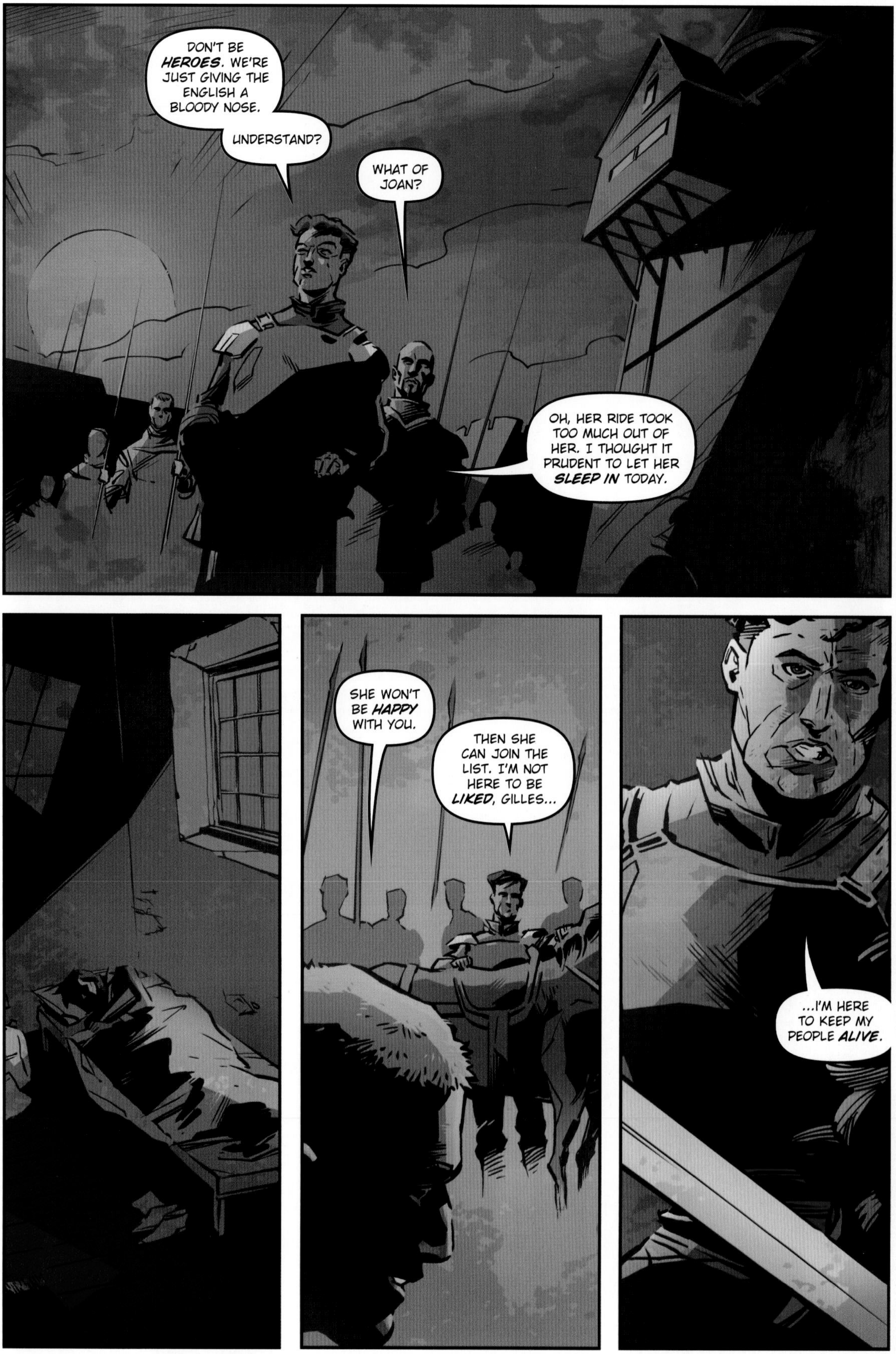
DON'T BE HEROES. WE'RE JUST GIVING THE ENGLISH A BLOODY NOSE.
UNDERSTAND?
WHAT OF JOAN?
OH, HER RIDE TOOK TOO MUCH OUT OF HER. I THOUGHT IT PRUDENT TO LET HER SLEEP IN TODAY.
SHE WON'T BE HAPPY WITH YOU.
THEN SHE CAN JOIN THE LIST. I'M NOT HERE TO BE LIKED, GILLES...
...I'M HERE TO KEEP MY PEOPLE ALIVE.

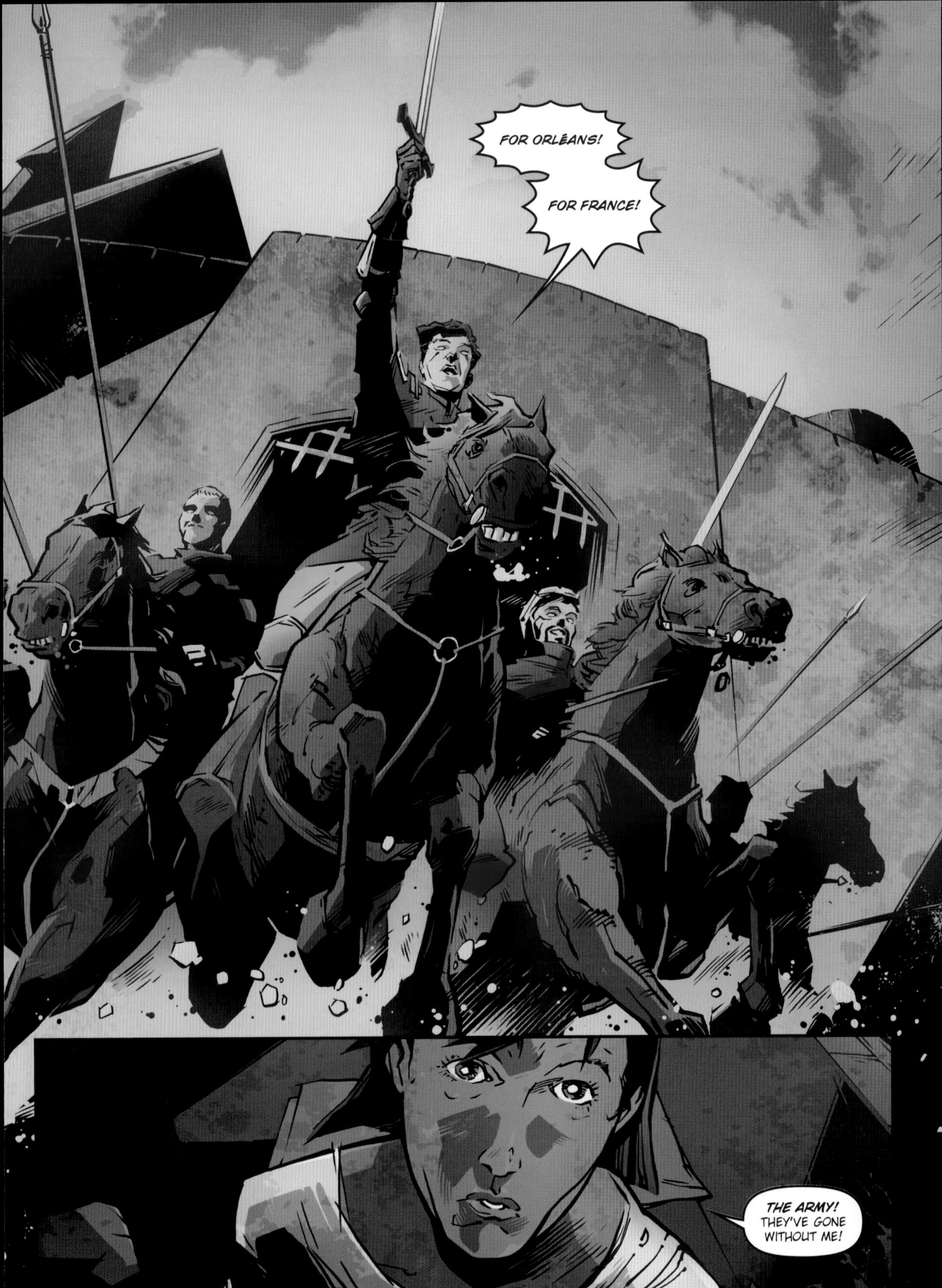
FOR ORLÉANS!
FOR FRANCE!
THE ARMY! THEY'VE GONE WITHOUT ME!

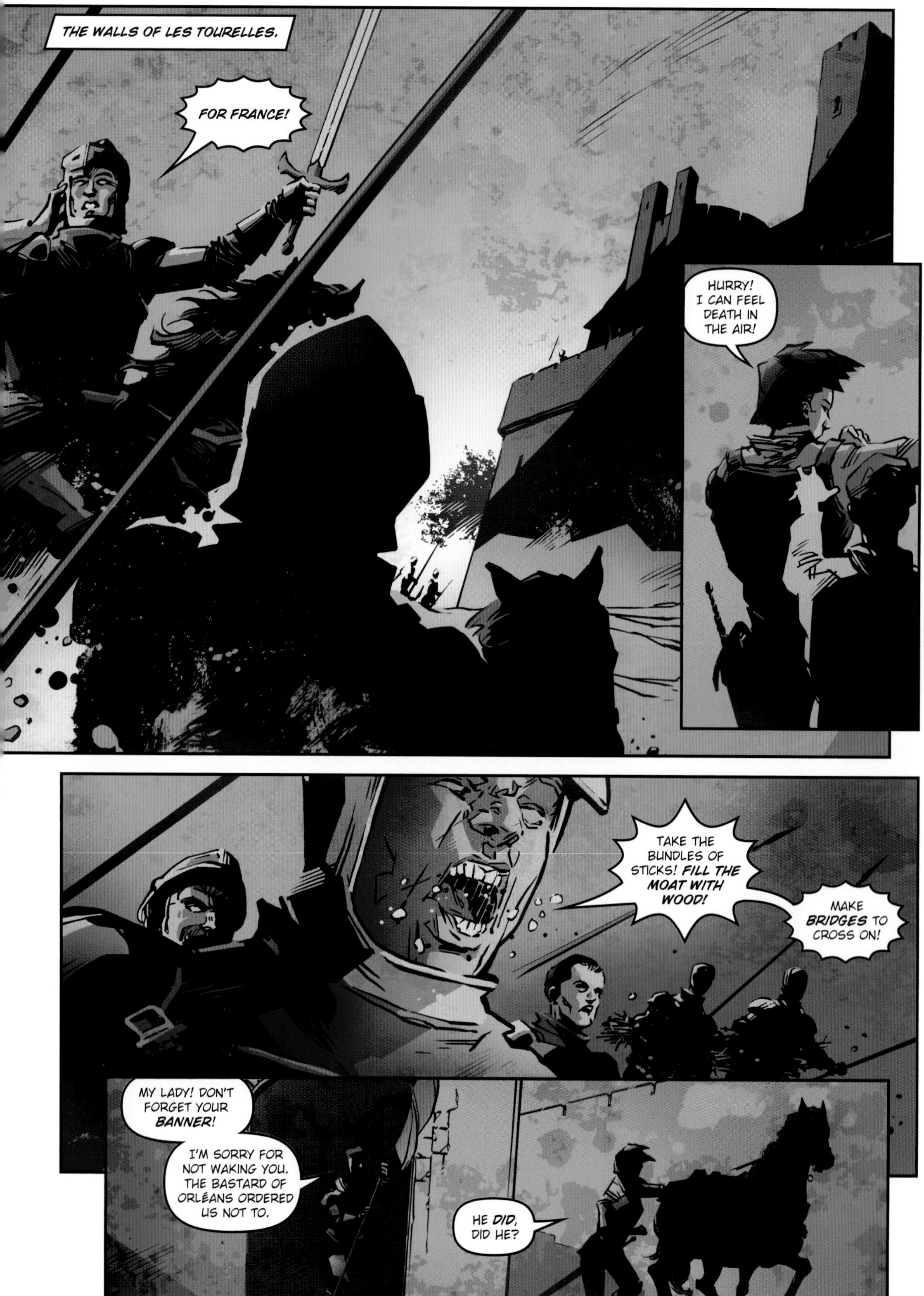
THE WALLS OF LES TOURELLES.
FOR FRANCE!
HURRY! I CAN FEEL DEATH IN THE AIR!
TAKE THE BUNDLES OF STICKS! FILL THE MOAT WITH WOOD!
MAKE BRIDGES TO CROSS ON!
MY LADY! DON'T FORGET YOUR BANNER!
I'M SORRY FOR NOT WAKING YOU. THE BASTARD OF ORLÉANS ORDERED US NOT TO.
HE DID, DID HE?

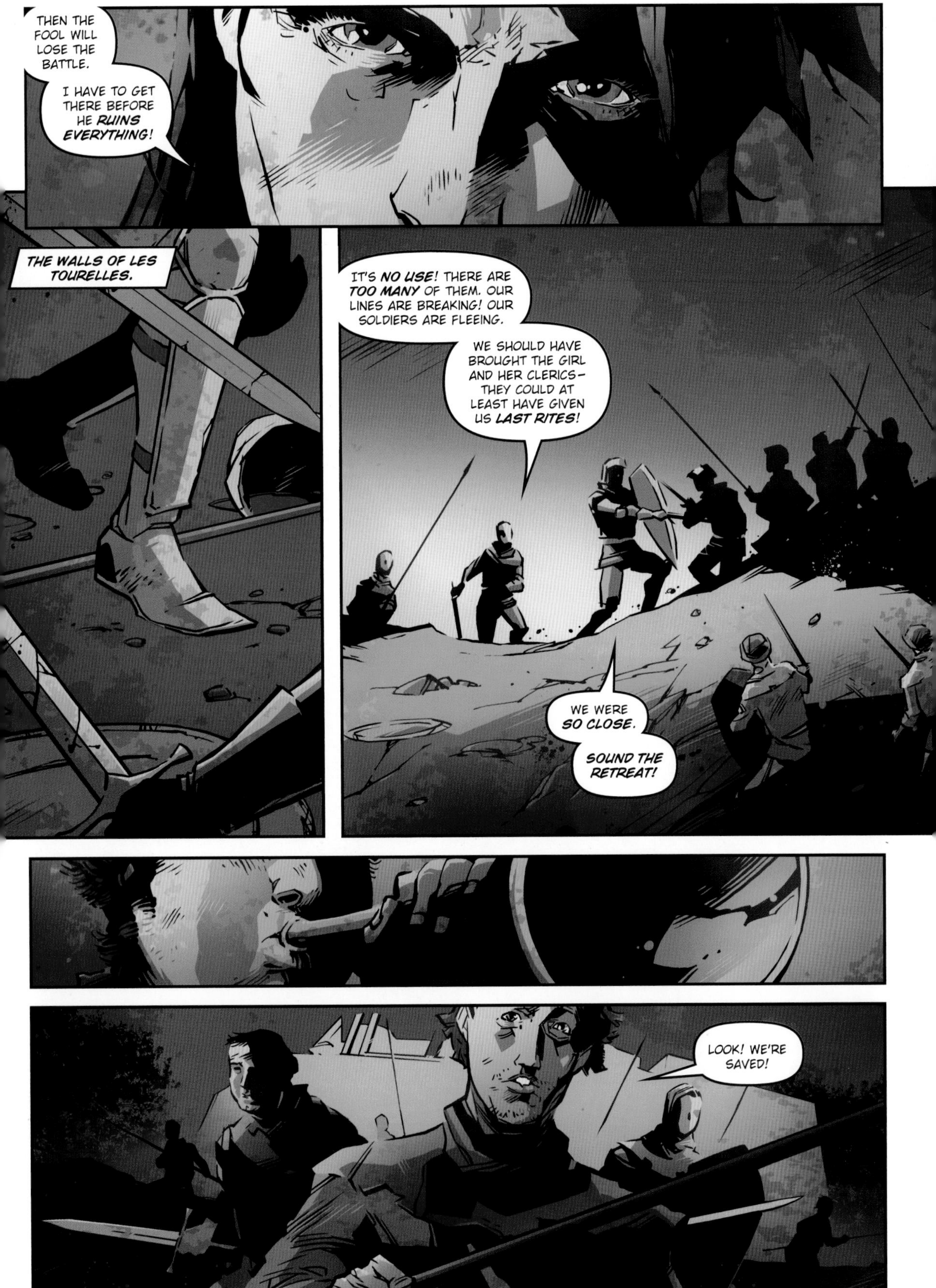
THEN THE FOOL WILL LOSE THE BATTLE.
I HAVE TO GET THERE BEFORE HE *RUINS EVERYTHING*!
THE WALLS OF LES TOURELLES.
IT'S *NO USE*! THERE ARE *TOO MANY* OF THEM. OUR LINES ARE BREAKING! OUR SOLDIERS ARE FLEEING.
WE SHOULD HAVE BROUGHT THE GIRL AND HER CLERICS— THEY COULD AT LEAST HAVE GIVEN US *LAST RITES*!
WE WERE *SO CLOSE*.
SOUND THE RETREAT!
LOOK! WE'RE SAVED!

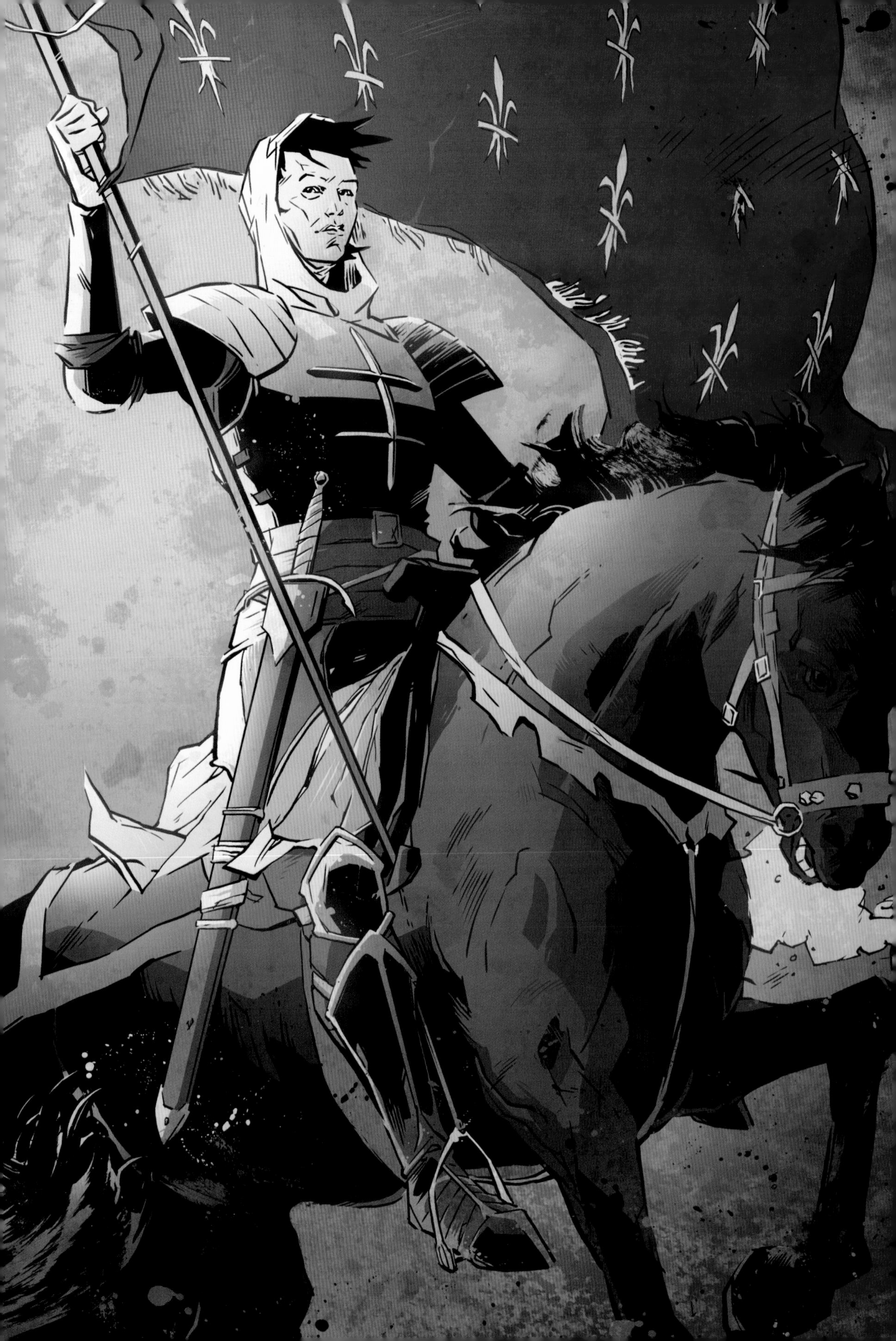

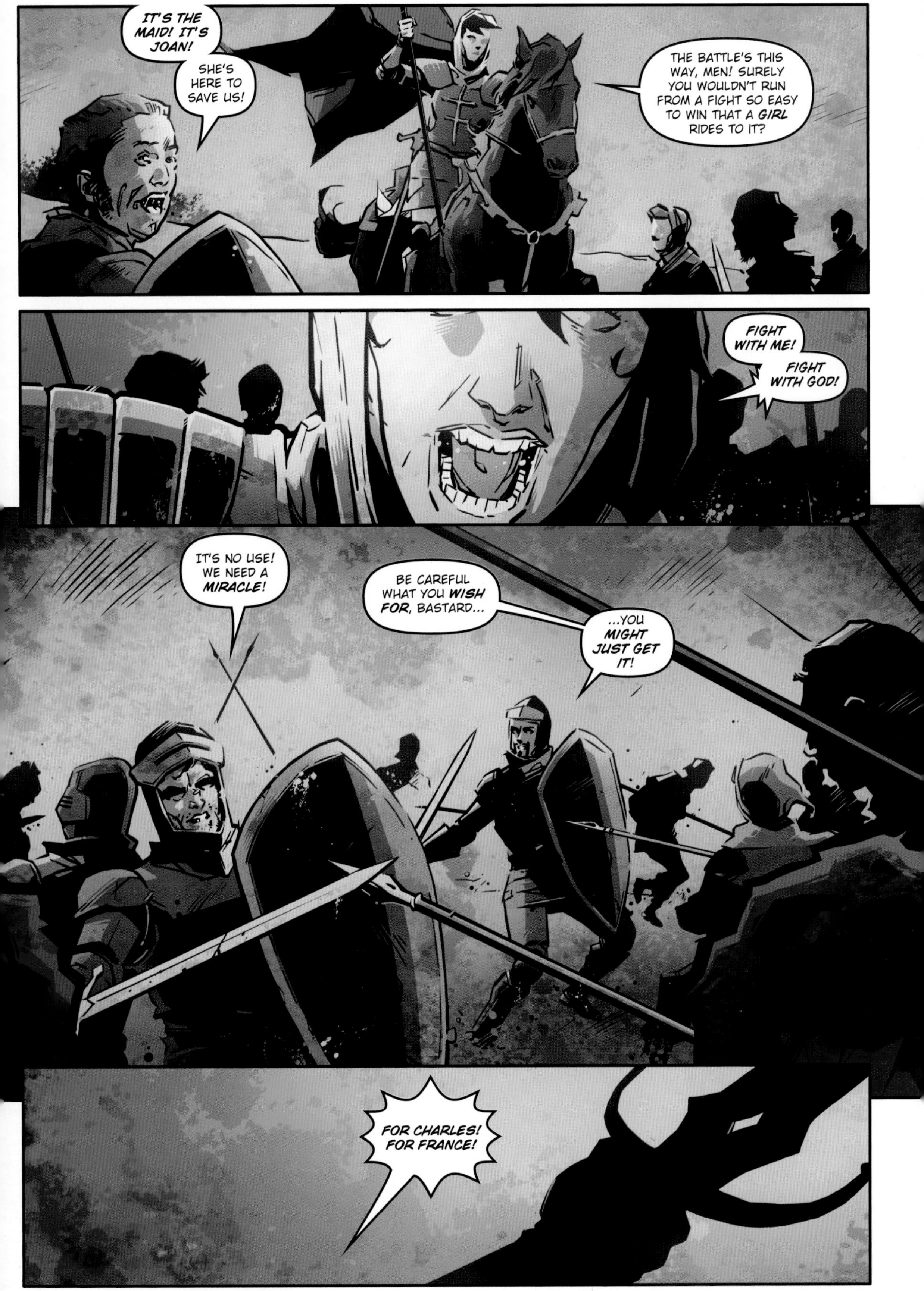
IT'S THE MAID! IT'S JOAN!
SHE'S HERE TO SAVE US!
THE BATTLE'S THIS WAY, MEN! SURELY YOU WOULDN'T RUN FROM A FIGHT SO EASY TO WIN THAT A GIRL RIDES TO IT?
FIGHT WITH ME!
FIGHT WITH GOD!
IT'S NO USE! WE NEED A MIRACLE!
BE CAREFUL WHAT YOU WISH FOR, BASTARD...
...YOU MIGHT JUST GET IT!
FOR CHARLES! FOR FRANCE!

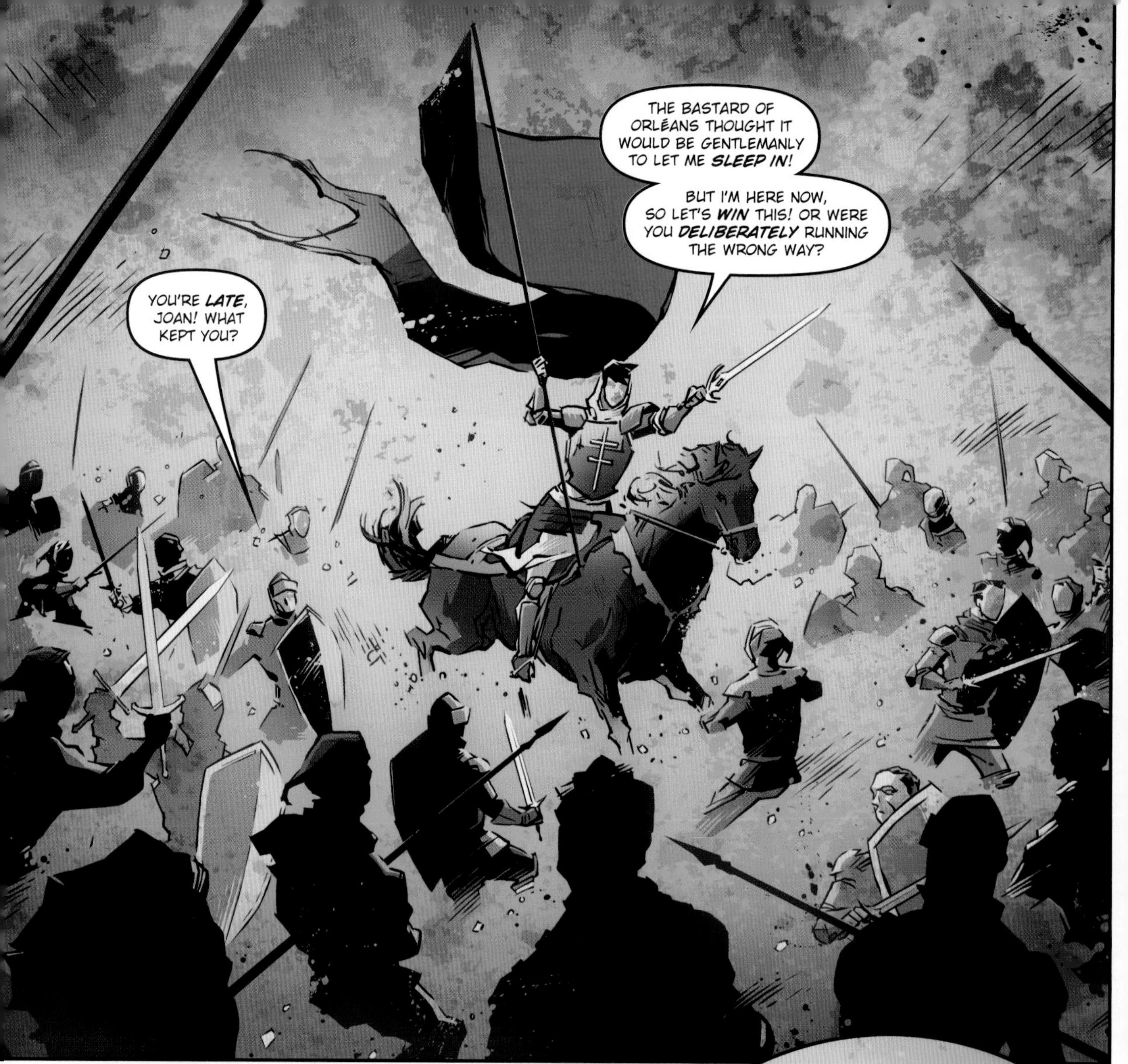
YOU'RE LATE, JOAN! WHAT KEPT YOU?
THE BASTARD OF ORLÉANS THOUGHT IT WOULD BE GENTLEMANLY TO LET ME SLEEP IN!
BUT I'M HERE NOW, SO LET'S WIN THIS! OR WERE YOU DELIBERATELY RUNNING THE WRONG WAY?
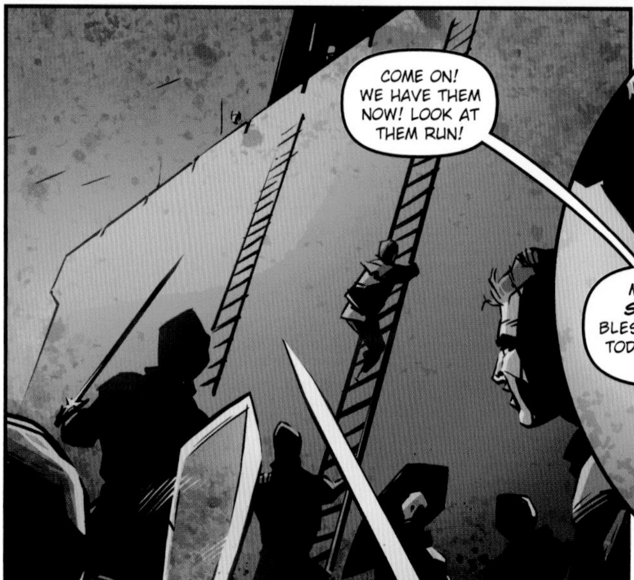
COME ON! WE HAVE THEM NOW! LOOK AT THEM RUN!
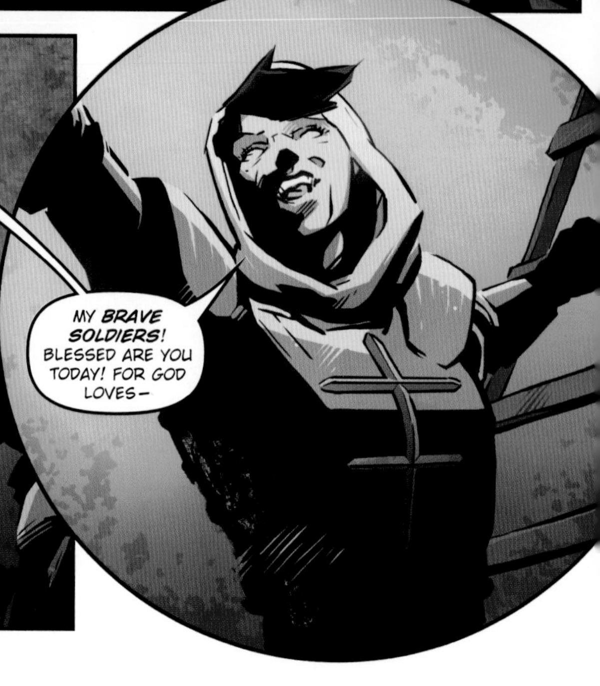
MY BRAVE SOLDIERS! BLESSED ARE YOU TODAY! FOR GOD LOVES—

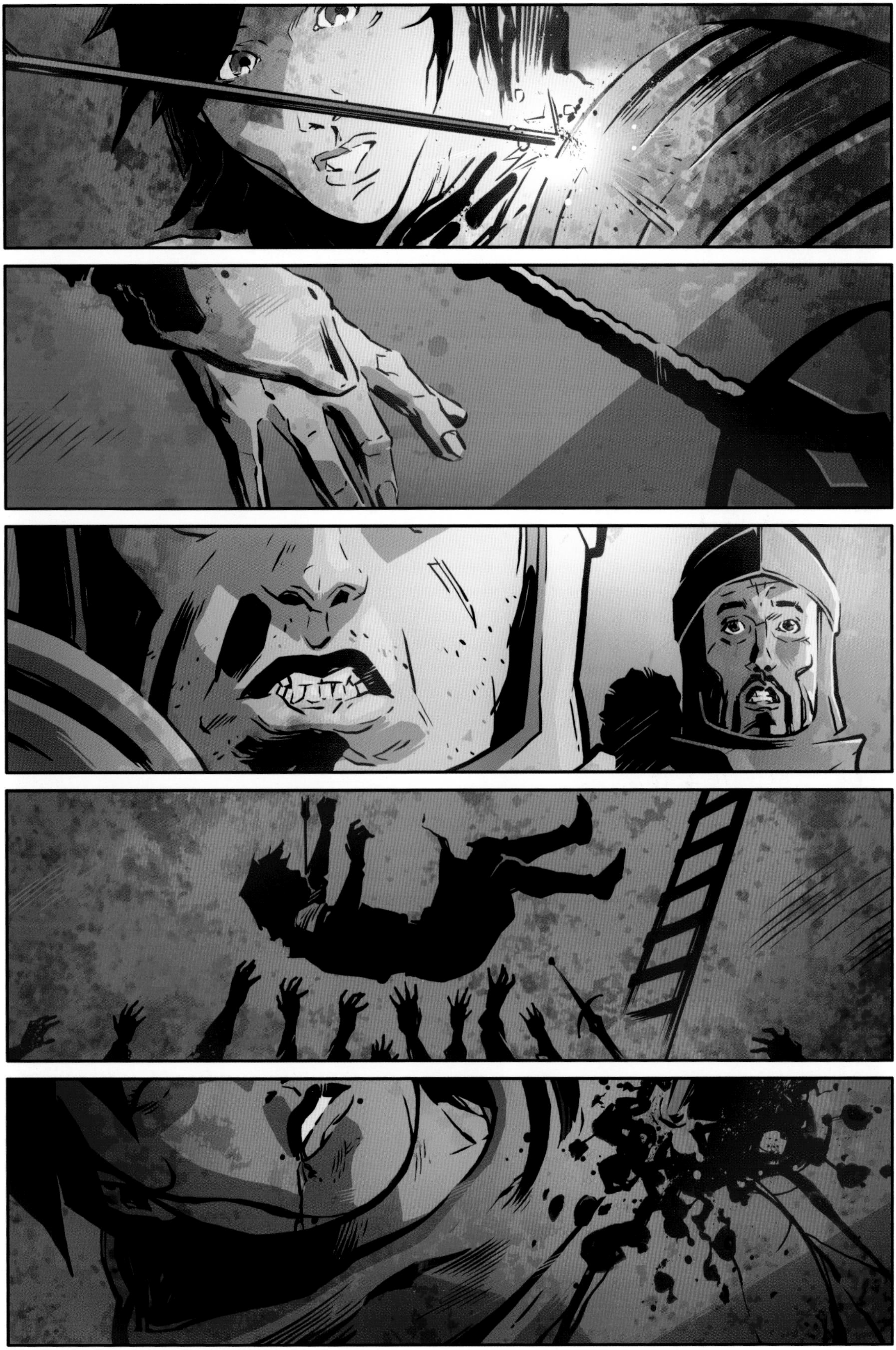

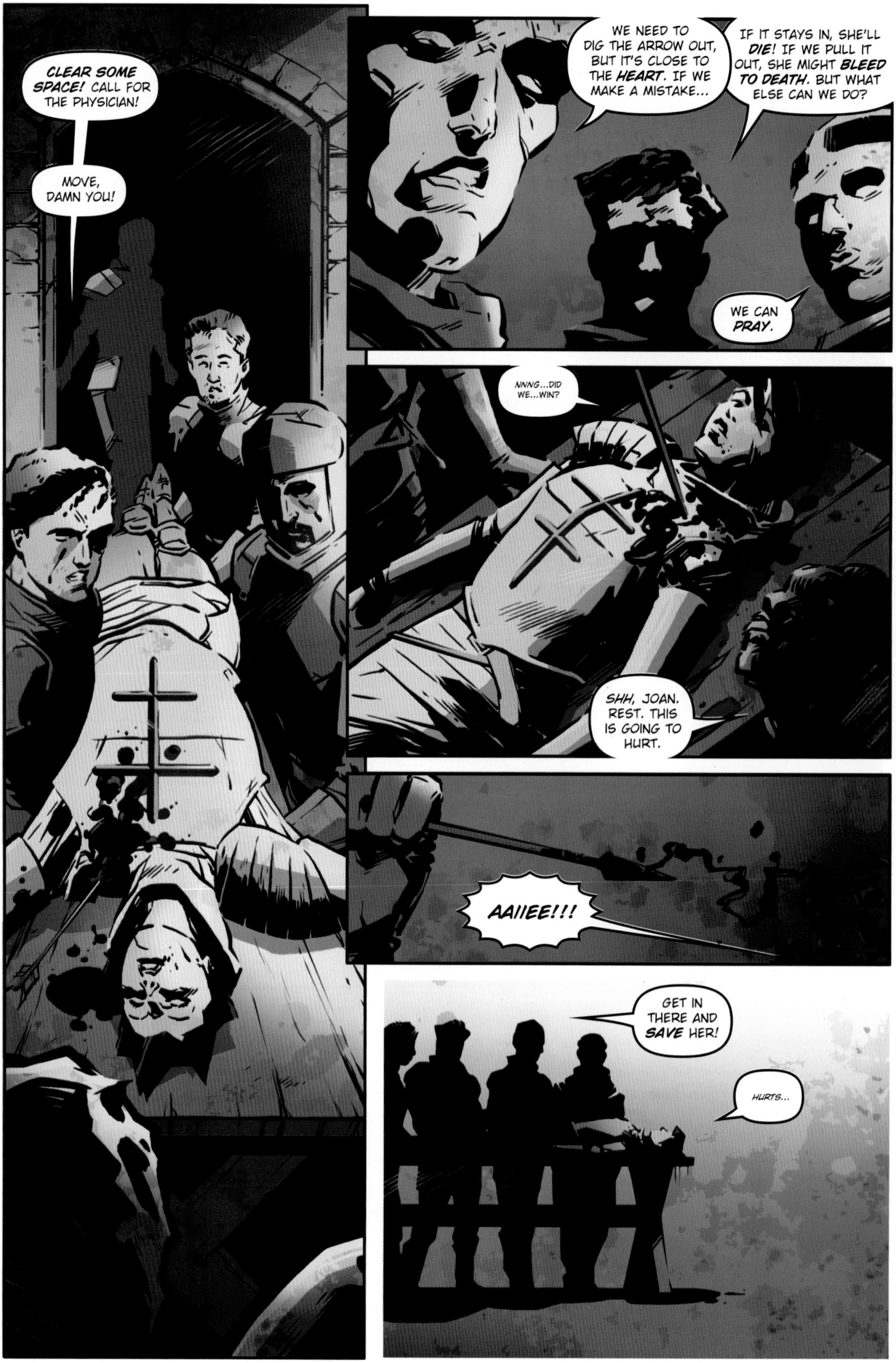
CLEAR SOME SPACE! CALL FOR THE PHYSICIAN!
MOVE, DAMN YOU!
WE NEED TO DIG THE ARROW OUT, BUT IT'S CLOSE TO THE HEART. IF WE MAKE A MISTAKE...
IF IT STAYS IN, SHE'LL DIE! IF WE PULL IT OUT, SHE MIGHT BLEED TO DEATH. BUT WHAT ELSE CAN WE DO?
WE CAN PRAY.
NNNG...DID WE...WIN?
SHH, JOAN. REST. THIS IS GOING TO HURT.
AAIIEE!!!
GET IN THERE AND SAVE HER!
HURTS...

MY LORD, I FEAR IT IS A **MORTAL** WOUND! I'VE SEEN MEN DIE FROM FAR LESS.

THE BEST I CAN DO IS MAKE HER **COMFORTABLE**— SHE WON'T LAST THE DAY!

I CAN'T... HEAR... WHAT DID... HE SAY...?

YOU NEED TO REST, JOAN. HERE, TAKE THIS...

...IT'S AN **OPIATE**— A DRUG THAT WILL **NUMB** ALL PAIN.

NO... NEED CLEAR HEAD... FOR FIGHTING...

THERE'S NO MORE FIGHTING FOR **YOU**, DEAR GIRL.

JUST **GLORY** AT THE LORD'S SIDE.

STOP... STANDING AROUND... GO ...FIGHT...

...

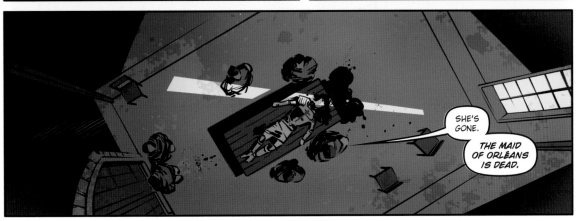

SHE'S GONE.

THE MAID OF ORLÉANS IS DEAD.

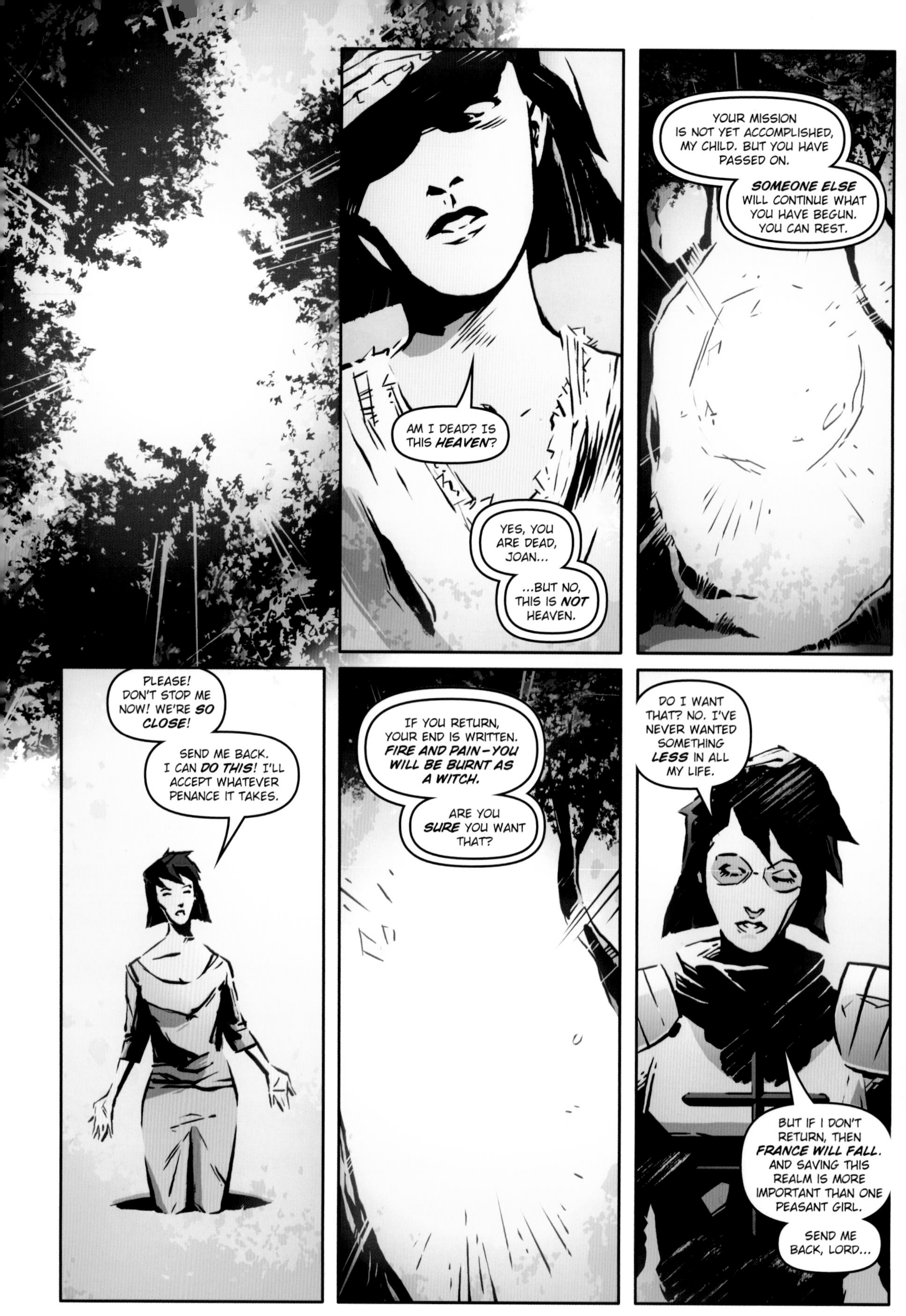
AM I DEAD? IS THIS HEAVEN?
YES, YOU ARE DEAD, JOAN...
...BUT NO, THIS IS NOT HEAVEN.
YOUR MISSION IS NOT YET ACCOMPLISHED, MY CHILD. BUT YOU HAVE PASSED ON.
SOMEONE ELSE WILL CONTINUE WHAT YOU HAVE BEGUN. YOU CAN REST.
PLEASE! DON'T STOP ME NOW! WE'RE SO CLOSE!
SEND ME BACK. I CAN DO THIS! I'LL ACCEPT WHATEVER PENANCE IT TAKES.
IF YOU RETURN, YOUR END IS WRITTEN. FIRE AND PAIN—YOU WILL BE BURNT AS A WITCH.
ARE YOU SURE YOU WANT THAT?
DO I WANT THAT? NO. I'VE NEVER WANTED SOMETHING LESS IN ALL MY LIFE.
BUT IF I DON'T RETURN, THEN FRANCE WILL FALL. AND SAVING THIS REALM IS MORE IMPORTANT THAN ONE PEASANT GIRL.
SEND ME BACK, LORD...

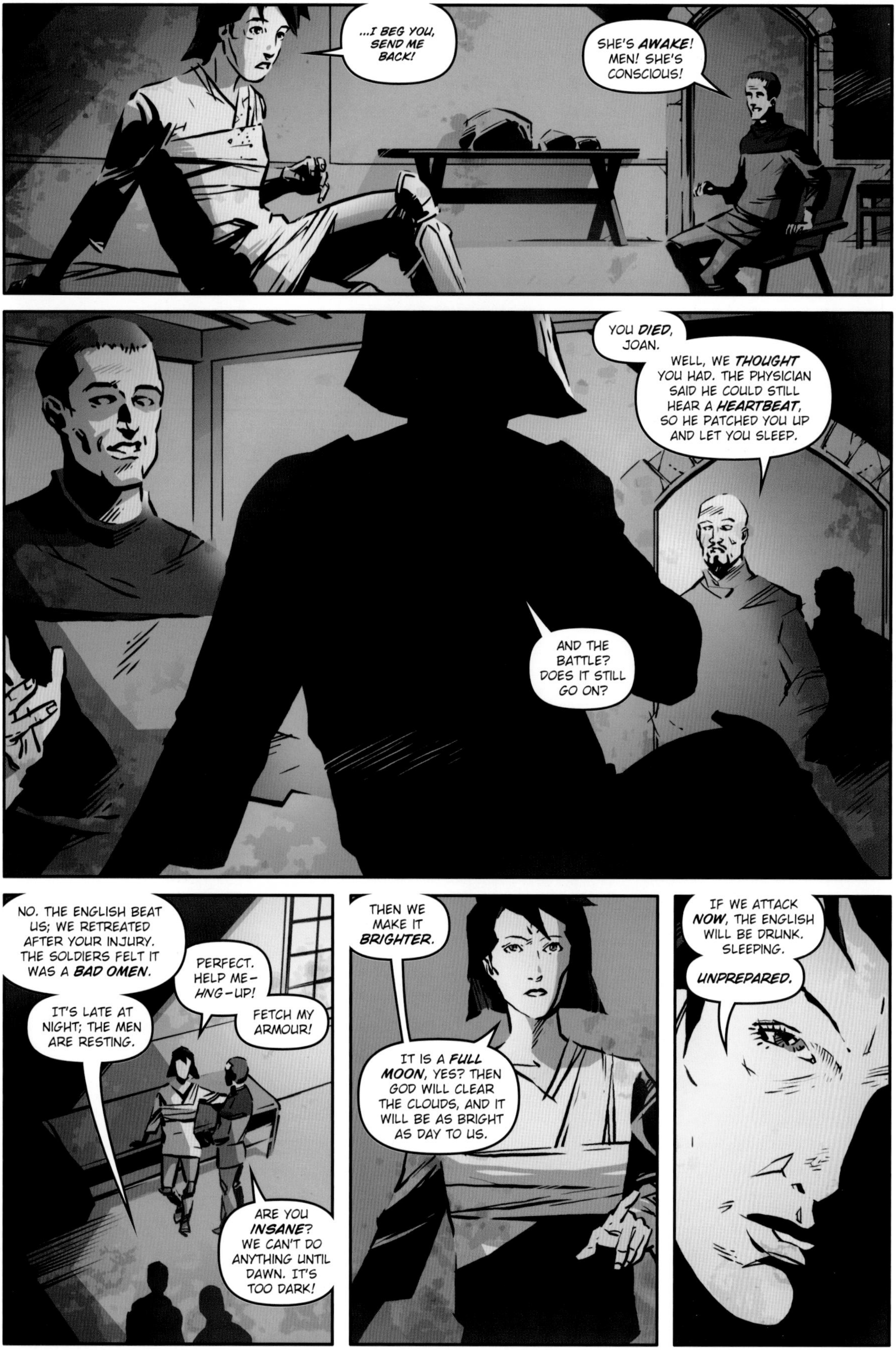
...I BEG YOU, SEND ME BACK!
SHE'S AWAKE! MEN! SHE'S CONSCIOUS!
YOU DIED, JOAN.
WELL, WE THOUGHT YOU HAD. THE PHYSICIAN SAID HE COULD STILL HEAR A HEARTBEAT, SO HE PATCHED YOU UP AND LET YOU SLEEP.
AND THE BATTLE? DOES IT STILL GO ON?
NO. THE ENGLISH BEAT US; WE RETREATED AFTER YOUR INJURY. THE SOLDIERS FELT IT WAS A BAD OMEN.
IT'S LATE AT NIGHT; THE MEN ARE RESTING.
PERFECT. HELP ME-HNG-UP!
FETCH MY ARMOUR!
ARE YOU INSANE? WE CAN'T DO ANYTHING UNTIL DAWN. IT'S TOO DARK!
THEN WE MAKE IT BRIGHTER.
IT IS A FULL MOON, YES? THEN GOD WILL CLEAR THE CLOUDS, AND IT WILL BE AS BRIGHT AS DAY TO US.
IF WE ATTACK NOW, THE ENGLISH WILL BE DRUNK. SLEEPING.
UNPREPARED.

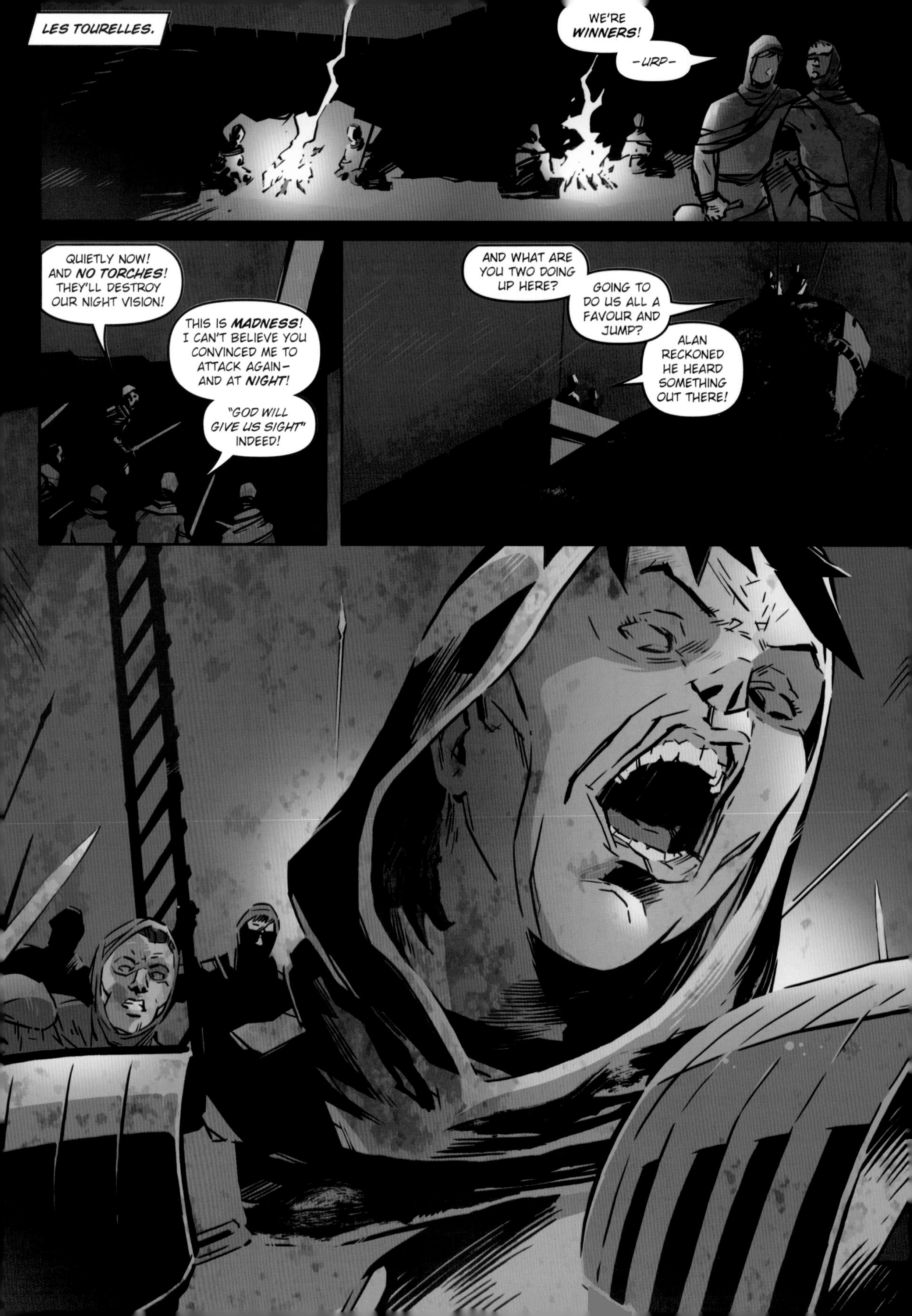
LES TOURELLES.
WE'RE WINNERS!
-URP-
QUIETLY NOW! AND NO TORCHES! THEY'LL DESTROY OUR NIGHT VISION!
THIS IS MADNESS! I CAN'T BELIEVE YOU CONVINCED ME TO ATTACK AGAIN– AND AT NIGHT!
"GOD WILL GIVE US SIGHT" INDEED!
AND WHAT ARE YOU TWO DOING UP HERE?
GOING TO DO US ALL A FAVOUR AND JUMP?
ALAN RECKONED HE HEARD SOMETHING OUT THERE!

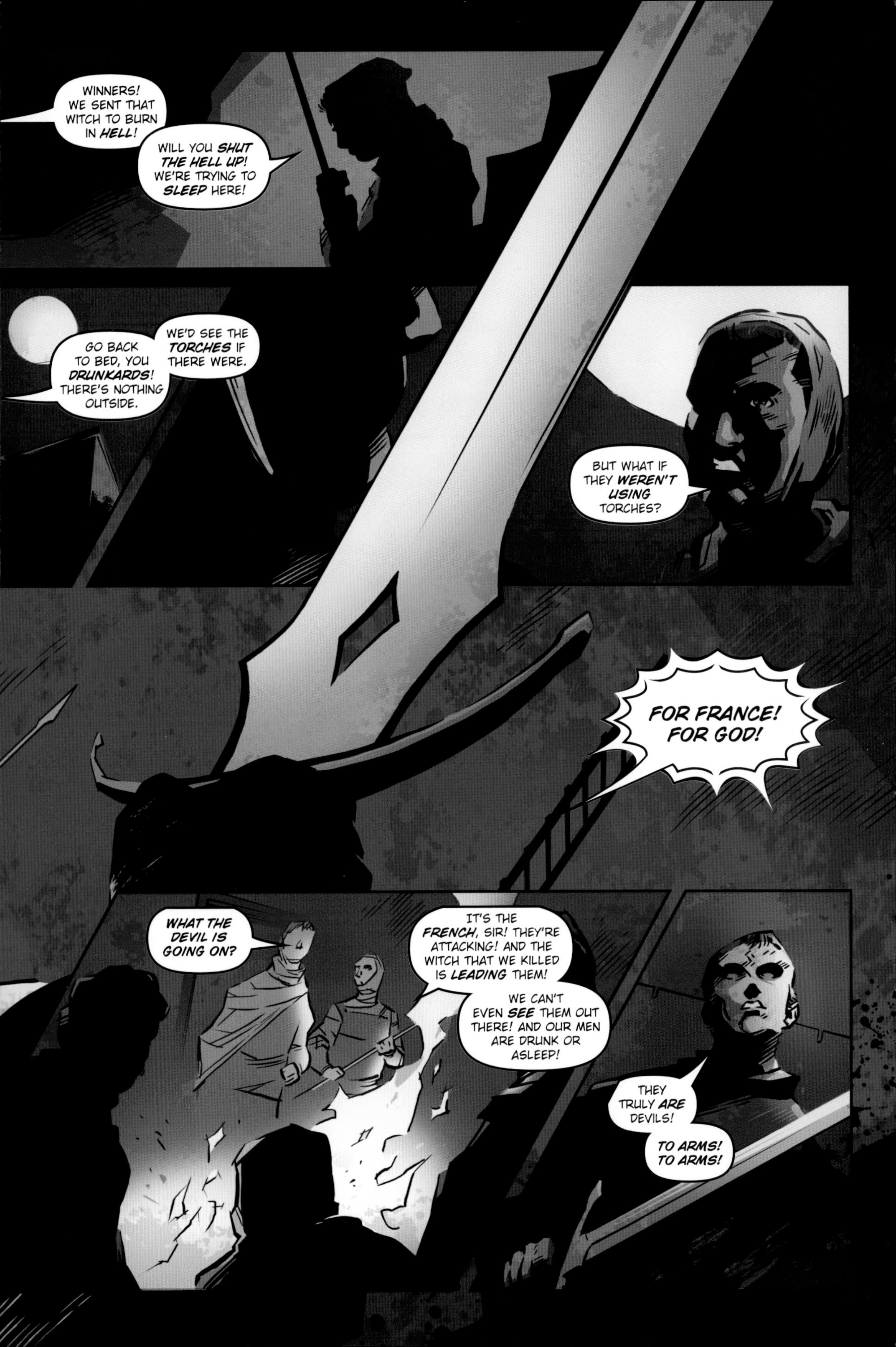
WINNERS! WE SENT THAT WITCH TO BURN IN HELL!
WILL YOU SHUT THE HELL UP! WE'RE TRYING TO SLEEP HERE!
GO BACK TO BED, YOU DRUNKARDS! THERE'S NOTHING OUTSIDE.
WE'D SEE THE TORCHES IF THERE WERE.
BUT WHAT IF THEY WEREN'T USING TORCHES?
FOR FRANCE! FOR GOD!
WHAT THE DEVIL IS GOING ON?
IT'S THE FRENCH, SIR! THEY'RE ATTACKING! AND THE WITCH THAT WE KILLED IS LEADING THEM!
WE CAN'T EVEN SEE THEM OUT THERE! AND OUR MEN ARE DRUNK OR ASLEEP!
THEY TRULY ARE DEVILS!
TO ARMS! TO ARMS!

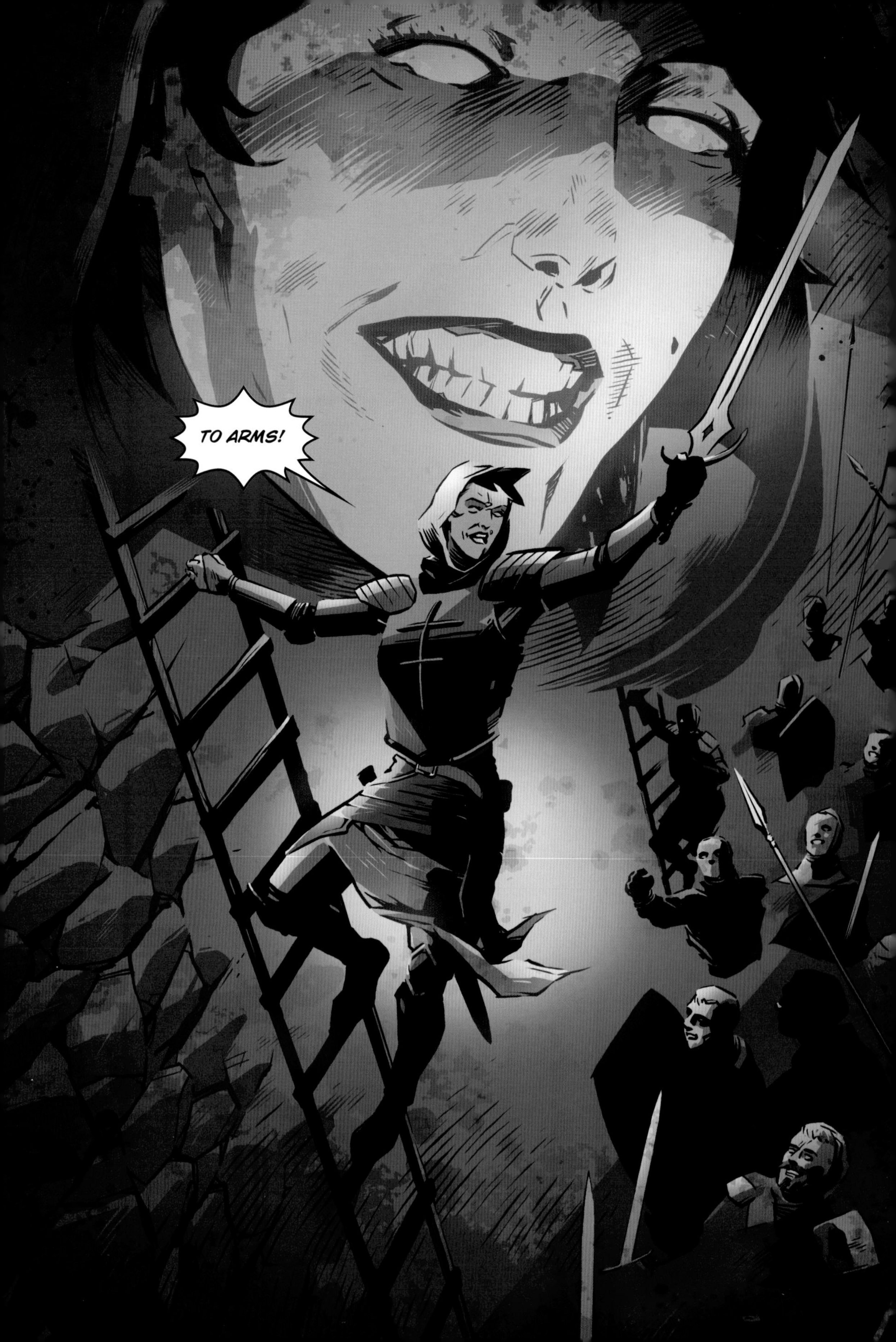
TO ARMS!

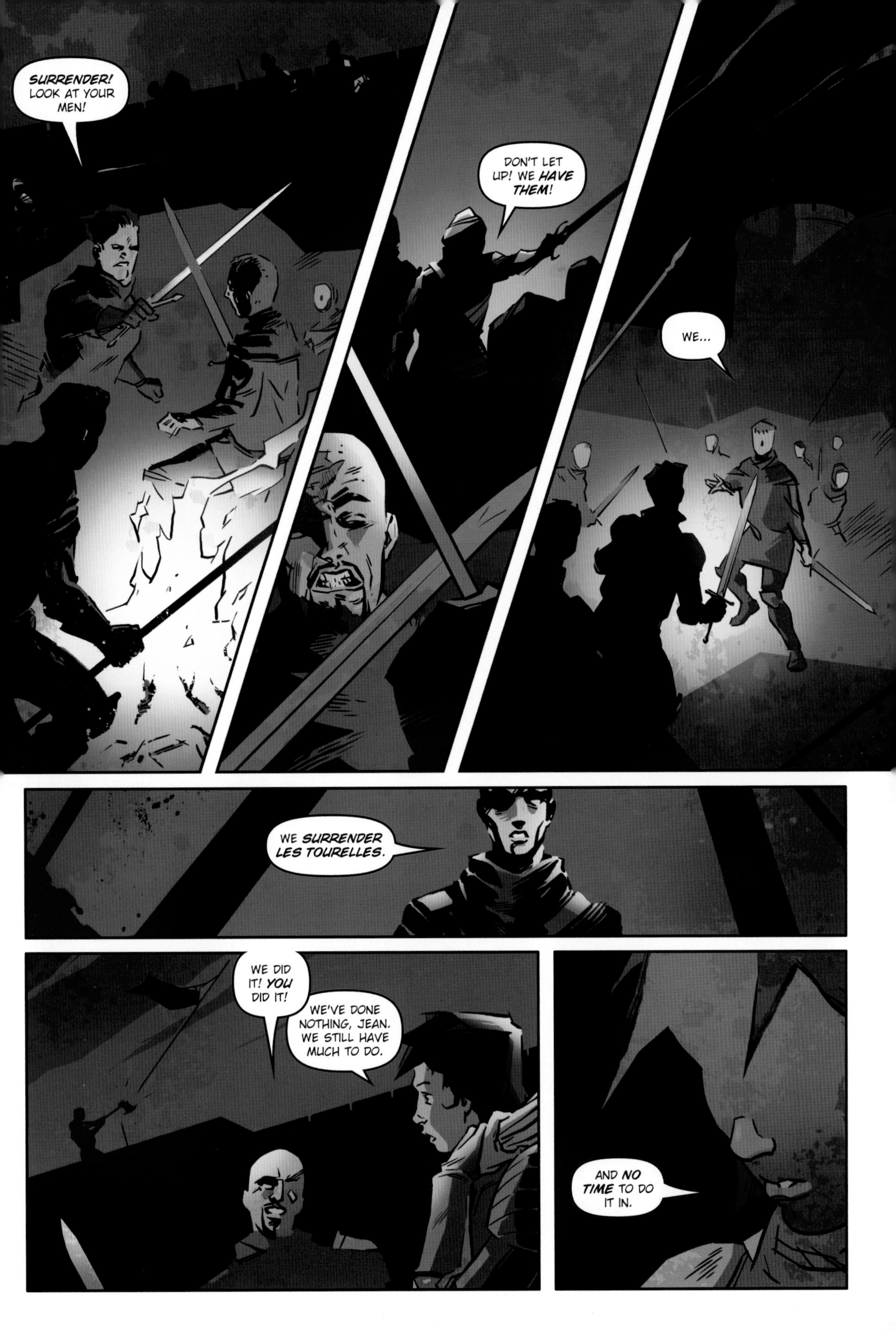
SURRENDER! LOOK AT YOUR MEN!
DON'T LET UP! WE HAVE THEM!
WE...
WE SURRENDER LES TOURELLES.
WE DID IT! YOU DID IT!
WE'VE DONE NOTHING, JEAN. WE STILL HAVE MUCH TO DO.
AND NO TIME TO DO IT IN.

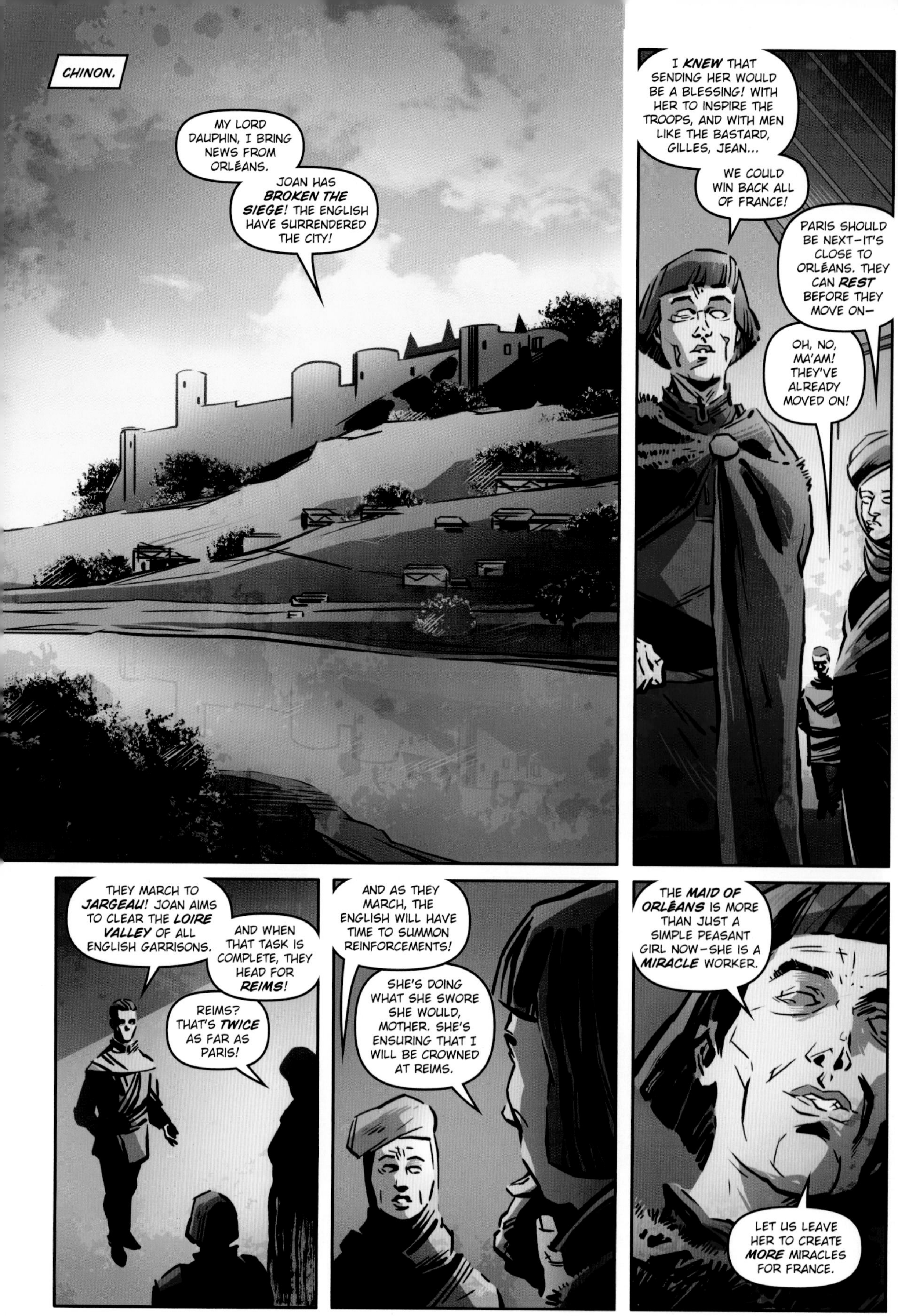

CHINON.
MY LORD DAUPHIN, I BRING NEWS FROM ORLÉANS.
JOAN HAS BROKEN THE SIEGE! THE ENGLISH HAVE SURRENDERED THE CITY!
I KNEW THAT SENDING HER WOULD BE A BLESSING! WITH HER TO INSPIRE THE TROOPS, AND WITH MEN LIKE THE BASTARD, GILLES, JEAN...
WE COULD WIN BACK ALL OF FRANCE!
PARIS SHOULD BE NEXT–IT'S CLOSE TO ORLÉANS. THEY CAN REST BEFORE THEY MOVE ON–
OH, NO, MA'AM! THEY'VE ALREADY MOVED ON!
THEY MARCH TO JARGEAU! JOAN AIMS TO CLEAR THE LOIRE VALLEY OF ALL ENGLISH GARRISONS.
AND WHEN THAT TASK IS COMPLETE, THEY HEAD FOR REIMS!
REIMS? THAT'S TWICE AS FAR AS PARIS!
AND AS THEY MARCH, THE ENGLISH WILL HAVE TIME TO SUMMON REINFORCEMENTS!
SHE'S DOING WHAT SHE SWORE SHE WOULD, MOTHER. SHE'S ENSURING THAT I WILL BE CROWNED AT REIMS.
THE MAID OF ORLÉANS IS MORE THAN JUST A SIMPLE PEASANT GIRL NOW–SHE IS A MIRACLE WORKER.
LET US LEAVE HER TO CREATE MORE MIRACLES FOR FRANCE.

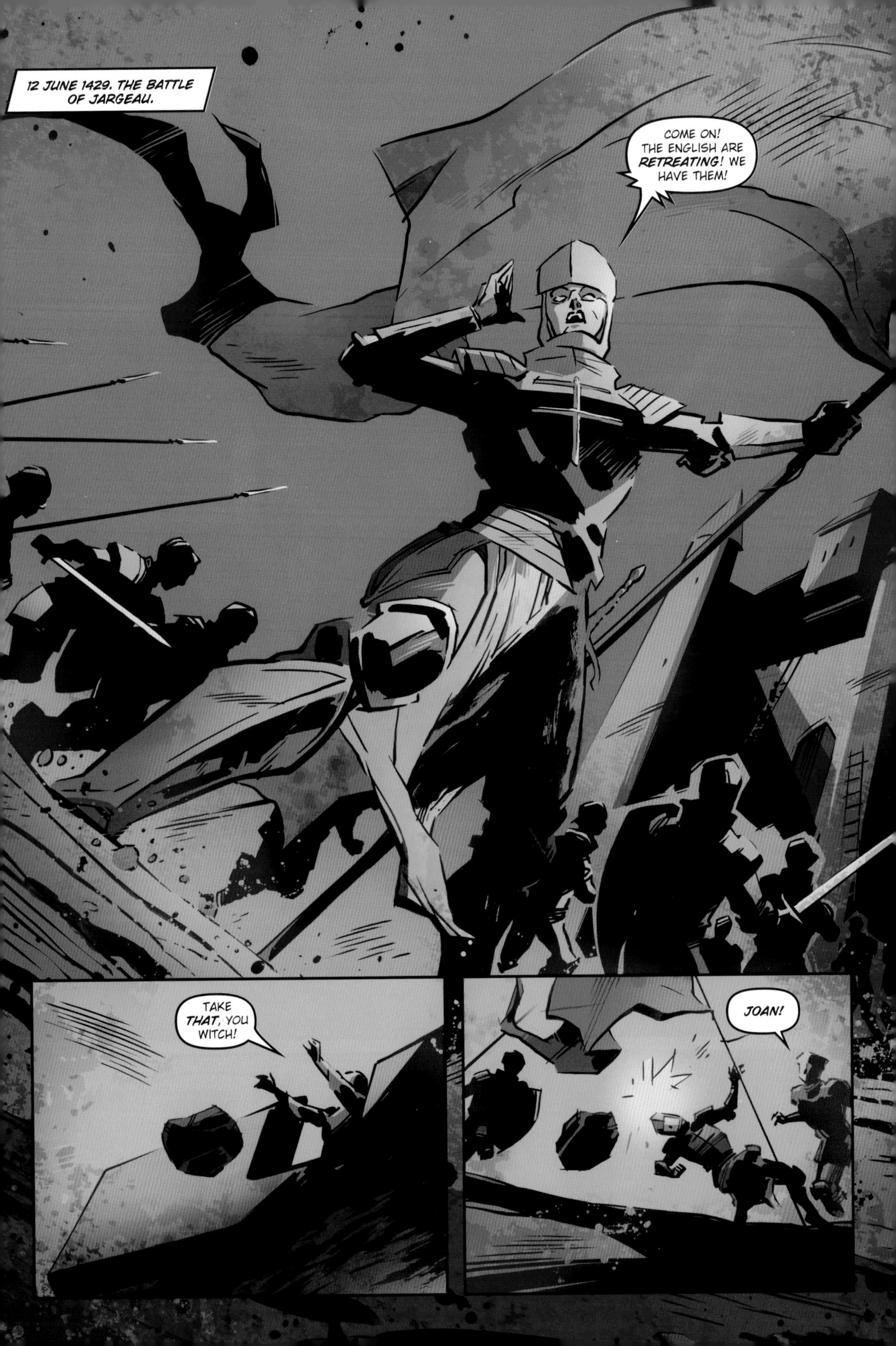
12 JUNE 1429. THE BATTLE OF JARGEAU.
COME ON! THE ENGLISH ARE RETREATING! WE HAVE THEM!
TAKE THAT, YOU WITCH!
JOAN!

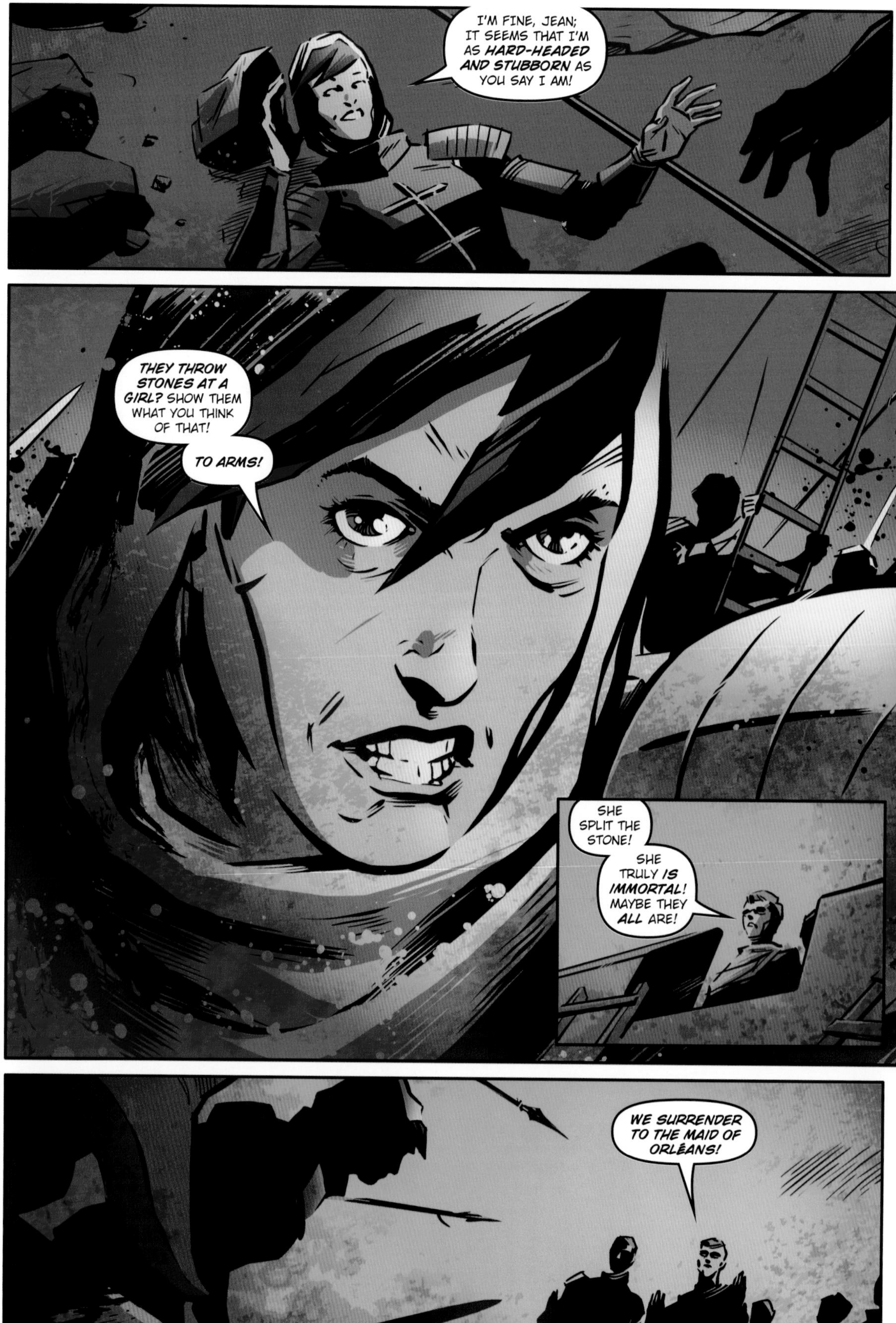
I'M FINE, JEAN; IT SEEMS THAT I'M AS HARD-HEADED AND STUBBORN AS YOU SAY I AM!
THEY THROW STONES AT A GIRL? SHOW THEM WHAT YOU THINK OF THAT!
TO ARMS!
SHE SPLIT THE STONE!
SHE TRULY IS IMMORTAL! MAYBE THEY ALL ARE!
WE SURRENDER TO THE MAID OF ORLÉANS!

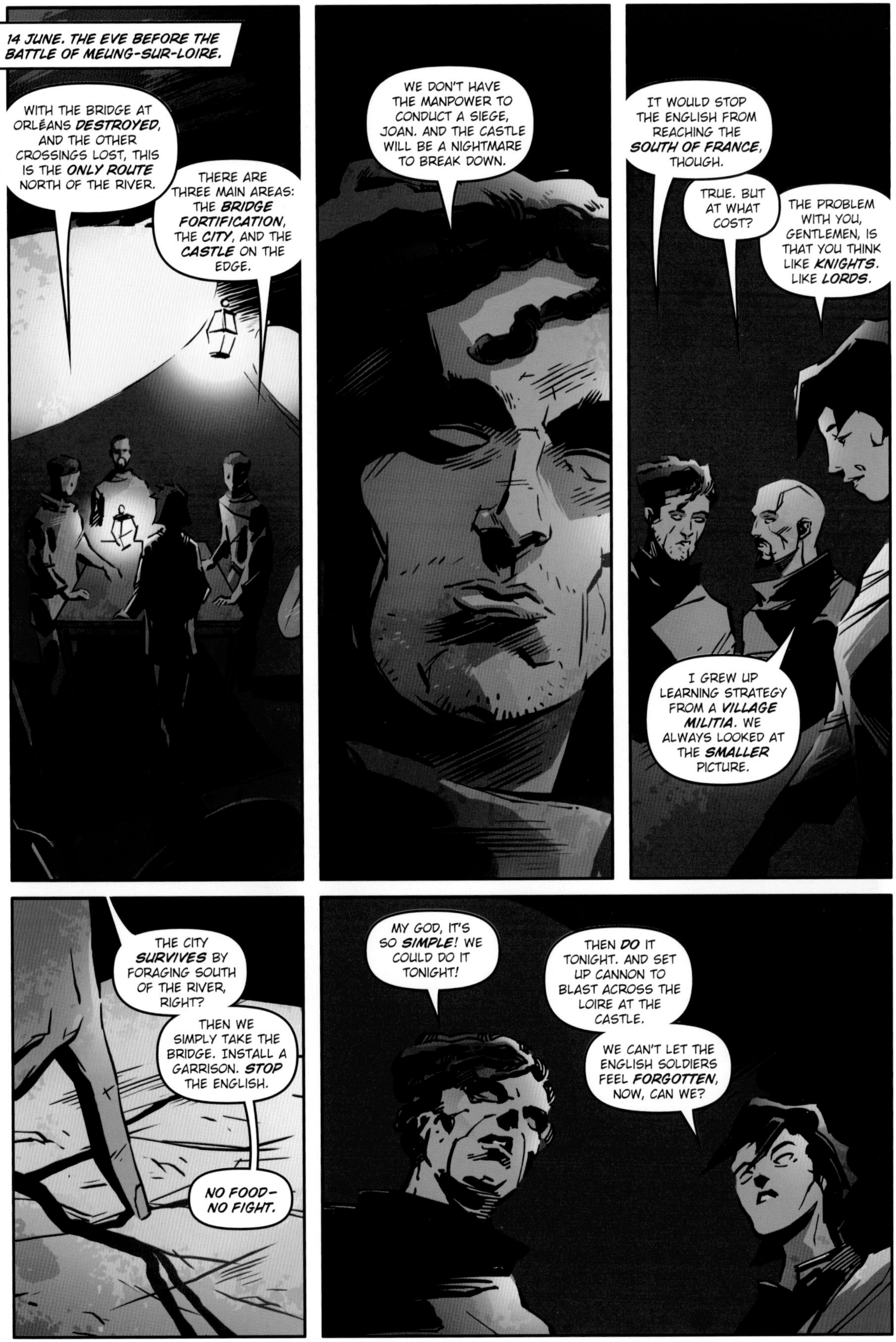

14 JUNE. THE EVE BEFORE THE BATTLE OF MEUNG-SUR-LOIRE.
WITH THE BRIDGE AT ORLÉANS DESTROYED, AND THE OTHER CROSSINGS LOST, THIS IS THE ONLY ROUTE NORTH OF THE RIVER.
THERE ARE THREE MAIN AREAS: THE BRIDGE FORTIFICATION, THE CITY, AND THE CASTLE ON THE EDGE.
WE DON'T HAVE THE MANPOWER TO CONDUCT A SIEGE, JOAN. AND THE CASTLE WILL BE A NIGHTMARE TO BREAK DOWN.
IT WOULD STOP THE ENGLISH FROM REACHING THE SOUTH OF FRANCE, THOUGH.
TRUE. BUT AT WHAT COST?
THE PROBLEM WITH YOU, GENTLEMEN, IS THAT YOU THINK LIKE KNIGHTS. LIKE LORDS.
I GREW UP LEARNING STRATEGY FROM A VILLAGE MILITIA. WE ALWAYS LOOKED AT THE SMALLER PICTURE.
THE CITY SURVIVES BY FORAGING SOUTH OF THE RIVER, RIGHT?
THEN WE SIMPLY TAKE THE BRIDGE. INSTALL A GARRISON. STOP THE ENGLISH.
NO FOOD— NO FIGHT.
MY GOD, IT'S SO SIMPLE! WE COULD DO IT TONIGHT!
THEN DO IT TONIGHT. AND SET UP CANNON TO BLAST ACROSS THE LOIRE AT THE CASTLE.
WE CAN'T LET THE ENGLISH SOLDIERS FEEL FORGOTTEN, NOW, CAN WE?

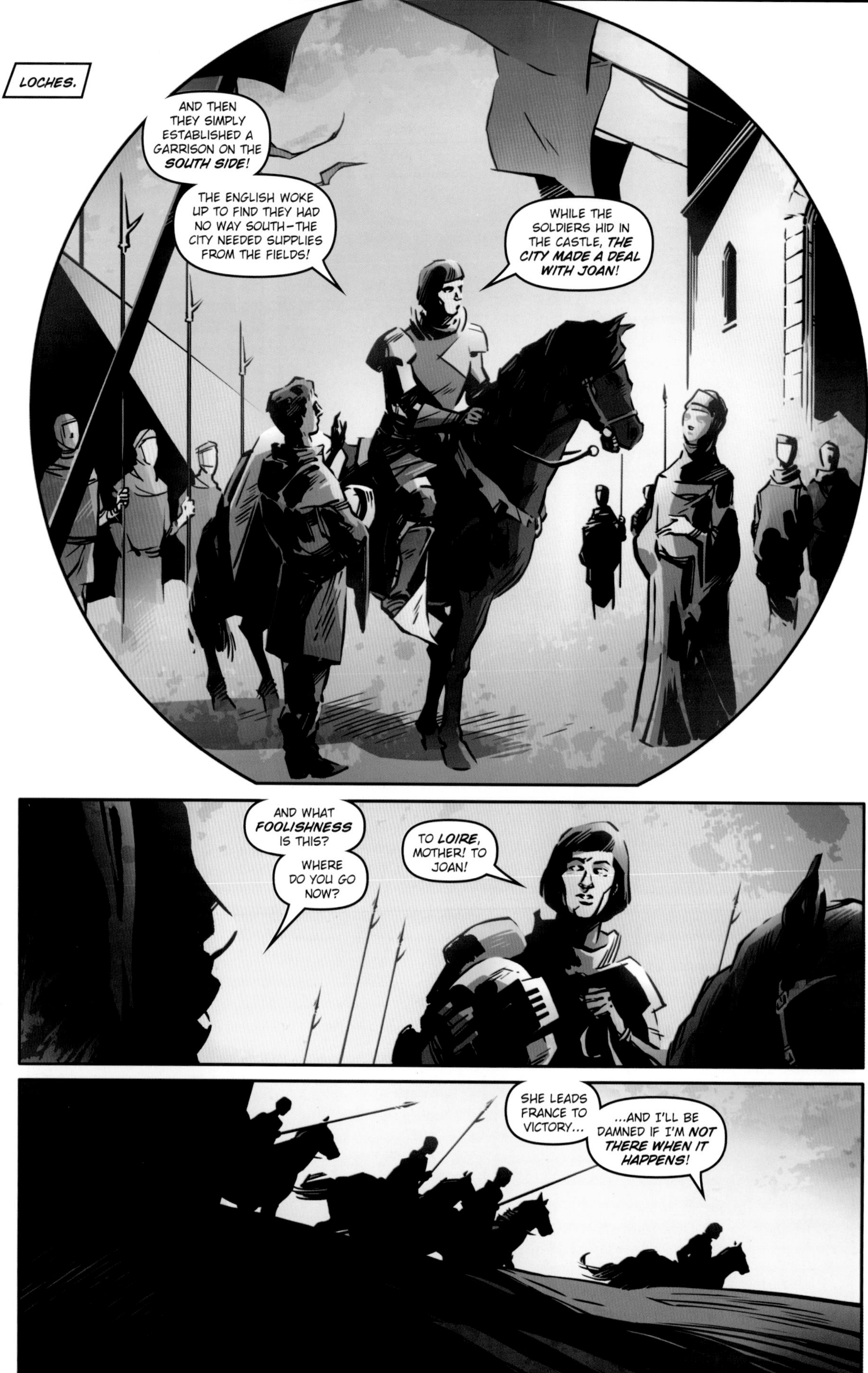
LOCHES.
AND THEN THEY SIMPLY ESTABLISHED A GARRISON ON THE SOUTH SIDE!
THE ENGLISH WOKE UP TO FIND THEY HAD NO WAY SOUTH—THE CITY NEEDED SUPPLIES FROM THE FIELDS!
WHILE THE SOLDIERS HID IN THE CASTLE, THE CITY MADE A DEAL WITH JOAN!
AND WHAT FOOLISHNESS IS THIS?
WHERE DO YOU GO NOW?
TO LOIRE, MOTHER! TO JOAN!
SHE LEADS FRANCE TO VICTORY...
...AND I'LL BE DAMNED IF I'M NOT THERE WHEN IT HAPPENS!

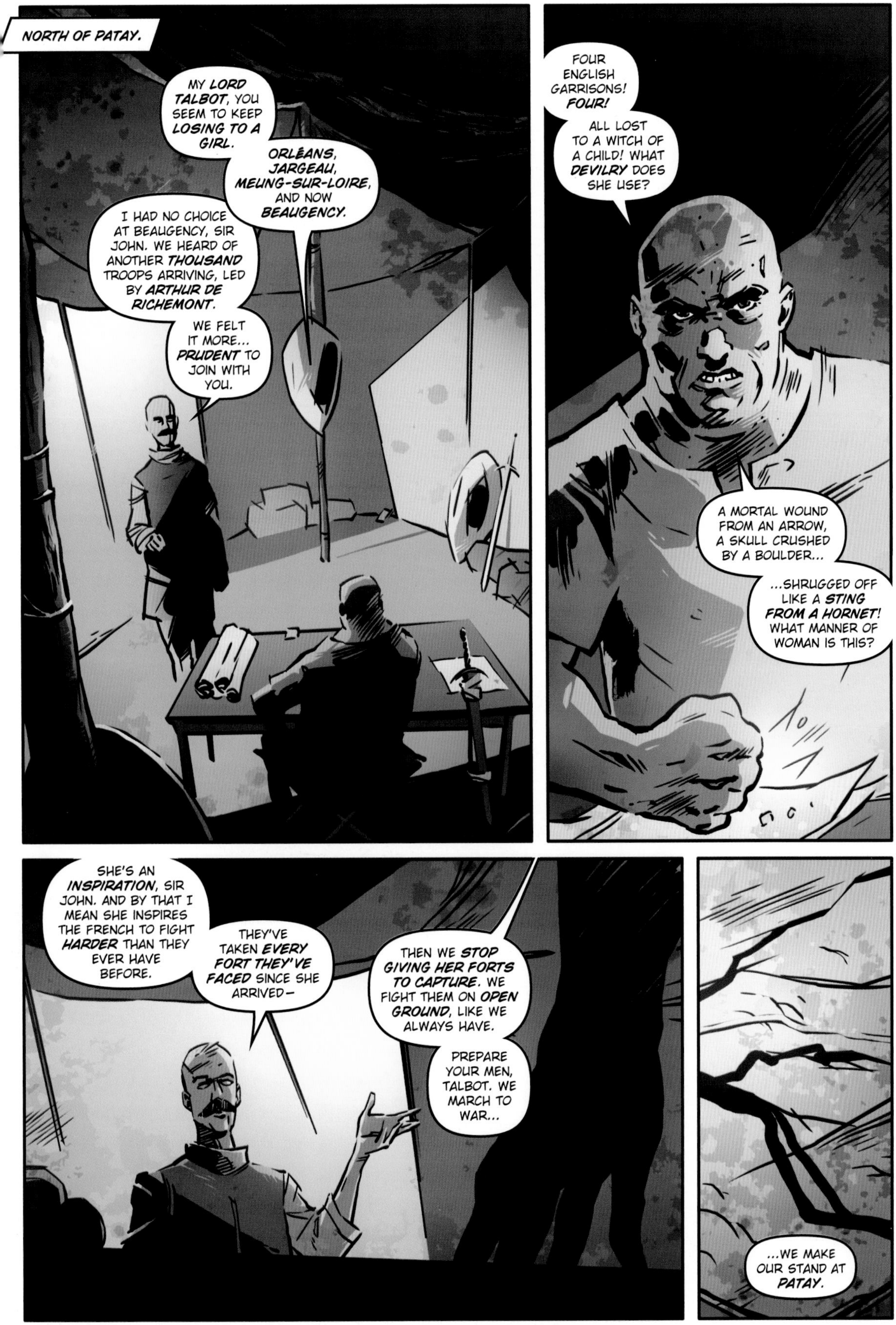
NORTH OF PATAY.
MY LORD TALBOT, YOU SEEM TO KEEP LOSING TO A GIRL.
ORLÉANS, JARGEAU, MEUNG-SUR-LOIRE, AND NOW BEAUGENCY.
I HAD NO CHOICE AT BEAUGENCY, SIR JOHN. WE HEARD OF ANOTHER THOUSAND TROOPS ARRIVING, LED BY ARTHUR DE RICHEMONT.
WE FELT IT MORE... PRUDENT TO JOIN WITH YOU.
FOUR ENGLISH GARRISONS! FOUR!
ALL LOST TO A WITCH OF A CHILD! WHAT DEVILRY DOES SHE USE?
A MORTAL WOUND FROM AN ARROW, A SKULL CRUSHED BY A BOULDER...
...SHRUGGED OFF LIKE A STING FROM A HORNET! WHAT MANNER OF WOMAN IS THIS?
SHE'S AN INSPIRATION, SIR JOHN. AND BY THAT I MEAN SHE INSPIRES THE FRENCH TO FIGHT HARDER THAN THEY EVER HAVE BEFORE.
THEY'VE TAKEN EVERY FORT THEY'VE FACED SINCE SHE ARRIVED—
THEN WE STOP GIVING HER FORTS TO CAPTURE. WE FIGHT THEM ON OPEN GROUND, LIKE WE ALWAYS HAVE.
PREPARE YOUR MEN, TALBOT. WE MARCH TO WAR...
...WE MAKE OUR STAND AT PATAY.

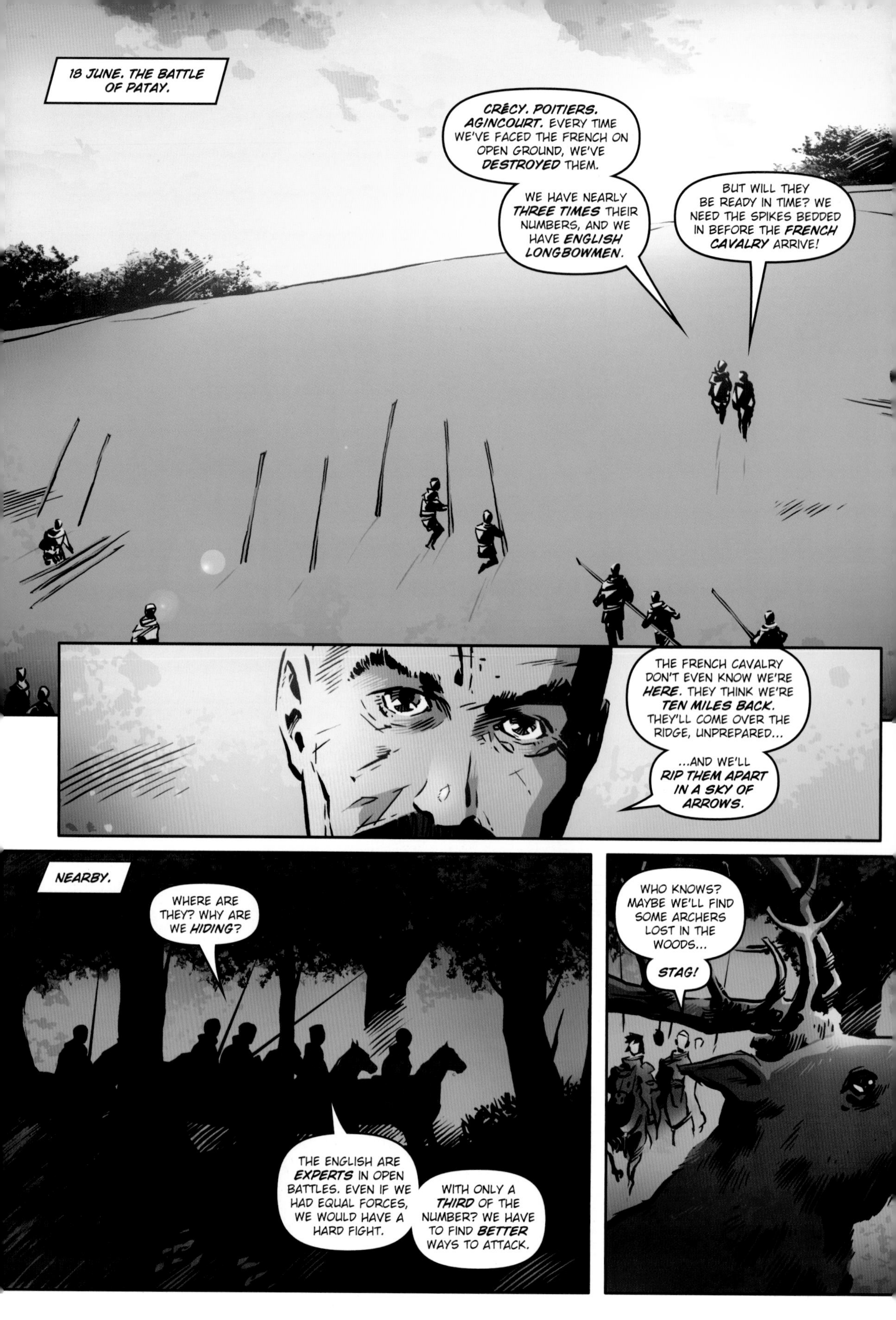
18 JUNE. THE BATTLE OF PATAY.
CRÊCY. POITIERS. AGINCOURT. EVERY TIME WE'VE FACED THE FRENCH ON OPEN GROUND, WE'VE DESTROYED THEM.
WE HAVE NEARLY THREE TIMES THEIR NUMBERS, AND WE HAVE ENGLISH LONGBOWMEN.
BUT WILL THEY BE READY IN TIME? WE NEED THE SPIKES BEDDED IN BEFORE THE FRENCH CAVALRY ARRIVE!
THE FRENCH CAVALRY DON'T EVEN KNOW WE'RE HERE. THEY THINK WE'RE TEN MILES BACK. THEY'LL COME OVER THE RIDGE, UNPREPARED...
...AND WE'LL RIP THEM APART IN A SKY OF ARROWS.
NEARBY.
WHERE ARE THEY? WHY ARE WE HIDING?
THE ENGLISH ARE EXPERTS IN OPEN BATTLES. EVEN IF WE HAD EQUAL FORCES, WE WOULD HAVE A HARD FIGHT.
WITH ONLY A THIRD OF THE NUMBER? WE HAVE TO FIND BETTER WAYS TO ATTACK.
WHO KNOWS? MAYBE WE'LL FIND SOME ARCHERS LOST IN THE WOODS...
STAG!

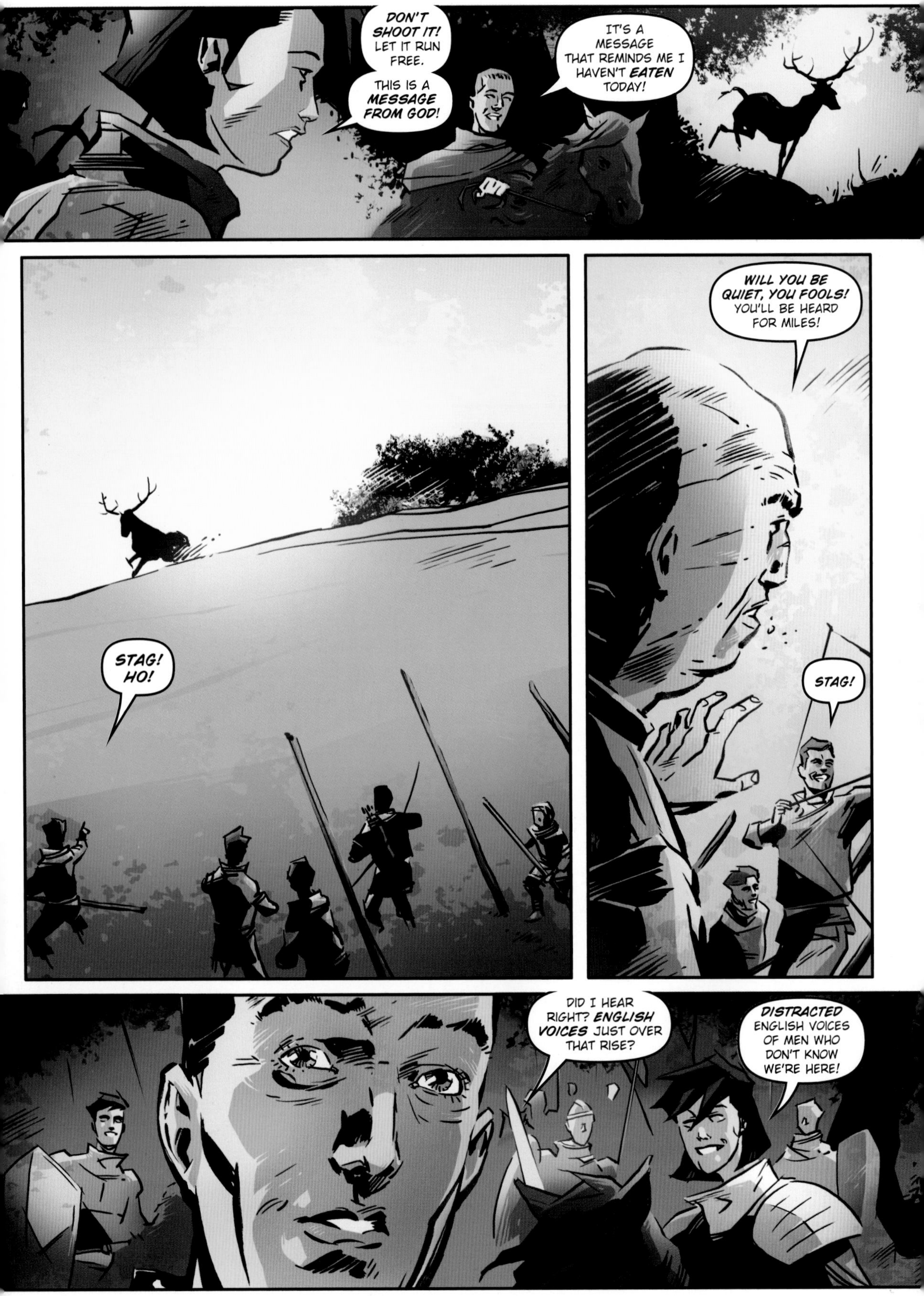
DON'T SHOOT IT! LET IT RUN FREE.
THIS IS A MESSAGE FROM GOD!
IT'S A MESSAGE THAT REMINDS ME I HAVEN'T EATEN TODAY!
STAG! HO!
WILL YOU BE QUIET, YOU FOOLS! YOU'LL BE HEARD FOR MILES!
STAG!
DID I HEAR RIGHT? ENGLISH VOICES JUST OVER THAT RISE?
DISTRACTED ENGLISH VOICES OF MEN WHO DON'T KNOW WE'RE HERE!

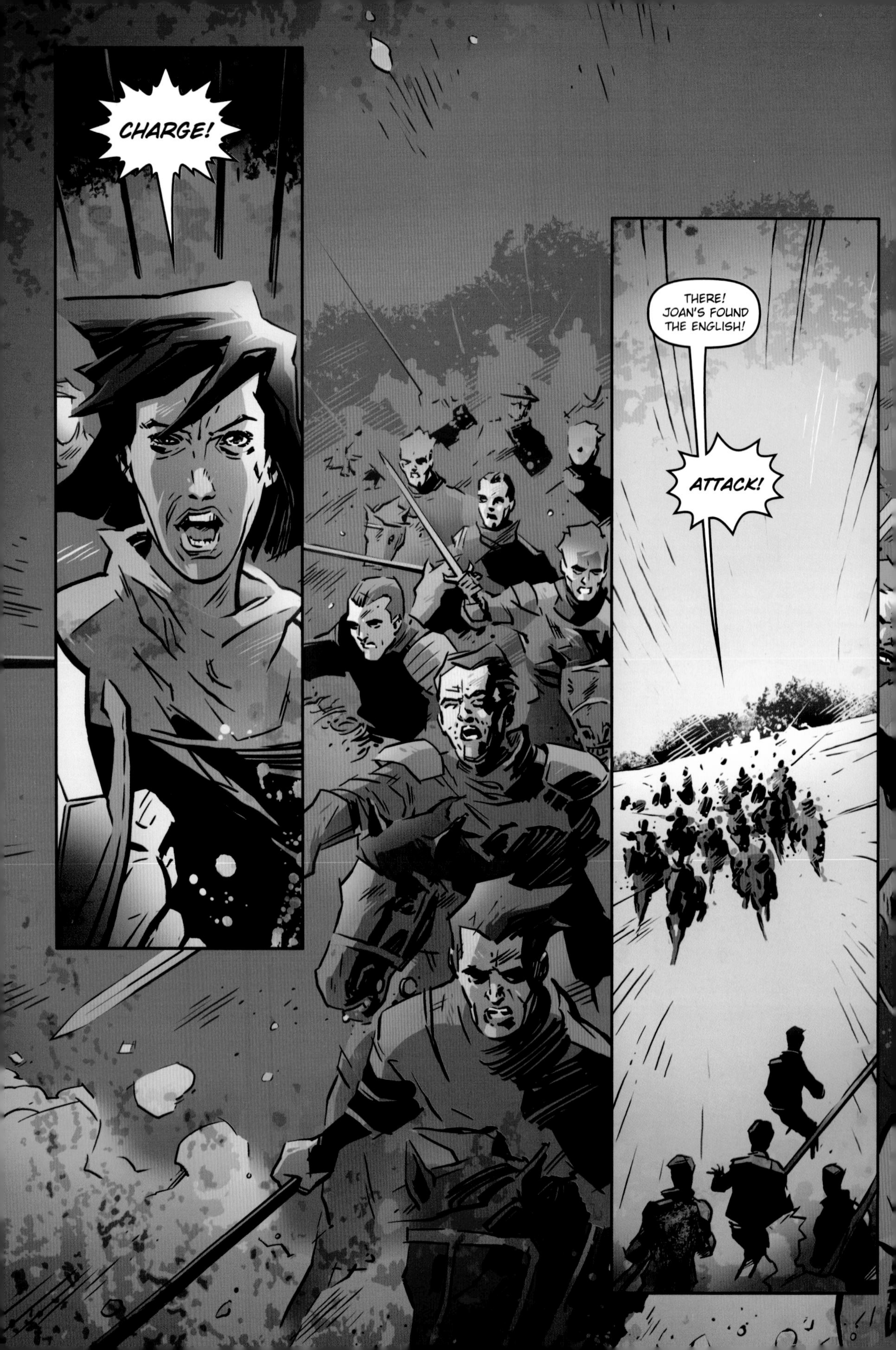
CHARGE!
THERE! JOAN'S FOUND THE ENGLISH!
ATTACK!

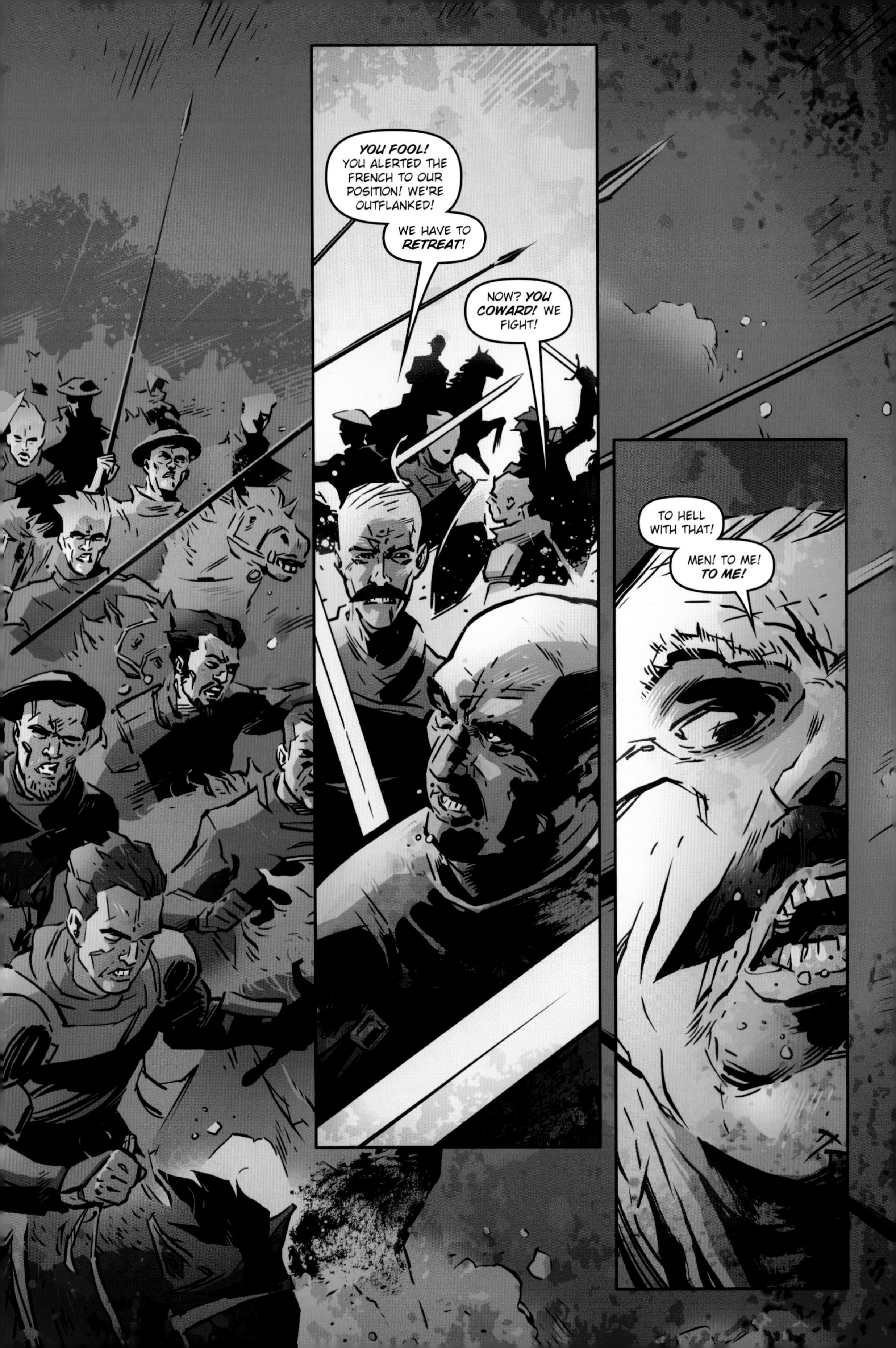
YOU FOOL! YOU ALERTED THE FRENCH TO OUR POSITION! WE'RE OUTFLANKED!
WE HAVE TO RETREAT!
NOW? YOU COWARD! WE FIGHT!
TO HELL WITH THAT!
MEN! TO ME! TO ME!

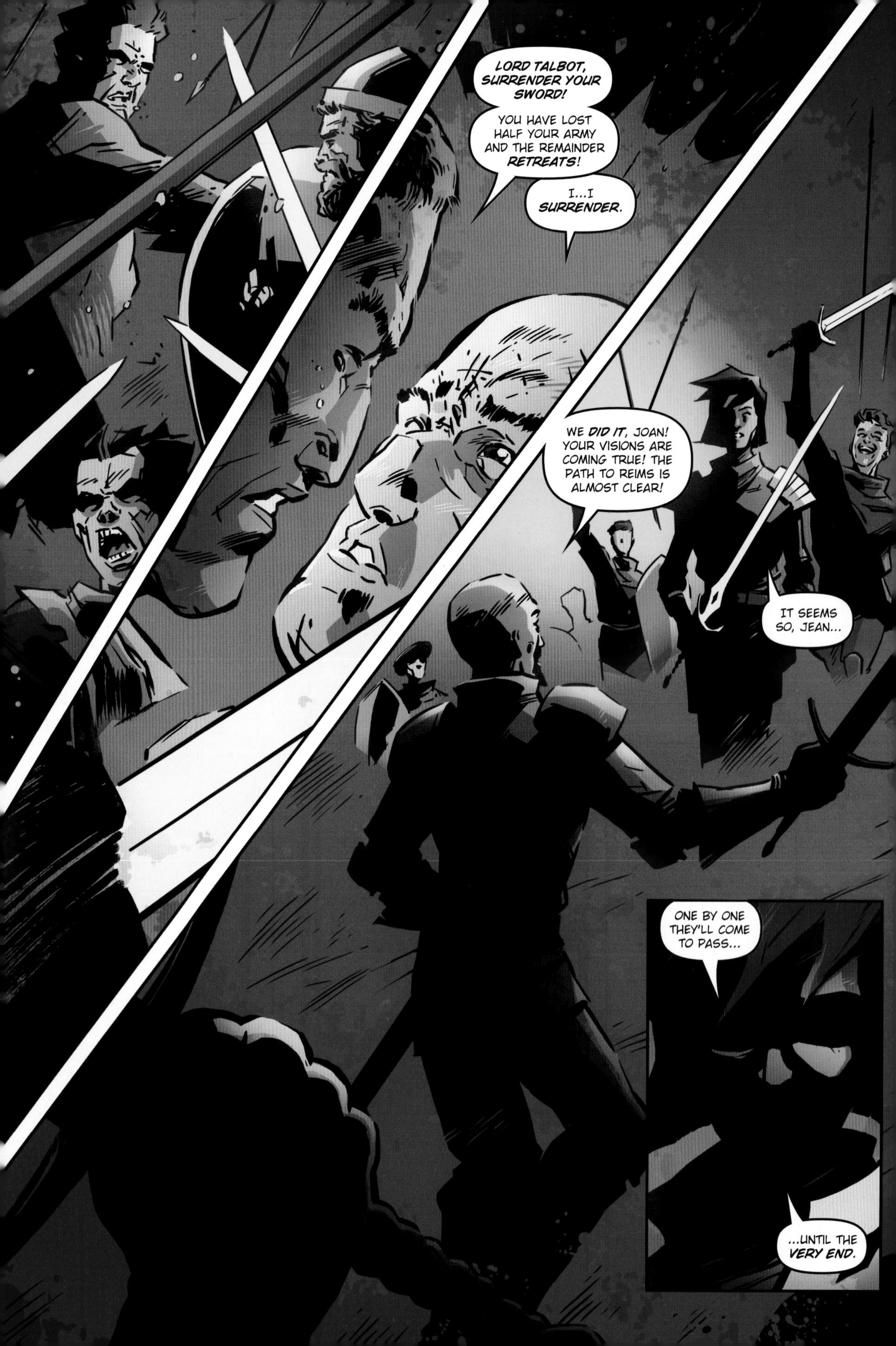
LORD TALBOT, SURRENDER YOUR SWORD!
YOU HAVE LOST HALF YOUR ARMY AND THE REMAINDER RETREATS!
I...I SURRENDER.
WE DID IT, JOAN! YOUR VISIONS ARE COMING TRUE! THE PATH TO REIMS IS ALMOST CLEAR!
IT SEEMS SO, JEAN...
ONE BY ONE THEY'LL COME TO PASS...
...UNTIL THE VERY END.

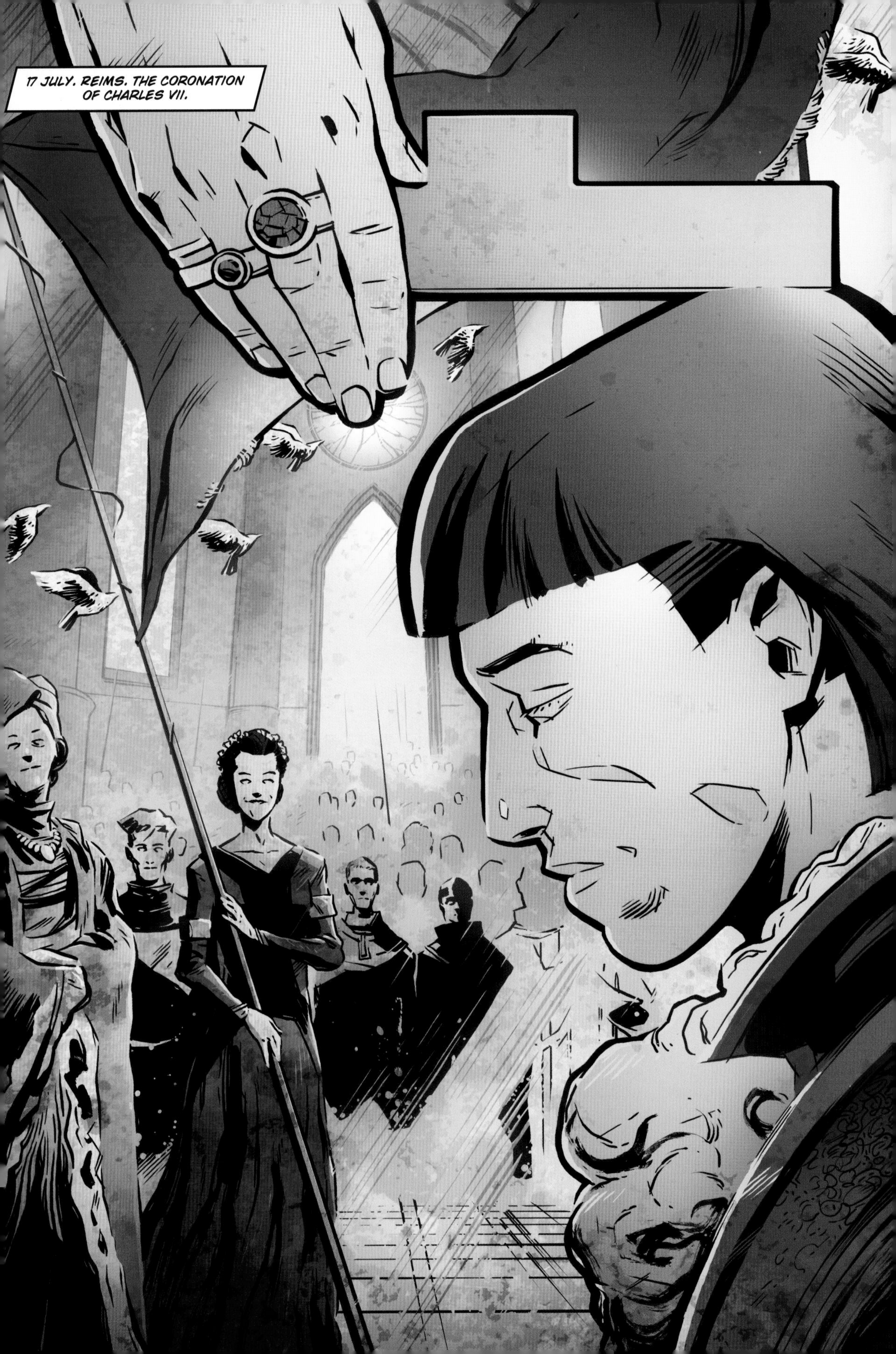
17 JULY. REIMS. THE CORONATION OF CHARLES VII.

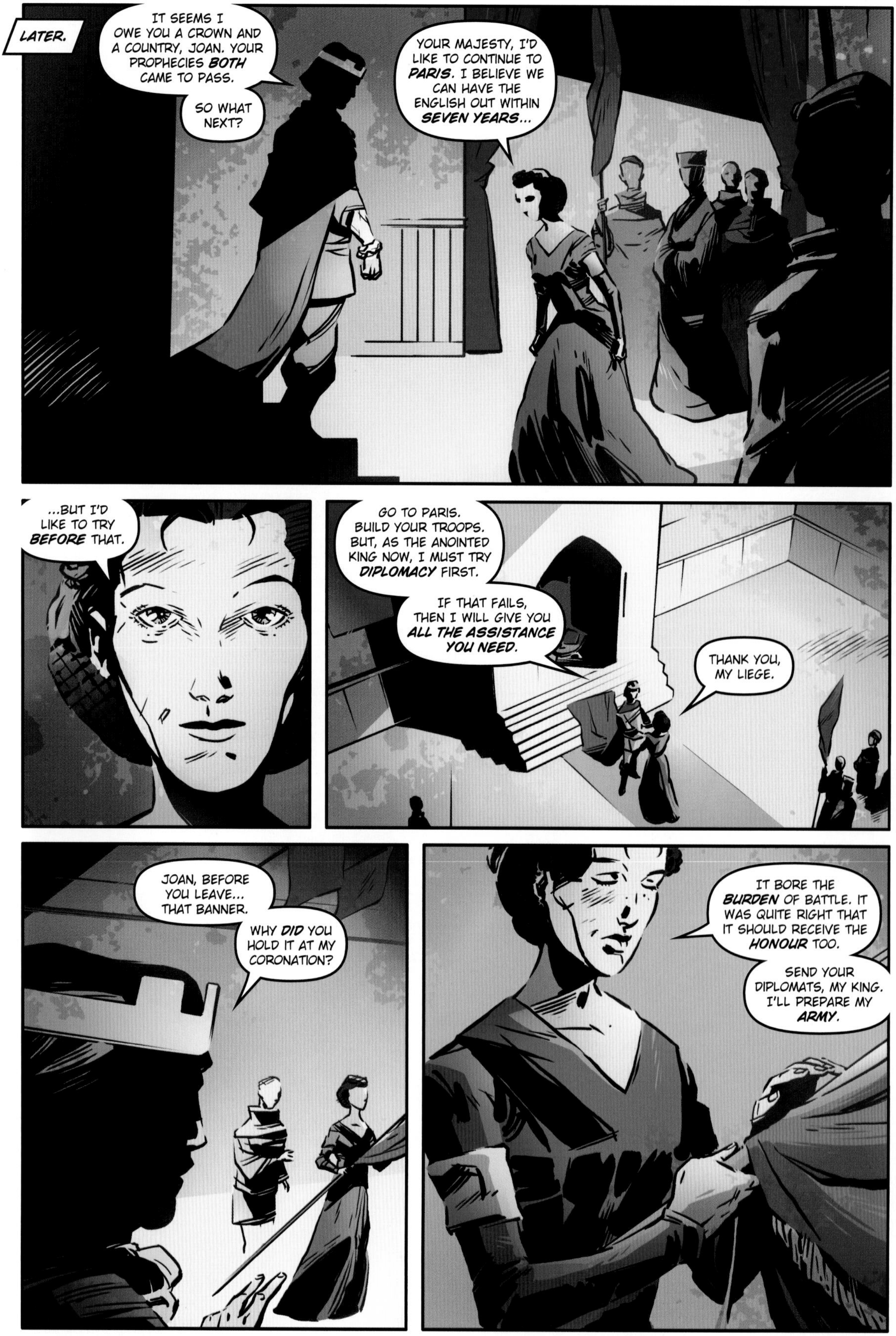
LATER.
IT SEEMS I OWE YOU A CROWN AND A COUNTRY, JOAN. YOUR PROPHECIES BOTH CAME TO PASS.
SO WHAT NEXT?
YOUR MAJESTY, I'D LIKE TO CONTINUE TO PARIS. I BELIEVE WE CAN HAVE THE ENGLISH OUT WITHIN SEVEN YEARS...
...BUT I'D LIKE TO TRY BEFORE THAT.
GO TO PARIS. BUILD YOUR TROOPS. BUT, AS THE ANOINTED KING NOW, I MUST TRY DIPLOMACY FIRST.
IF THAT FAILS, THEN I WILL GIVE YOU ALL THE ASSISTANCE YOU NEED.
THANK YOU, MY LIEGE.
JOAN, BEFORE YOU LEAVE... THAT BANNER.
WHY DID YOU HOLD IT AT MY CORONATION?
IT BORE THE BURDEN OF BATTLE. IT WAS QUITE RIGHT THAT IT SHOULD RECEIVE THE HONOUR TOO.
SEND YOUR DIPLOMATS, MY KING. I'LL PREPARE MY ARMY.

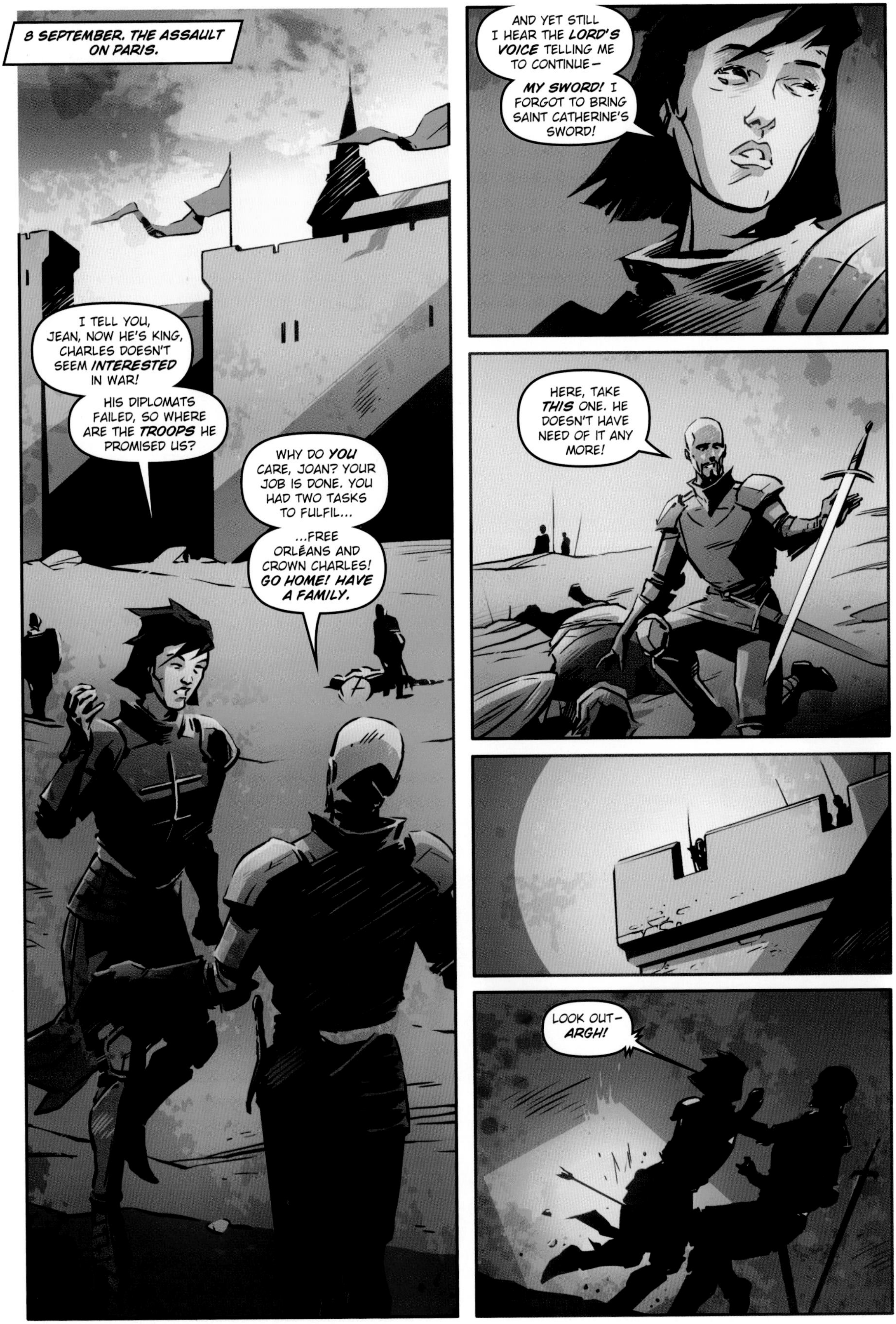
8 SEPTEMBER. THE ASSAULT ON PARIS.
I TELL YOU, JEAN, NOW HE'S KING, CHARLES DOESN'T SEEM INTERESTED IN WAR!
HIS DIPLOMATS FAILED, SO WHERE ARE THE TROOPS HE PROMISED US?
WHY DO YOU CARE, JOAN? YOUR JOB IS DONE. YOU HAD TWO TASKS TO FULFIL...
...FREE ORLÉANS AND CROWN CHARLES! GO HOME! HAVE A FAMILY.
AND YET STILL I HEAR THE LORD'S VOICE TELLING ME TO CONTINUE—
MY SWORD! I FORGOT TO BRING SAINT CATHERINE'S SWORD!
HERE, TAKE THIS ONE. HE DOESN'T HAVE NEED OF IT ANY MORE!
LOOK OUT—
ARGH!

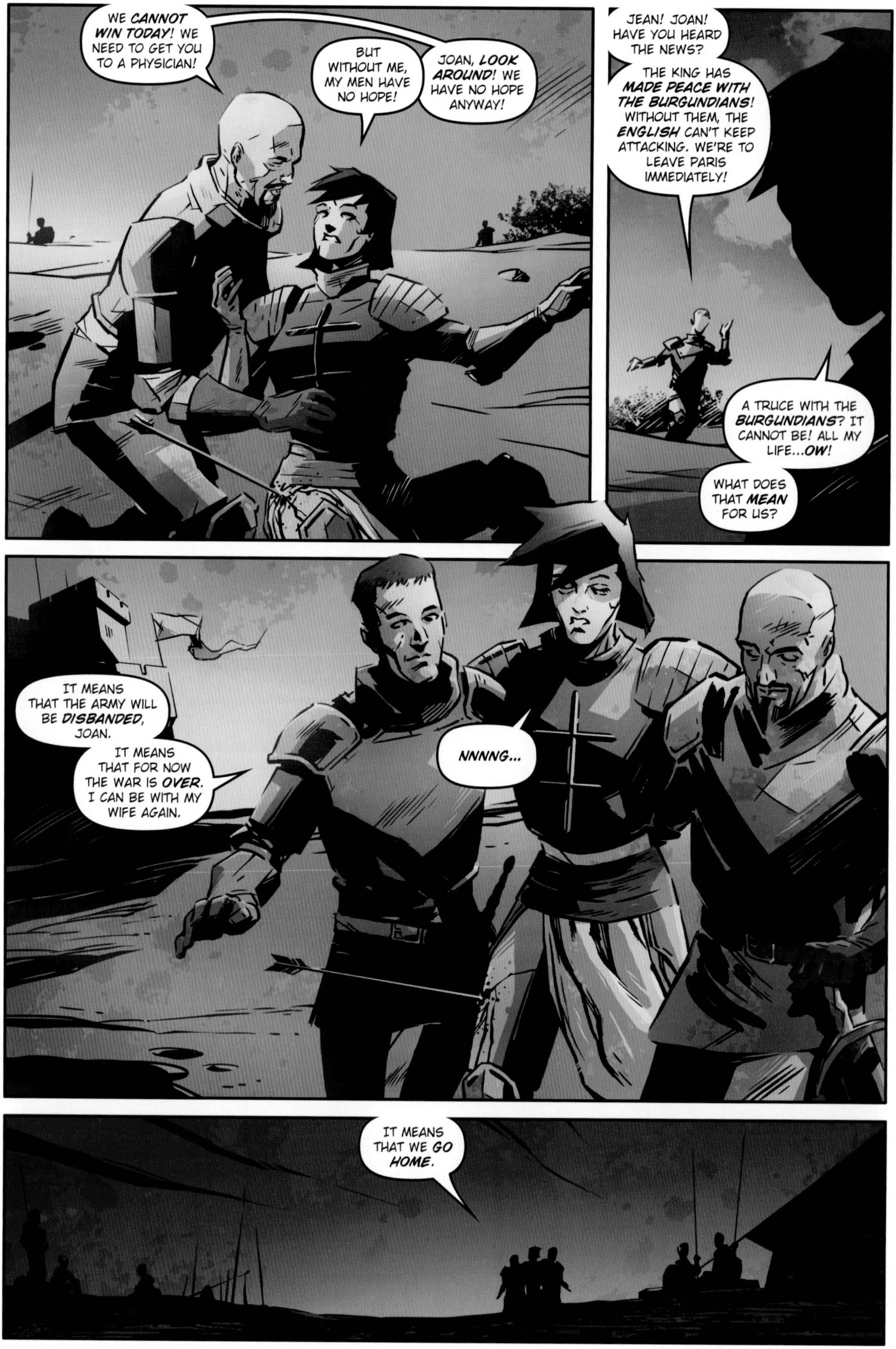

WE CANNOT WIN TODAY! WE NEED TO GET YOU TO A PHYSICIAN!
BUT WITHOUT ME, MY MEN HAVE NO HOPE!
JOAN, LOOK AROUND! WE HAVE NO HOPE ANYWAY!
JEAN! JOAN! HAVE YOU HEARD THE NEWS?
THE KING HAS MADE PEACE WITH THE BURGUNDIANS! WITHOUT THEM, THE ENGLISH CAN'T KEEP ATTACKING. WE'RE TO LEAVE PARIS IMMEDIATELY!
A TRUCE WITH THE BURGUNDIANS? IT CANNOT BE! ALL MY LIFE...OW!
WHAT DOES THAT MEAN FOR US?
IT MEANS THAT THE ARMY WILL BE DISBANDED, JOAN.
IT MEANS THAT FOR NOW THE WAR IS OVER. I CAN BE WITH MY WIFE AGAIN.
NNNNG...
IT MEANS THAT WE GO HOME.

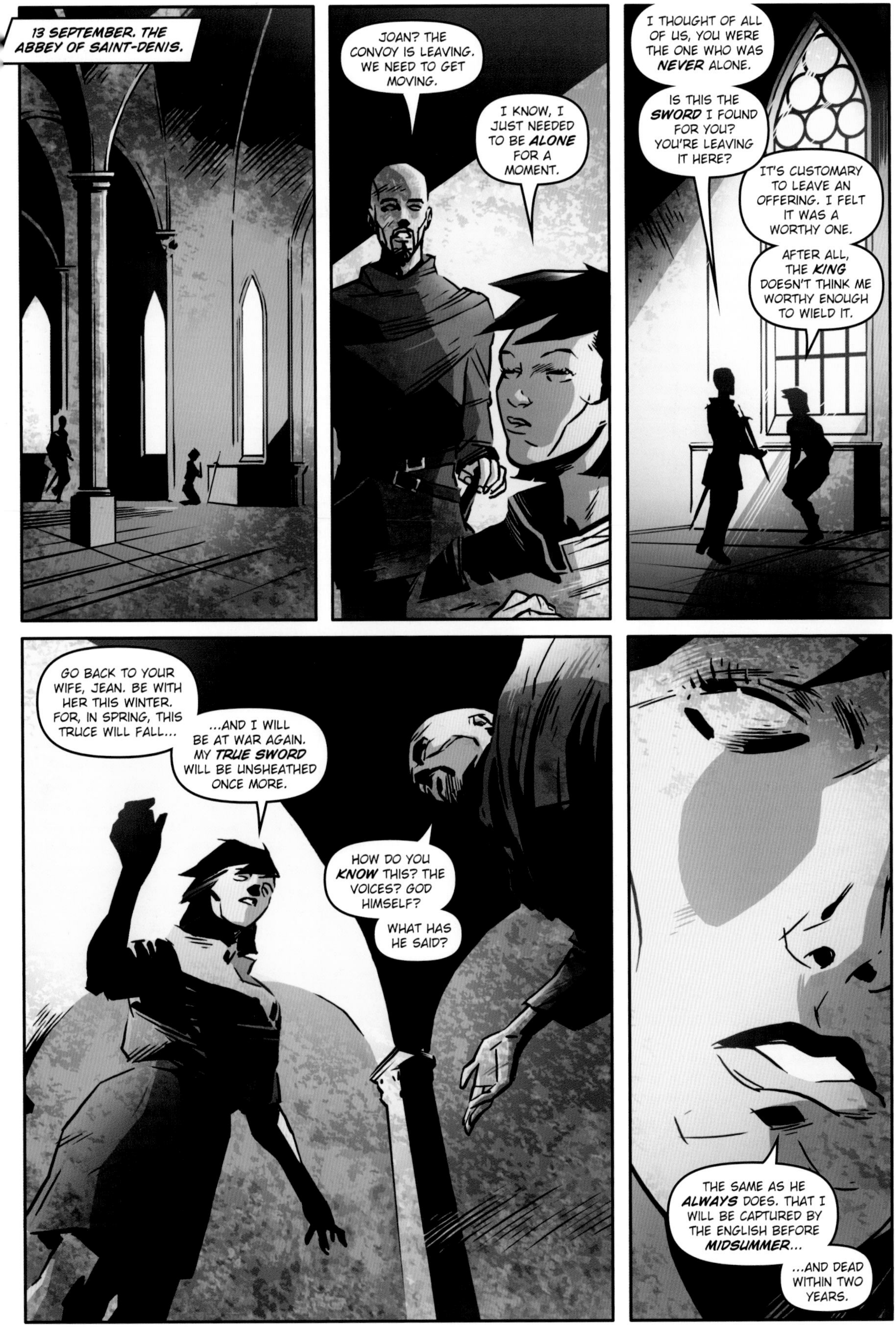

13 SEPTEMBER. THE ABBEY OF SAINT-DENIS.
JOAN? THE CONVOY IS LEAVING. WE NEED TO GET MOVING.
I KNOW, I JUST NEEDED TO BE **ALONE** FOR A MOMENT.
I THOUGHT OF ALL OF US, YOU WERE THE ONE WHO WAS **NEVER** ALONE.
IS THIS THE **SWORD** I FOUND FOR YOU? YOU'RE LEAVING IT HERE?
IT'S CUSTOMARY TO LEAVE AN OFFERING. I FELT IT WAS A WORTHY ONE.
AFTER ALL, THE **KING** DOESN'T THINK ME WORTHY ENOUGH TO WIELD IT.
GO BACK TO YOUR WIFE, JEAN. BE WITH HER THIS WINTER. FOR, IN SPRING, THIS TRUCE WILL FALL...
...AND I WILL BE AT WAR AGAIN. MY **TRUE SWORD** WILL BE UNSHEATHED ONCE MORE.
HOW DO YOU **KNOW** THIS? THE VOICES? GOD HIMSELF?
WHAT HAS HE SAID?
THE SAME AS HE **ALWAYS** DOES. THAT I WILL BE CAPTURED BY THE ENGLISH BEFORE **MIDSUMMER**...
...AND DEAD WITHIN TWO YEARS.

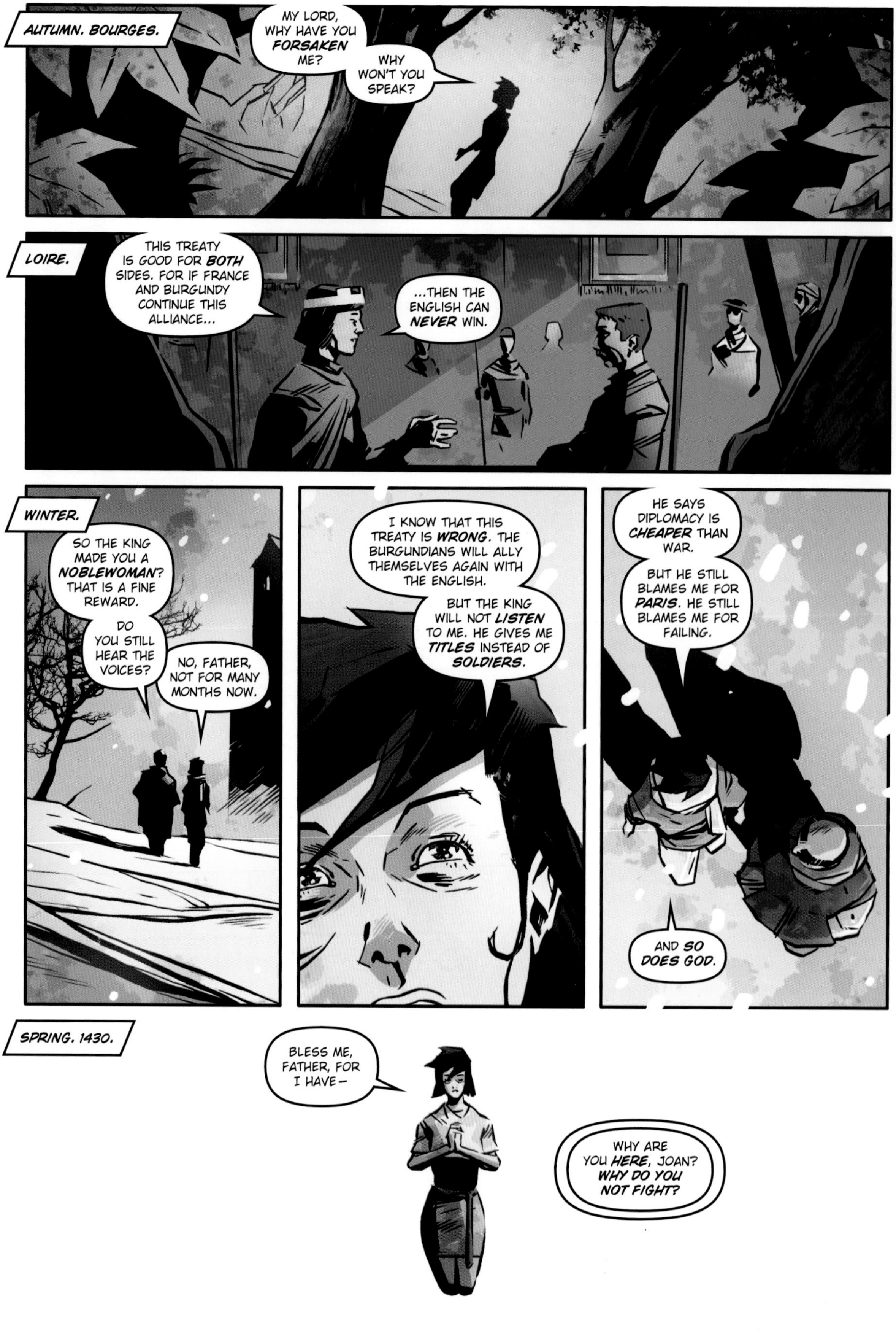
AUTUMN. BOURGES.
MY LORD, WHY HAVE YOU FORSAKEN ME?
WHY WON'T YOU SPEAK?
LOIRE.
THIS TREATY IS GOOD FOR BOTH SIDES. FOR IF FRANCE AND BURGUNDY CONTINUE THIS ALLIANCE...
...THEN THE ENGLISH CAN NEVER WIN.
WINTER.
SO THE KING MADE YOU A NOBLEWOMAN? THAT IS A FINE REWARD.
DO YOU STILL HEAR THE VOICES?
NO, FATHER, NOT FOR MANY MONTHS NOW.
I KNOW THAT THIS TREATY IS WRONG. THE BURGUNDIANS WILL ALLY THEMSELVES AGAIN WITH THE ENGLISH.
BUT THE KING WILL NOT LISTEN TO ME. HE GIVES ME TITLES INSTEAD OF SOLDIERS.
HE SAYS DIPLOMACY IS CHEAPER THAN WAR.
BUT HE STILL BLAMES ME FOR PARIS. HE STILL BLAMES ME FOR FAILING.
AND SO DOES GOD.
SPRING. 1430.
BLESS ME, FATHER, FOR I HAVE—
WHY ARE YOU HERE, JOAN? WHY DO YOU NOT FIGHT?

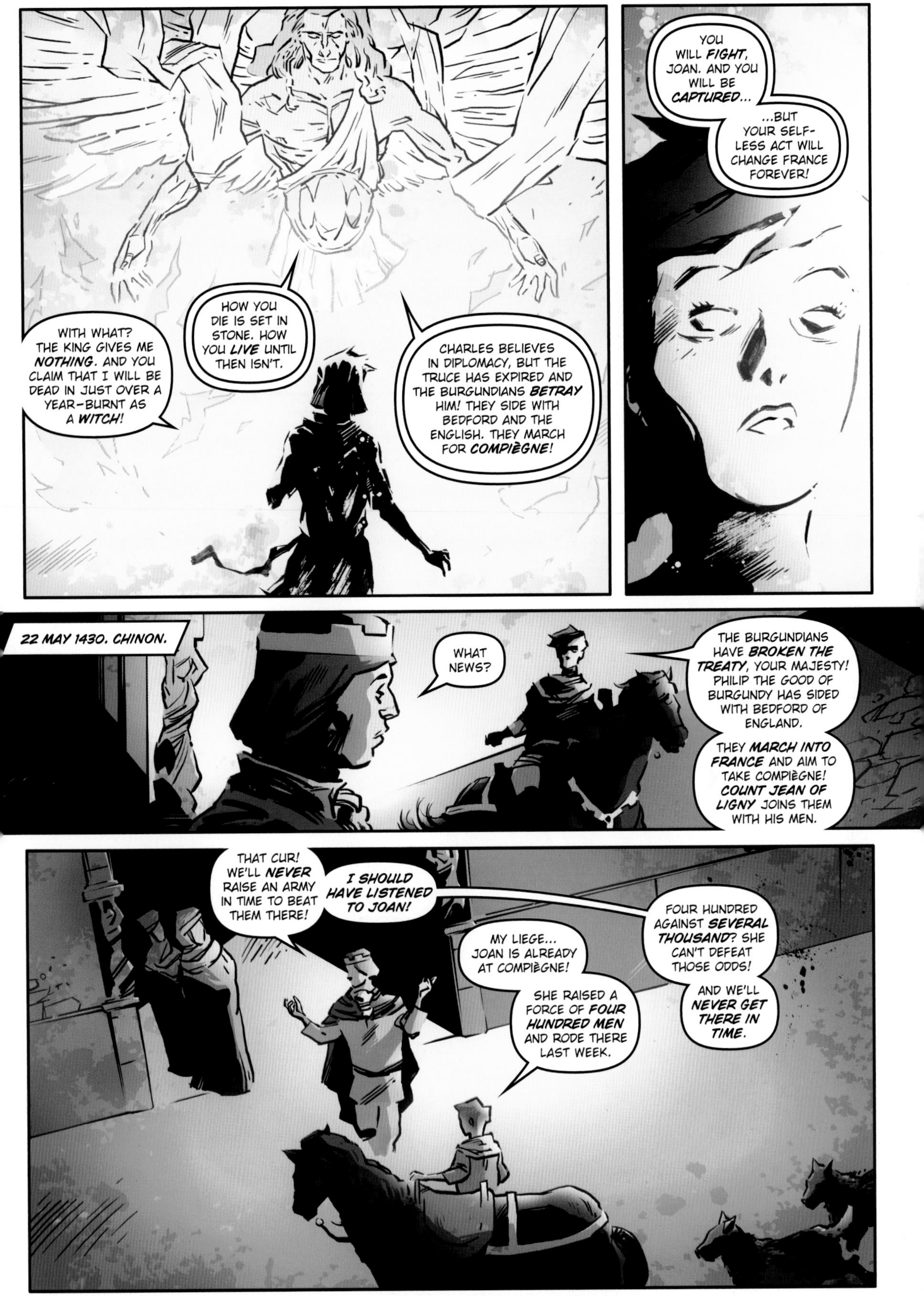

WITH WHAT? THE KING GIVES ME NOTHING. AND YOU CLAIM THAT I WILL BE DEAD IN JUST OVER A YEAR—BURNT AS A WITCH!
HOW YOU DIE IS SET IN STONE. HOW YOU LIVE UNTIL THEN ISN'T.
CHARLES BELIEVES IN DIPLOMACY, BUT THE TRUCE HAS EXPIRED AND THE BURGUNDIANS BETRAY HIM! THEY SIDE WITH BEDFORD AND THE ENGLISH. THEY MARCH FOR COMPIÈGNE!
YOU WILL FIGHT, JOAN. AND YOU WILL BE CAPTURED...
...BUT YOUR SELF-LESS ACT WILL CHANGE FRANCE FOREVER!
22 MAY 1430. CHINON.
WHAT NEWS?
THE BURGUNDIANS HAVE BROKEN THE TREATY, YOUR MAJESTY! PHILIP THE GOOD OF BURGUNDY HAS SIDED WITH BEDFORD OF ENGLAND.
THEY MARCH INTO FRANCE AND AIM TO TAKE COMPIÈGNE! COUNT JEAN OF LIGNY JOINS THEM WITH HIS MEN.
THAT CUR! WE'LL NEVER RAISE AN ARMY IN TIME TO BEAT THEM THERE!
I SHOULD HAVE LISTENED TO JOAN!
MY LIEGE... JOAN IS ALREADY AT COMPIÈGNE!
SHE RAISED A FORCE OF FOUR HUNDRED MEN AND RODE THERE LAST WEEK.
FOUR HUNDRED AGAINST SEVERAL THOUSAND? SHE CAN'T DEFEAT THOSE ODDS!
AND WE'LL NEVER GET THERE IN TIME.

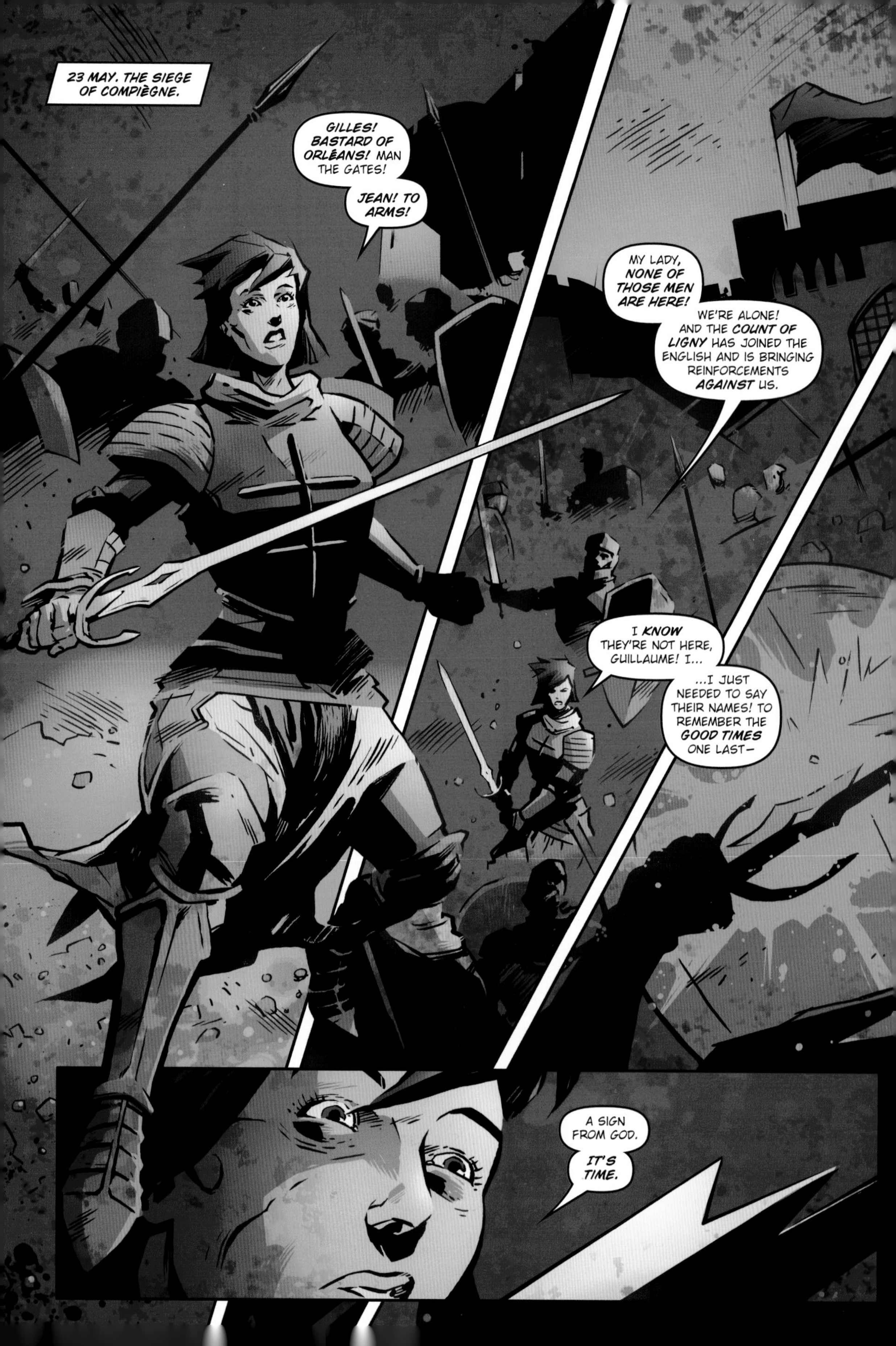
23 MAY. THE SIEGE OF COMPIÈGNE.
GILLES! BASTARD OF ORLÉANS! MAN THE GATES!
JEAN! TO ARMS!
MY LADY, NONE OF THOSE MEN ARE HERE!
WE'RE ALONE! AND THE COUNT OF LIGNY HAS JOINED THE ENGLISH AND IS BRINGING REINFORCEMENTS AGAINST US.
I KNOW THEY'RE NOT HERE, GUILLAUME! I...
...I JUST NEEDED TO SAY THEIR NAMES! TO REMEMBER THE GOOD TIMES ONE LAST—
A SIGN FROM GOD.
IT'S TIME.

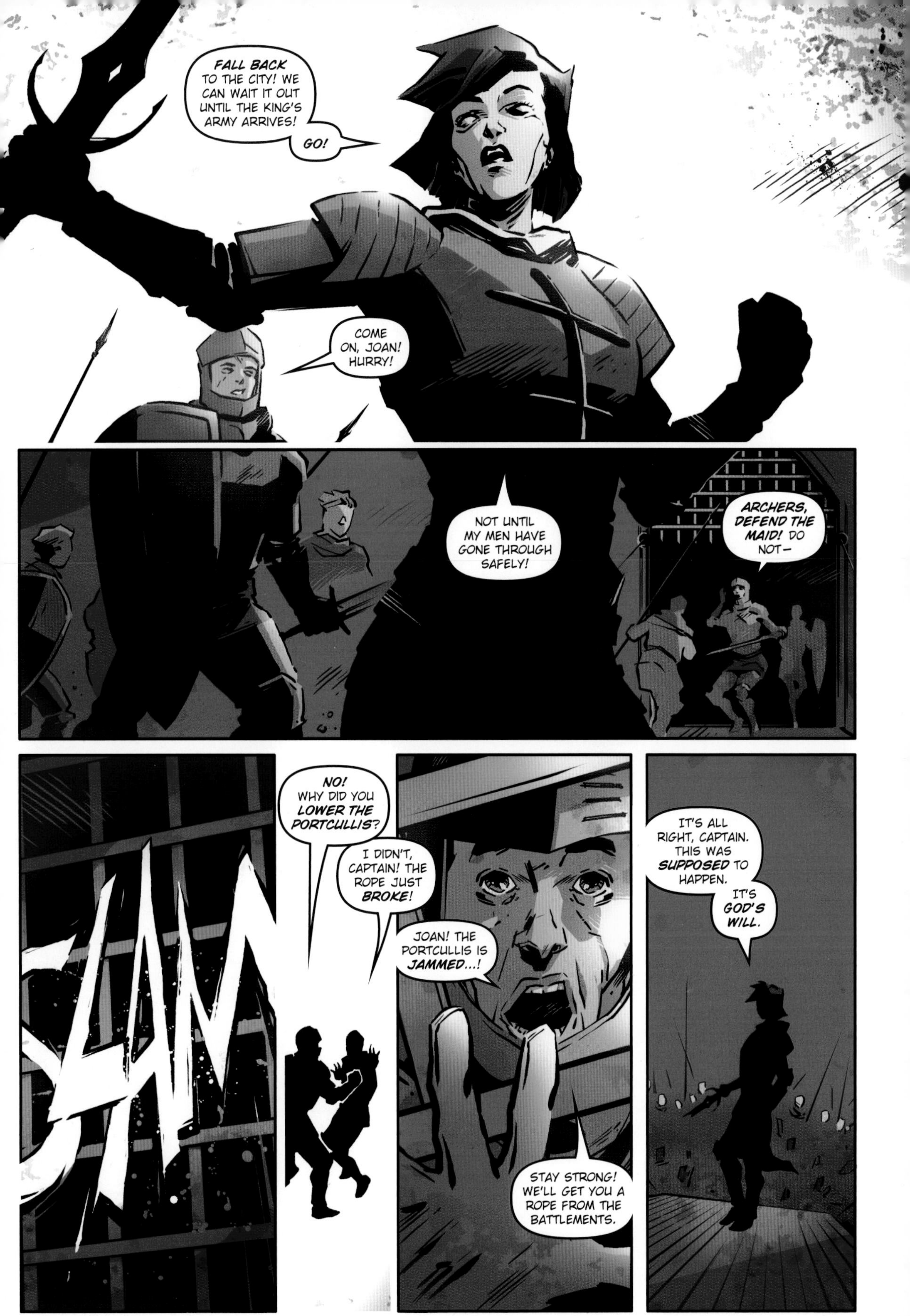
FALL BACK TO THE CITY! WE CAN WAIT IT OUT UNTIL THE KING'S ARMY ARRIVES!
GO!
COME ON, JOAN! HURRY!
NOT UNTIL MY MEN HAVE GONE THROUGH SAFELY!
ARCHERS, DEFEND THE MAID! DO NOT—
NO! WHY DID YOU LOWER THE PORTCULLIS?
I DIDN'T, CAPTAIN! THE ROPE JUST BROKE!
JOAN! THE PORTCULLIS IS JAMMED...!
STAY STRONG! WE'LL GET YOU A ROPE FROM THE BATTLEMENTS.
IT'S ALL RIGHT, CAPTAIN. THIS WAS SUPPOSED TO HAPPEN.
IT'S GOD'S WILL.

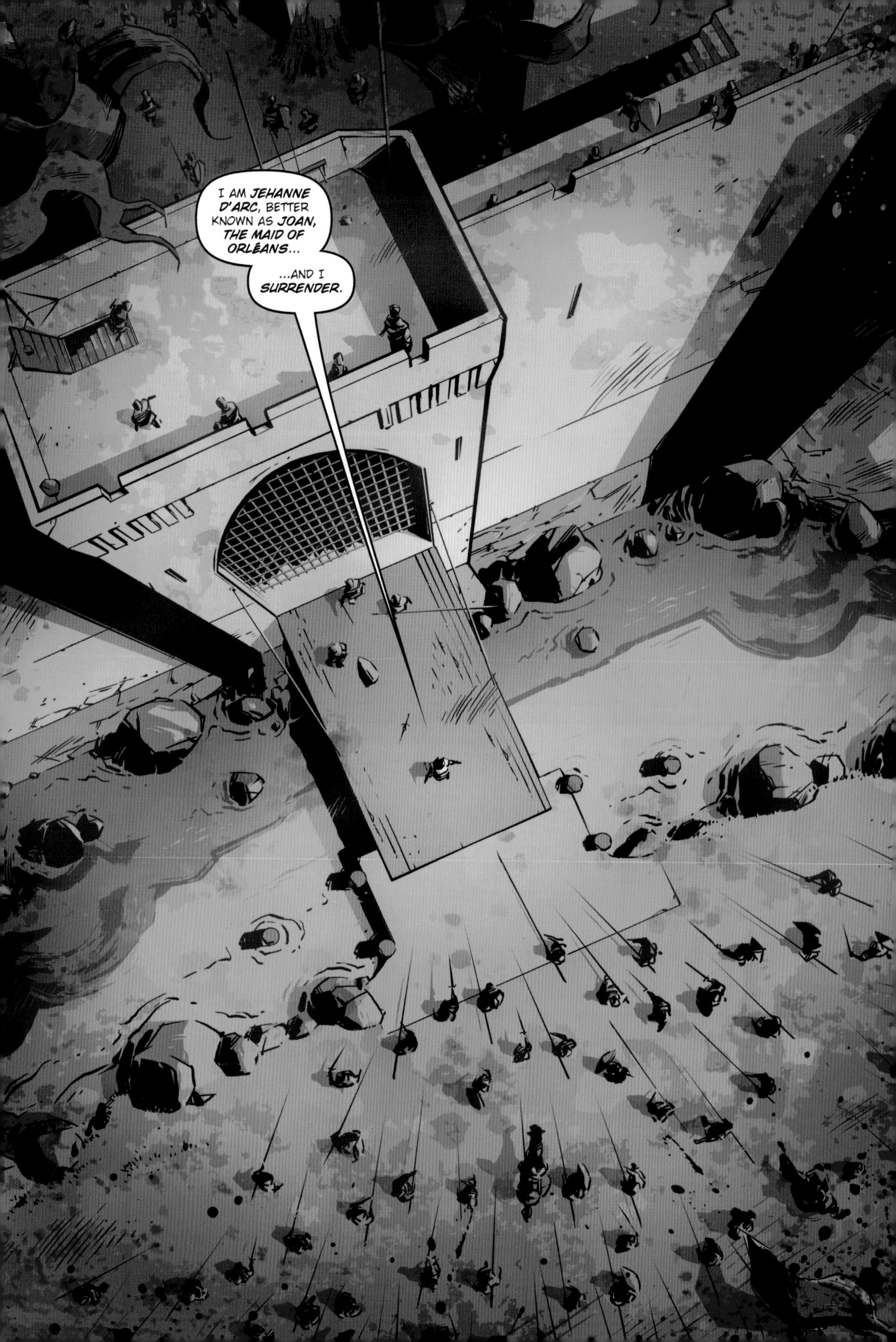
I AM JEHANNE D'ARC, BETTER KNOWN AS JOAN, THE MAID OF ORLÉANS...
...AND I SURRENDER.

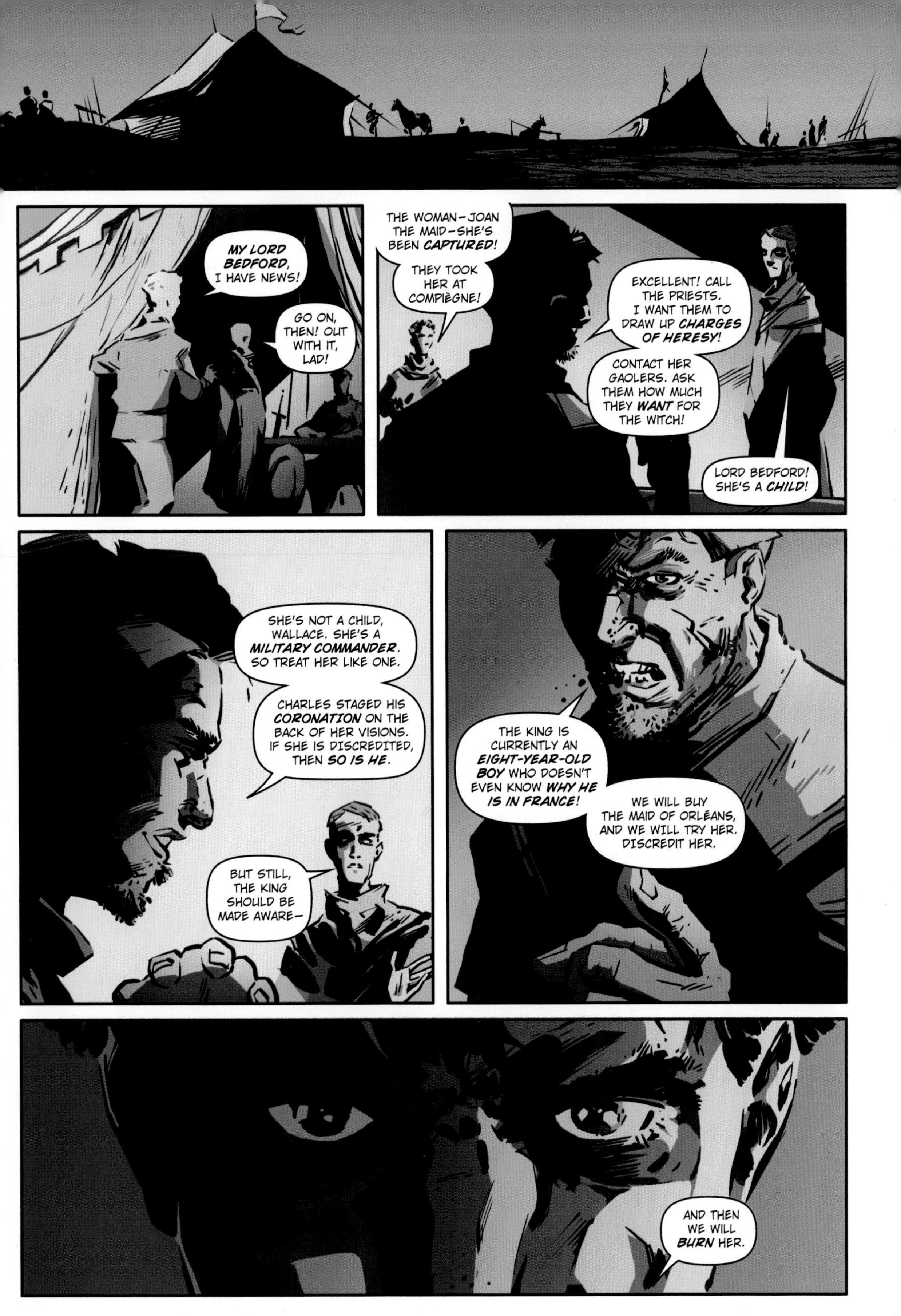
MY LORD BEDFORD, I HAVE NEWS!
GO ON, THEN! OUT WITH IT, LAD!
THE WOMAN—JOAN THE MAID—SHE'S BEEN CAPTURED!
THEY TOOK HER AT COMPIÈGNE!
EXCELLENT! CALL THE PRIESTS. I WANT THEM TO DRAW UP CHARGES OF HERESY!
CONTACT HER GAOLERS. ASK THEM HOW MUCH THEY WANT FOR THE WITCH!
LORD BEDFORD! SHE'S A CHILD!
SHE'S NOT A CHILD, WALLACE. SHE'S A MILITARY COMMANDER. SO TREAT HER LIKE ONE.
CHARLES STAGED HIS CORONATION ON THE BACK OF HER VISIONS. IF SHE IS DISCREDITED, THEN SO IS HE.
BUT STILL, THE KING SHOULD BE MADE AWARE—
THE KING IS CURRENTLY AN EIGHT-YEAR-OLD BOY WHO DOESN'T EVEN KNOW WHY HE IS IN FRANCE!
WE WILL BUY THE MAID OF ORLÉANS, AND WE WILL TRY HER. DISCREDIT HER.
AND THEN WE WILL BURN HER.

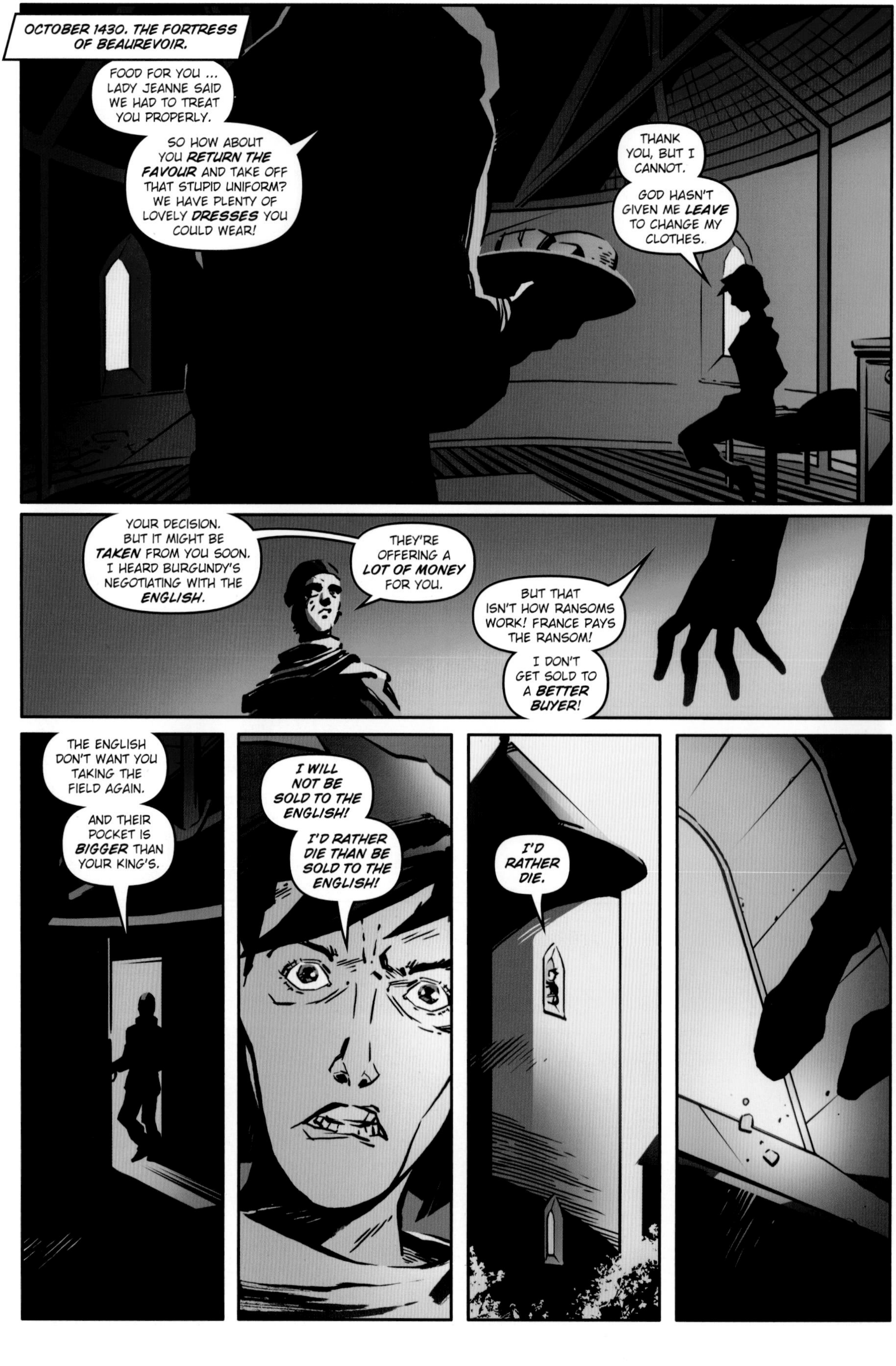
OCTOBER 1430. THE FORTRESS OF BEAUREVOIR.
FOOD FOR YOU ... LADY JEANNE SAID WE HAD TO TREAT YOU PROPERLY.
SO HOW ABOUT YOU RETURN THE FAVOUR AND TAKE OFF THAT STUPID UNIFORM? WE HAVE PLENTY OF LOVELY DRESSES YOU COULD WEAR!
THANK YOU, BUT I CANNOT.
GOD HASN'T GIVEN ME LEAVE TO CHANGE MY CLOTHES.
YOUR DECISION. BUT IT MIGHT BE TAKEN FROM YOU SOON. I HEARD BURGUNDY'S NEGOTIATING WITH THE ENGLISH.
THEY'RE OFFERING A LOT OF MONEY FOR YOU.
BUT THAT ISN'T HOW RANSOMS WORK! FRANCE PAYS THE RANSOM!
I DON'T GET SOLD TO A BETTER BUYER!
THE ENGLISH DON'T WANT YOU TAKING THE FIELD AGAIN.
AND THEIR POCKET IS BIGGER THAN YOUR KING'S.
I WILL NOT BE SOLD TO THE ENGLISH!
I'D RATHER DIE THAN BE SOLD TO THE ENGLISH!
I'D RATHER DIE.

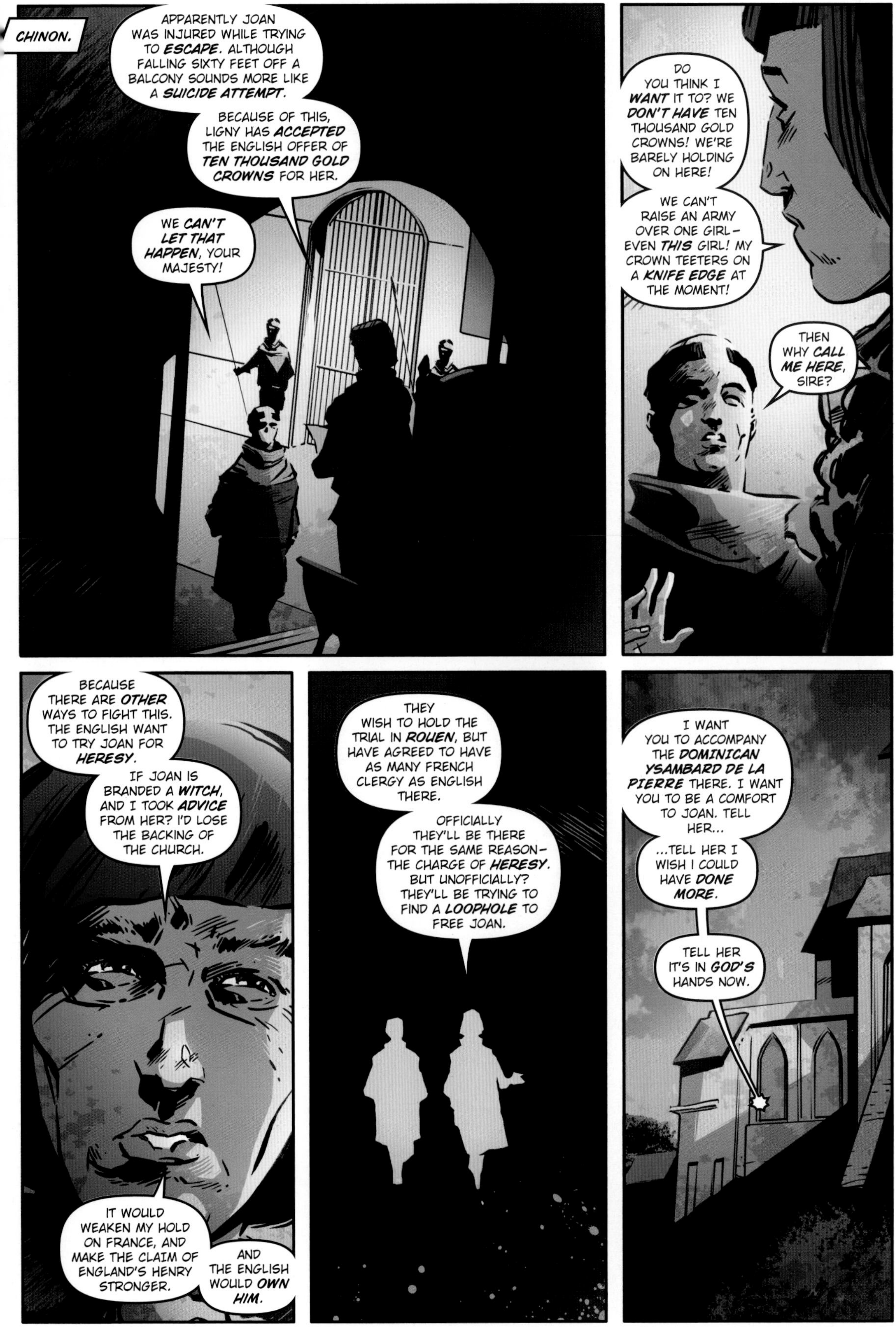
CHINON.
APPARENTLY JOAN WAS INJURED WHILE TRYING TO ESCAPE. ALTHOUGH FALLING SIXTY FEET OFF A BALCONY SOUNDS MORE LIKE A SUICIDE ATTEMPT.
BECAUSE OF THIS, LIGNY HAS ACCEPTED THE ENGLISH OFFER OF TEN THOUSAND GOLD CROWNS FOR HER.
WE CAN'T LET THAT HAPPEN, YOUR MAJESTY!
DO YOU THINK I WANT IT TO? WE DON'T HAVE TEN THOUSAND GOLD CROWNS! WE'RE BARELY HOLDING ON HERE!
WE CAN'T RAISE AN ARMY OVER ONE GIRL– EVEN THIS GIRL! MY CROWN TEETERS ON A KNIFE EDGE AT THE MOMENT!
THEN WHY CALL ME HERE, SIRE?
BECAUSE THERE ARE OTHER WAYS TO FIGHT THIS. THE ENGLISH WANT TO TRY JOAN FOR HERESY.
IF JOAN IS BRANDED A WITCH, AND I TOOK ADVICE FROM HER? I'D LOSE THE BACKING OF THE CHURCH.
IT WOULD WEAKEN MY HOLD ON FRANCE, AND MAKE THE CLAIM OF ENGLAND'S HENRY STRONGER.
AND THE ENGLISH WOULD OWN HIM.
THEY WISH TO HOLD THE TRIAL IN ROUEN, BUT HAVE AGREED TO HAVE AS MANY FRENCH CLERGY AS ENGLISH THERE.
OFFICIALLY THEY'LL BE THERE FOR THE SAME REASON– THE CHARGE OF HERESY. BUT UNOFFICIALLY? THEY'LL BE TRYING TO FIND A LOOPHOLE TO FREE JOAN.
I WANT YOU TO ACCOMPANY THE DOMINICAN YSAMBARD DE LA PIERRE THERE. I WANT YOU TO BE A COMFORT TO JOAN. TELL HER...
...TELL HER I WISH I COULD HAVE DONE MORE.
TELL HER IT'S IN GOD'S HANDS NOW.

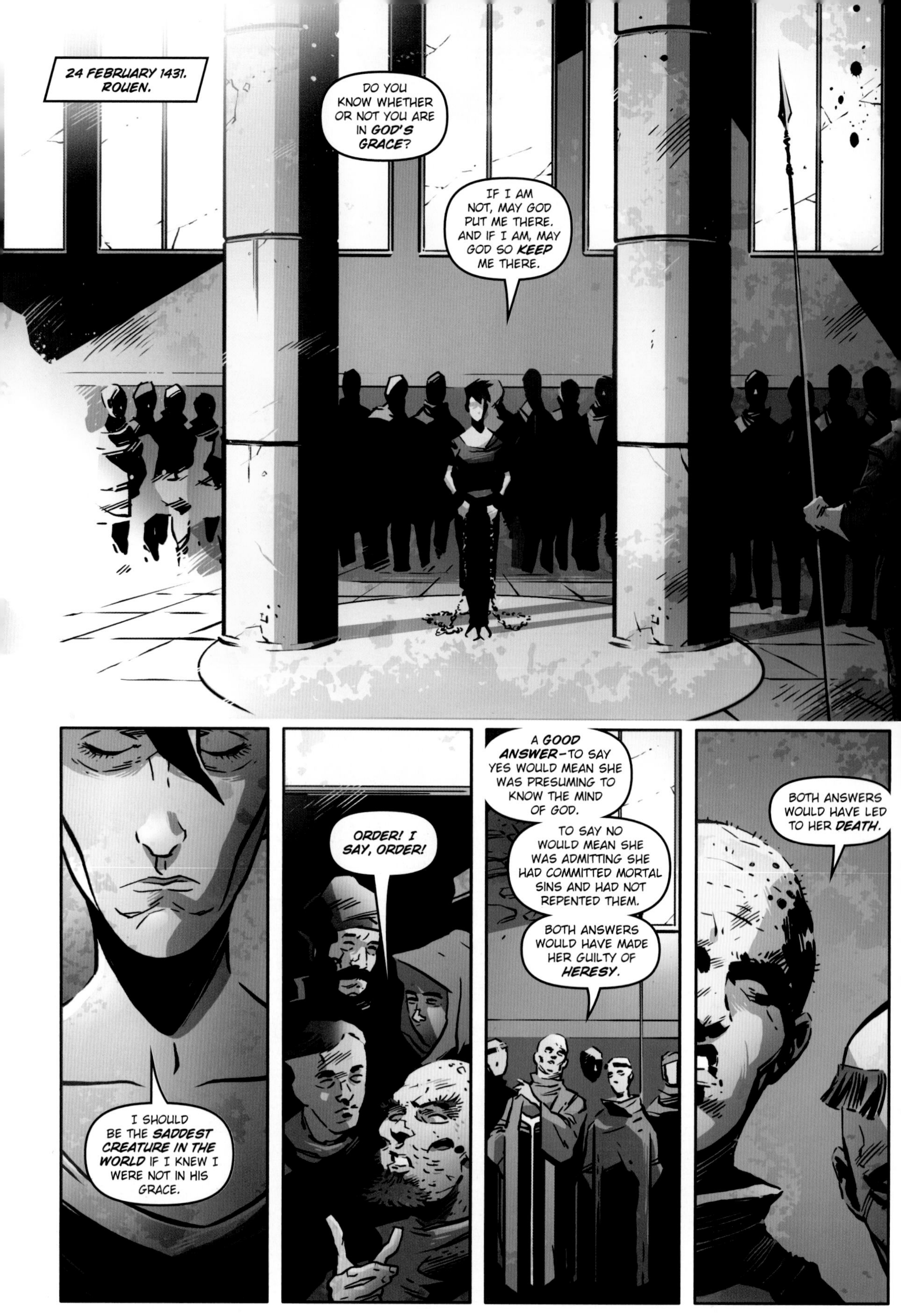
24 FEBRUARY 1431. ROUEN.
DO YOU KNOW WHETHER OR NOT YOU ARE IN GOD'S GRACE?
IF I AM NOT, MAY GOD PUT ME THERE. AND IF I AM, MAY GOD SO KEEP ME THERE.
I SHOULD BE THE SADDEST CREATURE IN THE WORLD IF I KNEW I WERE NOT IN HIS GRACE.
ORDER! I SAY, ORDER!
A GOOD ANSWER—TO SAY YES WOULD MEAN SHE WAS PRESUMING TO KNOW THE MIND OF GOD.
TO SAY NO WOULD MEAN SHE WAS ADMITTING SHE HAD COMMITTED MORTAL SINS AND HAD NOT REPENTED THEM.
BOTH ANSWERS WOULD HAVE MADE HER GUILTY OF HERESY.
BOTH ANSWERS WOULD HAVE LED TO HER DEATH.

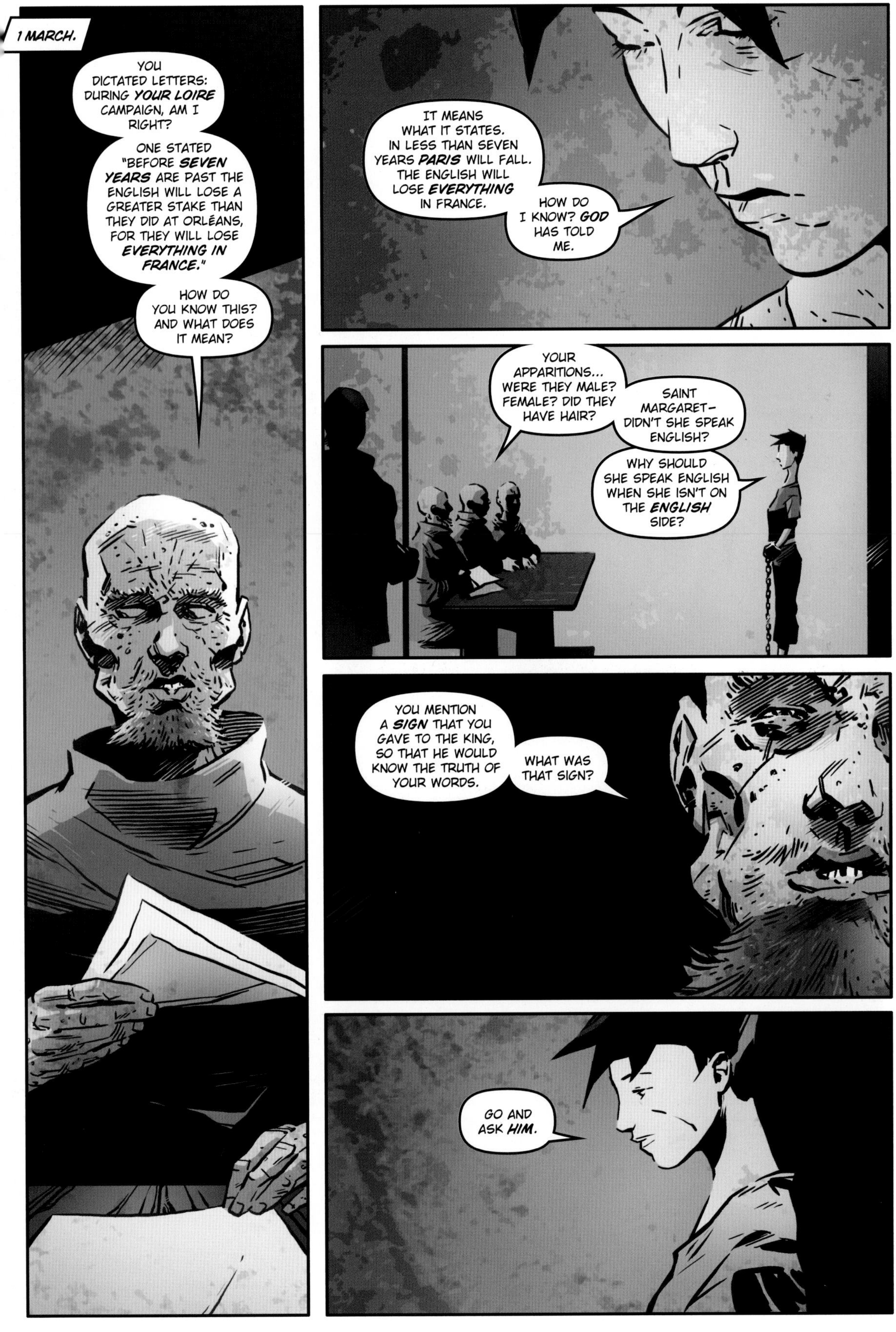
1 MARCH.
YOU DICTATED LETTERS: DURING YOUR LOIRE CAMPAIGN, AM I RIGHT?
ONE STATED "BEFORE SEVEN YEARS ARE PAST THE ENGLISH WILL LOSE A GREATER STAKE THAN THEY DID AT ORLÉANS, FOR THEY WILL LOSE EVERYTHING IN FRANCE."
HOW DO YOU KNOW THIS? AND WHAT DOES IT MEAN?
IT MEANS WHAT IT STATES. IN LESS THAN SEVEN YEARS PARIS WILL FALL. THE ENGLISH WILL LOSE EVERYTHING IN FRANCE.
HOW DO I KNOW? GOD HAS TOLD ME.
YOUR APPARITIONS... WERE THEY MALE? FEMALE? DID THEY HAVE HAIR?
SAINT MARGARET-DIDN'T SHE SPEAK ENGLISH?
WHY SHOULD SHE SPEAK ENGLISH WHEN SHE ISN'T ON THE ENGLISH SIDE?
YOU MENTION A SIGN THAT YOU GAVE TO THE KING, SO THAT HE WOULD KNOW THE TRUTH OF YOUR WORDS.
WHAT WAS THAT SIGN?
GO AND ASK HIM.

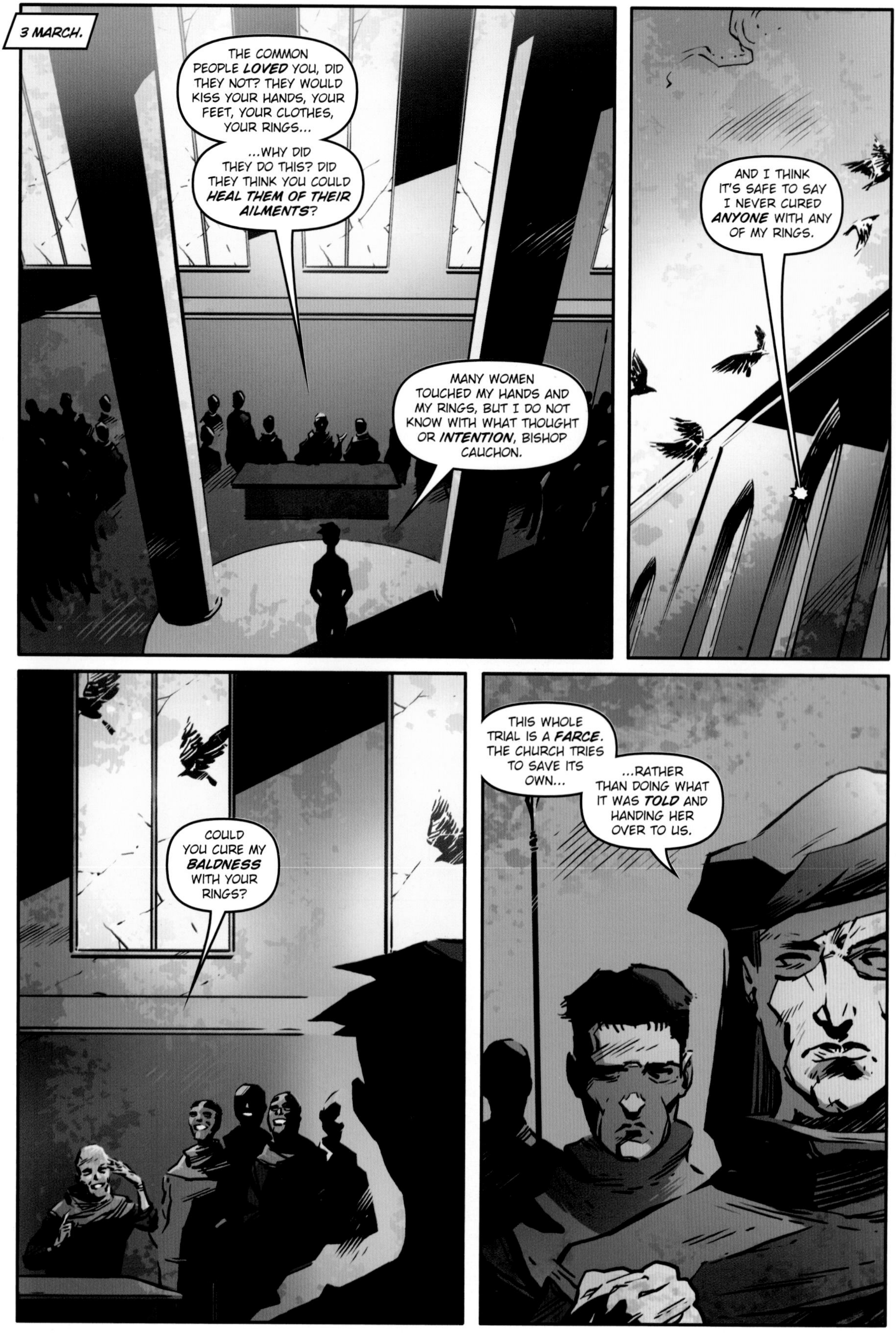
3 MARCH.
THE COMMON PEOPLE LOVED YOU, DID THEY NOT? THEY WOULD KISS YOUR HANDS, YOUR FEET, YOUR CLOTHES, YOUR RINGS...
...WHY DID THEY DO THIS? DID THEY THINK YOU COULD HEAL THEM OF THEIR AILMENTS?
MANY WOMEN TOUCHED MY HANDS AND MY RINGS, BUT I DO NOT KNOW WITH WHAT THOUGHT OR INTENTION, BISHOP CAUCHON.
AND I THINK IT'S SAFE TO SAY I NEVER CURED ANYONE WITH ANY OF MY RINGS.
COULD YOU CURE MY BALDNESS WITH YOUR RINGS?
THIS WHOLE TRIAL IS A FARCE. THE CHURCH TRIES TO SAVE ITS OWN...
...RATHER THAN DOING WHAT IT WAS TOLD AND HANDING HER OVER TO US.

YOU ALSO MET WITH *CATHERINE DE LA ROCHELLE*, A FRENCH MYSTIC WHO *ALSO* CLAIMS TO HAVE REVELATIONS FROM GOD.

SHE IS *NOTHING* – A FOLLY AND NOTHING MORE.

MY SAINTS TOLD ME SO.

WHILE YOU WERE AT *BEAUREVOIR*, YOU LEAPED SIXTY FEET FROM A BALCONY. YOU WERE BADLY INJURED...

...BUT WERE YOU TRYING TO ESCAPE OR *KILL* YOURSELF?

I LEAPED FROM FEAR OF THE ENGLISH, AND COMMENDED MYSELF TO GOD...

...FOR I WOULD RATHER *SURRENDER MY SOUL TO GOD* THAN FALL INTO THE HANDS OF THE ENGLISH.

I DON'T THINK THE GIRL *LIKES YOU*, MY LORD WARWICK.

SHE'LL LIKE ME EVEN *LESS* WHEN I *BURN HER*.

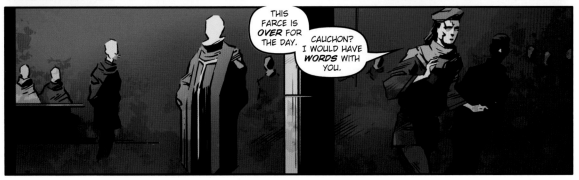

THIS FARCE IS *OVER* FOR THE DAY.

CAUCHON? I WOULD HAVE *WORDS* WITH YOU.

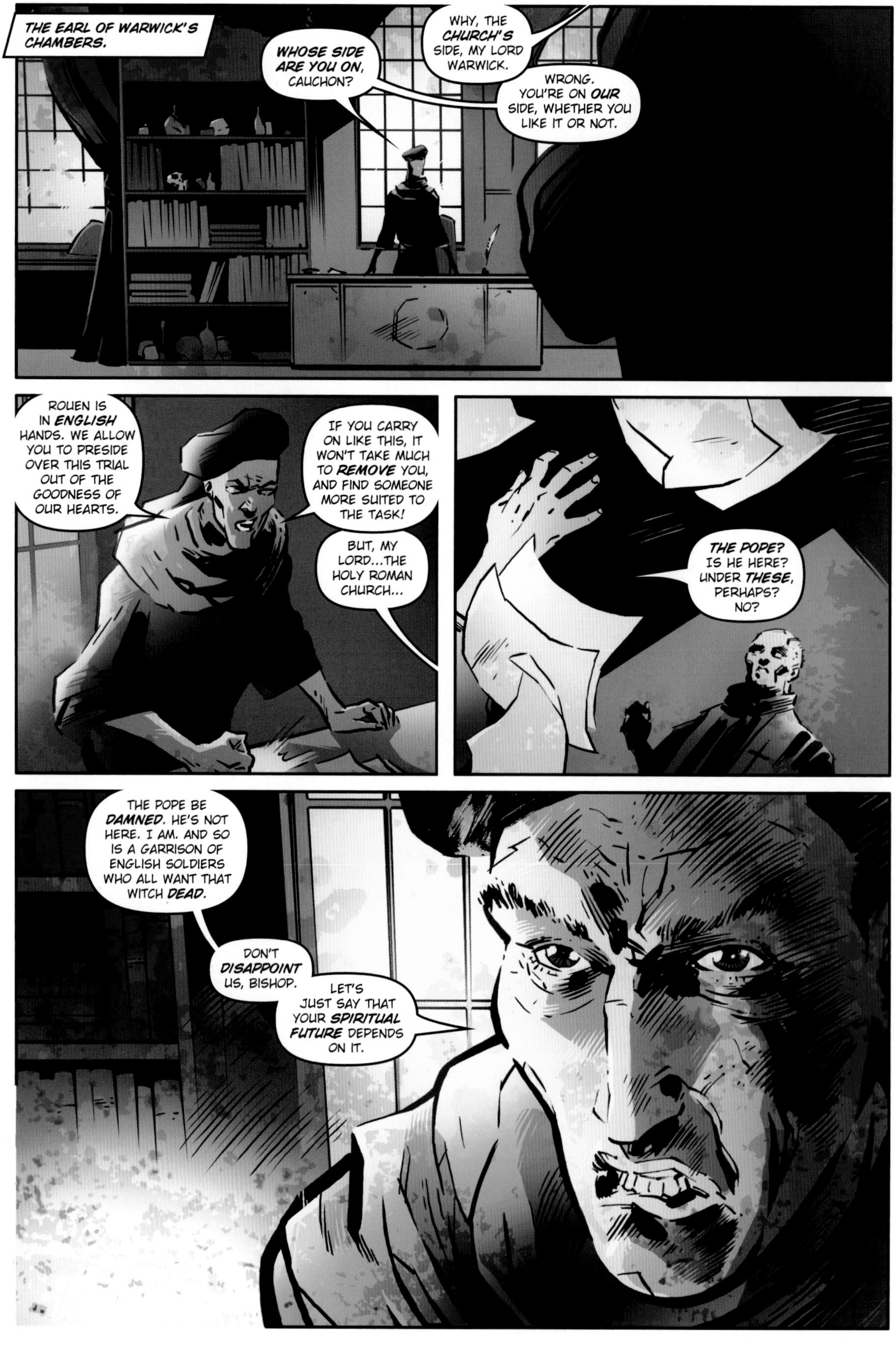
THE EARL OF WARWICK'S CHAMBERS.
WHOSE SIDE ARE YOU ON, CAUCHON?
WHY, THE CHURCH'S SIDE, MY LORD WARWICK.
WRONG. YOU'RE ON OUR SIDE, WHETHER YOU LIKE IT OR NOT.
ROUEN IS IN ENGLISH HANDS. WE ALLOW YOU TO PRESIDE OVER THIS TRIAL OUT OF THE GOODNESS OF OUR HEARTS.
IF YOU CARRY ON LIKE THIS, IT WON'T TAKE MUCH TO REMOVE YOU, AND FIND SOMEONE MORE SUITED TO THE TASK!
BUT, MY LORD...THE HOLY ROMAN CHURCH...
THE POPE? IS HE HERE? UNDER THESE, PERHAPS? NO?
THE POPE BE DAMNED. HE'S NOT HERE. I AM. AND SO IS A GARRISON OF ENGLISH SOLDIERS WHO ALL WANT THAT WITCH DEAD.
DON'T DISAPPOINT US, BISHOP.
LET'S JUST SAY THAT YOUR SPIRITUAL FUTURE DEPENDS ON IT.

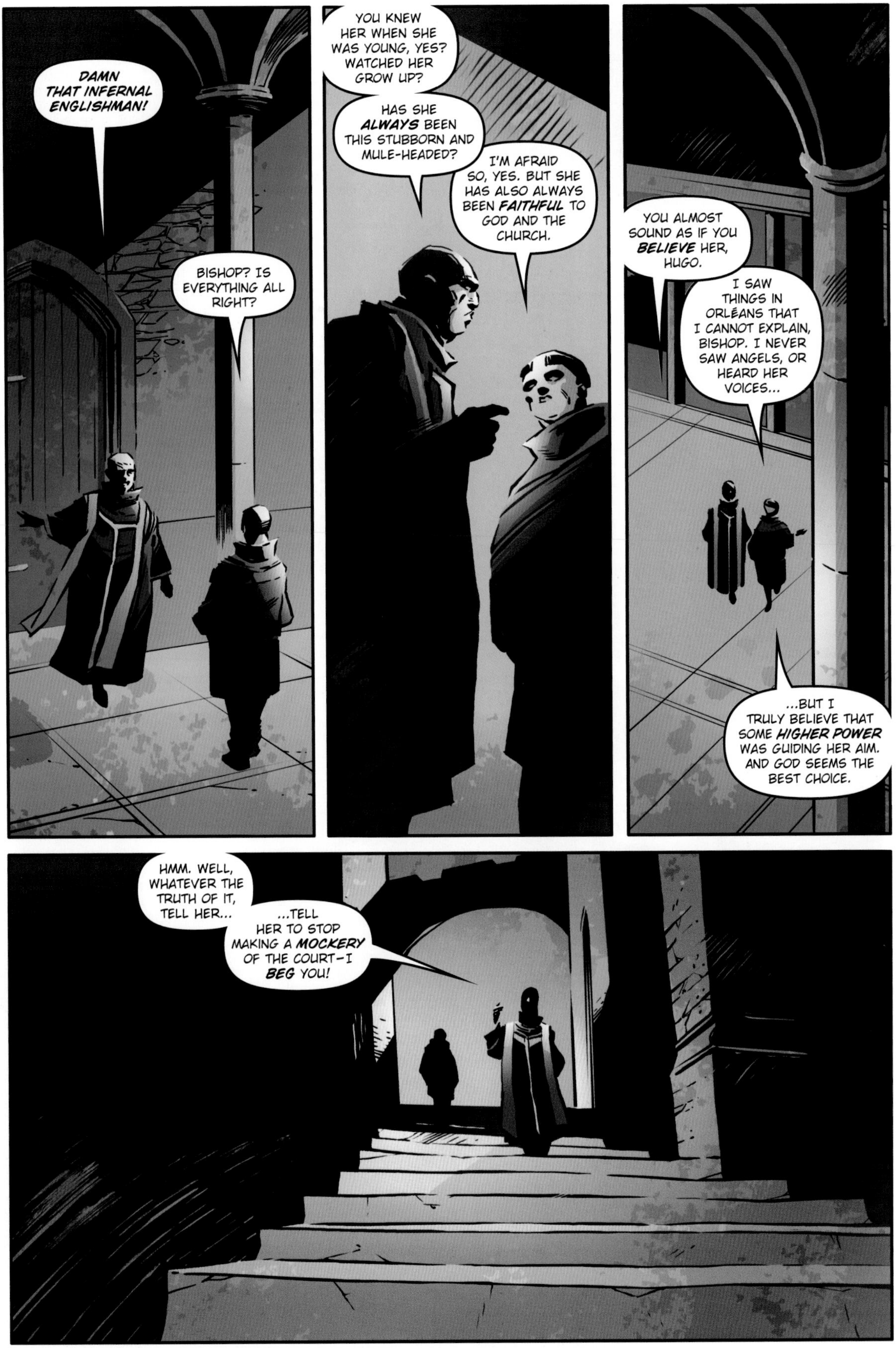
DAMN THAT INFERNAL ENGLISHMAN!
BISHOP? IS EVERYTHING ALL RIGHT?
YOU KNEW HER WHEN SHE WAS YOUNG, YES? WATCHED HER GROW UP?
HAS SHE ALWAYS BEEN THIS STUBBORN AND MULE-HEADED?
I'M AFRAID SO, YES. BUT SHE HAS ALSO ALWAYS BEEN FAITHFUL TO GOD AND THE CHURCH.
YOU ALMOST SOUND AS IF YOU BELIEVE HER, HUGO.
I SAW THINGS IN ORLÉANS THAT I CANNOT EXPLAIN, BISHOP. I NEVER SAW ANGELS, OR HEARD HER VOICES...
...BUT I TRULY BELIEVE THAT SOME HIGHER POWER WAS GUIDING HER AIM. AND GOD SEEMS THE BEST CHOICE.
HMM. WELL, WHATEVER THE TRUTH OF IT, TELL HER...
...TELL HER TO STOP MAKING A MOCKERY OF THE COURT—I BEG YOU!

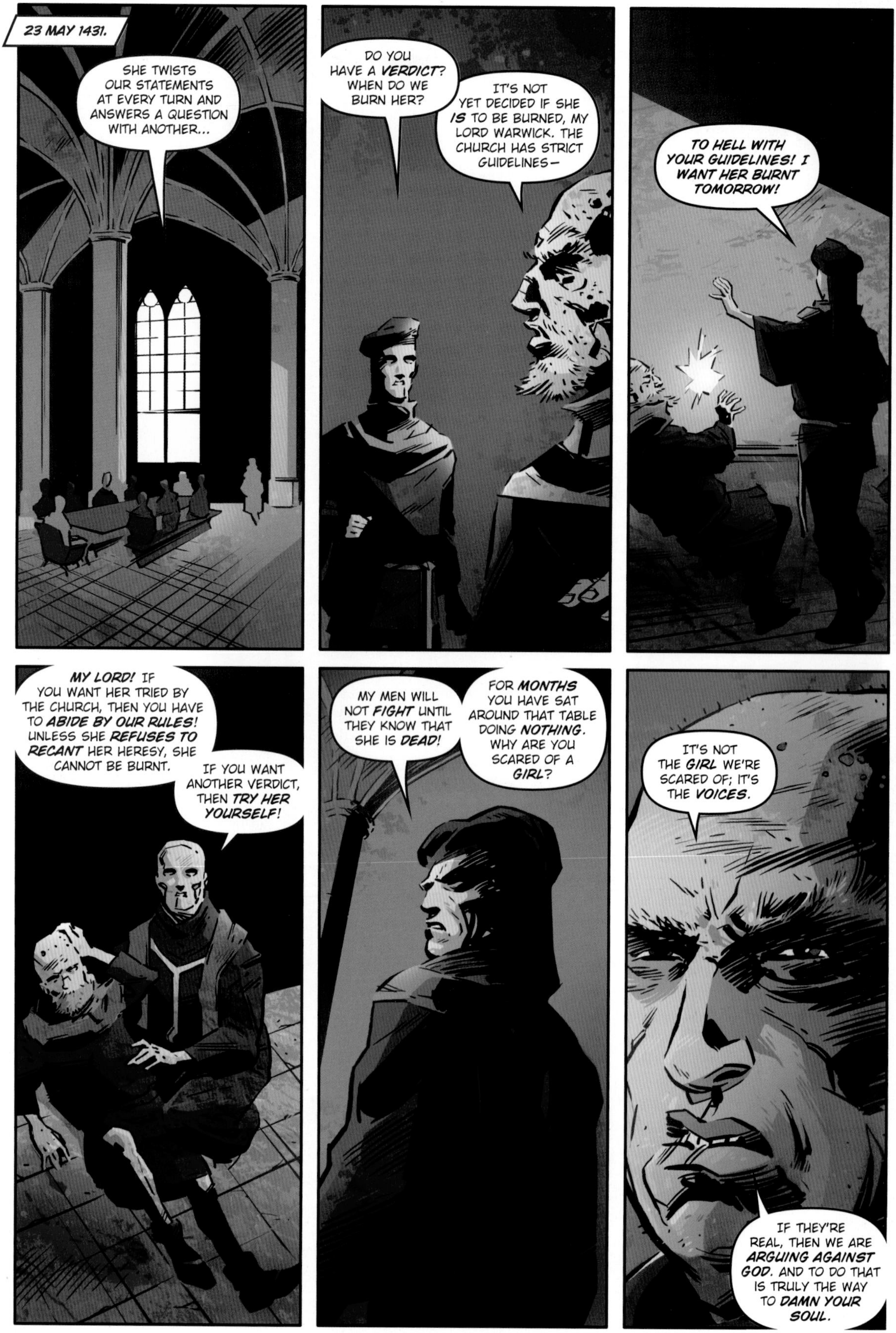

23 MAY 1431.
SHE TWISTS OUR STATEMENTS AT EVERY TURN AND ANSWERS A QUESTION WITH ANOTHER...
DO YOU HAVE A VERDICT? WHEN DO WE BURN HER?
IT'S NOT YET DECIDED IF SHE IS TO BE BURNED, MY LORD WARWICK. THE CHURCH HAS STRICT GUIDELINES—
TO HELL WITH YOUR GUIDELINES! I WANT HER BURNT TOMORROW!
MY LORD! IF YOU WANT HER TRIED BY THE CHURCH, THEN YOU HAVE TO ABIDE BY OUR RULES! UNLESS SHE REFUSES TO RECANT HER HERESY, SHE CANNOT BE BURNT.
IF YOU WANT ANOTHER VERDICT, THEN TRY HER YOURSELF!
MY MEN WILL NOT FIGHT UNTIL THEY KNOW THAT SHE IS DEAD!
FOR MONTHS YOU HAVE SAT AROUND THAT TABLE DOING NOTHING. WHY ARE YOU SCARED OF A GIRL?
IT'S NOT THE GIRL WE'RE SCARED OF; IT'S THE VOICES.
IF THEY'RE REAL, THEN WE ARE ARGUING AGAINST GOD. AND TO DO THAT IS TRULY THE WAY TO DAMN YOUR SOUL.

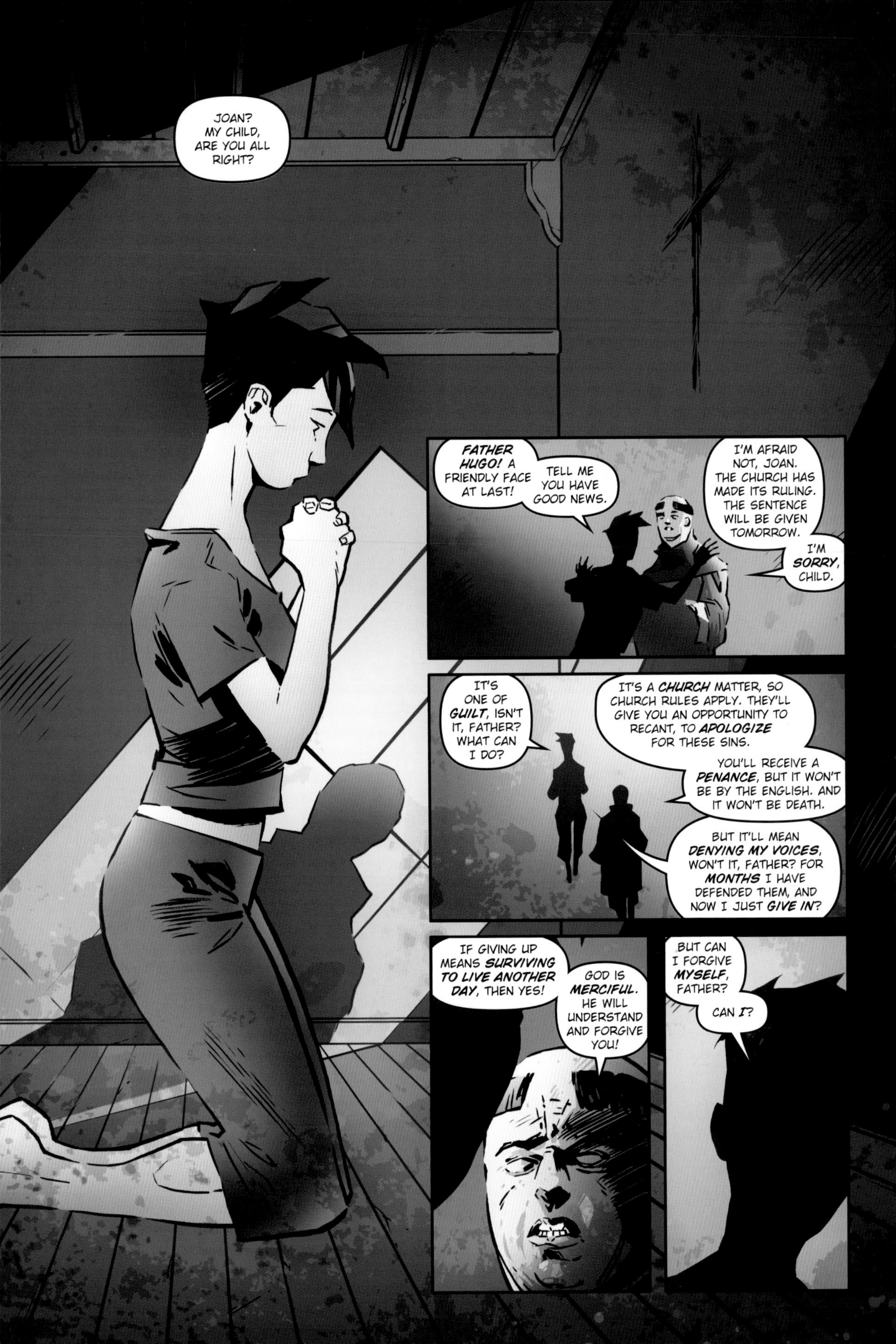
JOAN? MY CHILD, ARE YOU ALL RIGHT?
FATHER HUGO! A FRIENDLY FACE AT LAST!
TELL ME YOU HAVE GOOD NEWS.
I'M AFRAID NOT, JOAN. THE CHURCH HAS MADE ITS RULING. THE SENTENCE WILL BE GIVEN TOMORROW.
I'M SORRY, CHILD.
IT'S ONE OF GUILT, ISN'T IT, FATHER? WHAT CAN I DO?
IT'S A CHURCH MATTER, SO CHURCH RULES APPLY. THEY'LL GIVE YOU AN OPPORTUNITY TO RECANT, TO APOLOGIZE FOR THESE SINS.
YOU'LL RECEIVE A PENANCE, BUT IT WON'T BE BY THE ENGLISH. AND IT WON'T BE DEATH.
BUT IT'LL MEAN DENYING MY VOICES, WON'T IT, FATHER? FOR MONTHS I HAVE DEFENDED THEM, AND NOW I JUST GIVE IN?
IF GIVING UP MEANS SURVIVING TO LIVE ANOTHER DAY, THEN YES!
GOD IS MERCIFUL. HE WILL UNDERSTAND AND FORGIVE YOU!
BUT CAN I FORGIVE MYSELF, FATHER?
CAN I?

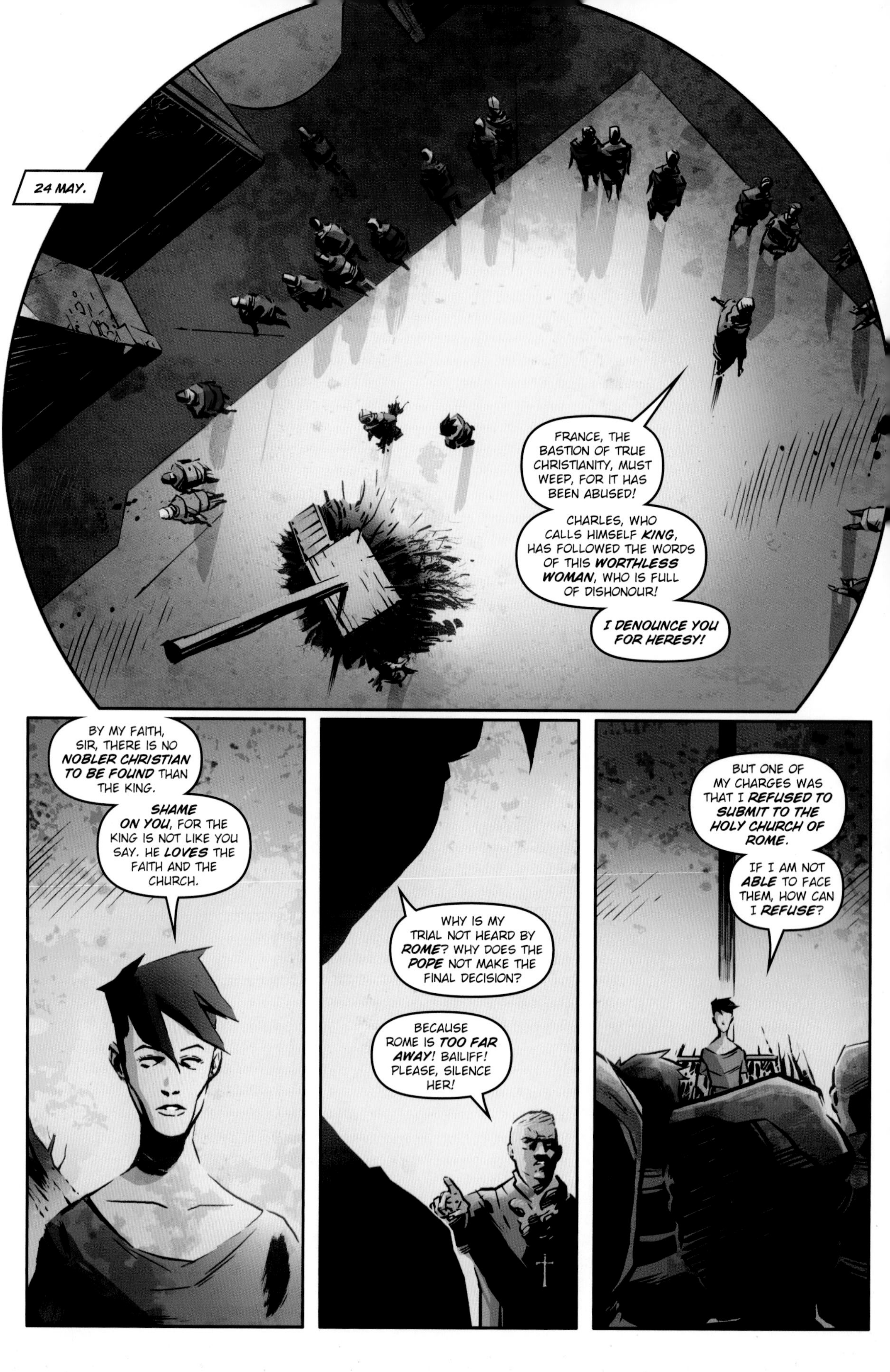
24 MAY.
FRANCE, THE BASTION OF TRUE CHRISTIANITY, MUST WEEP, FOR IT HAS BEEN ABUSED!
CHARLES, WHO CALLS HIMSELF KING, HAS FOLLOWED THE WORDS OF THIS WORTHLESS WOMAN, WHO IS FULL OF DISHONOUR!
I DENOUNCE YOU FOR HERESY!
BY MY FAITH, SIR, THERE IS NO NOBLER CHRISTIAN TO BE FOUND THAN THE KING.
SHAME ON YOU, FOR THE KING IS NOT LIKE YOU SAY. HE LOVES THE FAITH AND THE CHURCH.
WHY IS MY TRIAL NOT HEARD BY ROME? WHY DOES THE POPE NOT MAKE THE FINAL DECISION?
BECAUSE ROME IS TOO FAR AWAY! BAILIFF! PLEASE, SILENCE HER!
BUT ONE OF MY CHARGES WAS THAT I REFUSED TO SUBMIT TO THE HOLY CHURCH OF ROME.
IF I AM NOT ABLE TO FACE THEM, HOW CAN I REFUSE?

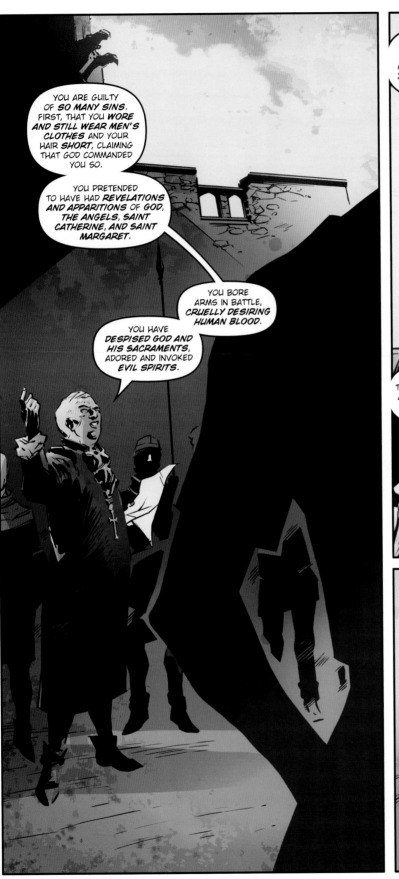

YOU ARE GUILTY OF **SO MANY SINS**. FIRST, THAT YOU **WORE AND STILL WEAR MEN'S CLOTHES** AND YOUR HAIR **SHORT**, CLAIMING THAT GOD COMMANDED YOU SO.

YOU PRETENDED TO HAVE HAD **REVELATIONS AND APPARITIONS** OF GOD, THE ANGELS, SAINT CATHERINE, AND SAINT MARGARET.

YOU BORE ARMS IN BATTLE, **CRUELLY DESIRING HUMAN BLOOD.**

YOU HAVE **DESPISED GOD AND HIS SACRAMENTS**, ADORED AND INVOKED **EVIL SPIRITS.**

THE LIST GOES ON. BUT THE CHURCH IS MERCIFUL. **RECANT YOUR SINS**, JOAN. APOLOGIZE.

REFUSE TO WEAR THESE CLOTHES AGAIN. **RENOUNCE HERESY** AND MAKE SUITABLE PENANCE...

...AND THE CHURCH WILL WELCOME YOU BACK INTO ITS BOSOM.

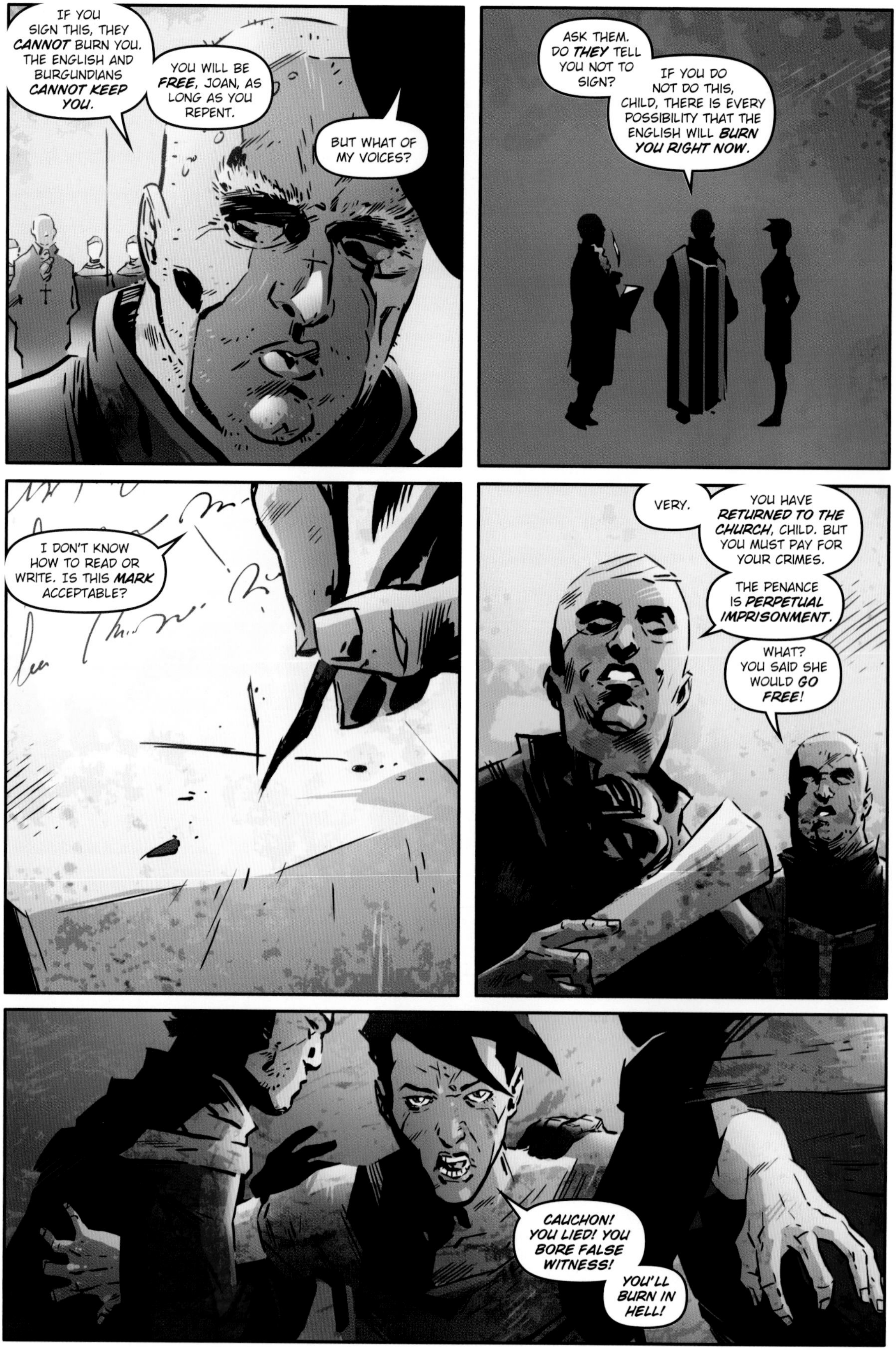
IF YOU SIGN THIS, THEY CANNOT BURN YOU. THE ENGLISH AND BURGUNDIANS CANNOT KEEP YOU.
YOU WILL BE FREE, JOAN, AS LONG AS YOU REPENT.
BUT WHAT OF MY VOICES?
ASK THEM. DO THEY TELL YOU NOT TO SIGN?
IF YOU DO NOT DO THIS, CHILD, THERE IS EVERY POSSIBILITY THAT THE ENGLISH WILL BURN YOU RIGHT NOW.
I DON'T KNOW HOW TO READ OR WRITE. IS THIS MARK ACCEPTABLE?
VERY.
YOU HAVE RETURNED TO THE CHURCH, CHILD. BUT YOU MUST PAY FOR YOUR CRIMES.
THE PENANCE IS PERPETUAL IMPRISONMENT.
WHAT? YOU SAID SHE WOULD GO FREE!
CAUCHON! YOU LIED! YOU BORE FALSE WITNESS!
YOU'LL BURN IN HELL!

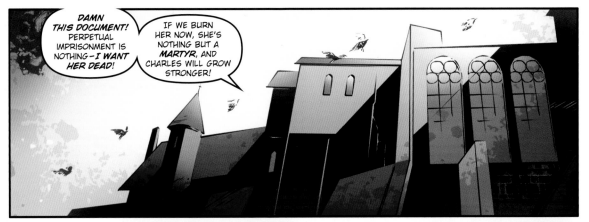

DAMN *THIS DOCUMENT!* PERPETUAL IMPRISONMENT IS NOTHING—*I WANT HER DEAD!*

IF WE BURN HER NOW, SHE'S NOTHING BUT A *MARTYR*, AND CHARLES WILL GROW STRONGER!

SHE'S EVEN TAKEN TO WEARING A *DRESS!* SAYS THAT SHE'S *REPENTING!*

DON'T WORRY, MY LORD WARWICK, WE'LL GET HER YET.

LOOK...

...SEE HOW SHE *SIGNED* THIS? SHE CLAIMS SHE CANNOT READ OR WRITE.

YET SHE SIGNED HER NAME TO *EVERY LETTER* SHE SENT LORD TALBOT AT ORLÉANS!

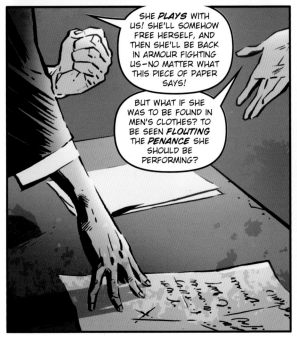

SHE *PLAYS* WITH US! SHE'LL SOMEHOW FREE HERSELF, AND THEN SHE'LL BE BACK IN ARMOUR FIGHTING US—NO MATTER WHAT THIS PIECE OF PAPER SAYS!

BUT WHAT IF SHE WAS TO BE FOUND IN MEN'S CLOTHES? TO BE SEEN *FLOUTING* THE *PENANCE* SHE SHOULD BE PERFORMING?

OH, TO GO AGAINST SUCH A DECREE AFTER WILLINGLY SIGNING IT, THAT WOULD BE *HERESY.*

MAKE IT SO.

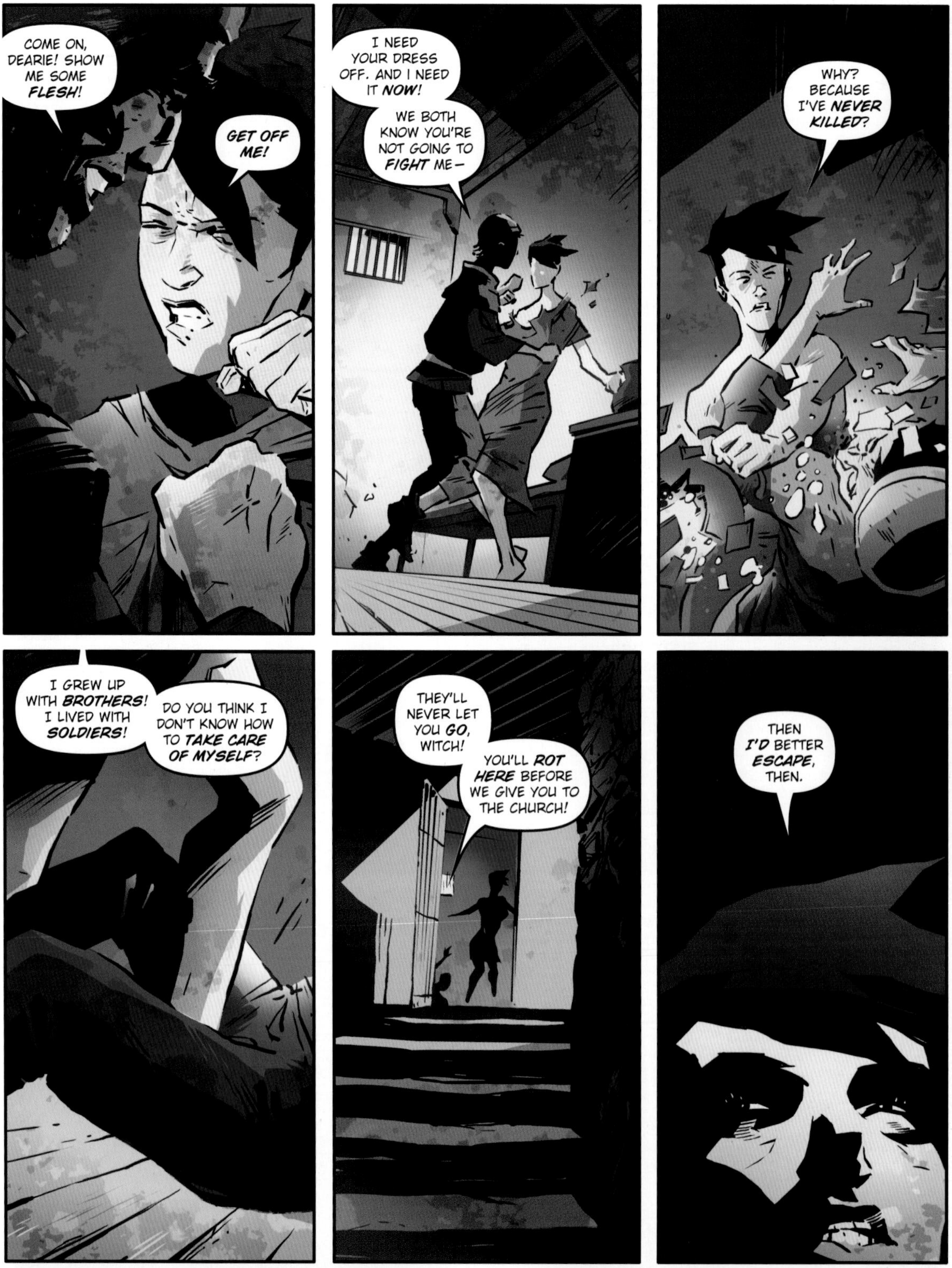
COME ON, DEARIE! SHOW ME SOME FLESH!
GET OFF ME!
I NEED YOUR DRESS OFF. AND I NEED IT NOW!
WE BOTH KNOW YOU'RE NOT GOING TO FIGHT ME—
WHY? BECAUSE I'VE NEVER KILLED?
I GREW UP WITH BROTHERS! I LIVED WITH SOLDIERS!
DO YOU THINK I DON'T KNOW HOW TO TAKE CARE OF MYSELF?
THEY'LL NEVER LET YOU GO, WITCH!
YOU'LL ROT HERE BEFORE WE GIVE YOU TO THE CHURCH!
THEN I'D BETTER ESCAPE, THEN.

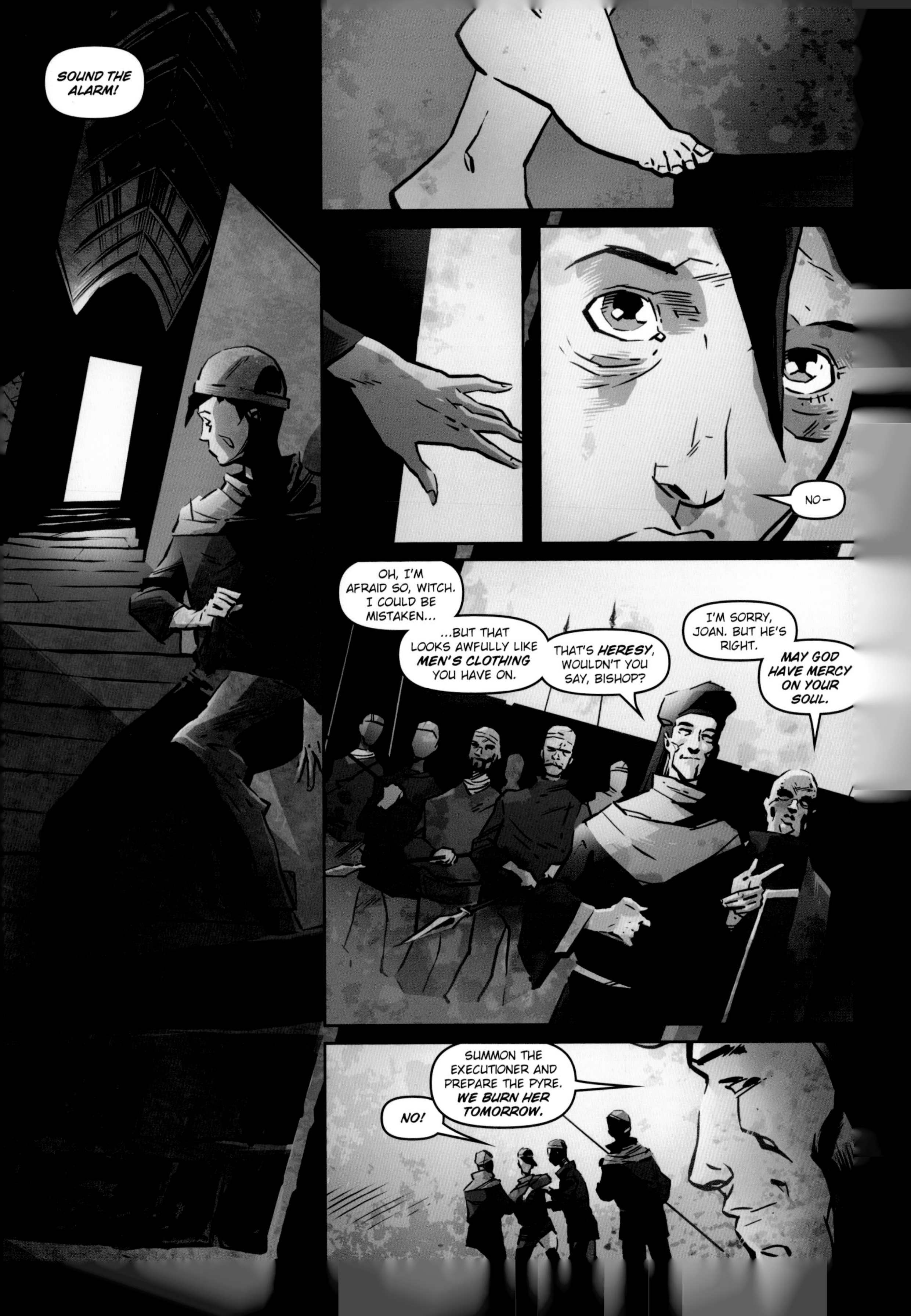
SOUND THE ALARM!
NO—
OH, I'M AFRAID SO, WITCH. I COULD BE MISTAKEN...
...BUT THAT LOOKS AWFULLY LIKE **MEN'S CLOTHING** YOU HAVE ON.
THAT'S **HERESY**, WOULDN'T YOU SAY, BISHOP?
I'M SORRY, JOAN. BUT HE'S RIGHT.
MAY GOD HAVE MERCY ON YOUR SOUL.
SUMMON THE EXECUTIONER AND PREPARE THE PYRE. **WE BURN HER TOMORROW.**
NO!

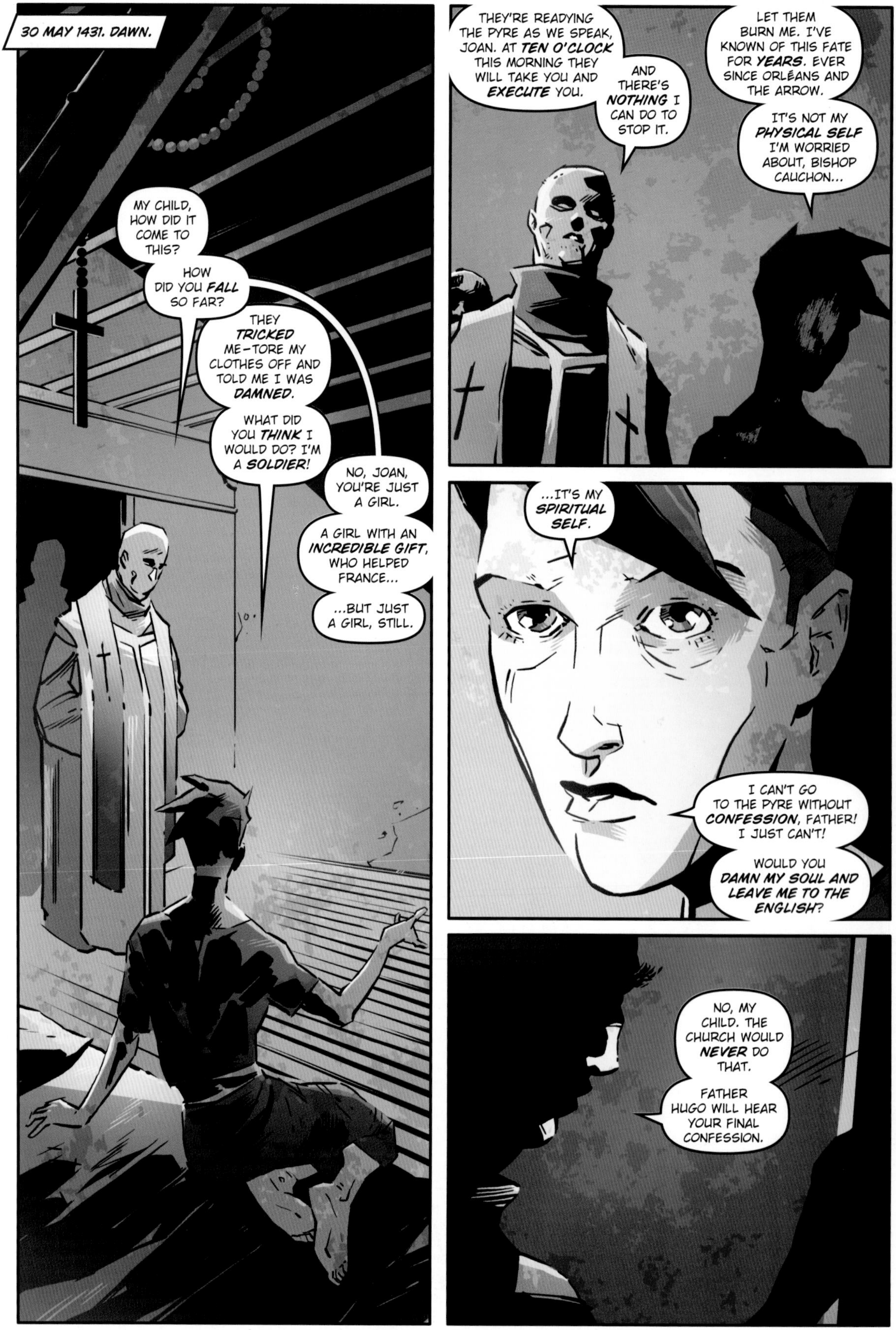
30 MAY 1431. DAWN.
MY CHILD, HOW DID IT COME TO THIS?
HOW DID YOU FALL SO FAR?
THEY TRICKED ME—TORE MY CLOTHES OFF AND TOLD ME I WAS DAMNED.
WHAT DID YOU THINK I WOULD DO? I'M A SOLDIER!
NO, JOAN, YOU'RE JUST A GIRL.
A GIRL WITH AN INCREDIBLE GIFT, WHO HELPED FRANCE...
...BUT JUST A GIRL, STILL.
THEY'RE READYING THE PYRE AS WE SPEAK, JOAN. AT TEN O'CLOCK THIS MORNING THEY WILL TAKE YOU AND EXECUTE YOU.
AND THERE'S NOTHING I CAN DO TO STOP IT.
LET THEM BURN ME. I'VE KNOWN OF THIS FATE FOR YEARS. EVER SINCE ORLÉANS AND THE ARROW.
IT'S NOT MY PHYSICAL SELF I'M WORRIED ABOUT, BISHOP CAUCHON...
...IT'S MY SPIRITUAL SELF.
I CAN'T GO TO THE PYRE WITHOUT CONFESSION, FATHER! I JUST CAN'T!
WOULD YOU DAMN MY SOUL AND LEAVE ME TO THE ENGLISH?
NO, MY CHILD. THE CHURCH WOULD NEVER DO THAT.
FATHER HUGO WILL HEAR YOUR FINAL CONFESSION.

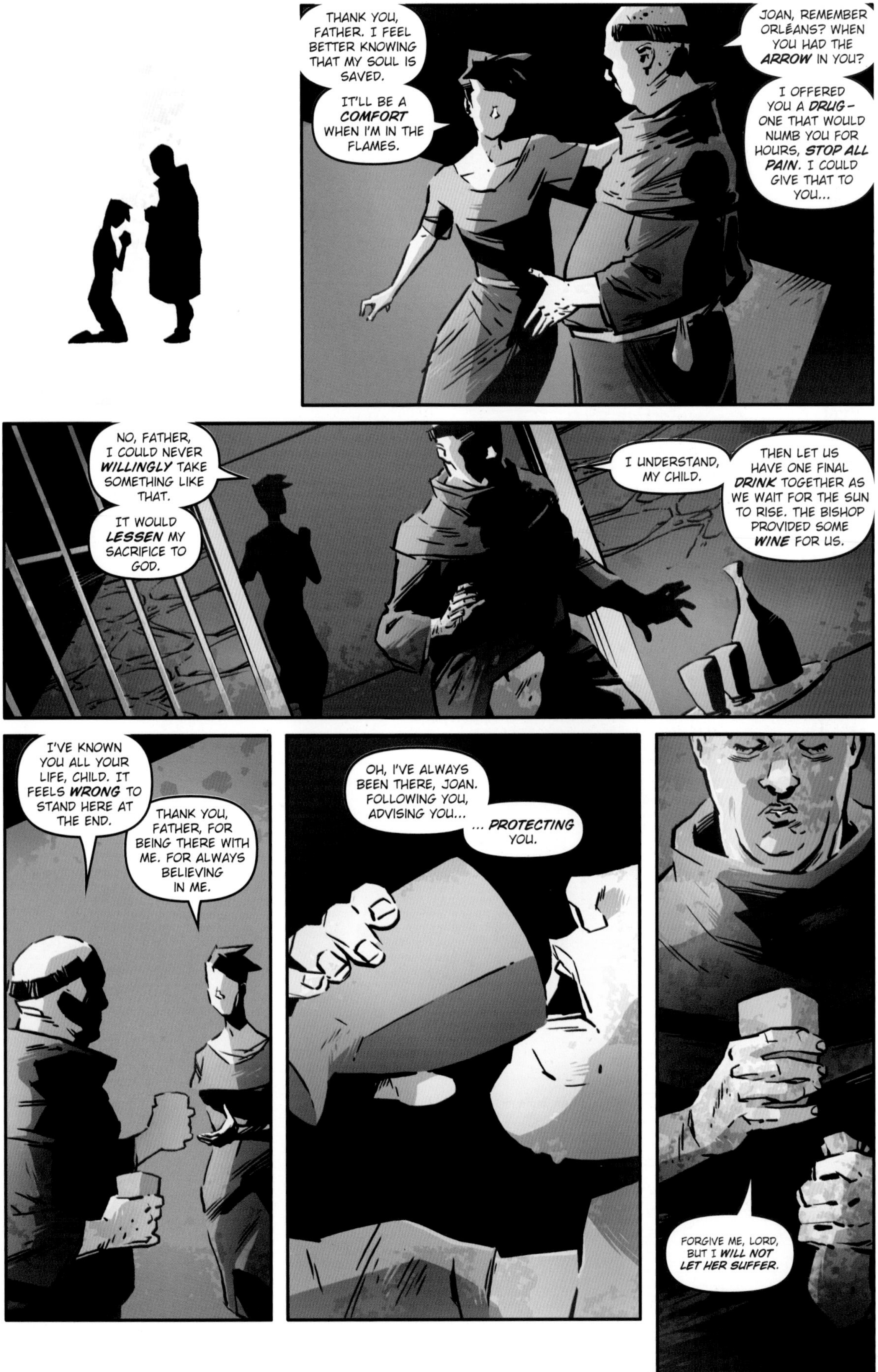
THANK YOU, FATHER. I FEEL BETTER KNOWING THAT MY SOUL IS SAVED.
IT'LL BE A COMFORT WHEN I'M IN THE FLAMES.
JOAN, REMEMBER ORLÉANS? WHEN YOU HAD THE ARROW IN YOU?
I OFFERED YOU A DRUG— ONE THAT WOULD NUMB YOU FOR HOURS, STOP ALL PAIN. I COULD GIVE THAT TO YOU...
NO, FATHER, I COULD NEVER WILLINGLY TAKE SOMETHING LIKE THAT.
IT WOULD LESSEN MY SACRIFICE TO GOD.
I UNDERSTAND, MY CHILD.
THEN LET US HAVE ONE FINAL DRINK TOGETHER AS WE WAIT FOR THE SUN TO RISE. THE BISHOP PROVIDED SOME WINE FOR US.
I'VE KNOWN YOU ALL YOUR LIFE, CHILD. IT FEELS WRONG TO STAND HERE AT THE END.
THANK YOU, FATHER, FOR BEING THERE WITH ME. FOR ALWAYS BELIEVING IN ME.
OH, I'VE ALWAYS BEEN THERE, JOAN. FOLLOWING YOU, ADVISING YOU...
... PROTECTING YOU.
FORGIVE ME, LORD, BUT I WILL NOT LET HER SUFFER.

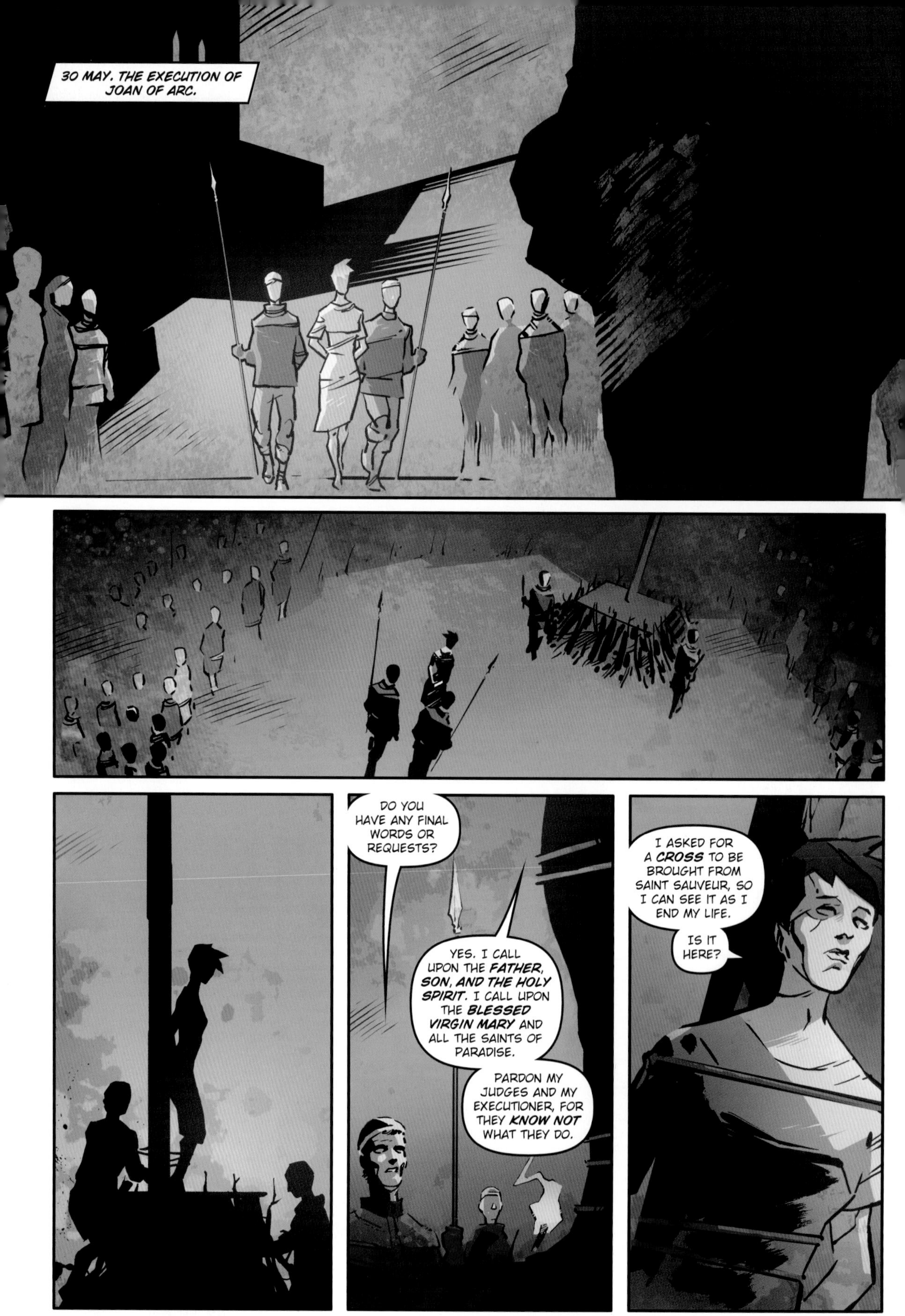
30 MAY. THE EXECUTION OF JOAN OF ARC.
DO YOU HAVE ANY FINAL WORDS OR REQUESTS?
YES. I CALL UPON THE FATHER, SON, AND THE HOLY SPIRIT. I CALL UPON THE BLESSED VIRGIN MARY AND ALL THE SAINTS OF PARADISE.
PARDON MY JUDGES AND MY EXECUTIONER, FOR THEY KNOW NOT WHAT THEY DO.
I ASKED FOR A CROSS TO BE BROUGHT FROM SAINT SAUVEUR, SO I CAN SEE IT AS I END MY LIFE.
IS IT HERE?

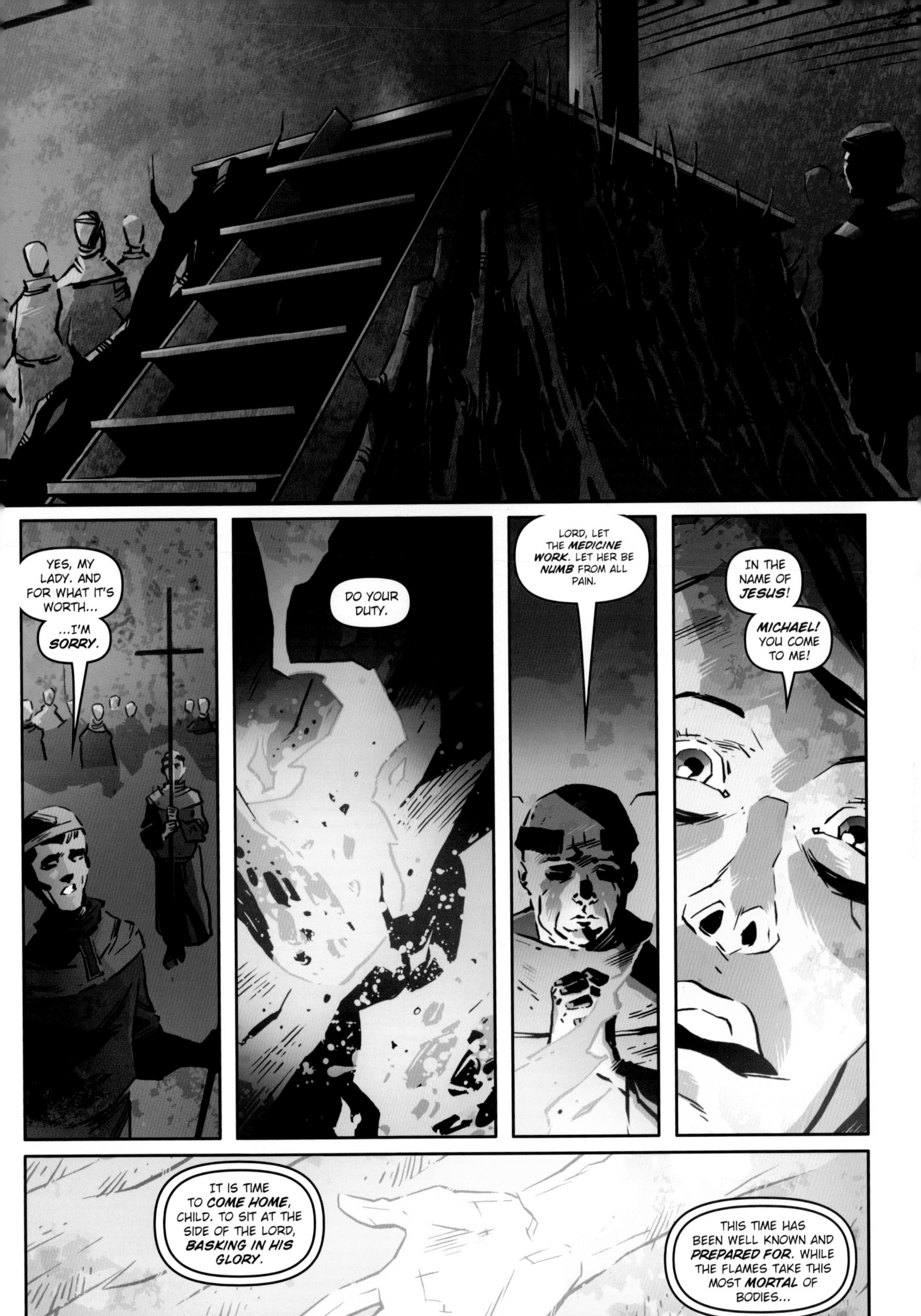
YES, MY LADY. AND FOR WHAT IT'S WORTH...
...I'M SORRY.
DO YOUR DUTY.
LORD, LET THE MEDICINE WORK. LET HER BE NUMB FROM ALL PAIN.
IN THE NAME OF JESUS!
MICHAEL! YOU COME TO ME!
IT IS TIME TO COME HOME, CHILD. TO SIT AT THE SIDE OF THE LORD, BASKING IN HIS GLORY.
THIS TIME HAS BEEN WELL KNOWN AND PREPARED FOR. WHILE THE FLAMES TAKE THIS MOST MORTAL OF BODIES...

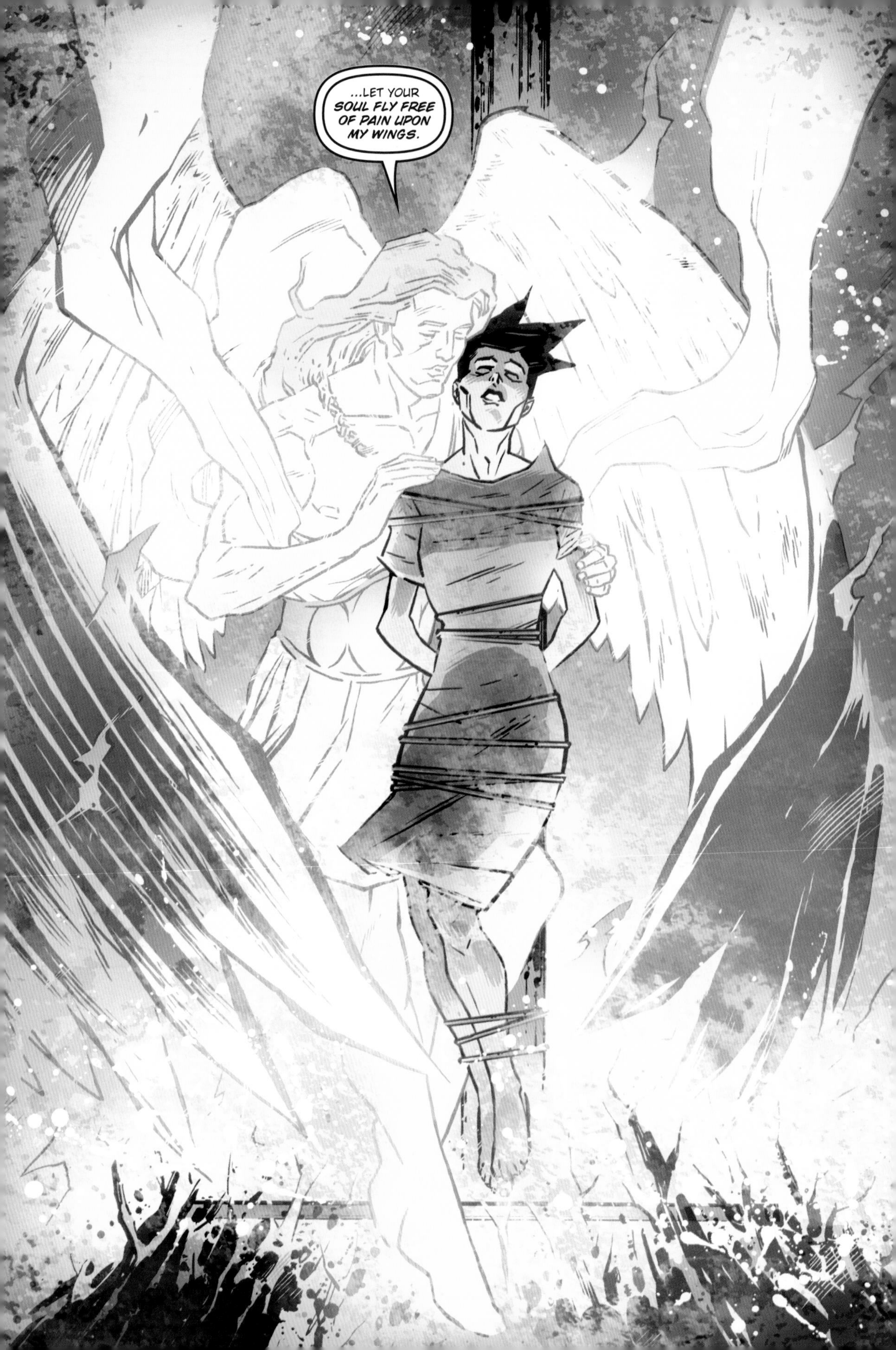
...LET YOUR SOUL FLY FREE OF PAIN UPON MY WINGS.

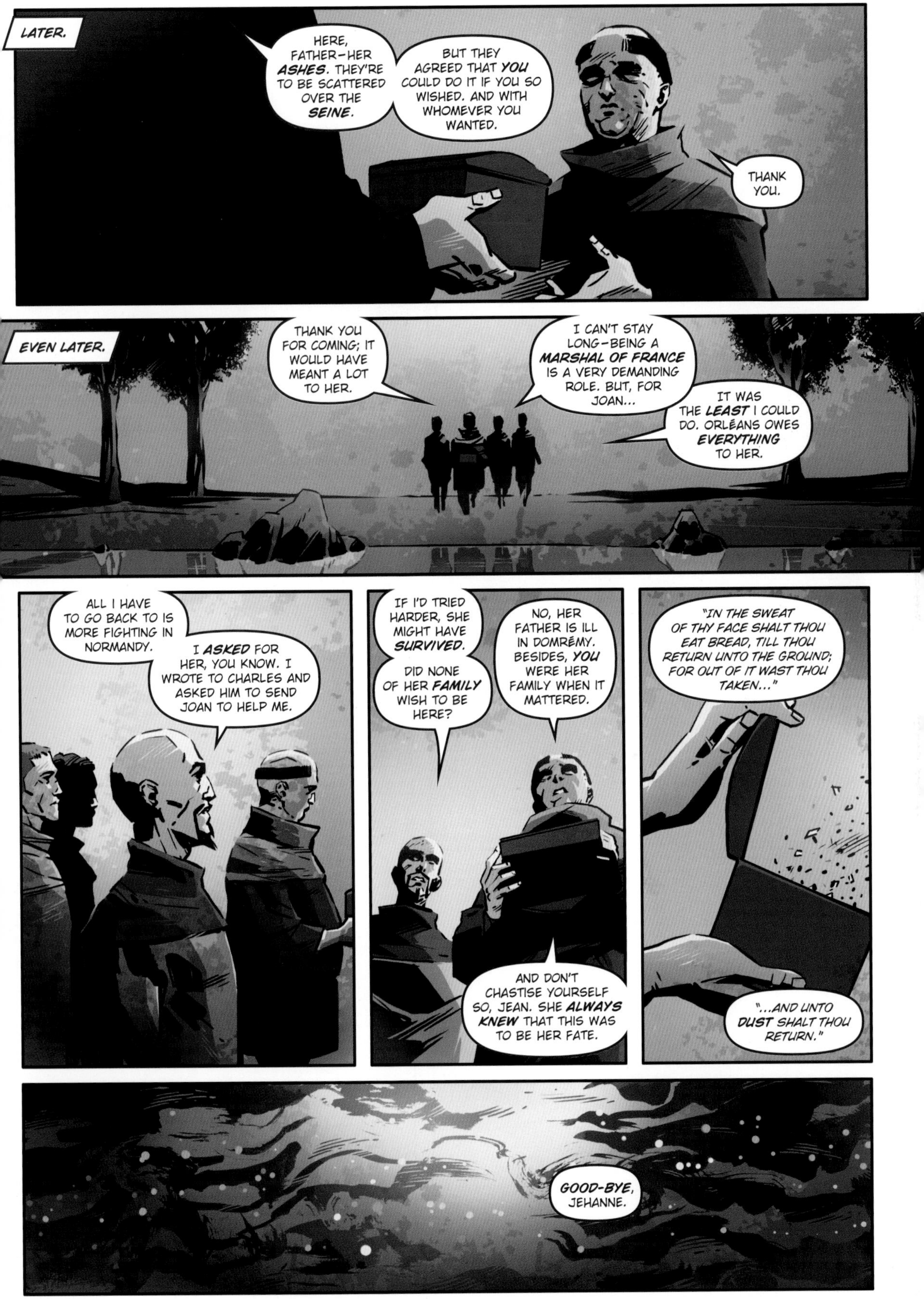
LATER.
HERE, FATHER—HER ASHES. THEY'RE TO BE SCATTERED OVER THE SEINE.
BUT THEY AGREED THAT YOU COULD DO IT IF YOU SO WISHED. AND WITH WHOMEVER YOU WANTED.
THANK YOU.
EVEN LATER.
THANK YOU FOR COMING; IT WOULD HAVE MEANT A LOT TO HER.
I CAN'T STAY LONG—BEING A MARSHAL OF FRANCE IS A VERY DEMANDING ROLE. BUT, FOR JOAN...
IT WAS THE LEAST I COULD DO. ORLÉANS OWES EVERYTHING TO HER.
ALL I HAVE TO GO BACK TO IS MORE FIGHTING IN NORMANDY.
I ASKED FOR HER, YOU KNOW. I WROTE TO CHARLES AND ASKED HIM TO SEND JOAN TO HELP ME.
IF I'D TRIED HARDER, SHE MIGHT HAVE SURVIVED.
DID NONE OF HER FAMILY WISH TO BE HERE?
NO, HER FATHER IS ILL IN DOMRÉMY. BESIDES, YOU WERE HER FAMILY WHEN IT MATTERED.
AND DON'T CHASTISE YOURSELF SO, JEAN. SHE ALWAYS KNEW THAT THIS WAS TO BE HER FATE.
"IN THE SWEAT OF THY FACE SHALT THOU EAT BREAD, TILL THOU RETURN UNTO THE GROUND; FOR OUT OF IT WAST THOU TAKEN..."
"...AND UNTO DUST SHALT THOU RETURN."
GOOD-BYE, JEHANNE.

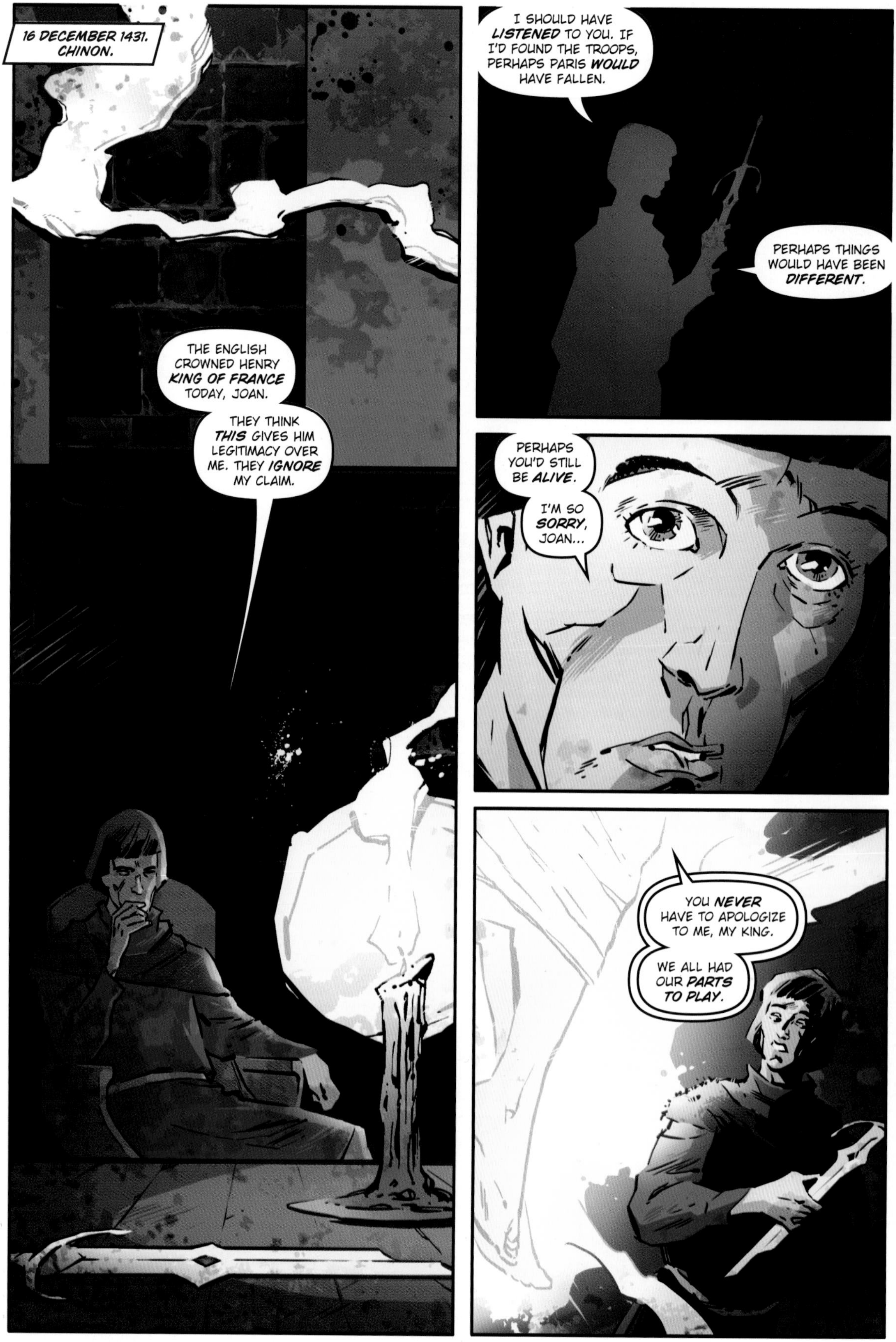
16 DECEMBER 1431. CHINON.
THE ENGLISH CROWNED HENRY KING OF FRANCE TODAY, JOAN.
THEY THINK THIS GIVES HIM LEGITIMACY OVER ME. THEY IGNORE MY CLAIM.
I SHOULD HAVE LISTENED TO YOU. IF I'D FOUND THE TROOPS, PERHAPS PARIS WOULD HAVE FALLEN.
PERHAPS THINGS WOULD HAVE BEEN DIFFERENT.
PERHAPS YOU'D STILL BE ALIVE.
I'M SO SORRY, JOAN...
YOU NEVER HAVE TO APOLOGIZE TO ME, MY KING.
WE ALL HAD OUR PARTS TO PLAY.

ARE YOU A GHOST? AN *ANGEL*?

NEITHER... JUST A *VISITOR*, SENT BY HER *LORD* TO CALM A MAN'S SPIRITS.

HELLO, CHARLES.

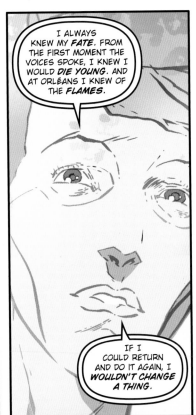

I ALWAYS KNEW MY *FATE*. FROM THE FIRST MOMENT THE VOICES SPOKE, I KNEW I WOULD *DIE YOUNG*. AND AT ORLÉANS I KNEW OF THE *FLAMES*.

IF I COULD RETURN AND DO IT AGAIN, I *WOULDN'T CHANGE A THING*.

BUT *YOU* NEED TO CHANGE. I GAVE YOU *FRANCE*, AND THE ENGLISH *TAKE IT BACK*.

BE THE KING I *BELIEVED* IN, CHARLES. *TAKE PARIS*. REGAIN YOUR LANDS.

PARIS? IT'S *UNDEFEATABLE!* THE ENGLISH WILL NEVER LOSE IT!

I TOLD YOU ONCE THAT PARIS WOULD FALL WITHIN *SEVEN YEARS*. DO YOU *STILL NOT BELIEVE ME*?

I AM AT *PEACE* NOW, MY KING.

SO, TOO, MUST *YOU* BE—FOR *FRANCE*.

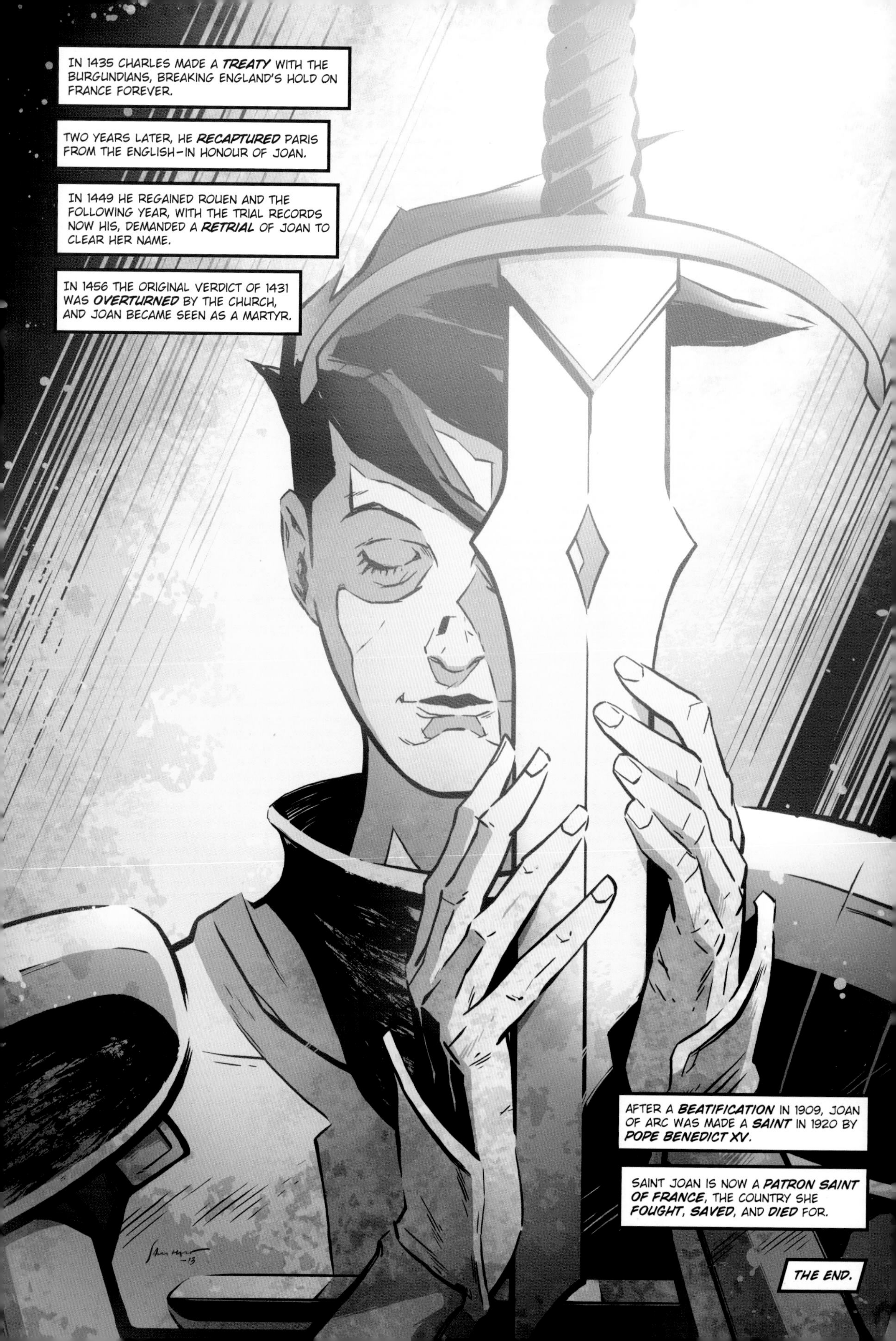
IN 1435 CHARLES MADE A TREATY WITH THE BURGUNDIANS, BREAKING ENGLAND'S HOLD ON FRANCE FOREVER.
TWO YEARS LATER, HE RECAPTURED PARIS FROM THE ENGLISH–IN HONOUR OF JOAN.
IN 1449 HE REGAINED ROUEN AND THE FOLLOWING YEAR, WITH THE TRIAL RECORDS NOW HIS, DEMANDED A RETRIAL OF JOAN TO CLEAR HER NAME.
IN 1456 THE ORIGINAL VERDICT OF 1431 WAS OVERTURNED BY THE CHURCH, AND JOAN BECAME SEEN AS A MARTYR.
AFTER A BEATIFICATION IN 1909, JOAN OF ARC WAS MADE A SAINT IN 1920 BY POPE BENEDICT XV.
SAINT JOAN IS NOW A PATRON SAINT OF FRANCE, THE COUNTRY SHE FOUGHT, SAVED, AND DIED FOR.
THE END.

TONY LEE

Tony Lee has written for many popular comic books, including
X-Men, *Doctor Who*, *Spider-Man*, *Starship Troopers*,
Wallace & Gromit, and *Shrek*. His adaptation of
Pride & Prejudice & Zombies: The Graphic Novel was a
New York Times bestseller. He is also the author of the young
adult graphic novels *Outlaw: The Legend of Robin Hood* and
Excalibur: The Legend of King Arthur. Tony Lee lives in London.

SAM HART

Sam Hart is a comic book artist and magazine illustrator who has worked on *Starship Troopers*, *Judge Dredd*, and *Brothers: The Fall of Lucifer*. He is the illustrator of Tony Lee's *Outlaw: The Legend of Robin Hood* and *Excalibur: The Legend of King Arthur*. Born in England, Sam Hart now lives and teaches comic art in Brazil.

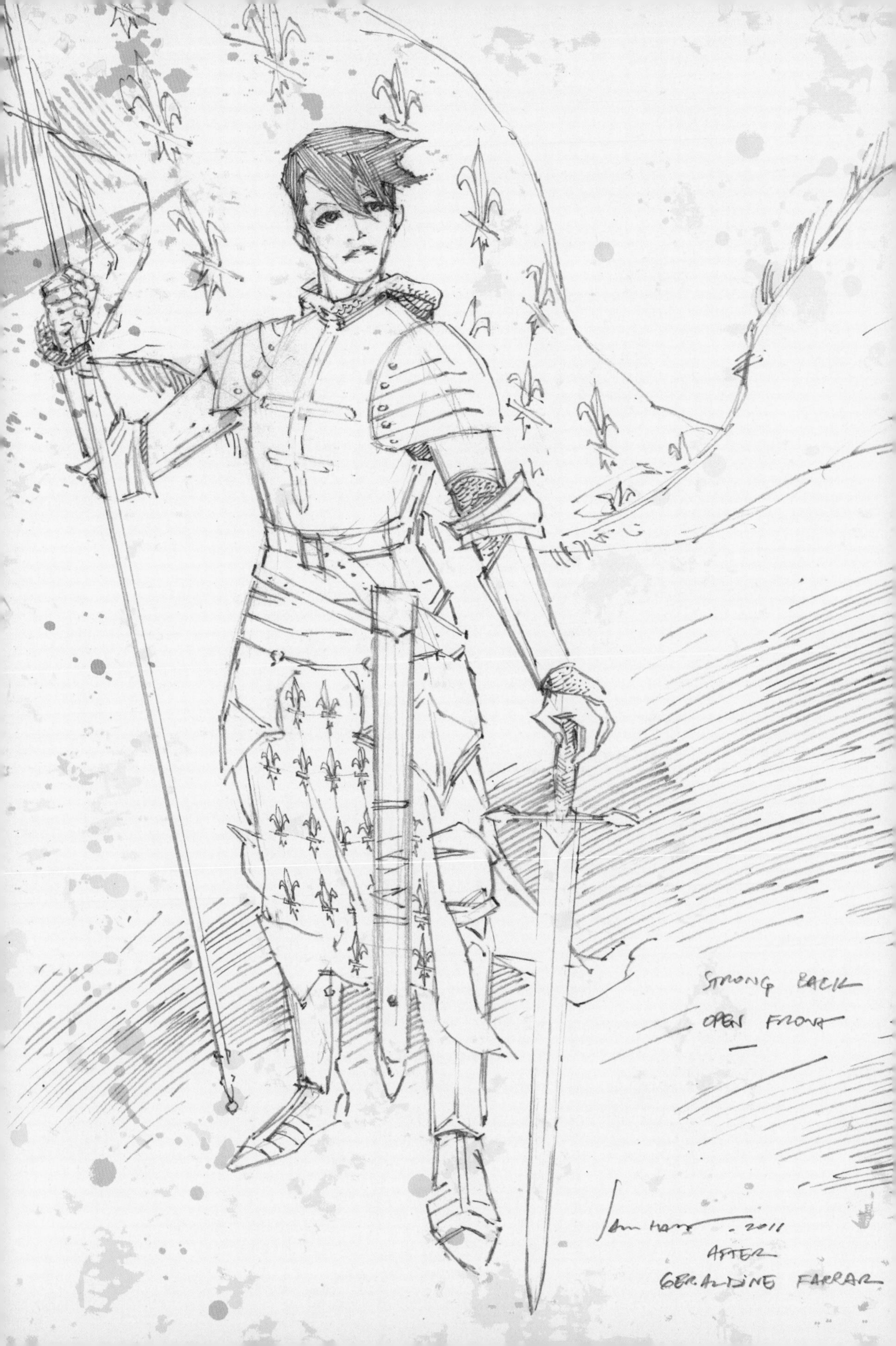
STRONG BACK
OPEN FRONT
2011
AFTER
GERALDINE FARRAR

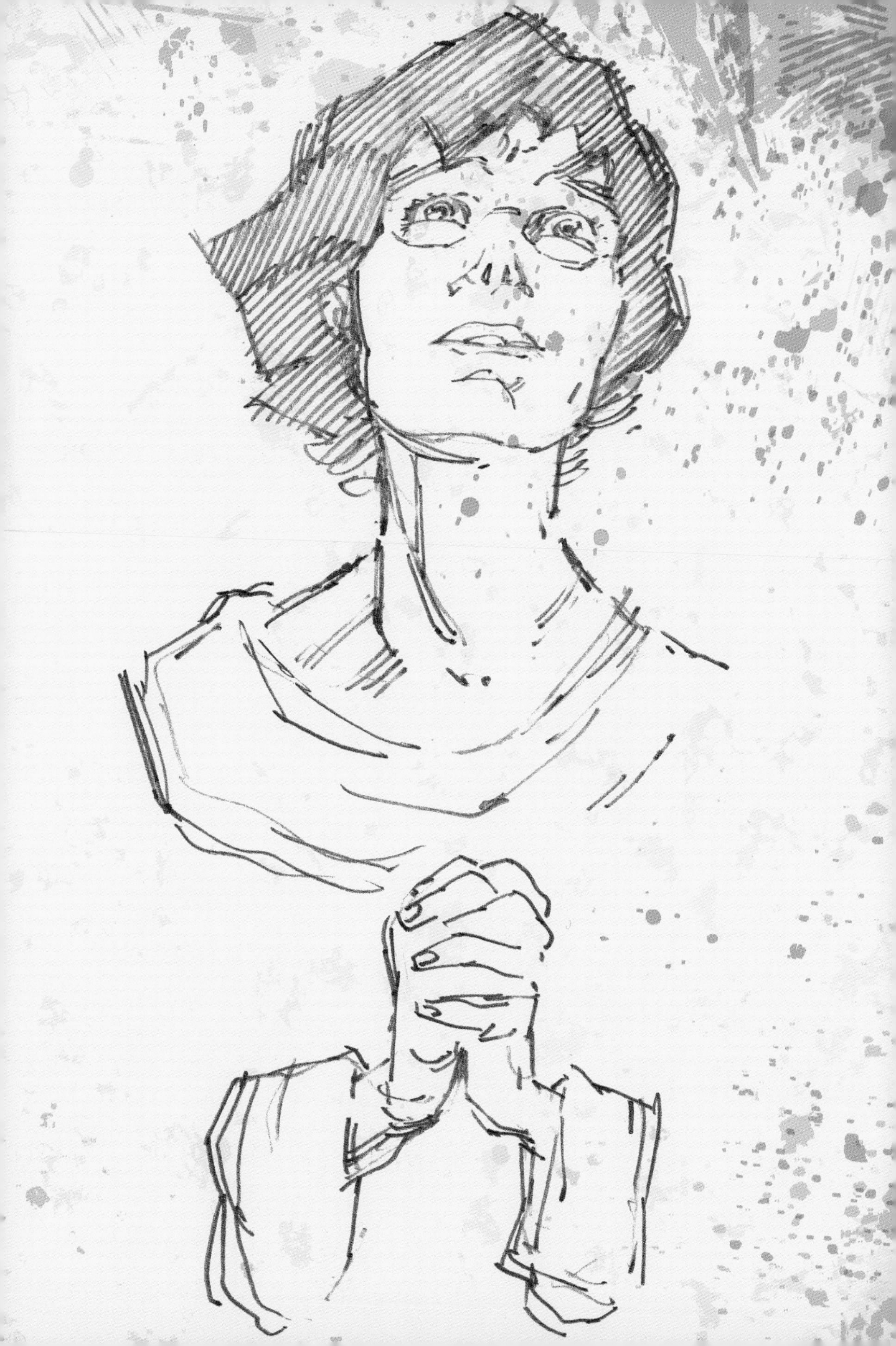

Text copyright © 2014 by Tony Lee
Illustrations copyright © 2014 by Sam Hart

First U.S. edition 2015

Library of Congress Catalog Card Number 2013957283
ISBN 978-0-7636-7613-1 (hardcover)
ISBN 978-0-7636-7614-8 (paperback)

SWT 20 19 18 17 16 15
10 9 8 7 6 5 4 3 2 1

Printed in Dongguan, Guangdong, China

This book was typeset in CCWildWords.
The illustrations were created digitally.

Candlewick Press
99 Dover Street
Somerville, Massachusetts 02144

visit us at www.candlewick.com